THE ECHO

OF

HIS FURY

THE ECHO OF HIS FURY

Copyright © 2025 by S.C. Makepeace.

For information contact: scmakepeaceauthor@gmail.com
https://www.scmakepeace.com

ISBN: 978-1-0683145-2-0

First Edition : May 2025

The Echo of His Fury

Fires of Irkalla

Book Two

S.C. Makepeace

This book contains strong language; graphic depictions of violence, torture, and death; and scenes of a sexual nature, which some readers may find upsetting. Additionally, this book includes content that may be especially unsettling for individuals with severe musophobia (fear of rats and mice).

To Bic,
Thank you for your unwavering
support and enthusiasm.

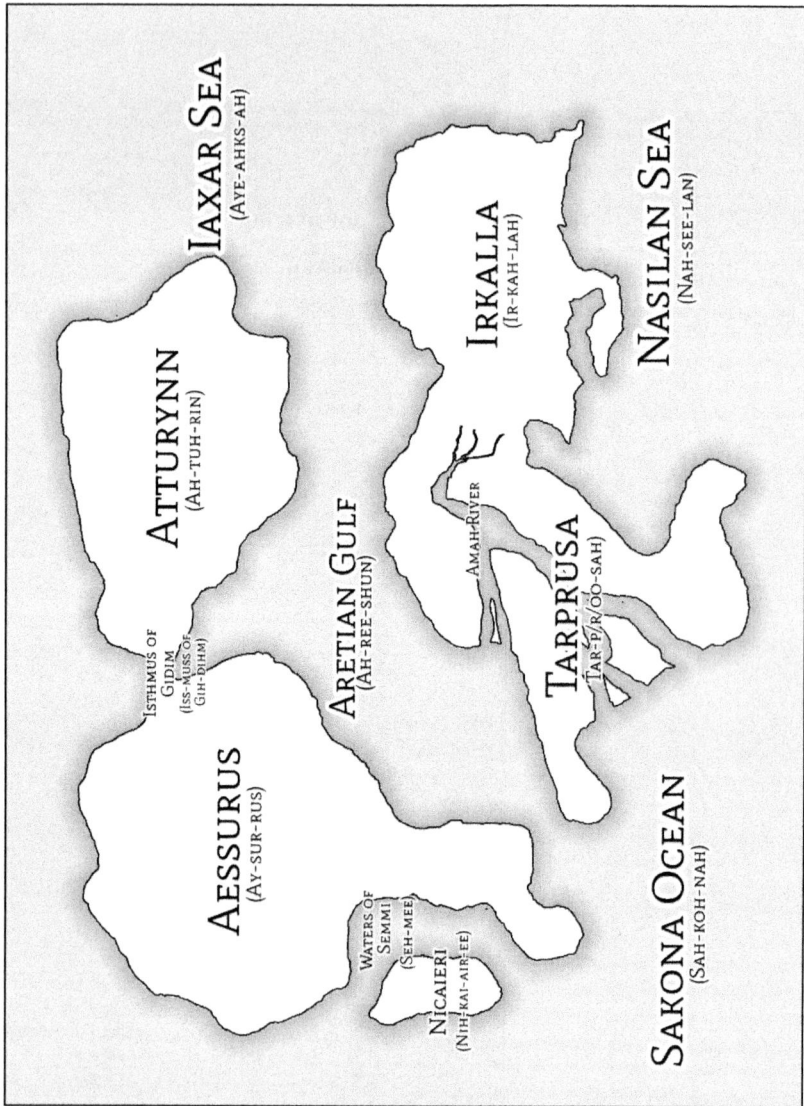

IAXAR SEA
(AYE-AHKS-AH)

NASILAN SEA
(NAH-SEE-LAN)

IRKALLA
(IR-KAH-LAH)

ATTURYNN
(AH-TUH-RIN)

ARETIAN GULF
(AH-REE-SHUN)

AMAH RIVER

TARPRUSA
(TAR-P/R/OO-SAH)

ISTHMUS OF GIDIM
(ISS-MUSS OF GIH-DIHM)

AESSURUS
(AY-SUR-RUS)

WATERS OF SEMMI
(SEH-MEE)

NICAIERI
(NIH-KAI-AIR-EE)

SAKONA OCEAN
(SAH-KOH-NAH)

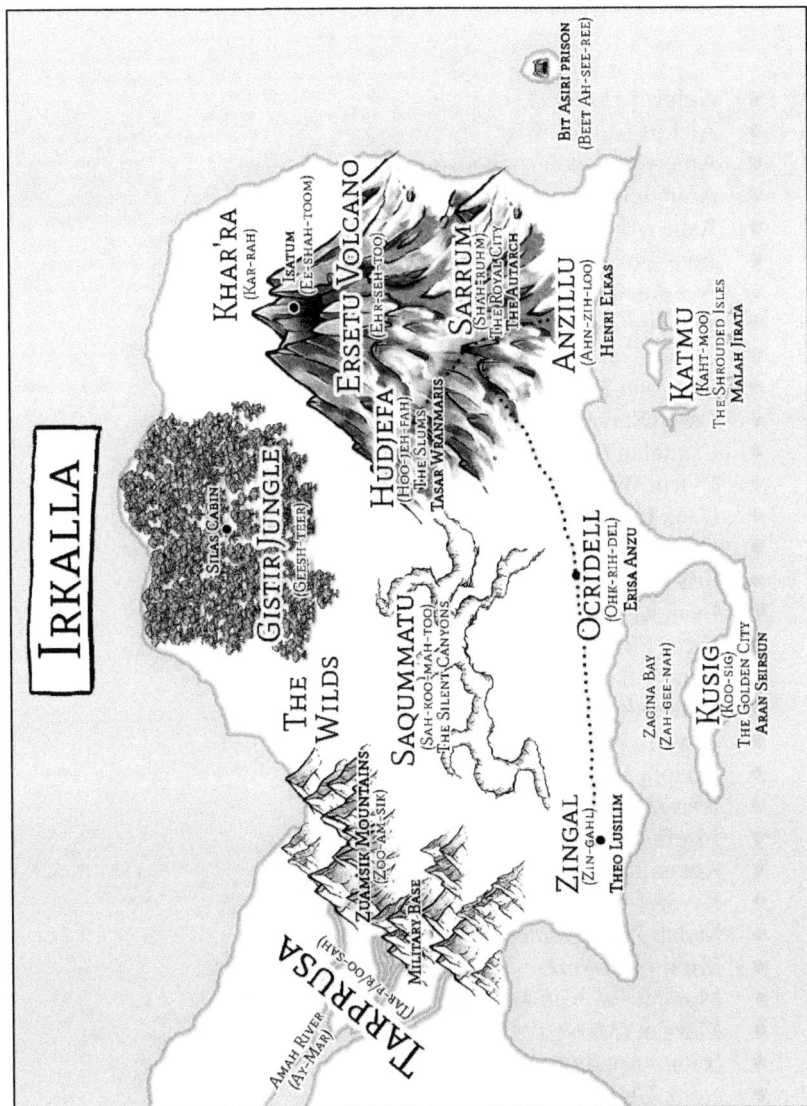

IRKALLA

THE WILDS

GISTIR JUNGLE
(GEESH-TEER)
• SILAS CABIN

KHAR'RA
(KAR-RAH)
• ISATUM
(EE-SHAH-TOOM)

ERSETU VOLCANO
(EHR-SEH-TOO)

HUDIEFA
(HOO-JEH-FAH)
THE SLUMS
TASAR WRANMARIS

SARRUM
(SHAH-RUHM)
THE ROYAL CITY
THE AUTARCH

ANZILLU
(AHN-ZIH-LOO)
HENRI ELKAS

ZUAMSIK MOUNTAINS
(ZOO-AM-SIK)

MILITARY BASE

SAQUMMATU
(SAH-KOO-MAH-TOO)
THE SILENT CANYONS

ZINGAL
(ZIN-GAHL)
THEO LUSILIM

OCRIDELL
(OHK-RIH-DEL)
ERISA ANZU

ZAGINA BAY
(ZAH-GEE-NAH)

KUSIG
(KOO-SIG)
THE GOLDEN CITY
ARAN SEIRSUN

KATMU
(KAHT-MOO)
THE SHROUDED ISLES
MALAH JIRATA

BIT ASIRI PRISON
(BEET AH-SEE-REE)

TARPRUSA
(TAR-P/R/OO-SAH)

AMAH RIVER
(AY-MAR)

Pronunciation Guide

- Aghna *(Ah-g-nah)*
- Alekos *(Ah-leh-kos)*
- ~~Amelyne Fedelis *(Ah-meh-lynn Feh-deh-lis)*~~
- Aran Seirsun *(Ah-ran See-er-sun)*
- Asila *(Ah-see-lah)*
- ~~Asor Jirata *(Ay-sor Jir-ah-tah)*~~
- ~~Ava Anzû *(Ay-vah Ahn-zoo)*~~
- ~~Bail Jirata *(Bayl Jih-rah-tah)*~~
- Calia *(Cah-lee-ah)*
- ~~Cameron Sangare *(Cam-er-on San-gar)*~~
- Casen Stavrou *(Kay-zen Stahv-row)*
- Csintalan *(Chin-tah-lan)*/The Autarch *(Aw-tark)*
- Cyfrin Wranmaris *(Kih-frin Ran-mah-ris)*
- Dana Lusilim *(Dah-nah Loo-sih-lim)*
- Diandra Lusilim *(Dee-ahn-drah Loo-sih-lim)*
- Erisa Anzû *(Eh-ris-ah Ahn-zoo)*
- ~~Evander Anzû *(Eh-van-dah Ahn-zoo)*~~
- Ezra *(Ehz-rah)*
- Henri Elkas *(Hen-ree El-kas)*
- ~~Hue Fedelis *(Hyoo Feh-deh-lis)*~~
- Ima *(Ee-mah)*
- Isodora *(Ee-soh-dor-ah)*
- Ivan *(Eye-vahn)*
- Josefine *(Joh-seh-feen)*
- Karasi Lusilim *(Kah-rah-see Loo-sih-lim)*
- ~~Kyron Lusilim *(Kai-ron Loo-sih-lim)*~~
- Malah Jirata *(Mah-lah Jih-rah-tah)*
- Mirai *(Mee-rai)*
- Morana *(Mor-ah-nah)*
- Morgan *(Mor-gahn)*
- ~~Natara Anzû *(Nah-tar-rah Ahn-zoo)*~~
- Nook Cularis *(Nuk Koo-lar-iss)*
- Omid *(Oh-meed)*
- Rania *(Rahn-ee-ah)*
- Samson *(Sam-son)*

- Silas *(Sigh-lass)*
- Sirrush *(Seer-ruh-sh)*
- Suenna *(Soo-eh-nah)*
- Tasar Wranmaris *(Tay-zar Ran-mah-ris)*
- Theo Lusilim *(Thee-oh Loo-sih-lim)*
- Tohnain *(Toh-nayn)*
- Tolani Seko *(Toh-lah-nee Say-koh)*
- Torin Sharru *(Toh-rin Shah-roo)*
- Vashti *(Vash-tee)*
- ~~Verrill Fedelis *(Veh-rill Feh-deh-lis)*~~
- ~~Zeti Anzû *(Zeh-tee Ahn-zoo)*~~

Gods and deities

- **Dumuzid** *(Doo-moo-zeed)* – god of agriculture
- **Ereshkigal** *(Eh-resh-kee-gahl)* – goddess of death, Queen of Irkalla
- **Geshtinanna** *(Gesh-tee-nah-nah)* – goddess of scribes and myths
- **Inanna** *(Ee-nah-nah)* – goddess of love, Queen of Heaven
- **Lamaštu** *(Lah-mash-too)* – demoness, ruler of monsters
- **Namtar** *(Nahm-tar)* – god of fate
- **Nanaya** *(Nah-nai-yah)* – goddess of love (lesser)
- **Nergal** *(Ner-gahl)* – god of war
- **Neti** *(Neh-tee)* – gatekeeper of Irkalla
- **Pazuzu** *(Pah-zoo-zoo)* – ruler of the wind

I need not ask for your throne of shadows, Ereshkigal, for it is mine by divine right. I may be Queen of the Heavens, but I know the underworld too. It is not enough to be deified by those of grace, when so many more live in sin. I will shatter the walls between life and death, and all who have passed through your hellish gates will fall to their knees before me. While you may dwell in the cold and silent night of Irkalla, dear sister, know that even the darkness must yield to the light.

Inanna, Goddess of Love and Queen of Heaven

Prologue

T hree hooded figures sat hunched around a single candle in a dark, damp room. Their curved spines were bent low, bowing their cloaked heads to the small, dancing flame.

"We are close, sisters," rasped one of the figures. Her voice was dry and throaty, but the tone was unmistakably triumphant.

"They acted as you foretold, Mirai," croaked another. "Though it was unfortunate about the boy, such a pretty face. They each cried so deliciously."

Mirai tilted her head up and the candlelight latched onto a smiling mouth of jagged, yellowing teeth. "We are not done with them yet, sisters. Erisa Anzû will seek our council once more. Where is she prowling, Ima?" she asked, turning to face the other woman.

"She is licking her wounds, biding her time."

"And what of Silas?" she pressed, ignoring the hisses of disdain that came from her companions at the mention of the name. "He has the power to ruin everything we've worked for."

"You know I cannot see him," Ima snarled. "He skulks beyond my Sight, but I can sense the shield remains with him."

"We must be careful, my sisters," said Mirai, "there is still much to lose. Every piece must be in play for Her to rise once more. And when she does, we ourselves must be ready."

As if hearing a silent command, the three women clasped their crooked, skeletal hands together and began to chant.

Chapter 1

Theo

B right light flickered against my eyelids, searing flashes of red across my vision. My mind was hazy, and without possessing the strength to open my eyes, I catalogued everything I knew.

Unfortunately, it wasn't a lot.

Every part of my body hurt, the hot air stank of flesh and waste, and I was almost certain that I was covered in my own vomit. The acidity of it coated the inside of my mouth, and my clothes were damp and sticky against my skin.

I had a vague memory of being held down, while Ezra poured spirits over my shoulder, causing me to retch before blacking out from the pain.

But what had come before that?

A muffled cry sounded somewhere to my left, punctuating the low groans and whimpers I hadn't realized surrounded me.

The noise triggered a memory; a flash of a knife inches from my face. A wooden hand, splintering under impact. Erisa hanging over the edge of the cliff, and Verrill falling.

As if the mental floodgates of my mind had opened, image after image cascaded back in, presenting a miserable timeline of my latest failures.

But I could only focus on one thing.

Karasi.

My eyes flew open, and I moved to sit up but found myself bound to some sort of makeshift palette. I was in a large tent, the fabric half-shredded and flapping in the breeze, allowing the sun to glare through intermittently.

Bodies lay around me, mostly injured soldiers from my own army. But there were a few dressed in pale blue uniforms, the exact shade of the Atturynnian flag. I had no idea why they would be here, though I was extremely grateful that they were. From my disjointed memories of the fight, I knew they had saved us.

I tried, and failed, to get up again. Roughly torn strips of fabric secured my injured leg in place, and I swore loudly from the pain in my right shoulder as I ripped them away.

A voice sounded inside the tent as I was working on the last knot, stilling my fingers.

"For goodness' sake, lie down, Theo, you'll reopen your stitches."

It was Karasi's voice.

My eyes shot to where she stood, only feet away from me, and I had to blink several times to ensure that I wasn't hallucinating. But the sight of my twin sister never wavered.

Maybe I was dreaming. Maybe I was mad.

"I'm here, Theo," she said softly, as though sensing my mental turmoil. Taking care not to jostle my leg, she moved to sit beside me.

"Karasi," I whispered senselessly, unable to get any other word out.

Her eyes filled with tears, and she threw her arms around my neck. "Oh Theo, I've missed you so much!" she choked out between sobs.

I ignored the fresh flare of pain she'd ignited in my shoulder and held her to me with my good arm, unable to believe that she was here. That she was real. Alive.

"What? How?" I spluttered. "Where have you been, Kara? We thought ..."

She pulled back and quickly wiped the tears from her cheeks, smearing dirt across her face. I took in the icy blue of her clothing, and the Atturynnian crest embroidered with silver thread on her shirt.

"I ..." Her voice trailed off as she noticed the blood seeping through the bandages on my shoulder, and she rose to retrieve a small medical box from the corner of the tent. "Sit still," she snapped as I tried to follow her movements, "there's not enough time to explain everything here. We need to leave as soon as possible."

My tattered shirt was already ripped away from my injury and Karasi tried to remove the soiled bandages, but her right hand was fumbling and awkward. It took me a few seconds to realize that her hand was wooden, made from dozens of small, interlinking pieces that moved like a real hand, each of them crafted in minute detail. Instead of a smooth, buffed surface, jagged splinters protruded from the back of the hand.

But of course it wasn't real. I felt foolish for not noticing it sooner, and for not making the connection that it was *that* wooden hand that had saved my life. I had received Karasi's real hand years ago, wrapped in a royal purple ribbon: a gift from the Autarch.

The memory was painful. Because it was Corbin. He had been the one to order the slaughter, and Erisa had wrapped that package.

Erisa. Where was she? Was she safe?

"I need help!" Karasi called out indignantly after failing to thread the needle for a third time.

Ezra appeared through the tent entrance before I could tell her it wasn't necessary. He was followed by a man I didn't recognize, who went to stand by Karasi.

"Good to see you're finally awake," Ezra said, his face drawn with exhaustion and grief. He took the needle and thread from my twin sister and began removing and replacing my broken stitches.

"How long have I been out?" I asked, fighting against the dizziness that warped the edges of my vision.

"Two nights. We need to start our retreat; we tried to tend to as many of the wounded as possible, but we aren't safe here out in the open."

"How is everyone?" I implored. "Nook? Didi?"

"Both fine," he said, and I let out a sigh of relief.

"And … Erisa?" My voice was barely audible through the

sudden tightness in my throat. "Ezra," I demanded when he didn't meet my gaze.

"She's gone, Theo," he said quietly, "she disappeared after …"

After she almost killed me. He didn't need to say the words for me to know what he was thinking.

"And she had better stay gone," the unfamiliar man grumbled in a thick northern accent. He looked up from where he was gently inspecting Karasi's wooden hand. His almost black eyes were glowering at me through the strands of icy blonde hair that fell across his dark eyebrows. A jagged scar ran down the left side of his face, darkened against his pale complexion. From his accent and the identical blue silks he was wearing, I guessed he, too, was from Atturynn.

"What do you mean by that?" I almost snarled at the stranger.

"I mean that had the Anzû bitch stayed long enough for me to catch her, I would have peeled the tissue from her bones. So, she better stay far away, because if I see her again, I'll kill her. And I'll do it slowly."

I wasn't even aware I was moving until Ezra was pulling me back down and Karasi was chastising me. My stomach twisted when I saw a flash of hurt cross her face at my defense of Erisa.

"Some brother you are," the stranger sneered, "protecting the woman who would have been responsible for your sister's death. You're deplorable."

His words hurt, because they were true. My sister had just returned from the grave, and I was defending her murderer. The hatred in his expression was nothing compared to what I felt for myself.

"That's enough, Torin," Karasi warned, and rose to her feet. "Let's speak outside."

"Karasi, wait!" I called. "Please, don't leave!"

"I'll explain everything later, Theo, I promise," she vowed with a small smile before exiting the tent, followed by Torin.

I watched her disappear in sheer disbelief, the utter shock of the discovery finally ebbing and giving way to the torrent of questions now swirling through my mind.

Where had she been all these years? How was she alive?

Erisa hadn't been overly detailed in recounting how she had killed my sister, but from the little she had said, I knew that Karasi surviving should have been an impossibility.

Ezra's hand was firm on my shoulder as he pushed me back down. "You can talk to her later, but I need to see to your stitches."

"What happened?" I said, not even sure exactly *what* I was asking about.

"She hasn't told any of us where she's been." My friend met my eyes for a brief second before returning back to his task. "We were overrun. If those soldiers from Atturynn hadn't shown up, we wouldn't have survived. The Autarch's men fled as soon as they arrived."

"He's—it's—the Autarch—*fuck*!" My tongue was tying itself in knots trying to tell Ezra who the Autarch was. He eyed me warily as I thought my words through carefully before uttering them. "The Autarch … We know him … Friend … Ocridell … Fighter." Forcing the words out felt like I was pulling a branding iron up my throat.

After a moment, Ezra's eyes widened. "Corbin?"

The muscles in my neck spasmed as I tried to nod, but by the way Ezra's eyes widened in disbelief, I knew he'd understood anyway. As soon as the information settled inside him, I felt the immediate release of the magic threatening to choke me.

And felt a different kind of torment take its place.

"Erisa didn't tell me," I muttered bitterly. "I'd talked about Corbin to her so many times and not once had she even tried to tell me who he was."

Ezra said nothing as he finished redressing my wound. He turned to leave the tent but paused when he was halfway outside. "For what it's worth, I don't think she meant to deceive you about that. I know it doesn't make any sense, but she wanted him dead; she wouldn't have let you tell him your plans if she knew who he was."

He was gone before I had to think of an answer.

❖ ❖ ❖

Though no one was certain where the Autarch and his men had gone, several reports claimed that they were journeying back to Katmu, likely wanting to regroup and plot their next attack.

I marched back to Zingal with the sad remains of my army, anxious to see the survivors safe within our own borders. The Atturynn forces joined us, led by Karasi's strange companion, Torin. Despite her promise, she had not been forthcoming with answers about her survival since I'd awoken, but did explain that she had convinced Torin to come to my aid when she had received word of my planned battle against the Autarch.

The closest I got to an answer from her was during the teary reunions she had shared with Didi and then my mother and Suenna. She had admitted that she was only alive because Torin had saved her, and although the man clearly didn't like me, I would never be able to express my gratitude toward him.

"It's not just my story to tell, Theo," she had said when I'd tried to push her for answers. "The Atturynnians—they're ... *guarded* about certain things, and I would be betraying those secrets if I told you the full story now. All that matters is that if it hadn't been for Torin, I wouldn't have survived."

I could accept that the details of where she had been didn't matter for now; she was alive. And she was back home. I was content with knowing that she'd tell me everything when she was ready.

"And there's been no movement across the channel?" I asked Tasar, almost two weeks after returning home.

"None that I've seen; Katmu's fleet hasn't moved. It looks like they're staying in the Isles for now."

We sat in my office, poring over the new scraps of information about the Autarch's movements. I shifted in my seat, the injuries in my leg and shoulder still paining me.

"And the Rats? Any news from them?" I skirted around the question I really wanted to ask.

"They're still chirping quietly," he said, meeting my gaze, "which means that they're still reporting to someone."

Early fall rain pelted against the windows, and I stared out to the gray skies, wondering where Erisa was. The Rats were loyal to her before Verrill's death, and now she would be in sole control over the network of spies.

But I had received nothing from her. Not a single message or note.

A fortnight had passed since I'd witnessed her singing on the side of that cliff and I could still feel the pull of that voice, as though she were in the room with me. She had concentrated her entire power onto the Autarch, and yet just the residual persuasion of her song had made me almost tear myself apart with the need to submit to her will.

I thought about how easily she could have been manipulating me for the entire time we had been together. Had any of my thoughts or impulses been my own? Or were they simply influenced by her beguiling machinations? Heat blazed angrily in my cheeks when my thoughts turned to anxiety about her wellbeing.

I was the biggest fool in all four realms. She had made it clear that she didn't want me, had been inches away from killing me, and yet I still wanted to comfort her. I knew she must be in torment over Verrill's death; he had been everything to her. I had always known that—that he would *always* come first, because I had *always* been left chasing after the leftovers of her affection for him. Even though the thought of her preference for the Fox still chafed, I mourned his loss for her. He was the last remainder of her family and childhood, the last piece to be stolen away by the Autarch.

"I've sent people out to try and ascertain her location," Tasar continued, "but the Feline was always a slippery creature. I've only heard rumors of rumors, which I'm sure you're already familiar with."

Of course I was. Despite knowing that any report I received would likely be fabricated or out of date, I had latched on to any scrap of information I had heard about Erisa's whereabouts, desperate for more.

"She won't be found until she wants to be," I grumbled, avoiding Tasar's sickening, pitying expression. I wanted to move the conversation on. "At least I won't have to reconsider your proposal now that we lost."

It was a poor jape, but Tasar still brightened at the words.

"Ah, but the war's not over yet, my friend. There's still hope."

Almost three years ago, Tasar had sent a letter requesting a marriage between his brother, Cyfrin, and my little sister, Diandra. I had dismissed the idea immediately, not only because the idea of forcing Didi to marry was deplorable, but because there was something unsettling about Cyfrin. However, I could never quite put my finger on what it was.

"The Autarch could have slaughtered half our men by now." I sighed, rubbing my eyes with the heels of my palms. "No one has seen or heard anything to suggest that they're still alive."

"But he might not have," Tasar countered. "Malah might be squirrelling them away, out of sight for now. You know how easily things are hidden within the mists."

His optimism should have cheered me, but it just seemed to sink my worries heavier in my gut. The majority of my army was still deep in enemy territory, locked away in the Shrouded Isles of Katmu. I didn't know if they were alive or dead. Despite attempting to send multiple Zingali Rats to gather any information, nothing got past the harbor in Anzillu.

Even if Malah Jirata had hidden them somewhere, there was no way someone without the knowledge …

"What did you say?" I asked, my attention snapping back to Tasar.

"The mists around Katmu hide all of the smuggling vessels on the smaller islands. You're the one who told me that."

Rising to my feet, I looked him directly in the eye, needing to judge his next words carefully.

"Tasar, are you with me?" I demanded.

"Would I be here if I wasn't?" he replied, but then seeing my expression he added, "Of course I am; he has my people too."

"I'm about to call a meeting with my court, which I'd like you to attend. But you're about to see something that you have to swear to keep quiet about."

Half an hour later, the table in the dining room was almost full, seating each of my trusted advisors: Nook, Ezra, Suenna, Didi, my mother, and Josephine. My circle of confidants had thinned since returning home, the betrayal of Corbin, Malah Jirata, *and* Aran Seirsun making me doubt my judgement.

Tasar sat opposite me and was inspecting the map of Irkalla I had laid out across the table. His head lifted when a light knock sounded at the door.

"Remember, Tasar," I warned, "not a word."

His response was lost in a gasp as he saw Karasi enter, followed—as always—by Torin. She gave a small smile to her old friend, her expression softening further at his wide eyes and open mouth.

"Kara," he breathed, rising to his feet and enveloping her into a fierce embrace. "I don't believe it, where have you been?" His words sounded thick as he half-sobbed them into her hair, gently clutching her dark curls in one hand.

All three of us had grown up as friends, but Karasi and Tasar had always been close. They shared the responsibility of being Lord and Lady of their respective districts and would lean upon one another to offer support. Tasar had been deeply hurt by her death, withdrawing into himself and rarely leaving Hudjefa.

A slight movement caught my eye, and I cast a swift glance at Torin. His hands were fisted and his jaw clenched as he watched the reunion with a vexed expression. His gaze tracked Tasar's hand in my sister's hair, the tension rippling off him in waves.

"It doesn't matter," Karasi said, pulling back from Tasar and shaking her head slightly. "I'm back now, but you must keep it a secret. The Autarch will come after me again if he knows that I'm still alive."

"I promise, Kara. You know you can trust me," he replied, reaching up as if to touch her again.

Tasar's hand faltered as Torin barged past the pair, seating himself at the end of the table.

"Are we going to start then?" the Atturynnian snapped. "The Autarch will have died of natural causes before you've begun your discussions."

"Of course," I said, gesturing for everyone to sit. Clearing my throat, I addressed the room. "The Autarch has our army. While we don't know exactly what's happened to them, I'm choosing to remain hopeful that he hasn't killed them all. I believe that if he had, we would have heard something of it. Instead, we're getting only silence from Katmu."

I leaned over to press a finger to where the Shrouded Isles were located on the map.

"Now, Tasar reminded me that the mists hide all of the smuggling vessels and cargo being brought to and from the islands."

"Filthy pirating scum, stealing from my lands," Torin grumbled.

I shot him a reproachful look before continuing. "We have Aran Seirsun locked away, meaning that if we're smart, we can gain control over the small remaining fleet he left in Kusig. Without their Lord, their defenses will be weakened. Manned with our men from the mountain barracks, we should be able to sail to Katmu, send in small numbers here, here, and here," I gestured to points across the islands, "to slip in unseen and recapture the prisoners."

"Are you out of your mind? What fresh nonsense is this?" Nook exclaimed. The shocked faces of the others echoed his sentiment.

Not quite the response I was hoping for.

"No one knows how to navigate those waters," Ezra said. "There's a reason you only find criminals crossing them, the ports are impossible to find unless you know where you're going."

"But I do know where I'm going," I countered, a grim smile stretching across my face. "Malah showed me the routes himself."

Chapter 2

Erisa

Erisa,

~~I know you're getting these letters, so stop ignoring me.~~
I know you're hurting, but I wish you'd just talk to me about it.
The reports I receive about your ruthless behavior around the
realm are the only indication I have that you're still alive.

~~Despite the nature of the contents, I fear the day that I'll stop~~
~~getting them.~~
~~I don't know how many times I can apologize for what happ~~

The situation concerning the armies is still precarious and I could
really use your help.

Please,
Theo

17 October

❖ ❖ ❖

I had never truly appreciated the possibility of loneliness.

The way grief subsides for the brief moments of revenge-
fueled rage, providing an intermission in the empty days that seem

to stretch out into a crepuscular, unremitting abyss.

For my entire life, I had been under the assumption that I had mastered the art of being alone; that I could function perfectly by relying on nobody but myself.

How ridiculously naive.

I supposed I had never truly counted Verrill as a separate person, rather considering us both two parts of a whole, neglecting to acknowledge the possibility that our separation was even feasible.

Even after the slaughter of our entire family, I had never been afraid that he would die. The thought had never even crossed my mind, because it was an impossibility. I still had a hard time believing that it was true; Verrill wouldn't leave me. He would fight the gods themselves before abandoning me.

But it had been weeks since I'd seen the light leave those warm, hazel eyes and weeks since I'd watched his body plummet toward the thrashing waves. I had since gone back to the cliff, carefully scaling the rock to where it met the cold seawater in a desperate attempt to find him. But there had been nothing, not a single scrap of evidence to suggest he'd ever been there.

The lack of discovery had caused a cruel, unwanted swell of hope to blossom in my chest. Because hadn't Theo also found nothing of Karasi? Her body had never been discovered, and he'd spent four years believing that she was dead. And yet, somehow, she had managed to survive.

I'd caught myself praying wretchedly to the gods that they would deliver Verrill back to me, begging Ereshkigal to let him go. That was when that merciless swell of hope had collapsed, laughing at my foolishness. The gods didn't owe me anything, and I'd never offered them enough respect to warrant such a gift.

Not like Theo; Ereshkigal's golden boy. Her rumored gift of redemption.

Bitterness curled my lip as I crumpled his latest pathetic plea for help into a ball and tossed it into a nearby torch sconce. Shadows danced across the walls of the narrow tunnel as the small flames consumed his inked words.

The streets of Šarrum were quiet now, and I could almost taste the apprehension and unease of the citizens in the air. Those residing in the royal city—the Autarch's domain—were left abandoned when he had fled to Katmu. Houses had already been raided by the Hudjefans, before Tasar had put a stop to it.

Now the wealthiest of Irkallians were at the mercy of the poorest.

Clinging to the shadows, I navigated my way through the familiar neighborhoods, remaining out of sight until I arrived at an inconspicuous wooden door of a plain little house. I slipped a key from my pocket and entered silently.

The house was dark and vacant, but my heart skipped a beat at the realization that it had been recently inhabited. Other than a thin sprinkling of dust decorating the simple furniture, it was clean and well kept.

This was one of the many properties Verrill and I owned throughout the realm, their locations unknown to anyone but ourselves. We would use them to store undisclosed shipments, house the Rats and would occasionally use them as places to stay when away from the Palace for extended periods of time. I had been searching each of them, one by one, to find out where Verrill had been staying before he died. He had been a known traitor, sympathetic to Theo's rebellion and therefore forced to flee his home at the Palace.

Barely breathing, I crept into the bedroom. The air was still with disuse, but I could see the signs of forgotten life. The bed was made, but the sheets were slightly crumpled. There were some folded clothes hung over the back of a small wooden chair in the corner of the room.

And leaning up against the wardrobe; a lyre.

The wood had been polished smooth, the surface waxed and gleaming. Every bend and contour of the instrument was as familiar to me as my own limbs and seeing it felt like breathing in a forgotten scent, the associated memories flooding my vision and spilling down my cheeks.

I barely registered my silent tears as I crossed the room, reaching out a hand to delicately run my fingers over Verrill's lyre. My breath caught at the soft twang of the strings.

Without realizing how I got there, I found myself lying on the bed, clutching the sheets and pillow to my face, breathing in the faded scent of sage and juniper. All of my tightly wound composure snapped, and I sobbed and screamed into the cold blankets, falling apart at the seams. The stitches holding me together were fraying and unravelling too fast, leaving me incapable of pulling myself together again.

❖ ❖ ❖

"Excuse me, miss … some letters for you. I swear I didn't read them."

I looked down to where a little boy of no more than ten was tugging on the skirt of my dress. His face was too thin, lacking the childish roundness of his peers and his dirty clothes were threadbare.

A small, brown ribbon was tied to a buttonhole in his baggy shirt.

"How old are you, little Rat?"

"I'm not little." He lifted his chin in defiance. "I'll be eight in two months."

Was it impressive for a child of seven to be able to read strategic correspondence? I didn't know enough about children to be certain.

He held out the letters to me, clutching them in his small hand. I recognized one of them as a Rat's replication of sealed correspondence, but the other was sealed with an unfamiliar crest imprinted in the wax. The boy's hand was shaking slightly, betraying his outward confidence. It was obvious he hadn't been doing this for long.

"Where are your parents?" I asked, taking the letters from him and slipping them into my pocket.

His lower lip trembled, and his dark, wide eyes filled with tears. His voice was barely above a whisper when he finally spoke. "Gone," was all he said.

"And you can read and write?"

"Yes," he said proudly. "I've read four big books with no pictures, and I know my letters *and* my numbers."

I had never been particularly fond of children; they were

noisy and sticky and generally poor company to keep. But I found that the thought of leaving him to continue fending for himself disturbed me.

"What's your name?"

"Farzin."

"Are you hungry?"

He looked at me warily as he nodded.

"Come with me, little Rat," I said, trying and failing to make my voice sound like a soft suggestion rather than a demand.

He hesitated. "No, thank you. I don't know you and nothing is ever given for free. And … and you haven't paid me for your letters."

"Very wise words," I commended, and pressed a silver coin into his hand. "That should be more than enough for now. But I have another job for you, one that requires you to be cleaned up with a full belly."

Farzin gaped at the coin, before nodding eagerly. He fell into step behind me as I made my way through the bustling bazaar in the heart of Anzillu.

The district had been split into two, with Henri Elkas retreating with his dwindling army to hold the harbor and the coastline. The remaining citizens thrived without their Lord; their spirits buoyed with the possibility of a new era. Henri had always been firm with his people, and had learned the hard way what happened when those forced into fighting were given an opportunity to rebel.

Tasar's brother, Cyfrin Wranmaris had infiltrated Henri's ranks not two weeks after the battle in Ocridell, and had planted dangerous ideas amongst the fighters. Those ideas had spread like wildfire, resulting in almost half of Henri's men defecting to return home. The remainder likely stayed out of fear alone. Unlike the people of Šarrum, those in Anzillu embraced Theo's insurrection with ease, rallying behind his schemes and denouncing their Lord and Autarch.

"Stay close, little Rat," I called to Farzin when he'd stopped to gaze longingly at one of the food stalls roasting chicken legs over a small fire. He bounded to my side instantly and looked questioningly at the door I'd stopped to knock at.

A graying woman with bright, cunning eyes answered. She took one look at me and attempted to slam the door shut in my face. I caught it with my boot just in time, jamming it into the frame.

I tutted. "Don't be rude, Aghna. I'm here to collect a debt."

I tapped a finger against one of the silver bands tattooed around my right forearm, pleased to see that my collection once again reached my elbow.

Aghna gripped the door tightly for a moment, as though contemplating her options before opening it and inviting me inside. The apartment was spacious, adjoined to the bakery next door and smelled of freshly baked bread and cakes.

She scowled, gesturing for me to sit at a small table in the kitchen. "What do you want, Feline?"

Even though I wasn't wearing my veil, her recognition didn't surprise me; I had worked with Aghna enough times before.

Farzin halted at her words, staring up at me with wide, fearful eyes.

I tried to fix my face with a kind smile. "Don't be afraid, if I was going to hurt you, don't you think I would have done so on the journey here?"

He didn't look convinced.

"This is Farzin," I said, gesturing to the frightened boy before turning back to Aghna. "You're going to let him stay here. He's going to be collecting other strays to join him, and I need someone to look after them."

"You want him to bring other children here? What are you going to do to them?" she asked hesitantly.

"Orphans," I corrected, "there seems to be an influx of them recently. And my plans for them are none of your business. Your job is to look after them."

"Why me?"

"You have the space," I said, watching her wrinkled hands nervously smooth over the front of her apron. "I know the powder you used to store in those back rooms wasn't flour or sugar, so you have no use for them now. And besides, you must be lonely here without Frank. I expect them to be fed, bathed, and clothed as well as you would your own children. I'll be checking in regularly."

"These are difficult times, Feline. Even if business *was* booming, there would be little chance of my finances stretching to accommodate this request."

"This isn't a request," I reminded her. "But don't worry, I'll be covering the costs. You'll have more than enough. Understood?"

Begrudgingly, she nodded—and the second she did, I felt my arm burn and the bargain mark disappear.

"Perfect," I said, standing and making my way back out. I stopped to address Farzin, who was still standing in the corner of the room. "Be good, little Rat. I'll see you again very soon."

I was almost out the door when the aged woman appeared beside me.

"Don't expect me to believe you're doing this out of the goodness of your heart, Feline. You have an agenda."

"It's called an investment, Aghna," I snapped. "Seeing as you're also one of mine, you should be familiar with the concept."

I was out onto the street before she could respond, making my way back to the small boarding house I'd been staying in for the past few nights. As soon as I was back in my room, I retrieved the crumpled, unfamiliar letter from my pocket and unfolded it.

Miss E A,

Unfortunately, we have not had anyone admitted matching that description. Nor have we seen any item that would remotely resemble the one you are looking for.

I understand your desire for anonymity, but, if you do not reveal any supplementary details or give us an incentive, I'm afraid I cannot provide you with any additional information on this matter.

I wish you luck with your search.

Sincerely,
Casen Stavrou, Governor of Bīt Asiri Prison

24 October

"Fuck," I whispered, crushing the letter in my hand.

Though I hadn't expected much, the prison was one of my last resorts for finding Silas. He was a slippery bastard, somehow managing to evade the Rats at every turn. No matter how many spies I sent out, each of them came back empty handed.

It was as if he had simply disappeared. Which I wouldn't have cared about, except for the fact that he still had the shield. The one object that would defeat the Autarch. And as my need for revenge was the only thing currently keeping me sane, I was desperate to get my hands on it.

Anxiety ricocheted around my chest at the thought of failing. Silas was ruining my plans, and I was running out of options. I needed that shield. I needed Geshtinanna's stylus—the real one. And I needed to get to Katmu; to finally take my revenge.

Pulling in deep, steadying breaths, I mentally sorted through the subjects of my retribution. Aran's disloyalty was almost expected, I wouldn't waste too much time on killing him. Malah's betrayal stung; I had truly believed that we were friends. He had worked with Verrill and I, partied and danced with us and Asila, and had welcomed me into his inner circle from the very beginning of his Lordship. And yet, he had lied and abandoned us when we needed him most, stealing Asila away in the process.

But my anger toward Malah paled in comparison to what I felt for Csintalan. I had spent ten years looking up to him as though he were a second father to me. Verrill and I had considered him our hero and savior for pulling us out of the burning rubble and giving our lives purpose and meaning again. He had trained us, loved us, treated us as though we were his own children, and had given us everything we could possibly want. But all that time, he had been lying to our faces, pretending to put the blame on others for the ruin of our family, when it lay solely with him. And then he killed Verrill.

Yes, Malah was going to die, but Csintalan was going to be very, very sorry.

❖ ❖ ❖

The strange necklace in my hand glistened in the morning sun that cut through the eerie misty atmosphere enshrouding Khar'ra. Evenly spaced around a thin chain were small, golden leaves; so detailed and delicate that they were entirely lifelike, as though they'd been caught falling from a tree at the end of summertime. The leaves were separated by small elaborate beads of lapis lazuli, the blue contrasting beautifully against the shining gold. The intricate surface of the beads depicted images so tiny I could barely make them out. There was no clasp, just an unending circle of leaves and chiseled blue. Brushing my thumb over a carved face in the lapis stone, I realized that I had never seen anything like this before. This piece of jewelry was old; crafted in a time that had long since been forgotten.

As expected, Silas' cabin had been completely empty, but I had forced myself to make the detour anyway, just in case. It was in the same state of disarray as the last time I'd searched it months ago, but something about the quiet stillness had made me uneasy. Without touching anything, I'd inspected the house again and found nothing noticeably different except for the necklace.

As I rode through the streets of Khar'ra, I traced the splendent surface of the leaves, wondering if I'd made a mistake in stealing it. I assumed it belonged to the woman he'd hidden away when I'd first visited with Theo. Which meant at least *she* had returned to the cabin. I was certain I hadn't missed this before.

Tucking the necklace into my pocket, I continued through the city toward the small wooden gate that marked the entrance to the Beldam's sanctum. It was already open, as if they had been expecting me, and I urged my horse on to cross the narrow bridge that would lead me to Ereshkigal's temple.

None of the usual young acolytes were present as the twisted temple came into view and the sight of the empty grounds made my skin crawl with unease. Though I hadn't expected a warm welcome after my previous visit, I had been prepared for at least some resistance. This all felt a little too easy.

I tied my horse loosely to the fence, leaving the option of a quick escape, and walked briskly up the steps toward the temple door that arched high above my head. Without hesitation, I barged it open, striding through and into the dark room beyond. I hadn't made it two full strides before the jarring voice of one of the Beldams surrounded me.

"You are not welcome here, Erisa Anzû."

And yet, you still let me in, I thought dryly.

"You pledged your support to Theo," I reminded them, continuing into the center of the room to sit in front of the single burning candle. "We're on the same side. Give me the information I seek, and I won't need to return again."

I could just about make out the three shadows of the old women before they stepped into the meagre illumination produced by the small flame. Thankfully, their hoods were up, concealing the gruesome faces that lay beneath. They sat in unison, lowering to the floor opposite me.

"We support Theodoraxion Lusilim's claim to the realm of Irkalla," corrected the one in the middle, "not you. Especially as you are no longer allied with him."

"You want the Autarch dead," I countered, "you wouldn't have helped us in the first place if that wasn't the case. If you give me the information I need, I'll kill him, and you can appoint any oaf you like to take his place."

"It is a shame about your Fox," the haggard old bat on the left croaked, as though I hadn't even spoken. "He was such a pretty thing, but foolish nonetheless. We showed him what would happen eventually if he continued on the path, and yet he chose to walk it anyway."

I ground my teeth at the mention of Verrill, urgently clawing my rising temper down into submission. They were testing me as they had during my previous trip, wanting me to lash out and rage to avoid giving me answers.

But I was determined to succeed where I'd failed before. I remained silent, despite my desperation to know what she meant. As far as I was aware, Verrill had only visited the Beldam's once, with Theo and myself.

"You wish to find Silas," the woman in the middle stated after an age of heavy silence.

"I wish to find the shield," I clarified.

The one on the right cackled beneath her hood. "You will not kill the Autarch with an incomplete shield, stupid girl. You need the stylus crafted for Geshtinanna."

"But I need to find the shield to complete it," I argued through gritted teeth.

"You are not welcome here, Erisa Anzû," repeated the middle woman. "We do not give information for nothing, and after your last visit, you cannot expect to get answers from us."

I considered using my newfound powers against them. I'd always been able to send intentions and emotions out with my voice, but before the battle in Ocridell I never knew I'd be able to directly control someone before. I could still feel the bitter taste of Csintalan's will on my tongue, fighting to regain authority as his body obeyed my command.

But I was still too green, too unpracticed with the gift. I wasn't even sure if I could do it again. And I was almost certain that these women harnessed a different kind of power, that if I tried and failed to control them, it would be the last thing I ever did.

"What do you want?" I asked them.

"Make a deal with us," she offered, reaching a corpse-like hand from beneath her robes toward me. "We will answer three questions in return for a debt."

My mouth seemed to fill with sand. I hadn't owed a debt to anyone since before the fall of my family. I collected bargains instead of giving them, relishing in the power it gave me. I refused to relinquish that to anyone else, to enable anyone to have that level of control over me.

"No."

Had it been anyone other than these three witches, I would have considered the deal. I was desperate, but I knew without a shadow of a doubt that if I was to agree, their collection price would be steeper than I could afford.

And even when it seems like you have nothing left to lose, that's when you have everything to gain.

"Then you must leave," she said, folding her boney arm back into her robes. Though I couldn't see her empty eye sockets or the blue eye tattooed onto her forehead, I knew she was watching me intently.

"Is there nothing else I can give you?" I asked, without making a move to stand. I could feel the gazes of all three sisters penetrate beneath my skin as they searched my past, present and future.

The gold and lapis lazuli necklace in my pocket seemed to burn under their scrutiny.

"Tell us how you summoned Silas during the battle in Ocridell," rasped the figure on the left. "He eludes the Sight."

"If I knew how to do that, I wouldn't have needed to waste my time coming here," I snapped. "Silas made sure that only *I* could read the words with the power to call him, and that once they'd been spoken aloud, they'd be forgotten. The words vanished off the paper as soon as he'd answered the call."

Trying to calm the swell of anger racing up my throat, I rose to my feet. If they couldn't even see Silas, there was no point in asking them where the shield was. This trip had been a waste of time. I should have just gone straight to Aran Seirsun as I had previously planned.

The Beldams stood too, their dark gray cloaks revealing nothing of the hideous creatures beneath.

"You'll leave now, Lady Anzû," announced the sister on the

right. Her hunched form uncurled to her full height, which matched my own and I took an involuntary step back. "If you want to find Geshtinanna's stylus before Silas does, you cannot idle away the hours with dreams of revenge. Silas is looking for it, and if he finds it before you do, your chance will be lost forever."

I paused. "What would he want with the stylus?"

A croaking answer came from beneath the hood on the left. "He never wanted you to complete the shield. Once you placed the relics into their designated settings, they became untouchable."

"If it is not placed, then the stylus can be destroyed," said the one on the right, still towering above her sisters. "You will ask for our council once more, Feline. But remember, we will not give you something for nothing."

The Beldams' words taunted me on the ride back toward Ersetu. I hadn't even considered the possibility that Silas would be trying to disrupt Theo's plans by destroying his ability to use the shield against the Autarch. He had made his aversion to the scheme known to Theo from the beginning, but had never indicated that he would actively plot against his friend.

I tried to shift my thoughts away from Theo as I approached the new opening in the volcano that would lead me to Hudjefa. I couldn't let myself get distracted now that I knew the consequences of delaying my actions.

If I wanted to kill Csintalan, I needed to find Aran Seirsun and force him to reveal the location of the stylus. Once I had it, I could find the shield and complete it. Then, seeing as Theo's army was in a state of disarray, I'd need to utilize Aran's fleet to cross the channel to Katmu.

As I arrived at the Wranmaris estate, I noticed Tasar's brother, Cyfrin, was listening to a whispered message from a young man, who tapped the shell of his ear, before scurrying back out of the stable block.

Cyfrin beamed at me. "Feline, what a pleasant surprise." He lifted the back of my hand to his lips before stepping back to admire the horse I'd stolen from Anzillu a week prior. His alert, pale green eyes sparkled. "What a beauty."

"Look after her for me," I said, "I need to take a tram."

"Of course. Where are you going?" He grinned, as though he already knew the answer. The smattering of copper freckles across his cheeks shifted with the movement. "I'll arrange for one to depart immediately."

"I'm going to Zingal."

Chapter 3

Theo

T he metal doorframe was cool against my back where I leaned against it, closing my eyes to try and collect myself. My heart hammered in my chest, showing no sign of slowing its relentless pace. I was nervous; anxious about what awaited me on the other side of the door.

The sound of Aran's screams reaching all the way up from the underground cellar could only mean one thing; Erisa was here.

I hadn't seen her since the battle in Ocridell, when she had blamed me for Verrill's death and tried to sink a dagger into my face in reparation. The menacing beauty of her features twisted into that hateful rage was the vision I saw each night before I went to sleep.

Easing the door open, I crept slowly down the stone steps toward the cells. The air was cold and damp, contrasting with the early fall heat outside.

"You can't have it," Aran whimpered from the end cell. There were only three in total, and I could count on one hand the number of times they'd actually been used to hold prisoners. The rusted metal door was cracked ajar, and I peered through, not wanting to betray my presence.

"Tell me where it is, and I'll let you keep this fingernail." Erisa loomed over Aran like a menacing spirit, her dark veil of silken hair enclosing his face.

I drank in the sight of her greedily, as though she were the first drop of rain across parched plains. Even in her simple black riding clothes, she stole the breath from my lungs.

She jerked her arm back suddenly and Aran's wails filled my ears. He flailed in his chair, pulling fruitlessly at the restraints securing his wrists and ankles. I had avoided coming down into the cells since we'd brought him here, not wanting to even look at the man who had been complicit in the Autarch's schemes.

In *Corbin's* schemes.

I pushed the wretched thought away and focused on the scene in front of me instead. Aran had lost all of his golden shine since the battle. His hair was limp and dirty, darkened by the filth coating the rest of him, and his skin looked pallid and greasy. Blood dripped from a few of his fingers and pooled on the floor around a missing toe.

"This all could've been avoided, Aran," Erisa said, leaning herself lazily against the wall opposite him. "If only you had made better choices."

"I'm loyal to the Autarch," Aran hissed, "something you would know nothing about."

He spat at her, and his head whipped to the side as she lunged forward and backhanded him faster than my eyes could track.

"And where did that loyalty get you?" she sneered. "Is he coming to rescue you from this disgusting hovel? Is he going to reward your loyalty with anything other than a knife in the chest? I *was* loyal to him, Aran, more loyal than you could ever dream of being. I gave him everything and he still betrayed me."

Aran's lip curled in disgust. "Maybe you just outlived your usefulness. I'm not surprised he wanted to cut you off after you let the enemy crawl between your legs. Was the Fox so terrible in bed that you needed to—"

His words were interrupted by the scream that tore from his throat as a dagger landed in his kneecap.

"Don't you dare speak of him." Erisa's voice was chilling; I tried to look at her expression, but she had her back to me as she stalked toward her captive.

"I've always hated you both," Aran grunted through gritted teeth. "Even when you were younger, you were arrogant swines, using the Rats to stick your noses where they didn't belong."

"Maybe you and your darling *Mama* shouldn't have had anything to hide then, and we wouldn't have had an issue all those years ago."

"I told you then that you'd be sorry for what you did to her." Aran looked up at her with a hatred that only made her smile.

She let out a cold, cruel laugh. "Oh, how you must *love* the irony that I killed her for the same reason I would commit treason myself, I just didn't know it yet."

His eyes widened on the blade she trailed up this throat. "She'll be the one laughing in the end, I made sure of it," he said, with a trembling voice.

The honed edge stopped at his jawline as Erisa froze. She tilted her head to the side, assessing him for a few seconds before her face split into the most exquisite smile.

A sharp breath left me at the sight, causing her head to snap up and her gaze to fix on mine. The smile dropped instantly into a scowl and her bright yellow eyes flamed orange with disdain.

"I should've known you'd be eavesdropping like a timid shrew, Theo. Too scared to announce your presence," she said venomously.

"You're trespassing, Feline. Aran is my prisoner to interrogate, not yours."

The formality of my words almost pained me, but since the battle, she'd made it extremely clear that she couldn't care less about our relationship or alliance.

"No matter," she jeered, looking me quickly up and down before starting toward me at the door, "I've got what I came for."

My hand wrapped around her wrist as she moved to pass me, and I pulled her to a stop. The scent of jasmine and orange assaulted me, and I couldn't stop myself from leaning in closer to breathe it in.

"I know you've been looking for him, seeking vengeance," I murmured into her ear. "You'll only get to him with my help, but I need yours too. Please, Sunflower, just work with me on this."

Her nails drew blood as she ripped my hand from her wrist, disappearing up the stairs without a sound.

"You should've finished her off when you had the chance, Lord Lusilim," Aran labored, his sallow complexion drained further from the pain and blood loss. "Not that I blame you; even

I would've taken her for a tumble before slitting her throat."

I heard one of his pearly white teeth fall to the floor as I punched him in the face.

❖ ❖ ❖

"What do you mean, you had business to attend to?" my mother demanded later that evening when Karasi and Torin reappeared in the parlor, after their unexpected absence that had lasted for almost two weeks. Shortly after they had left, the Atturynnian fleet had also departed, disappearing into Tarprusan waters and out of sight.

"Exactly that, mother," she huffed, taking off her sodden cloak to hang it by the hearth. "I left you a note to say I would be gone for a few days."

"And I suppose that makes it okay then," my mother said, sending an accusatory scowl toward Torin, whose expression remained blank and unchanged. "We've only just got you back."

A warm, nostalgic heat spread through my chest at the familiar bickering, soothing an ache that I hadn't known was still there. Seeing my twin sister alive and well, with a frustrated flush to her cheeks as she argued with our mother over trivial matters, was more amusing that I remembered. And having my family united once more was a gift I would never take for granted again.

"I'm sorry for tricking you all," Karasi began sadly, "I had to make my death look believable—"

"The reason for which you'll still refuse to give, no doubt," Didi grumbled quietly.

"—but I *didn't* die all those years ago. I have a life, I have things I need to do." She paused for a moment. "I only risked coming back because Theo needed my help."

We locked eyes for a moment, and I wished she could see the gratitude I felt for her in my expression. The entire army would have been slaughtered had she not come to aid us.

Even though it had been weeks since the battle in Ocridell, she had still not explained exactly how she'd known I was making a move against the Autarch. She'd only said that word spread between the realms faster than a forest fire.

My mother opened her mouth to speak but Karasi held up her left hand to stop her, before letting out a shaky sigh.

"I found out about the Autarch … about Corbin," she confessed quietly, ignoring the hurt cries of betrayal Didi and my mother stifled at the mention of the name. I had managed to tell the rest of my family about Corbin's treachery similar to the way I'd told Ezra; forcing my way through it.

Karasi continued. "He's the reason I went missing before Theo returned from Tarprusa, he had me locked in Bīt Asiri Prison." Her voice shook slightly as she looked at her strange companion. "Torin helped me get out. After Corbin realized I was gone, he tricked me, sending the Feline to … dispose of me."

The brief silence was shattered by my mother's keening over Karasi's treatment at the hand of the man who had mourned her with us, knowing he was the reason for our grief. My twin allowed our mother to fuss over her and weep into her dark curls.

My mind spun with this new information. Not much was known—or made public—about Bīt Asiri Prison, but everyone knew that only the foulest in the realm were sent there. And once you were admitted within its walls, there was no way out.

Reaching into my pocket, I pulled out her beloved charm bracelet and handed it to her. Her eyes widened in disbelief as she took it from me and fastened it onto her wooden hand, slipping the ring over the middle finger. Its surface was no longer marred by splinters, but smooth and gleaming.

"Where did you get it?" she asked, looking up at me. Her eyes were the exact mirrors of my own; the Lusilim green we'd all inherited from our father. "I thought the Autarch had found it."

She fumbled with the broken locket clasp, glancing up at Torin when she realized that it was empty. He was focusing on the fragile trinket as though it were a ghost that haunted his nightmares.

"The stone is gone. Eri—we fixed it, like you said to do," I informed her, a grin tugging at a corner of my mouth, "though your instructions left a lot to be desired."

Karasi gave me a questioning look. "My instructions?"

"The note you left with the stone, in the locket on your bracelet. You told me that I already knew who *he* was—I'm assuming that was Corbin—and that I needed to fix the stone."

"Ah," she flicked her gaze back to Torin for a second, "that, er … that note wasn't meant for you, Theo."

"But you addressed it to T …" I faltered, my question trailing off as I looked over to where Torin had raised an amused, scarred brow. "Well, I guess that explains why I couldn't make sense of it."

"I'm sorry, Theo," she said with a sympathetic smile, "there was so much going on at that time and I—"

She broke off as Ezra's voice called out from the kitchen,

"Theo."

He appeared in the doorway a second later, and my now racing heart dropped with disappointment at the unfamiliar man who accompanied him. For a brief second, I'd secretly hoped that he'd caught Erisa lurking somewhere and had dragged her inside.

"He said he had a message for Torin and refused to let anyone else deliver it," Ezra grumbled, gutting his chin to the stranger. Though he wasn't particularly tall or muscular, his presence was striking and exigent. His dark skin contrasted with his light blue eyes so decidedly that the effect was astonishing.

"Samson." Torin grinned, embracing the man with an uncharacteristic warmth.

Though I had tried multiple times to engage in conversation with Torin since Ocridell, he'd remained quiet, giving expressionless, monosyllabic responses to everyone except Karasi. Had I not seen how his attention would fixate solely on my sister, and her unique ability to pry emotions from his inscrutable features, I would've thought him incapable of any expression at all. I was shocked to hear the fondness in his voice now, which I'd assumed he reserved only for her.

"I have news from your sister, Your Highness," Samson announced in the chiming accent of the northern kingdoms. He glanced around the room at my family and friends, no doubt seeing the shocked expression on each of our faces. "Perhaps there is somewhere private we can go to discuss?"

Torin looked at Karasi intently, a silent conversation communicated between them. Torin nodded once, before turning and leading Samson out of the room.

"Karasi, what the fuck is going on?" I demanded. "Who is he?"

"Prince Torin Sharru of Atturynn, second in line to the throne," she answered, a hint of pride lifting her chin.

I had too many questions to voice, I didn't even know where to begin. If I thought logically about this new development, it explained how so many Atturynnians were able to come to our aid, but I couldn't even begin to imagine how he and Karasi had become allies.

The spare heirs of the northern kingdoms weren't often a topic of conversation in Irkalla, and I knew too little about the popularity of names over there to have made Torin stand out as unique. But surely *someone* here had to have made the connection.

A quick glance around the room told me that that wasn't the case.

"You need to explain," I said to my sister. "I've been patient with you, allowed you to keep the secrets of the past four years to yourself, but this is too far. What are you doing with the Prince of Atturynn? Are they planning on invading Irkalla?"

"Of course not," she snapped. "Torin helped me escape, he saved my life and kept me hidden from the Autarch. He's here in Irkalla because I asked him to come and help you. You should be singing his praises for saving you, when he could have easily left you to your fate. Especially when he had Aessurus to deal with."

"Are you two … involved?"

"No." Her tone was final, daring me to push that particular subject further.

"He *is* grateful," my mother assured, "we all are. But you

must see how confusing this is for us. You haven't given us any explanation apart from the fact that Torin is the reason you're alive. And I see the way you two are together—"

"He belongs to somebody else, mother," she interrupted. "I don't want to talk about it anymore. I came back to help defeat the Autarch once and for all, to finally get revenge on Corbin for everything he put me through."

❖ ❖ ❖

The map of Irkalla covered the surface of the large table in the dining room, with small paper weights holding down the corners. My closest friends and confidants were seated around it, joined by Karasi, Torin, and Samson, who had returned after an hour of private discussions the night before.

I tried not to think about my sister's involvement with Atturynn, or what she could've possibly promised them in return for coming to my aid. She denied giving any explanation about it, saying only that she owed them nothing. Even if that were true, her refusal to promise me that she would stay in Zingal made me nervous.

"This is no longer my home," she'd said earlier that morning, after I'd arranged a decorator to come and talk to her about renovating her room. It had remained vacant for the years she'd been away, and I had thought she might like to have a fresh start. Her words were a blow, and despite my best efforts, I couldn't help harboring less than amicable feelings toward the Prince of Atturynn. I had no doubt that he was behind it.

Even though the shock of her return had worn off, interacting with my twin sister now was strange. I had mourned her for years, familiarizing myself with life without her. She had changed too; she was tougher, stronger than when she had left Irkalla behind. She had built a new life for herself, so different from the one she'd left me in that it felt as though I barely knew her anymore.

"Most of Aran's accessible fleet is still moored in Zagina Bay at Kusig's northern anchorage," Ezra said, leaning over the table to tap his finger on the district border in the lower half of the map. "He sent most of them to Katmu before the battle, but from the reports we've been getting, it should just about be enough."

I nodded. "Excellent, we'll trickle in slowly when the mists are at their thickest to try and avoid as much unwanted attention as possible. I'll go in the first wave, to spread the word amongst our men and women that they need to be ready for the second wave to collect them. If we relay the vessels effectively, we should have just enough to get them all out."

"You shouldn't be going in there at all, Theo," Nook said, a disapproving look souring his perpetually playful expression. "If they capture you, the entire operation fails, and Zingal will be taken."

"Zingal has its Lady back, I'm no longer Lord," I replied, looking at Karasi.

"Absolutely not!" she shot back. "The realm thinks I'm dead, and I've got no desire to change that, nor do I want to be Lady again."

"I'm not sure it works like that, Kara," I argued, but decided to drop the matter at her scathing look. We could discuss it later. "Now, we've been through the plan enough times, is everyone certain on their role?"

They all nodded and rose to their feet to follow me out of the room.

A dark-haired woman was waiting in the hallway. It was Vashti, one of Nook's most frequent lovers, and her eyes lit up when she saw him exit after me. The pair had met when she'd treated his wounds after one of our silly escapades in the Zuamsik mountains had resulted in him almost lancing his arm off. She had berated him for his foolishness, and he'd been entranced with the medic ever since.

She pulled him into the parlor to whisper something into his ear, and I was about to protest that we were in a hurry, when a grin almost split his face in two. Everyone stopped to watch as he lifted her up and spun her around, the joy practically radiating off them both.

He turned to face us. "We're going to have a baby!" he cheered, proudly placing a hand on Vashti's abdomen.

Within seconds, the pair were flooded with hugs and congratulations, and I could feel my cheeks pulling themselves into the first real smile I'd had in ages. I glanced over to Ezra, not surprised to find him beaming as he locked eyes with Nook. I had never fully understood their relationship, but I knew that Ezra was truly happy for Nook in this moment.

I clapped Nook on the shoulder and pressed a kiss to Vashti's cheek in congratulations, burying my sense of trepidation that this news had come at an inauspicious time. Bringing a child into the potential of war was less than ideal.

"You can stay behind," I told my friend, even though the

thought of doing this without him pained me. "We can find someone else to cover your role."

"Don't be absurd, of course I'm coming," he exclaimed, before taking Vashti's hand and pulling her away from the crowd. "Let me just say goodbye and I'll meet you out there."

The weather had turned in the last week and the fall air was unusually bitter. Rain pelted relentlessly against our cloaks as we waited at the platform in the center of Zingal for the tram to arrive. Despite the cold, the exaltation from Nook's happy news still warmed us through, and there were smiles among the men and woman as the news traveled between them.

Now that Tasar had full control over the network, the trams no longer ran on regular schedules, and would only be sent with direct approval from Hudjefa. I'd written to Tasar asking for one to be sent days ago, along with my hopes that his men would be safely returned to him soon.

I had brought thirty of my best fighters with me—ones that knew how to sail—and tasked them to choose small crews of their own, who would be taking subsequent trams to join us throughout the night. Even though the city was in a state of lockdown without its Lord, we had to stagger our arrival in Kusig as much as possible to avoid notice.

The tram came into view, the wood paneling groaning slightly as it looped around the platform toward us. We began jogging to match the pace, before leaping into the different carriages and continuing up toward Ersetu.

"It's freezing," Didi whined, wiping the wet hair from her forehead before she pulled her cloak tighter around her shoulders.

"Here," I said, withdrawing my dry scarf from beneath my own cloak and wrapping it around her neck, and pulling it up to cover her ears too. "Do you still have the letter?"

She only rolled her eyes at the question I'd repeated three times already. I had tasked her with hand-delivering the details of our plan to Tasar, not trusting it to the Rats. Even though I wanted Didi to remain in Zingal, I didn't have anyone else I could trust to carry out the task, and I knew Tasar would keep her safe. She would have to carry on into the volcano alone.

Not that she couldn't take care of herself. I'd made a bad habit of underestimating my sisters, and it was time I started giving them the opportunity to hold their own.

I gave Didi a quick kiss on the forehead before joining the rest of my soldiers in leaping out of the carriage and onto the platform in Ocridell. Immediately, we retreated into the long unkempt grass at the edge of the area, before filtering out in small groups to begin our trudge through the deteriorating city toward Kusig.

My feet were soaked and blistering by the time we made it to the edge of Ocridell. We stood on the battleground, poised at the entrance of the descent down the cliff toward the Golden City. The steep, winding path was quiet and void of travelers, but I knew that despite our best efforts, anyone watching the road would notice us immediately.

Since Aran's capture during the battle, the Autarch had sent forces to *protect* the people of Kusig; keeping them locked inside to prevent the citizens from turning themselves over to me, for the sake of their Lord. They were trapped in their homes, their every move likely watched and monitored.

Eventually, we reached the closed gilded gates of the city and skirted around the tall limestone wall encasing the border, being mindful of the waves lashing at the jagged rocks to our right. Sheltered by the smooth, pale stone, we waited for the second and third groups to join us from the tramline and began our journey anew.

The freshly healed wound in my leg throbbed angrily as we started to walk again. The rocky path was thin and slippery, pulling at my muscles enough to make me wince. It took two hours for the first of the ships to appear in the dark waters.

I raised a hand to signal for my companions to halt behind me and watched intently at the small flames flickering in the hands of the Autarch's guards patrolling the edge of the port. With the rain clouds obscuring the moon, I knew I had to get closer in order to proceed.

"Wait here," I whispered to Nook, who held the rest of them back as I crept forward, clinging to the side of the wall.

The guards remained still as I approached, sitting on the steps that led up to the city in a staggered formation. It wasn't until I was only a few feet away that the flames from their torches illuminated what I'd missed from afar.

Instead of sitting, the small group of men and women were sprawled across the stairs, each of them sporting a lethal wound that had made for a swift and silent death. My stomach clenched at the sight. Even though it was unfortunate that these people had been slaughtered, I wasn't about to mourn the opportunity we'd just been given.

Hadn't we also been prepared to achieve our goal by whatever means necessary? Though I had to wonder who had decided to make our job easier. Either this was a trap, or there was another horse in this race.

Careful not to slip on the trickles of blood seeping down the steps, I walked up to the nearest guard and pulled the torch free from where it had been lodged in between their leg and the step. I extracted a small vial from within my cloak and walked over to a large, wooden weapon rack and carefully poured the fluid from the vial, covering as much of the wood as possible.

Retreating back to the waterfront, I waved the torch slowly, using the flame to signal Nook without attracting the notice of the guards further into the harbor. Based on their movement, I assumed they were still alive.

Silently, Nook, Ezra and I filtered everyone into large rowboats and pushed off into the frigid water, taking care to avoid any areas of light that might give us away. By the time we reached the first of the ships, my adrenaline had spiked, soaring to snap everything into sharp focus. We spread ourselves between the hulking vessels, scrambling up onto the decks in the darkness.

I could see dawn approaching in the lightening of the eastern horizon and became anxious to set sail. Finally, a series of three rhythmic taps sounded along each of the ships, indicating that everyone was in place. That they were all waiting for my signal.

Ezra offered me a bow, the largest in my collection and I took it, hefting the weight of it in my arms and ignoring the twinge of pain in my right shoulder. He offered the arrow next, and I aimed, readjusting the course to account for the force and direction of the wind. It took him three attempts to strike a small flame with the damp matches, but the head of the arrow caught successfully, burning brightly enough to heat my face.

I let it fly, holding my breath as we all watched it burn through the night air like a comet and land in the shadows of the quay. The weapon rack ignited immediately in an explosion of light that spread along the wooden railings and splashed sparks across the steps.

The instant the guards started running toward the commotion, the sails were raised and the ships lurched in unison, ready to make our escape.

"So far, so good," murmured Suenna, who was bouncing anxiously on the balls of her feet, clutching the railing.

"It won't last long," I replied, "but hopefully enough to get us—"

A loud, blaring horn interrupted my musings, as though in mockery of the words I was saying. They'd seen us far sooner than we had prepared for, but there was nothing to do but keep going. Shouts among my fighters rang out as the first projectile was launched, smashing into the side of the ship in front of my own, causing it to sway violently from side to side.

More missiles kept falling, until the sky rained with boulders and debris. I heard the screams as the first ship started to go under and saw the carnage unfolding as the next ship caught alight, one of the flaming projectiles finally managing to catch onto the sodden wood.

"DROP THE LADDERS!" I yelled, hearing the order be repeated down the line of ships. I leaned over the railing to release the ladder that unraveled into the tumultuous water below. It stretched toward the flailing bodies, and I willed them to make contact before becoming swept away by the waves.

Most of them didn't.

We lost three ships and saved less than half of the soldiers that had fallen overboard. Despite cursing them for our losses, I silently thanked the gods for the gust of icy wind that propelled us forward, and out of Zagina Bay.

Chapter 4

Theo

The ship groaned and creaked as it rocked against the waves. The Nasilan Sea was famous for its roiling waters and violent storms. I briefly watched dawn break through the small, cracked window in my cabin, before the ship crested the wave and slammed back down onto the correct course. I traced the split glass with a finger, more evidence of the attack we'd barely escaped and a harsh reminder of those we'd left behind in the dark, frigid water of Zagina Bay.

"We all knew the risks," Ezra said from behind me, placing my small, damp bag onto the table beside the thin bed. "No one expected us to succeed without losses."

Despite knowing that he was right, I'd still foolishly hoped that we'd accomplish the impossible. I yearned to speak to Corbin, as I had so many times before when I needed guidance, and the reminder of his betrayal felt like a physical slap across the face. For at least a decade, he'd been leading that perverse double life. I was unable to reconcile the monster who had plotted to murder

Karasi with the man who had helped raise us, pretending to love us like we were family.

At my lack of response, Ezra vacated the cabin, leaving me to my thoughts. I stripped off my wet clothes, hoping to find something dry in my bag. I rifled through the contents, pulling on various, slightly damp, garments, when the faint scent of jasmine hit me like a blow to the chest. It was so unexpected that I staggered on my feet, my balance already shaky from the movement of the ship.

The offending item was a linen shirt, and images of the creamy fabric contrasting against Erisa's tawny, sun-kissed skin flooded my mind without permission. I could recall the way she'd been sprawled across the rumpled sheets of my bed, sunlight filtering through the parted curtains to coax the deep, rich tones from her inky hair. Even swamped in my too-large shirt, she'd been a perfect vision.

I swore loudly, balling the fabric up and throwing it across the small room. I allowed the anger and fury I felt toward Erisa to rise and wash over the grief I knew lay beneath. I wanted to bury any evidence of the heartbreak she'd caused me.

For what seemed like the hundredth time, I felt like a fool. Like the biggest fool to have ever existed. How quickly she'd turned on me; to go from waking up in my arms to flying toward me with a poisoned dagger. Then she'd left without so much as a farewell. She hadn't even bothered to return any of my letters, completely cutting me off as though our time together had meant nothing at all.

I had risked my life to save hers, and it still hadn't been

enough.

I should have let her fall from that cliff, I thought bitterly, but regretted the idea as soon as it had formed. Saving her that day wasn't a choice, failing hadn't been an option; especially when I knew the cost of that loss. I'd felt it every time I'd awoken from the very same nightmare that had haunted me for months before it had manifested itself into reality.

I sat on the bed, curling my knees up and fisting my hair in my hands, pulling at the roots to try and distract myself from spiraling. Anguish lashed at me, thriving in Erisa's absence while a small, cruel part of me mocked the misery, insisting that I deserved this agony. After all, what could I have possibly expected from betraying the memory of my twin sister and falling in love with the woman who had murdered her?

But when that empty, aching pain in my chest didn't subside, I embraced the latest wave of self-loathing, as I retrieved the crumpled shirt from the floor and returned to the bed, falling asleep with the sweet aroma of happier memories settling deep into my lungs.

❖ ❖ ❖

After a fitful, broken sleep during the day, I ventured onto the deck of the ship that was glowing golden in the setting sun. We had anchored to the south of Katmu, remaining close enough to access the islands during the night, but remaining far enough away to not be recognized.

Suenna and Ezra were standing at the bow, taking it in turns to look through a spyglass at the distant Shrouded Isles. They had a crumpled diagram of the seven islands in front of them.

"Have the mists begun to settle yet?" I asked as I approached them.

"Not enough," Suenna replied, handing me the spyglass. I shook my head, trusting her judgement more than my own. She'd spent years on the water as a child, and I had next to no experience at sea that didn't include staying in plush cabins as a paying customer seeking passage.

"It shouldn't take too much longer though," agreed Ezra, turning to me and gesturing to the scrawled map. "Where exactly did Malah take you?"

"Here," I said, drawing a line with my finger around the southeastern island of Katmu, "there's a dock on the west, located here, but the entire southern and western coast is completely concealed in mist. The next one is here." I pointed to the northern tip of the southern, middle island. "There's another smuggling port hidden between two sea stacks. From there, we need to sail around and down toward these caves," I traced across the map, ending on the island to the far left, "they're dotted along the eastern coast. The mist will be thin between them, so we'll need to be quick."

"And what if our people are being kept on the main island? Or one of the northern ones?" Ezra asked, voicing the concern we'd all asked multiple times before.

"That's why I'm going in first," I said, "to find out where they are and how we can get to them." I looked to Suenna. "You'll need to wait until you receive word from me to know how to proceed."

She nodded, and gave me a small, forced smile before

heading below deck to get some food.

Ezra chuckled. "She's annoyed you're leaving us behind, and that you're letting Nook go with you instead of her."

"I need her here to command the fleet, and I need you to help organize the distribution of the army when we rescue them. I don't have anyone else I can trust."

He nodded, sighing sadly as though he too was thinking about how much each recent betrayal had cost us. "You'll always have us, Theo," he promised, meeting my gaze, "until the end."

My skin pricked at the words I hadn't heard since our last battle in Tarprusa. Nook, Ezra, Suenna, and I had repeated the phrase before every fight, and even Silas had caught on to the habit eventually. And though I expected that for him *the end* meant something entirely different, he'd always made the vow with such conviction that we'd felt it in our bones.

"Until the end," I repeated, feeling my heart swell with love for my friend, who always seemed to know exactly the right thing to say, even when that meant saying nothing at all.

As night dragged a dark veil over the pale evening sky, the energy on the ship crackled with anticipation of the coming mission. Planks were lowered between the ships to allow Ezra and Suenna to move to their stations, and for Nook and me to begin our advance on Katmu. Our team was small, joined by one of my army's lieutenants, Omid, and his four selected crew members.

We approached the mists slowly, silently cutting through the water toward the opaque barrier that seemed to swirl in anticipation of our arrival. As the first damp tendrils reached out to caress the prow of the ship, the anchor was dropped, and the rowboat was prepared to be lowered into the calm waters below.

"I'll be in and out as quickly as possible," I said to Nook as I joined Omid in the rowboat. "If you don't hear from me within twelve hours, head straight back to the others and begin your retreat."

He rolled his eyes at the repetition of the plan we'd been memorizing for the past week.

"Remember, if you're caught, just start explaining the mechanics of that field plough you built last year and you'll bore them to death," he jested with a wink. It wasn't until we started our descent to the water that he grabbed my forearm, his perpetual humor vanishing from his face. "Be careful, Theo. I mean it."

I nodded, holding his moonlit stare until we sank into the water and the mist slowly concealed him from view. The soft, cold vapor coated my exposed skin, causing the hairs on the back of my neck to rise.

The impression of being watched consumed me, and I looked around anxiously, despite not being able to see my own hands in front of my face. Though the night was bright and cloudless, the mist polluted the air into a milky darkness that seemed to stretch on endlessly.

How many deaths have you caused, Lord Lusilim? it taunted. *How much blood is on your hands?*

I tried to shake the whispers from my head, but they were persistent and nagging. The faceless entity that protected the Isles was known for its cruel remarks, and many sailors had been driven to madness when lost in it for too long.

Your sister would never have come back if not for your

failures. She'd rather pretend to be dead than waste any more time on you.

Everything was right there in front of you, and you were too stupid to see it.

A soft, pained groan escaped Omid. I tried to speak, to offer a word of comfort, but my throat was thick, the heavy depression glueing my mouth shut and my eyes closed. I quickened my pace, ignoring the protest in my shoulder as I lifted the oars from the water and plunged them back down with a renewed vigor. We needed to get out of the mist.

Even Erisa knew to leave you. How pathetic you must be, when even the friendless Feline has no use for you.

Grinding my teeth together, I focused all my attention on the task at hand, praying that the fog would dissipate. It felt like we'd been stuck in the confines of this rowboat for hours.

She has no one left, and she still doesn't want you.

As quick as it had come, the mist cleared, and I let out a long sigh of relief. Omid trembled slightly, and his eyes were wide, but even in the moonlight, I could see him quickly regaining composure.

"I'll never get used to that," I murmured. He only shook his head in agreement, as if not trusting himself to speak yet.

The steep cliff face of the island towered above us, and we approached the looming rock steadily. We needed to get away from the wall of mist quickly, to avoid the contrast of our dark boat against the unnaturally pale backdrop. I set my sights on the small, dark cove ahead.

The currents swirling around and between the islands of

Katmu caught us suddenly, temporarily stealing control of the boat. I plunged the oars in deeper, attempting to stabilize our course and redirect us away from the jagged rocks the tide was luring us toward.

Every muscle in my body bunched and burned with exertion as we navigated along the path Malah had shown me during my last visit to Katmu. The small flickering lights of lanterns guided me toward our destination.

"Get the rope ready," I muttered to Omid, making sure my voice was barely audible above the flow of the water. Any louder and I was sure it would carry over the surface, alerting anyone keeping watch within the cove.

As soon as we were about to pass the last of the larger rocks jutting out from the water, Omid threw the rope, lassoing it around a natural cleat in the stone. He grunted with the effort it took to haul us in, finally making it off the rapid current and securing us to the rock. It was the perfect place to remain mostly hidden from the cove. I'd suggested removing the taller stones to Malah, to enable better visibility, but was glad to find that he hadn't taken my advice.

"Keep out of sight," I ordered, "I'll be back as soon as I can. Don't take any unnecessary risks."

He wrung his hands nervously. "You remember that too."

Nodding, I pulled off my coat and lowered myself into the water, bracing myself for the cold. To my surprise, it was a pleasant temperature, almost warm against the chill air. I waded around the boat, keeping only my head above the water as I let the current pull me toward the cove.

I kept to the shadows as I approached, trying not to think about the sea snakes I knew lurked in the shallows around the southern islands. A large boat was just docking within the sheltered bay, and I swam beneath the wobbling wooden planks of the walkways to observe from the edge of the cove. Voices became distinct when I reached the boundary of the small boatyard, and I could just about make out the faces of the few individuals in the dim light.

There were three men sitting on barrels around a small fire, roasting skewers of fish and playing a game of dice. They were each wearing plain, seaworn clothes unified with a badge sewn onto their chests: Katmu's key in a navy-blue shield, indicating that they were part of Malah's Coastguard.

They all looked up as a woman walked down the gangway from the newly docked boat. She looked to be approaching middle aged, her skin tanned and weathered from the sun, the golden hue of it obscured by the colorful tattoos stretching up her arms.

"What have you got for us tonight, Morgan?" one of the men called out to her.

She smirked when she met them at the fire. "That depends, are you going to let me trade?"

"For a price, same as always." He held out his hand to take the small bag of coins she had pulled from her trouser pocket. He jutted his chin toward her boat. "So, anything interesting?"

"Goods from the Cedar Forest," she replied cryptically.

He raised his eyebrows in surprise, but didn't seem concerned about pressing her for information about the illicit contents of her cargo hold. "All the way from Atturynn, eh? No wonder we haven't seen you around these last few weeks."

She casually helped herself to a piece of roasting fish from one of the men's skewers, seeming familiar with each of them.

"Nice to know you missed me." Morgan winked and started walking back toward her boat. "I've got someone coming to collect the load in the morning, then I'm dropping the rest of the goods at the Stacks for another buyer."

I had to stifle a gasp as I felt something brush against my leg. I kicked out beneath the water, hoping that I could scare away whatever lurked beneath the surface without making a splash.

"You can't stay here," another of the men called after her, and they all rose to their feet to follow. "We're being watched heavier than ever right now. We'll help you unload the cargo, but your boat needs to be kept out of the cove."

I waited until they had all reached the boat before pulling myself up onto the dock platform, hoping that their combined voices would muffle the sound of my soaked clothes dripping onto the floor. Cringing at the squelching of my shoes, I crept into the tunnel entrance at the rear of the cove, trying to stay away from the sconces lighting the walls.

The walkway was crudely made; a narrow passage hurriedly carved from the stone and propped up with thick supporting beams that looked as weary as I felt.

Before I had even made it a hundred paces into the tunnel, I heard footsteps behind me. Sucking in a breath, I plastered myself to the wall of a small alcove hidden in shadow. I was suddenly grateful for the condensation dripping from the ceilings which concealed the water I'd traipsed across the floor.

I recognized the man who passed me as one of the guards from the fire, and followed him cautiously, waiting until he had turned around the corners before tracing his steps. Although I knew that following him would increase my chances of being caught, I had no idea where I was going, and was never going to be able to find out any information of value by aimlessly wandering the tunnels.

The man's raised voice echoed against the barren walls. "Oi, look lively you lazy gits, I've got a job for you! You lot there, come with me."

I stayed back, hidden behind a natural bulge in the stone as he pointed in front of him to someone out of view. When I heard his footsteps coming back my way—accompanied by several more—I pressed myself back even further into the stone.

Almost a dozen individuals passed by without seeing me, following the guard, until a young man at the end of the line turned his head as he walked by. His eyes widened when he saw me, and I recognized him as a field soldier from my own army. He was from one of the fishing villages on the western coast of Zingal and had been among the first to sign up to fight for me against the Autarch.

"Zak, what are you doing?" I breathed, shocked, as his hand clasped around my wrist and he pulled me to the back of the group.

"There are more guards in there with the others, you'd be walking right into the trap," he whispered, shrugging off his filthy cloak and handing it to me to disguise my dripping clothes.

"Where's the rest of the—" my question faltered as he pressed a finger to his lips and shook his head. He tapped the shoulders of the two men in front of us, and after managing to control their shocked expressions, silently alerted the next in the group.

By the time we made it to the cove, I was in the center of the procession, hidden in the middle, with a new worn hat and dirt smudged along my face. I gripped one of the women by the arm to stop her as we stepped onto the walkway.

"Can you swim?" I breathed in her ear. When she nodded, I hurriedly continued, "Omid is waiting in a rowboat outside the cove. He's roped to one of the larger stones, but you'll be able to see it from the water. Go back with him and tell Nook where the rest of you are located in the tunnels and I'll make sure they're ready to leave when he comes."

Her eyes widened in silent response. She dropped back from the group and slipped behind a stack of barrels. I coughed to disguise the sound of the soft splash as she entered the water, but it wasn't necessary, we were almost at the large boat at the other end of the cove.

"Now," the guard called suddenly, halting us, "what you need you to do, is move the goods from inside the cargo hold and back out to the docks. I'm going to get another group to transfer them into the caves. The boys will see you do it right." He jutted his chin toward the other guards still standing and chatting to Morgan.

"In here," she said, gesturing us to follow her down into the belly of the boat to where crates were stacked one on top of the other, filling the entire space. At the front were partially obscured cages, each with a different strange noise emanating from it. I picked up the first and a low, throaty hiss came from within, paired with a snapping of teeth as I tried to look through the breathing holes in the top of the cage.

"What are you doing here, Lord Lusilim?" Zak murmured as we started to form a chain of bodies to pass the crates along. "If they find out you're here, the Autarch will have you locked away, I've heard them talking about it."

I glanced around, making sure none of the guards were in earshot. "I needed to come and find out where he's hiding you all. Is the rest of the army here on this island?"

Zak kept his voice low. "No. No one has come or gone from this island since before the battle. The army was split into three when we first arrived in Katmu to spread between the southern islands to try and tackle the piracy here. We were prepared to set sail for the fight against the Autarch, but the ships never came for us. As far as I know, the other two divisions are still in the other smuggling hotspots. They don't even bother locking us in cells because they know that without boats, there's nowhere for us to go. Even the strongest swimmers can't go up against the currents between here and the mainland."

"And you've had no contact with anyone since then?"

He shook his head. "All the information we get is from the Coastguard. There are a few of us who are friendly with them, and they'll relay information. That's how we heard about the battle and about Malah and Aran's betrayal." His face twisted in disgust briefly before he leaned in closer. "The Coastguard aren't happy about siding with the Autarch. They were tricked by Lord Jirata too, but they won't say a bad word about him. If you're thinking about trying to sway them, it won't work; they're loyal to him."

He paused again. "But they aren't loyal to the Autarch."

I let his words simmer in my mind as we finished unloading the last of the stolen animals off the boat and looked at the remaining crates, which were to be delivered elsewhere. The contents forced me to do a double take. Neat stacks of chopped, reddish-brown wood lay tied and secured in each crate.

"Wood?" I puzzled out loud, but even as I said the word I knew that this was no ordinary timber. I ran a hand over the coarse bark, admiring the rich color. There was a thrum of energy that seemed to pulse up my fingers where they made contact with the surreptitious surface. The emanation made me feel cold and almost … mournful?

"It's from the Cedar Forest," the man to my right explained. "The smugglers have been bringing more wood and creatures from Atturynn every few weeks. I don't know why, but there's something special about the trees that grow there. No one knows who picks it up though, as it's usually sent to the Stacks. These logs have been cut short, but we've had to shift almost entire tree trunks before."

"The Stacks?"

"It's the port on the lower middle island between the sea stacks," Zak answered.

Though I'd had a hunch, having it confirmed made my heart race. I would have to take a gamble now and hope that it paid off.

"I want you to spread the word that tomorrow night at midnight, there will be ships here to collect you." I rushed through the words as quickly and quietly as I dared. "You must do whatever it takes to get everyone out and into the cove, where the

Seirsun fleet will be coming in one by one to pick you up. You'll get further instructions from those in charge of the ships."

I didn't have time for them to overcome their shock before I started to move. I could already hear the closest guard coming down to the back of the ship to check for any remaining cargo. Ignoring the wood splintering into my hands, I pushed my way into a stack of crates and knelt to hide.

"What are you doing?" Zak hissed, frantically looking from me to the approaching guard.

"Tell Nook I've gone to the Stacks."

He swore under his breath and was gone from my view for a second, before a heavy, musty sack was thrown over my head, concealing me completely.

Chapter 5

Theo

The boat lurched over the small, choppy waves that separated the southern islands of Katmu, and I was grateful that I had never fallen prey to motion sickness. If I had, the confines of the stuffy, scratchy fabric concealing me might have been overwhelming. The cargo hold had remained silent since the boat had set sail from the cove, but I had remained hidden in case anyone came down to carry out an inspection.

Though the boat moved swiftly, more than an hour had passed before it finally slowed on what I hoped was the approach to the Stacks. Cautiously, I removed the sack from my body, shivering slightly as the cooler air touched my still-damp clothes.

There was a small, rudimentary window fixed into the side of the ship, and from the moonlight I could just make out the layered stone of the towering sea stacks that dominated our course. Their monumental size grew as we approached, and soon I was unable to see the top from my restricted viewpoint.

A sudden jolt informed me that the boat had made port, and

I quickly slid into a gap between two piles of crates. The quiet thrum of energy being emitted from the wood all around me intensified, as though it was feeding off my anticipation and amplifying it.

I heard the gangplank lower and groan as people boarded the boat and followed the rising sound of their footsteps as they approached the cargo hold. From the small gaps between the crates, I watched dozens of men and women enter, working hard to shift the contents onto land. Though I didn't see anyone I knew personally, I recognized these people. My heart warmed at seeing the sun-kissed brawn of the Zingali soldiers, working in harmony with their leaner and paler Hudjefan comrades, united as one.

A loud series of clatters sounded from the deck above, and I made use of the distraction, slipping out of my hiding place and picking up a crate for myself. I kept my head down as I joined the others in their task, hauling the wood across the narrow bridge connecting the Stacks to the main bulk of the island. In the dim light, I evaded notice, keeping my gaze lowered and mouth shut.

Sporadic snippets of hushed conversation reached me during the task, and with a few gentle prompts, I learned that the rest of the army was being kept on the most southwestern island. There had been contact made between the soldiers here and those kept at the Stacks via the visszhangok nesting in the cliffs.

It was a common method of communication used in the coastal regions of Zingal. Fishermen would use the echoing calls of the birds to send messages and warnings to each other in the water. A visszhangok would copy a call made from a predator and repeat it back to its flock to alert them of its presence, at the same time, it would confuse the predator into thinking that there were more of its kind nearby.

The news that the birds inhabited the Isles almost made me giddy, and I sent a silent prayer of thanks to the gods for opening up another avenue in my scheme. Everything was going to plan so far; I'd managed to locate where my army was being held and collected enough information to form a basic plan to extract them. But I felt uneasy. Malah had shown me how to infiltrate these three locations in my last visit to Katmu, and it seemed suspicious that he hadn't moved my people elsewhere. I knew that they were likely being used as bait, but I had to at least *try* to bring them home.

"Hey!" I called softly to a tall, muscular woman I recognized from the mountain barracks. We were in a holding room, piling the last of the wood-filled crates into tidy rows. The air surrounding them was choking and sorrowful.

The woman's dark eyes widened as she looked at me properly for the first time, and she looked around us quickly before whispering, "Lord Lusilim?"

"Shh." I pressed a finger to my lips. "Tell me, are the rest of you locked up, or can you move freely? Are you all well?"

She stared at me in disbelief for a second before hurriedly answering, her voice barely audible. "We aren't chained up or locked in dungeons, but we aren't allowed to roam outside of the lodging cells. They've cramped us into small rooms and taken away anything that could be used as a weapon, but they need us fed and watered to carry out the constant tasks. Not much has changed since we first arrived, but since the Isles locked down, they've watched us closely. We're mostly fine, but there have been a number of people who have rebelled and have paid the consequences for it."

I nodded, understanding from her grim expression exactly *how* they had paid. Despite her last point, I was glad to hear that they hadn't been starved.

"I need you to go back to the others and spread the word that there are ships coming," I breathed. "I don't know when, but you must all be ready when they arrive. I want everyone off this Island, leave no one behind."

"We're leaving?" Her eyes widened once more, hope filling them with a glossy shine.

I smiled. "If all goes to plan, you'll be home by the end of the week. Now, how can I get to the visszhangok?"

❖ ❖ ❖

Sweat coated my brow as I scaled the final edge of the cliff. The visszhangok were notorious for nesting in the hardest to reach places, laying their eggs behind small, jagged lips in the rock face. I had scrambled up to the very top of the island alone, following the rushed directions given to me by the soldier. She had tried to insist on coming with me to show me the way, but I hadn't wanted to risk her absence being noticed.

She had taken me to the narrow opening they had discovered and gradually widened in one of the chambers near the surface. The crevice was just wide enough for me to crawl through and from there I'd blindly made my way up to the top of the island in the dark, gripping desperately to the sparse shrubbery and slippery tree roots.

Dawn was brightening the sky when I saw the first of the visszhangok, the pale iridescent sheen of its feathers stark against the dark greenery. I looked away from it, purposefully avoiding eye contact and pretended to slink quietly through the bushes. A cool breeze whipped at my face, the salt from the ocean stinging my cheeks. I dared a few more steps toward the edge of the cliff and was rewarded by rustling sounds to my left and right.

I didn't need to look up to know that more of the pale birds had begun to watch me, assessing how much of a danger I posed to their flock. I whistled the short, discrete tune we used to test the communication channel in Zingal.

Anyone there?

As soon as I'd made the noise, a few of the birds launched themselves into the sky, luring me away from the nests. As soon as I began to follow, I heard the whistled tune echoing around me. Even though I had used this same method many times before, it was still unnerving and disorienting. There was no way to know where the sound was coming from.

Wanting to create some distance between me and the sheer drop in front of me, I retreated back a healthy distance and sat concealed by a small mountain willow and waited. The echoed tune faded after a few minutes and there was no sound but the blustering wind and the crash of the ocean below.

The sun had crested the eastern horizon, and I'd crept toward the birds and repeated the message twice before I heard the response. My heart stuttered in relief as I heard the faint, distant echoing whistle answering my own.

Receiving.

Once again, I skulked toward the nesting visszhangok, waited for the telltale rustling of feathers and started sounding out a message consisting of coos punctuated with clicks and yips. I kept it as short as possible, trying to use the limited vocabulary to convey the message.

Lusilim. Boat coming. Prepare.

There was no delay in the response this time.

Unclear. Repeat.

I repeated the message until the visszhangok were mimicking it flawlessly, down to the rough scrape of my voice that had developed from my lack of water. Weary from exhaustion and hunger, I collapsed down to the ground and waited with bated breath.

As soon as the whispers of the answering echoes reached me, I was unable to stop the grin from spreading across my face.

Received.

❖ ❖ ❖

Despite looking a bit worn out and in need of a decent bath, I was pleasantly surprised to find that the rest of my army based at the Stacks were generally in good health. There were complaints about how they had been kept isolated from the rest of the realm, and I'd had many people asking after family members in Zingal and comrades at the other islands. They had hidden me within their ranks, sharing rations and clothes to help me blend in.

As the second night approached, the energy amongst the men and women was charged and volatile. I'd sent more silent prayers to the gods in the last week than I had in my entire life and for now at least, they seemed to be listening, if not answering. Malah's guards had been distracted or lazy enough in each inspection to fail at discovering my presence. And my people had listened eagerly to my instructions on how best to aid each other when the boats came.

There had been no sign or sound that the troops from the first island had been liberated, but it was more secluded than the rest of Katmu. I just had to hope that the communication channels had been disrupted thoroughly enough between the islands. Though there was no way of knowing if or when Nook was going to send the ships to us, I had to believe that everything so far had gone according to plan.

As darkness fell, the already charged energy amongst the camp was almost visible as it pinged off the walls. Word had spread rapidly through the ranks, and everyone was ready and waiting. Tasar's people had gelled seamlessly with my own, and I could see real kinships had developed between them; they acted and behaved as one.

When the first warning horn blared through the silence of the Stacks, everyone launched into action. The small, hidden cache of weapons were distributed amongst the best fighters, who led the way down to the port, cutting down any member of Malah's Coastguard that stood in their way. I had hoped that we could avoid bloodshed wherever possible, but even I was unable to temper the desperation for freedom that drove these men and women forward.

I followed within the ranks, letting the most experienced

soldiers lead the way through the unfamiliar tunnels and passageways. Malah's men couldn't hide their surprise at the hordes of soldiers who had broken free from their ill-equipped holding cells. They certainly weren't prepared for the fleet of warships funneling in on the swirling current. Cannons were launched too late, and the Coastguard moving to man the defenses found themselves overpowered and outnumbered. As the ships approached the docks, gangways were flung between them, creating a chained route from the nearest ship to the furthest.

As planned, before the first ship had even fully stopped, unarmed soldiers were flinging themselves aboard and running across the gangways. Everyone was aware of the time restraints. We had so little of it before reinforcements would arrive and block our exit.

I ran alongside a group heading up to the top of the tallest sea stack, where we met the guards sprinting up to light the distress beacon. If they succeeded in lighting it, it would alert the other islands to our presence. My legs burned from the climb, and I dodged on instinct as a guard thrust his sword in my direction. I was too exhausted for a fight, but adrenaline fueled me, propelling me forward with an attack of my own. He lunged again, trying to knock the dagger from my hand, but I twisted at the last second, shoving him toward the edge of the cliff. He lost his footing, but there wasn't time to watch him fall.

I rushed forward to help the others destroy the large beacon used to call for aid. Ropes had been thrown around the metal grating and several people were pulling it down from its wooden pole. I joined the effort, heaving all my weight into the task before the pole splintered and cracked, allowing the beacon to fall and be rolled over the edge and into the dark waters below.

Shouts were echoing off the Stacks as we ran back down to the docks. Soldiers filtered quickly onto the line of ships, the strongest fighters clearing the way, battling against the Coastguard with everything they had. The sheer number of them more than made up for their lack of weapons.

Another distant horn blared from the rest of the fleet waiting outside of the Stacks, signaling that it was time to leave. Either reinforcements were on their way, or they had already arrived. Simultaneously, the warships raised their sails once more and prepared to escape. The sight caused a flurry of panic, fights were abandoned, and people were pushing and shoving each other out of the way to board the ships.

Despite trying to think rationally, it was hard not to also get swept up in the chaos, and I could practically see my heart hammering through my chest at the thought of being left behind.

Now that the Coastguard were no longer outnumbered, their actions were bolder. They'd begun to block the way to the departing ships, giving chase to those that slipped past. A few of them had replaced the slaughtered operators of the catapults and ammunition had begun to rain down on the nearest ships. If we didn't leave soon, the chain would be broken, and our escape would be impossible.

"This way, my Lord," panted a young man to my left, "there's another way down." I let him pull on my sleeve as I followed him with the rest of the dwindling group that had remained at my side. Instead of taking the steps that were blocked by a group of Malah's guards, we jumped down some perilously slippery outcroppings of rocks to reach the ledge above the docks.

"RETREAT!" I yelled to the remaining soldiers, still putting up a brave fight to allow the rest to flee. There were too many guards on the docks now, and they were already attempting to board the last ship, which was slowly moving back, the gangway splintered uselessly into the water, courtesy of the catapults. I called out again, "Quick! Up the smugglers walkway!"

Then we were all running in unison, along the slippery ledge that would bring us almost level with the deck of the ship. It was how pirates would slip on and off boats without being noticed. The men and women already aboard the ship cleared from the side of the deck, allowing us space to jump.

The end of the ledge approached all too fast and the breath caught in my lungs as I leapt, suspended in midair for an eternity, before my feet hit the solid wood of the deck. My knees buckled and I rolled, carried forward with the momentum. Frantic hands grabbed me and pulled me out of the way before the next soldier could land on me.

The commotion was disorientating, and it took a long moment for me to collect myself after I'd been pulled to my feet and for the adrenaline to begin ebbing away. I looked up in time to see the last woman jump from the ledge. The boat had moved past the rock, and the distance was almost too far. My heart skipped as she flew, only managing to grasp onto the rope netting hanging from the stern. Instantly, she was helped up by the others and relief made my knees weak once more.

We'd done it.

Cannons fired from the ship toward the other vessels in the docks, making it impossible for Malah's men to leave. And with the ruined beacon, they would be unable to signal to the other islands until new boats arrived for the shift change the following day.

A quick glance at the retreating docks was enough to dampen any sense of victory in a second. Bodies lay strewn across the wooden walkways. Brave soldiers who had fought to the death so that others had a chance of escape. I needed to go back for them, to take their bodies home to their families and ensure their names were known throughout Zingal and Hudjefa.

But I knew that was impossible. And the guilt felt like a hot knife twisting in my gut.

❖ ❖ ❖

Nook and Ezra had executed the plan flawlessly. There had only been a small number of Coastguard on the first island, and the army had overpowered them and forced them onto the boats to be taken as prisoners to ensure they couldn't raise the alarm.

Even though we'd gone through every part of it in minute detail before we left Zingal, I was still astonished to find out how many solders they'd already saved. Many of them were already on ships back home under Suenna's command, packed in so tightly there was barely room for them to move. They were to sail to the fishing dock on the Zingali coast, which would have been cleared by Josefine, with the help of Torin, and Karasi when she could stay hidden.

"And if you pull another stunt like that, I'll leave you

behind," Nook griped, continuing his chastisement for not following the plan myself.

"I know it was a foolish risk to take," I acknowledged, "but I saw an opportunity to infiltrate the Stacks and get the soldiers out there before the first island could raise the alarm."

"And if you'd been captured?" Ezra said, his expression telling me that he too, was unimpressed with the surprise developments. "The plan was for you to retreat after visiting the first island and take them one at a time. When we heard that you'd moved on to the second, we had to rush the plan to get to you as soon as possible."

"And I had every faith in you both." I tried to grin, but the smile fell from my face at their expressions. "I'm sorry. I shouldn't have acted so rashly."

Fortunately, the pair weren't known for holding grudges, so the conversation turned quickly to the final stage. We were already approaching the third and final island with the remainder of the fleet. Tension and unease were thick in the air. We barely had enough ships to transport the rest of the army, and apart from the visszhangok delivering my message, no one had been able to make contact with them at all.

We approached the most southwestern island of Katmu quickly, without trying to be stealthy. We didn't have the luxury of time to be cautious, instead banking on the waning darkness of the night to conceal us as much as possible. Rowboats were already prepared and waiting to be dropped.

"My Lord!" one of the crew shouted, pointing back the way we'd come. "They've signaled the attack!"

A large, gleaming flame crowned the top of the Stacks. Somehow, they'd managed to ignite a makeshift beacon and call for help.

"We proceed as planned," I called back. "If they haven't already, it won't be long before they realize the first island has been compromised too. We won't get another chance."

The moment we entered the shallows, I plunged into the water in my own boat, hauling the oars with a frenzied desperation. Warning sirens blared, shattering the quiet, signaling that the Coastguard knew we were here, and that they were ready. We now had even less time than before, but I intended on making the most of every second.

Shouts and splashes soon overpowered the sirens as hundreds, if not thousands of my soldiers fled into the water to meet the rowboats. The sight of them made my heart swell, and my boat lurched as they began to clamber inside.

"Is everyone on the beach?" I called to one of the men helping to haul the others inside. I recognized him as one of the stable hands who used to work at Josefine's estate for her father. He had a split lip and blood trickled from a cut across his eyebrow.

"Yes," he panted, "we've been … waiting … As soon as we … heard the siren … we started fighting … the Coastguard."

When the boat was unable to fit another person in, I shouted, "Everyone, pick up an oar!" They obeyed without hesitation, barely flinching when the first of the arrows flew, and continued propelling the boat back toward the ships.

A few brave individuals stayed back to help me retrieve more from the shore, the stable hand included. We managed three trips back to the ships before the arrows ceased and the stones began to fall. Several of the boats were damaged, and the ruthless waves were soon weaponizing the splintered wood and floating bodies. During the next two relays, I learned that, like on the previous island, a number of soldiers had stayed behind to fight off Malah's Coastguard, allowing the rest of the army to retreat to the beach at the first sight of the rowboats.

I wouldn't let them down this time.

As we approached the beach once more, I focused my eyes on the shadows of the caves, where the beach met the towering cliff face. The darkness was punctuated with flashes of metal reflecting off the waning moonlight and the fires of the torches.

"Get on another boat!" I yelled to my exhausted companion, "I'm going to help the others on the shore."

His response was lost in the commotion, and as soon as I felt the beach jolt against the boat, I was in the water, hauling it up onto the sand. I didn't spare a single glance behind me as I began to run, ignoring the burn in my legs as they sank into the sand.

The fighting had been contained to two caverns—one at the base of the cliff, and another about halfway up. In the upper cavern, my soldiers were holding back the Coastguard, preventing them from firing more missiles at the rowboats and from climbing higher to reach the distress beacon that would trigger Katmu's failsafe to protect the main island. I picked up a discarded sword and charged toward the nearest cave, where Malah's men were being pushed back deeper into the stone.

"Now, Marie!" several of them shouted.

As soon as I saw what they were doing, I changed course,

scrambling up onto a ledge to help the woman battling against the lever to the portcullis. Her face was almost purple with exertion as she pulled against the rusted metal, welded motionless with age and sea spray. Even with our combined strength, it wouldn't budge. Hauling the sword above my head, I brought it down hard against the rusted hinge securing the thick chain.

When nothing happened, I brought it down again. Over and over until the weak metal groaned and eventually surrendered to the pull.

I heard the portcullis slam down into the stone and the enervated cries of victory from my soldiers below as they slew the remaining Coastguard who had been caught on the wrong side and took care of any others attempting to lift it back up. No one spared me a second glance as they fled from the gate toward the last remaining boats in the water.

Instead of following them, I charged to the far edge of the beach and began up the slippery steps that led to the catapults. But by the time I'd made it up the first flight, the small remainder of my army were barreling down toward me in a desperate attempt to flee. At the bottom of the steps, I looked up to see the cause of the commotion. My pounding heart plummeted as I took in the hordes of Coastguard filtering toward the catapult clearing, across the narrow wooden bridges connecting the cave entrances.

I took off back down toward the last remaining boat gently bobbing against the sand. It was manned by a single soldier; the brave stable hand. He was helping the rest of his comrades into the last boat when his face turned his face up toward the cliff and his expression turned to horror.

The failsafe beacon had been lit; a blue, driftwood fire with a small cylinder of mirror shards revolving above it, refracting the vibrant light in multiple directions at once. Members of the Coastguard were already rushing over the narrow, wooden bridge from the catapults toward another ledge at the other end of the cove, where a large capstan sat ready to haul the thick chain up out of the water between the cove and the main island.

The chain was designed to keep unwelcome ships from infiltrating the main Citadel, protecting the heart of Katmu. But they weren't trying to keep anything out now. The chain was being raised to trap the entire fleet inside.

"GO!" I bellowed to the stable hand, charging toward them as fast as I could manage. "I'll swim out to you!" But I knew the battered rowboat wouldn't make it in time. Nook knew what that signal meant, and he knew that he would need to leave immediately.

Hands grasped the back of my collar as someone caught up with me, their weight sending me careening down into the sand. Shifting back onto my knees, I tried to rear my head back, but my arms were pinned behind my back and rope looped around my ankles. Two more Coastguards ran into the water after the rowboat, trying to haul it back to shore.

For a split second, a flash of light demanded my attention, and I saw a figure kick the mirrored beacon over the edge of the cliff and slice the throat of the guard manning it. My heaving breaths caught as I watched the figure follow the others onto the wooden bridge before deftly slicing through the rope attaching it to the cliff face.

Immediately, the bridge went slack and began to swing down toward the beach. The members of the Coastguard who had been running to the capstan plummeted into the water, with loose planks of wood falling in after them.

I looked up in time to see the figure briefly glance from me to my fleeing soldiers, before raising a hand and throwing a blade into the remaining guard trying to seize the boat. Before the bridge would swing further, the figure dropped into the waves, reemerging a few feet from the battered vessel, where she was hauled up into safety.

Because before she had even lifted the hood of her cloak, I knew who it was. She'd made a choice to kill the guard holding the boat, and not the one who had hold of me.

How had she even managed to get to Katmu?

More guards piled on top of me, but I was already rendered motionless by the strange pair of eyes fading in the distance toward the safety of the fleet.

Erisa was leaving me here to die.

Chapter 6

Erisa

Replication of sealed correspondence
Lord Jirata,
Should an attempt be made to liberate the rebel soldiers from your islands, I expect every effort to be made to thwart the endeavor.

I want Theodoraxion Lusilim taken <u>alive</u>. Put down anyone else who stands in your way. And should you manage to ensnare the Feline, I demand to be notified at once. She is to be apprehended but treated with the utmost respect until I am called.

If I detect the slightest hint of betrayal, I will not hesitate to remind you what you stand to lose.

Sincerely,
Your Autarch

5 November
Copy made 7 November

❖ ❖ ❖

"We should go back," the young man repeated, looking to the others in the boat helplessly. Blood was crusted to his brow, and he looked as though he hadn't slept in weeks.

I knew the feeling well.

"You'll be no use to him dead," I snapped, "and if you don't pick up the pace, we'll never make it to the ship in time."

"I'd rather die alongside my Lord than run away and abandon him."

"I told you; they won't kill him. You'd be dying for nothing."

The other soldiers were uneasy too. They didn't trust me, but any fool could see the impossibility of helping Theo now. Katmu's Coastguard had swarmed the beach around him, and Malah himself had made an appearance on the shore. The sight of him almost made me agree to turn back, but we weren't out of danger yet.

I turned to look at the ships retreating from the Isles. I'd destroyed the route to the capstan from this island and the distress beacon, but the signal had already been received. The chain was being raised from the other end; the distant flashes of glistening metal reflecting red in the early morning light gave it away.

"They're going to leave without us," someone fretted, throwing another anxious glance at the last remaining warship sitting within the cove.

But the ship wasn't moving farther away, if anything it was coming toward us, close enough for me to make out the individuals moving frantically on the deck.

"Quick," I called, hauling the oar with a renewed vigor, "row as fast as you can, they're waiting for us! They must think Theo is on board."

Rope ladders were dropped as we approached; lifelines that felt torturously unobtainable with every wave that pushed us back. But relief was still a long way off, even as my hands closed around the rough material and began hauling myself up the side of the hulking vessel.

"Where is he?" Nook growled, grabbing fistfuls of my soaked cloak before I'd even stepped on board. "How are you even here?"

I shrugged out of his grasp. "The fool got himself captured, and if we don't make it over the chain, we will be too."

I neglected to mention that if the Autarch succeeded in capturing me now, all hope for Theo and his rebellion would be lost.

Nook ripped at his red hair, looking desperately between the hundreds of soldiers on the ship, and the shore where Theo remained alone, as though the answers were held in the roiling waves that separated the two.

"FUCK!" he shouted, the agony of his decision clear as it rang over the deck. "Raise the sails!"

He knocked into my shoulder as he barged past, and I quickly turned from his face, pretending not to see the tears spilling down his cheeks.

With the abundance of soldiers on board, the process of setting sail was swift. But even as the ship slowly began to move, our apprehension regarding the chain didn't subside. Despite the nearest end failing to be raised, the chain between Katmu's main island and the most southwestern one would soon become taught, and we had yet to reach the safety of the other side.

From the portside deck, I could just make out the small ripples being made on the water's surface, as the metal links were dredged from the seabed.

"Full sail!" I heard Nook cry as the glistening chain came into view from the water some few hundred feet away. It would have been a ridiculous order at any other time; we were already going too fast for the tight confines of the rocky channel, risking wreckage on one of the jagged outcroppings of broken cliff breaking through the surface of the water.

But we were already out of time.

I rushed to aid the soldiers seeing to the sails, who were fumbling at the knots with trembling fingers. A few swore as I sliced a dagger cleanly through the binds, causing the sails to billow and catch on the wind. The ship lurched forward, and I could hear Nook calling out orders from where he stood at the wheel.

We were halfway over the chain when it snagged on the keel, causing me to lose my footing. Wood groaned ominously beneath us, and I felt my face turn as green as those of the rest of the soldiers around me when the stern of the ship started to lift out of the water.

"Hold on!" Nook shouted, and with a splintering crash, the ship shot forward, the prow crashing into the waves and spraying the deck with sea foam. The chain whipped up behind us, snapping off part of the rudder with a deafening crack.

A celebratory cheer rang out through the ranks, and I hurried to the back of the deck to lean over the railing, catching the last sight of Theo before we sailed around the cliff face and out of view.

The beach was swarming with Malah's Coastguard, and I could just about make out a kneeling form in the center of the mass. If I looked hard enough, I could almost see the look of betrayal burning into me from the shore.

I'd made a choice not to save Theo tonight. He hadn't been able to see how close the Coastguard were behind him, but I knew that if I'd cut down the man holding him, his men on the rowboat wouldn't have gotten away.

I told myself that my decision was based on numbers alone; that I was saving twenty soldiers instead of one.

But as we rounded the coast and the accusatory burn of Theo's glare faded from view, I knew it was a lie. I could've landed on the beach and died trying to help him fight his way off the island.

Instead, I chose to save myself.

❖ ❖ ❖

I had hoped to disembark swiftly and without notice as soon as we reached Zingal's main fishing bay, with the intention of avoiding Theo's friends and family. Nook, however, had a different plan in mind.

"Get off me," I snapped, pulling at my wrists from where they were clasped tightly in his hands. "We both know I could take you down in seconds. Save yourself the embarrassment."

He ignored the warning, only tightening his grip and staring forward toward the shore with a steely expression. "You'll have to explain yourself to the others, same as me." His eyes followed a flock of pale birds circling the approaching coast, as though he was listening to their peculiar song.

Despite knowing that I could, I didn't attempt to escape. The journey back to the mainland had been uncomfortable to say the least. I'd kept to myself as much as was possible on the overcrowded ship, perching high in the crow's nest, preferring the biting cold over the scalding glares of the soldiers. Word had quickly spread amongst them that I was partly, if not wholly, responsible for leaving their Lord behind.

Usually, I wouldn't have let it bother me. As the Feline, I was accustomed to being feared instead of liked, but something about their betrayed expressions had guilt lashing at my conscience. There had been a painful *lack* in Nook's countenance since we'd set sail. There was no added malice or disdain when he looked at me, but a decided deficiency of his usual carefree cheerfulness that forced me to remain by his side as we disembarked.

As we were the last to arrive, the process of dealing with the influx of soldiers back into Zingal was already underway, led by Josefine. Her annoying, high-pitched voice somehow managed to carry across the entire docking yard to grate on the last of my nerves.

The rest of Theo's council were waiting at the entrance to the market clearing, each face a poorly concealed mask of confusion when they couldn't find their Lord. They didn't even try to hide the fury that replaced it when their gazes landed on me.

"He was captured," Ezra deduced, his eyes not straying from Nook's face, which fell as he nodded in confirmation.

Dana and Didi's cries were lost in the sharp slap of Suenna striking me hard across the face. In the brief second it took for the small black spots dotting my vision to clear, she'd raised her hand once more.

"I gave you a free pass the first time," I snarled, batting her arm to the side and placing the hood of my cloak back over my head, "you won't be getting another."

Dana's voice was shrill and panicked. "Where is Theo?"

"We should discuss this back at the house," Ezra cautioned, looking around at who could be overhearing the conversation. Not that it mattered, everyone in the realm was probably already aware about the current misfortunes of the Zingali Lord.

"No!" Dana demanded, "you tell me where my boy is *right now*, Nook Cularis!"

"He was on the beach ..." Nook's voice trembled. "I told him not to pull anything like that again ... but I had to make the call." He swiped furiously at a tear on his cheek. "I left him behind."

"Is he dead? Is that why you left him?"

Nook winced at her words, causing her shrieks to double in intensity.

"Nook had no choice; I was the one who left Theo on that beach. And he's not dead," I interjected, "Malah is under orders to keep him alive."

No one seemed surprised, and their expressions of hatred deepened now that the blame could be shifted from Nook to me.

"And we're supposed to trust *you*, are we?" demanded Suenna, "the double agent who somehow always *miraculously* manages to survive, especially when leaving others behind."

A flashing vision of Verrill falling from my arms had me almost doubling over in pain before I forced it from my mind. Squaring my shoulders, I met her hard, brown eyes.

"If Theo dies, his newly liberated army will rally against the Autarch, whose own army is surrounded on all land sides. He can't afford to create a martyr, and letting Theo become one was never his intention. And more importantly," I paused, glancing between each of them, "the Autarch is using him as bait."

"Bait?" Ezra asked, his cool expression lacking its usual warmth.

"We shouldn't be talking about this out in the open," I replied, walking past them in the direction of the wagons carting the soldiers toward the city.

I arrived at the Lusilim estate before the others and climbed the familiar route of jagged rocks up the side of the house to slip noiselessly into Theo's room. Purposefully ignoring the bed and various items of his lying about, I entered the bathing chamber and began to fill the tub.

I had spied around the estate for days before they'd left for Katmu, but I hadn't dared to venture upstairs into the rooms Theo and I had spent so many months in before the battle in Ocridell. They'd been the happiest months I'd had in years.

When I was finished scrubbing the past week from my skin and my wet hair was braided down my back, I returned to the bedroom. I paused at the closet, not wanting to open the doors. Even though I knew my clothes had likely been moved or replaced in my absence, I was still strangely reluctant to see it. But the cold air creeping into the room forced me to open the doors, and to my surprise, they were still there, exactly as I'd left them.

My face heated with an unexpected wave of relief, which I tried to stifle as I put on a clean pair of trousers and a fresh shirt. The room smelled faintly of cedar and ginger, and I allowed myself a brief moment of inhalation before the guilt took over once more.

How many hours had I spent inhaling this scent while I should have been with Verrill?

And now … now I wondered if I'd ever experience it again after abandoning Theo on that beach, leaving him to face the horde of Malah's Coastguard alone. The sight of him kneeling in the sand with his hands and feet bound obscured my vision.

I knew from the look in his eyes that he'd never forgive me.

Raised voices filtered out from the parlor, growing louder as I crept closer to the open doorway, almost tripping over the travel bags someone had left in the hall. Theo's friends and family were having a heated discussion about how best to rescue him from Katmu.

"If you think they're going to keep him on that island, you're sorely mistaken," I chimed in, striding into the room. "They'll have already taken him to the Citadel on the main island until the Autarch can see him. And I wouldn't be surprised if he decided to move Theo again after that; Katmu is hardly known for its impenetrable defense, as demonstrated by your ridiculous plan."

Every pair of eyes was pinned to me, and I took notice of the crowded room. Nook, Ezra, and Suenna, predictably accompanied by Dana and Didi. Josefine was also present, as well as Theo's very undead twin sister, Karasi.

Even though I knew from seeing her briefly on the cliff in Ocridell that she was somehow alive, it was still unnerving to have her stand before me.

Behind her were two unfamiliar men, the two of them almost complete opposites of each other. The dark skin and black hair of one contrasted with the paleness of the other, apart from their eyes. While the dark-haired man had the bluest eyes I'd ever seen, the white-haired man's appeared completely black.

Black and full of rage. He was almost trembling, and looked at me with a hatred so intense, I thought he might actually be about to keel over.

What a strange man, he clearly has some issues.

Happy to look away from the grisly scar on his face, I shrugged off the thought and addressed Karasi directly. "I'm not going to apologize for killing you, because clearly I didn't do a good enough job." I waved a hand to gesture to her very-much-alive form. "I was only following the order I'd been given by the Autarch, but I'm ... *glad* to see that you survived."

Happy would have been overkill.

The disturbed, pale man lurched toward me; murderous intent written clearly across his features. My daggers were already secured in my hands, but before he could reach me Karasi's voice halted him.

"Torin, stop!" she snapped, yanking on the sleeve of his coat to pull him back to her side like an obedient pup. She turned her gaze back to me, the shade of green so familiar, but with an icy disdain I'd never seen in Theo's. "I accept your half-assed apology, but purely for the sake of moving this conversation on to finding my brother. We'll need to work together on this."

Based on the fact that Karasi's unhinged companion—*Torin*—looked as though he'd blow steam from his nose if I mentioned that I didn't actually apologize, I decided to let the matter go.

"Work together?" Josefine shrilled, the pitch of it so high I was surprised anyone other than the dogs could hear it. "She's the reason he's stuck there! And are we all forgetting that she tried to kill him in Ocridell?"

I struggled not to roll my eyes. "You weren't even *there* in Ocridell, and besides, if I wanted Theo dead, it would have happened already. I will get him out of there, but I need you all to stay out of my way."

There was an uproar from the parade of clowns, but Nook's voice rang out louder than the others.

"We're supposed to just leave it with you, are we?" he asked sardonically. "After you had the chance to get to him on the beach and chose to leave instead."

"It was either him or me," I lied smoothly, "and being the most useful of the two, I chose myself. Now, you can complain all you want, but every single one of you knows that I'm the best chance you've got at getting him back alive. You'll just have to trust me."

Suenna scoffed, her eyebrows almost reaching her hairline. "I wouldn't trust you to fasten my cloak without swiping the buttons!"

"I think we'll take our chances," Ezra added coolly.

Each of them wore the same expression of disdain—apart

from Torin, who was practically frothing at the mouth—and I turned my back to the group and left them to their scheming.

I knew there was nothing I could do to convince them that I was their best hope. Because I *was* going to get Theo out, I *needed* to. Csintalan had told Malah that he wanted me alive, and he was clearly planning to use Theo as bait to lure me into a trap. The knowledge that I would recover him was the only reason I was able to leave him there. I was certain that wherever Theo had been taken, the Autarch would be there too. And this time, I'd make him pay for taking someone else from me.

The approaching evening air was cold against the too-thin fabric of my summer clothing, and I regretted not taking some of Theo's thicker garments with me when departing from the Lusilim estate.

The barn door creaked in the wind as I moved to bridle one of the horses from the stable. The almost inaudible crunch of hay underfoot alerted me to the person's presence, and I had barely a second to duck beneath the long arm sweeping through the air where I'd just been.

Whirling around, I blocked the second attack with my forearm and brought my leg up to deliver a sharp, quick kick to the side of the man's knee. He staggered for a second, but that was all I needed to make a series of fast, calculated jabs to his pressure points. He was by no means an unskilled fighter, and his determination made him all the more lethal. But I had spent the last decade fending for myself, and the last few weeks had been the worst of them.

As soon as I landed a swift punch to his throat, he stumbled back, and his hood fell to reveal a head of almost white, ash blond hair. I was hardly surprised to discover that it was Torin who was trying to kill me, but I was unsure what I'd done to offend him so badly.

He flew at me again, pure hatred sparkling in his dark eyes. He was incredibly tall, even more so than Theo, and almost as muscular. But there was a calculating, snakelike precision to his movements that Theo would never have been able to replicate. I feinted left, pushing out with my arm to drive his momentum forward and into the stable door. It swung open, and Torin lost his balance, toppling to the floor and spooking several of the horses.

In his moment of disarray, I was able to loop a halter around his feet, giving me enough time to extract his knives, each of which had given me several shallow cuts across my arms.

Not wanting to give him a chance to right himself, I quickly untied the horse I'd bridled and pulled it toward the entrance of the barn. I'd have to go without a saddle for now.

I could hear him scrambling after me as I mounted.

"I will get you one day, Erisa Anzû." Torin's deep voice followed me out into the cold air. "On my honor as a Sharru, you will pay for your crimes."

His words continued to prickle across my skin as I rode fast toward the Zingali border, refusing to stop until I was certain no one was following my trail.

Torin Sharru. One of the princes of Atturynn, though I couldn't remember which. That explained his arrogance and puffed-up air of importance. It didn't explain his desire to kill me, but from the way he seemed to hover around Karasi, I could make a pretty good guess.

Stars were sprinkled across the dark, cloudless sky as I rode on toward the volcano and I couldn't help but think about Torin's threat. Whether it was the Prince of Atturynn who came to deliver my final blow, or if it came from one of the many others I'd wronged, I knew that that day was approaching. And if Torin was right, and I was destined to pay for every crime, the cost would be steep.

But there were things I needed to do before I settled that bill, and they all included adding to it.

Chapter 7

Erisa

Feline,
You asked to be alerted immediately about any news regarding the Rats at Anzillu Harbor. I'm writing to inform you that one of them managed to make it halfway across the channel hidden among the food sacks being shipped to Katmu's main island.

Unfortunately, in order to escape discovery, they had to abandon the mission and swim back to the harbor. But they swore they saw the failsafe beacon, giving orders to raise the chain. No one is certain what this means, but I will, of course, update you as soon as I know.

Additionally, there has been movement detected within the Palace. It has been empty since the Autarch vacated it, but a torch was seen moving around within the walls.
Alekos

10 November

❖ ❖ ❖

Upon first glance, Anzillu bazaar was the same frenzied, writhing mass of color and heat it always had been, but the closer I got to the heart of the market, the more anxious the energy became.

"What's happened?" I asked Aghna when she opened the door to her bakery. It was stifling inside from the blaring heat of the ovens, but the smell was heavenly. I seated myself at her kitchen table and snagged one of the spiced muffins cooling on racks across the top.

"The Elkas estate has been destroyed, it fell down only a few hours ago," she said, twitching the threadbare curtains back over the grubby windows. "And word has it that the Autarch is on the move, his army dispersed, with only the remainder retreating to the edge of the Harbor after a fire was started throughout the camp."

"Fell down? The entire estate?" When she nodded, I pressed, "And the fire, who started it?"

"No one knows, though I imagine it will have been one of Wranmaris' men, they've been getting bolder since they took over Šarrum, there's already been countless riots throughout the wealthier areas."

It was possible, but I didn't think this was down to Tasar. I would have to go and inspect the damage for myself.

A pair of dark eyes, half-covered by some shaggy black curls, peeked out from behind the kitchen door.

I smiled. "Hello, little Rat. Come here and let me look at you."

Farzin gingerly stepped into view and approached me slowly, as though ready to flee at any second. He looked a lot healthier than when I'd left him with Aghna a few weeks ago, with rounder cheeks and cleaner clothes.

"Hello, Feline," he said bravely, holding his chin high to mask his nervousness.

"Would you like to accompany me on a job today?" I asked, trying to keep my voice gentle. In an attempt to entice him, I added, "If you're good, I'll buy you a treat from the market."

He nodded eagerly at that, and ran to the door, propping it open and tapping his foot impatiently.

I used the journey to Henri Elkas' estate to question Farzin about his stay at the bakery and learned that he was now one of twelve orphans staying with Aghna—or *Aggie* as they called her. Aided by my prompts, he told me that she fed, clothed, and bathed them, but he pouted when relaying that she was strict about bedtimes.

"Candles out, children," he mocked in an uncanny impression of Aghna's croaking tone.

"And the other children," I said, "where did you find them?"

"Most are from the volcano. They don't have homes no more either, got blown up with the trams and their parents didn't come back from the fighting … like mine."

We continued in silence until we reached the Elkas estate, and I pretended not to see Farzin wiping his eyes or hear his muted sniffles. If I'd known what to say, I would have tried to comfort the small boy, but I knew from experience that no words could make up for the loss of your family.

Henri Elkas was a paranoid man, so seeing his estate without its usual swarm of over-armed guards was unsettling. At first, I was curious about why there weren't people making the most of the absent security and looting the place, but as we approached, I understood why.

Not only was the building in ruins, but there was a strange sickly feeling in the air that intensified as we drew nearer. I was suddenly claustrophobic, which made no sense, as the Elkas estate was situated just outside of Ersetu, nestled against the side of the volcano, with nothing but open sky above.

"I don't like it here," mumbled Farzin, who was shuffling behind me, awkwardly huddled against the backs of my legs.

"Don't worry, little Rat," I said, "nothing can hurt you when you're with me."

At least, I hope not.

The entire mansion looked as though it had exploded from a single room on the left side of the plot, where only two of the walls remained standing. The charge of the air was almost unbearable as we reached the heart of the detonation. I had never paid much attention to the residual magic that had remained after the supposed fall of the gods, but this felt like raw, primitive power, unbridled and lashing out without restraint.

I had felt something similar when fusing the two pieces of the Orb of Nanaya together, but that felt like a mere prickle of static dancing across my skin compared to the lightning bolts now firing from every pore.

Farzin cried out and retreated to the perimeter of the house, eyes wide and hands trembling slightly. If I had known what would be here, I wouldn't have brought him with me.

I began to hum a low, steady tune, throwing the influence of it out toward the young boy. Immediately, I felt his fear of the house, could taste the sickly sweetness of it coating my tongue. I hummed a little louder, gently manipulating his fear and apprehension into something else, molding it into a soothing calmness that eased the rapid pace of his heart. His drawn brow smoothed, and he watched a beetle fly past his face before turning and bounding after it, his distress completely forgotten.

Broken glass crunched beneath the soles of my boots as I entered the remnants of the room. I recognized it as Henri's vault of hidden treasures. He was known for hoarding rare and ancient collectibles, items from the days of the gods, cursed relics and syphons of magic. I had only seen this room once before, when I broke in to steal Nergal's shield. Whether the shield had *actually* belonged to the god of war, I didn't know—or particularly care— but there was undeniably something *other* about it. Just like there was with the other relics Theo and I had collected, in our attempt to end the Autarch.

Despite the disarray of the rest of the estate, this room had somehow remained in order. A few of the paintings were hanging off center and the rows of golden pencils sat on one of the desks were no longer meticulously straightened, but everything else appeared to be just as I remembered it.

Due to the overwhelming pressure building in my head from the heavy press of air around me, I turned to leave after a quick scan of the room. A flash of metal caught my attention. I recognized the weapon immediately as Sharur, the supposedly enchanted mace that had the power to destroy anything.

It was rumored to be indestructible, which was why armorers and blacksmiths across the four realms used its likeness as a stamp of superior quality. It was also rumored to have been wielded by one of the lesser gods, whose name I'd long since forgotten.

Despite the popularity of its likeness, I had no idea it was a real weapon. I could feel the thrum of power emanating from it— this was no replica. And if anyone would have hoarded the real thing, it was Henri Elkas.

I didn't remember seeing it during my last visit to this room, and the sight of it now stopped me in my tracks. The weapon was made from solid bronze, with ancient inscriptions etched into the surface. They spiraled up toward the head of the mace, where two winged lions crouched side by side, roaring in opposite directions.

It was one of the only items in the room that appeared to have been misplaced; instead of being tucked away in a designated spot, it lay discarded beneath the desk. And as soon as I noticed it, I was certain that this was the reason for the excruciating charge in the air.

Because the length of the mace was bent. Something had broken the only indestructible weapon ever rumored to exist.

❖ ❖ ❖

By the time my head had finally stopped spinning, Farzin and I were almost at the harbor. The walk had been long, since the trams were no longer running on a schedule, but my companion hadn't complained once.

The smell of burning wood and canvas fabric was thick in the air as the port came into view, overpowering the usual stench of fish. Tendrils of smoke still lingered from a few of the tents across the expansive encampment, though the smoldering remains hadn't deterred people from scavenging anything of value left behind.

At the far end of the harbor, I could just make out the remnants of the Autarch's army barricading themselves into the port, in a clearly desperate act of self-preservation. Now that his half of Theo's army had been recovered from Katmu, if Tasar was so inclined, he would have little trouble reclaiming the port and being in sole control over the entire harbor.

I crouched down to Farzin's height and pointed to a small house a few hundred paces away from the perimeter of the camp.

"You see that house there, with the red door?" I asked him. When he nodded, I continued, "A very important Rat is staying in that house. I need you to run over there and tell the man to meet me by the entrance to the port."

He smiled eagerly at the task and sprinted away. Clouds of soot dispersed into the air as I moved closer to watch the Autarch's army in more detail, paying particular interest to the way they moved their remaining food stores from one of the harbor warehouses onto a large ship, moored alongside the port. Several dozen barrels were lined up, ready to be loaded. I was sitting on a charred bench, obscured by the flapping remnants of a tent, when I heard someone approach from behind.

"Feline," Alekos greeted stiffly, his gray eyes widening at my unveiled face before darting around the quiet ruins of the harbor. Farzin skipped to my side; his smile bright at accomplishing his task.

"Sit," I instructed the older man, nodding to the bench beside me. Alekos obeyed and ran a hand through his thinning dark hair.

He had been one of Verrill's personal Rats, operating for the Fox so secretly that even I had only seen him a few times in my life. After Verrill died, Alekos had written to me directly, ensuring that his loyalty did not waver, even though the Fox was gone.

"You look older since the last time I saw you," I stated, noting the new wrinkles and slightly gray tinge to his olive complexion.

Alekos chuckled. "It's been a tough few months. Life outside the Palace is hard, especially at times like this. I'm sure you would agree."

I considered his words for a moment. "You mentioned someone was at the Palace, who was it? It won't allow just anyone to enter."

When Verrill and I had first arrived at the Palace, Csintalan had informed us that it had its own protective wards that would prohibit unwelcome guests from entering. I had shivered at the press of those wards against my skin as I walked through the gates for the first time.

"They didn't stick around long enough to be identified. But as far as I could tell, it was only one person, and the visit was too quick for them to be aimlessly looting."

Immediately, I thought of Csintalan. I had received no confirmation on his whereabouts, but I was certain he had to be on one of Katmu's islands. For him to somehow travel back to the Palace would be no easy feat.

"And you've had no word from the Rats in Katmu?" I asked.

"Nothing. There's a handful of us who used pigeons to transport unimportant notes for the Fox, but since the Autarch had

Elkas' men lock down the harbor, I've received nothing. I'm assuming any birds coming in from over the channel are shot down."

Pigeons were common enough for correspondence, but their lack of security made them ill-equipped for sensitive information. Where pigeons failed, Verrill's Rats had thrived.

"If your birds were to make it over the channel, would they still be able to find their destination?"

"I don't see why not," Alekos mused, "they're resourceful creatures."

I looked out toward the sea, where Katmu was just a mass of green and brown on the horizon. The body of water separating the two districts was usually nothing. But with no way to cross, it suddenly became everything. If I could just make contact with a few of the Rats, I'd be able to flesh out the plan I had begun to form.

I turned to Alekos. "I have a job for you."

❖ ❖ ❖

Tasar had never looked so displeased to see me. Granted he'd only seen my face a handful of times, but the shock of it seemed to disturb him more with each visit.

The thought unsettled me slightly. While I thoroughly enjoyed not having to worry about my veil, I knew that soon, more people would start connecting my face to the Feline, and any freedom I had in the kingdom would be shattered.

"Try not to jump for joy, Tasar," I drawled, "I'm only here for a quick visit."

"And yet, I don't remember inviting you for a 'quick visit' into my home," he said quietly, through gritted teeth.

A quick glance at his small desk and threadbare rug had me biting back a remark that I'd seen horses with nicer homes. But then I remembered that my own was a flattened pile of charred rubble.

I raised an eyebrow, sensing from his scowl that he had more to say.

"I have been allied with the Lusilim family since I was a child," he began, "and although I wasn't as close to Theo, I still accepted his decision to trust you. I thought he was foolish at first, of course, but I admit, you surprised me, Feline." He rubbed his face with work-worn hands. "I'm disappointed in myself for beginning to trust you, too. When I heard that you tried to kill him after the battle in Ocridell, I almost didn't believe it. After everything you and the Fox had done to aid us over the summer months."

He paused for a moment, as though trying to choose his next words. In an attempt to keep the meeting successful, I refrained from rolling my eyes but was unable to keep the disinterest in his lecture from showing on my face.

I guess my veil did have its uses after all, I decided.

"I don't believe that you're still working for the Autarch, but I do find it interesting that once again, Theo's life is in danger because of you. I've heard how you were there in Katmu, and that even though you could've freed him, you encouraged the others to leave him there, alone and in the hands of the enemy."

I raised a brow. "Are you done?"

"I just want you to know that whatever you're planning on asking of me, if I agree, it *won't* be for you," Tasar snapped. "If you can turn on Theo, I have no doubt of you double crossing me, no matter how friendly you are with my brother. And I've heard about what the Autarch had you do; I'll never forgive you for killing Karasi."

I scoffed. "Oh please, we both know that she's not even dead."

He spluttered on whatever he was going to say, clearly taken aback by the fact that I knew Theo's twin sister hadn't died when I threw her over the edge of the Silent Canyons. I knew from my Rats that Theo had included Tasar in a few of his council meetings where Karasi had been present. He was a fool for trusting yet another district Lord after being betrayed by both Malah Jirata and Aran Seirsun.

"I've come here offering you an opportunity," I announced. "Not that I should be helping you now, given how rude you've been, but I will nonetheless." He waited silently for me to continue. "You're probably aware of the fire that destroyed the encampment at Anzillu Harbor. I was there yesterday and saw the state the Autarch's army was in. If you were to call your forces back from Zingal, you'd be able to take control over the entire harbor within the day."

Tasar considered my words carefully. "I think my people have been through enough already," he said. "Half were held hostage in Katmu, and the other half were ambushed in Ocridell. They've only just returned, I can't ask them to fight another battle, especially when they decided to follow Theo, not me."

"So, all they've been through has been for nothing, then? They decided that they wanted to follow Theo for themselves, they wanted to fight to make Irkalla a better place. Taking control of the harbor is a step in the right direction, you'd take over the channel in the same way you've been managing the trams. And besides, I'd hardly call it a battle, I've seen more vigor in a one-wheeled cart than in those poor bastards abandoned at the port. They're practically begging to give it up."

Tasar stared out of his grimy window and onto the torchlit cavern beyond. "Control of the channel would only be possible if I held both the harbor in Anzillu and the one on Katmu's main island."

"Not necessarily," I mused, tracing a crack in the ancient leather chair I was sitting on. "You'd only need to know the exact time and location to sail to when making a crossing. If the right people were working at a specific mooring location, you'd be in and out without any trouble."

Tasar stood up and began to pace, retracing a worn line in the faded rug. His voice was tense when he finally spoke. "And I suppose you have the *right people* in place? Communication with Katmu has been cut off for weeks."

Did he think I was devoid of sense? Of course I would have handled the logistics before coming to him. I'd devised the scheme myself, though I needed a few of the littler orphans staying at Aghna's to help me carry it out.

"I'm working on it," I said simply. "This time tomorrow, I should be back in contact with some of my Rats in Katmu. Malah's men are not loyal to the Autarch, Tasar, and they aren't happy with

Malah for allowing him to take over their district."

"And what are you getting out of this?" he shot back, giving me a searching look. "I've never known you do something for nothing. You've freely given me information that will benefit me, without asking anything in return. I don't trust it."

"We're on the same side. No one wants to take down the Autarch more than me."

He snorted. "And me giving you access to Katmu is going to let you do that, is it? I'm sure he's just sat on the shore of the main island waiting for you to show up."

"No, but get me over to Katmu and I'll rescue Theo."

Tasar's pacing finally stopped. He turned to look at me, his dark eyes serious in a way I'd never seen them before. "You have a plan?"

Before I could answer, a knock sounded at the door and Farzin poked his head around the frame. As soon as he met my eye, he came bounding into the room, grinning from ear to ear.

"A letter for you, Feline," he said, and I was surprised that he'd managed to unglue his jaw from the sheer volume of toffee I'd seen him and the other children inhale after I'd returned them to Aghna's house. The note had been scribbled quickly, but I knew from the handwriting that it had come from Alekos.

Feline,

As you predicted, the children made for an excellent distraction. We successfully stashed the birds amongst the provisions. I've got three of my best on board in Anzillu uniforms to ensure they are released without fail, as soon as they make port.

Updates to follow.
A

I looked at Tasar, a slow smile spreading across my face. "I do now."

Chapter 8

Theo

Time seemed to warp, crawling by so slowly from lack of stimulation and yet rushing past at a blinding speed from the dread of my impending death.

Because I was sure I was going to die in this pit of shit.

Water dripped from the ceiling of the cave down the back of my neck, soaking the dirty, sodden shirt I'd been wearing since being captured on that beach.

I was cold, hungry, and aching. My shoulders had long since gone numb from my hands being chained to the wall behind my back, and even if I'd had the space to stand up, I doubt that my legs would manage it.

It was impossible for me to know how long I'd been down here. After the Coastguard had hauled me to my feet on the beach and secured me in enough rope to take down a dragon, I'd been thrown onto a boat and taken to where I guessed was the main island, beneath the citadel and into the dungeons.

Malah had been there when I had arrived, the flame of the

torch lighting up the sadness on his face. His carefree youthfulness had been lost to aged worry and responsibility. He'd waited until I was securely shackled to the wall before sending the guards outside and crouching down beside me.

"I'm sorry, my friend, I did all I could," he'd whispered. "This was the only way." He'd paused, looking at the door for a second before turning back. "They got away. All of your ships, they got away."

Even if I hadn't been gagged, I wouldn't have had time to reply before he left the cold, dark cell without another word.

I hadn't seen him since.

But his words had stayed with me. All of the ships had made it out of Katmu. My army was finally free. I had to believe it was true.

❖ ❖ ❖

I woke with a start, the sound of the metal door scraping against the stone floor jarring me from my sleep. Blinding torch light flooded the dank cave and seared into my retinas, making it impossible to see who had entered. When the guards remembered to bring me food, it was usually done by a single candle, so my eyes had grown used to the darkness.

I squinted against the fiery onslaught, trying to make out the faces behind the flame, when a cold, deep voice filled the cell.

"Theodoraxion Lusilim. How the mighty have fallen."

The Autarch.

"Corbin," I tried to growl around the strip of fabric in my mouth, but my tongue felt tied, and it twisted the word into a garbled mess.

My eyes adjusted enough to see a large black crow mask looming over me. The sharp beak shone ominously in the orange light. The smug bastard gave a half chuckle, half sigh, as though he found my current state of degradation both amusing and sorrowful. Malah was beside him, holding the torch, and I tried to catch his gaze, but he wouldn't meet my eyes. Coward.

Was he working against the Autarch? Now that I'd had time to think about it, his Coastguard hadn't put up much of a fight, and he'd left my army in the three weakest locations in his district, after giving me the knowledge on how to exploit them.

"He looks terrible, Malah, haven't you been feeding him?"

"I was not aware of his condition, Your Grace," Malah answered. His voice was steady, but he was anxiously tugging at the cuff of his sleeve. "As per your instructions, I've not been to visit him. This is the first time I've been down here in years; I could never stomach the smell for very long."

I wasn't sure why Malah was lying about not coming to see me, but despite how much he may deserve it, I didn't betray his secret. Maybe I'd hallucinated the encounter.

"I'd like to thank you, Theo," Corbin was saying, and I turned my attention back to him, focusing my glare through the black mesh covering his eyes. "Though I hadn't exactly planned on Malah's asinine Coastguard losing control of your forces, I still got my desired outcome. I'm sorry to say that you played right into my little trap."

He didn't sound sorry at all. I wanted to rage. I wanted to scream at him, demanding how he could do this to me. He'd practically been part of the family for decades. The restraints bit against my wrists as I pulled against them, desperate to get to the old man. He needed to pay.

"I'm afraid you'll just wear yourself out doing that." He sighed, and reached down to pull the rag from my mouth. I resisted the urge to try and bite him, instead licking at the corners of my mouth which had become dry and cracked from the gag.

"Where is she, Theo?" Corbin asked, his tone taking on a seriousness that took me back to his lessons during my childhood. "My lovely Feline is nowhere to be found, and I'd like you to tell me where she's hiding."

I remained silent. Even if she hadn't left me for dead, and even if I had any idea about the dark, miserable corner of the realm she hid herself in, I wouldn't give this man anything ever again.

"You know, she was playing you all along," he said. "Before you'd even been introduced, I'd given her instructions to weasel her way into your life by using whatever methods she deemed necessary. Such an enchanting gift, that siren song of hers. One would barely even know when they were under her spell. Wouldn't you agree?"

I clenched my teeth so hard they threatened to crack. He was trying to get inside my head, to make me doubt everything that had happened between Erisa and me. But this wasn't the first time I'd considered the possibility that everything had been a lie, and I'd had days—at least I thought it had been days—to ruminate over her betrayal.

Corbin wasn't saying anything I hadn't already reflected on. I'd tortured myself by going over every single interaction. And even though I knew he was trying to make me doubt, somehow hearing about Erisa's betrayal out loud hurt even more.

The fact that the man I looked up to as an uncle had used her to get to me made me feel sick. How much had she told him? Was there ever a time when she hadn't been playing us both to suit her own agenda? Had she ever been on my side, even for a single second?

"I know the Feline better than she knows herself," Corbin continued, "the Fox's death would have upset her greatly. She's not thinking clearly, she needs me right now. And I know you care about her, so tell me where she is and all of this," he gestured to where I lay chained on the floor, "can be forgotten."

"If you know that traitorous bitch so well, why do you need me to tell you where she is?" I croaked, my voice cracking from misuse.

The kick to my stomach was swift, and air wheezed from my lungs like wind through an old bellows. My body curled in on itself as much as it could with my arms still bound behind me.

"I will not tolerate your disrespect. Tell me where she is, or your stay here will start to become rather unpleasant."

He raised his hands slightly, palms facing up. For a moment nothing happened, but then I began to feel the little nips and bites at my ankles. I tried to kick out, but more rats seemed to swarm around me, nibbling at my clothes.

Corbin cleared his throat, and the vermin dispersed immediately.

"Think on it, Lord Lusilim," he said. "I'll be back."

And he had been back. Again and again, until I screamed

THE ECHO OF HIS FURY

through my gag as the little teeth buried themselves into my skin, over and over. I'd tried to fight my way out, but the shackles were secure, and he'd rewarded my efforts by stamping on my bound hands, breaking my fingers.

After the fourth visit, Corbin had begun leaving a single candle in the center of the cell, with the wick giving me just enough time to read the latest prints before the wick ran out.

DISTRESS BEACON ACTIVATED

EARLY THIS MORNING, MULTIPLE DISTRESS SIGNALS WERE SIGHTED AMONG THE ISLANDS OF KATMU, AND IT HAS BEEN VERIFIED THAT THE DEFENSE CHAIN WAS RAISED. THE FAILSAFE MECHANISM PROVIDES PROTECTION FOR KATMU'S MAIN ISLAND, WHERE LORD MALAH JIRATA RESIDES.

ALTHOUGH THE REASON BEHIND THESE ACTIONS REMAINS UNKNOWN, SOURCES HAVE CONFIRMED THAT THE CITADEL WAS NOT BREACHED AND THAT THE DISTRICT REMAINS UNITED. WAS IT SIMPLY A PRACTICE DRILL OR WAS THERE A MORE EXTREME REASON FOR THE PRECAUTIONARY MEASURES?

REBEL LEADER APPREHENDED

THEO LUSILIM, LORD OF ZINGAL, HAS BEEN CAPTURED IN KATMU BY OUR MIGHTY AUTARCH. THE INSURGENT WAS INCARCERATED DURING A SCHEME TO RECAPTURE AND FURTHER RADICALIZE HIS ARMY OF "FOLLOWERS" WHO HAD PREVIOUSLY SOUGHT SANCTION IN KATMU, AFTER BEING FORCED TO PLAY A PART IN 'LUSILIM'S TRAITOROUS WAR.'

FORTUNATELY FOR US ALL, THE AUTARCH OUTSMARTED THE OVERGROWN TROUBLEMAKER IN OCRIDELL, FORCING LUSILIM TO RETURN HOME WITH HIS TAIL BETWEEN HIS LEGS. ALTHOUGH NO FURTHER DETAILS HAVE BEEN RELEASED ABOUT THIS NEW ATTACK, SOURCES REMAIN CERTAIN THAT HE NO LONGER POSES A DANGER TO OUR BELOVED IRKALLA.

My existence was slowly becoming unbearable, and I yearned for the days when I lay neglected and forgotten in the dark. Even in sleep I could no longer get any reprieve. Every time I lost consciousness, Erisa would haunt my nightmares.

She was relentless in her mission to ruin me completely. Each time she would appear in my cell, so real I could almost smell the wild jasmine and citrus of her perfume. She would come to my side, melting away the chains binding me to the wall. She'd massage the knots from my strained shoulders, warming me from the inside out with sweet words and peppered kisses across my neck and cheeks.

And each time, she would move to face me, coming in so close that I could taste her breath on my lips.

"Such a fool," she'd say, before plunging a dagger deep into my gut, chuckling as she twisted it.

✥ ✥ ✥

LORD LUSILIM CONSORTING WITH PIRATES

DURING HIS RECENT UNSUCCESSFUL ATTACK ON KATMU, THEO LUSILIM WAS CAPTURED WHILST ATTEMPTING TO "LIBERATE" HIS FOLLOWING. IT HAS SINCE COME TO LIGHT THAT HE NOT ONLY KNEW OF THE POPULAR SMUGGLING ROUTES USED BY PIRATES AND CRIMINALS, BUT THAT HE ALSO COMMANDED A FLEET OF STOLEN SHIPS, BELONGING TO OUR GOLDEN LORD OF KUSIG, ARAN SEIRSUN.

LORD SEIRSUN IS STILL RUMORED TO BE MISSING. AFTER HIS HEROIC DISPLAY OF BRAVERY ON THE BATTLEFIELD IN OCRIDELL, THE LORD DISAPPEARED AND HAS YET TO BE SEEN IN PUBLIC SINCE THE CONFLICT. TO THOSE CONCERNED, HOWEVER, OUR ILLUSTRIOUS AUTARCH HAS ASSURED US THAT ARAN IS ALIVE AND WELL ON THE ROAD TO RECOVERY.

✥ ✥ ✥

"Theo," Erisa cooed, stroking my cheek softly with the backs of her knuckles. "Come on, Theo, it's time to go."

Light haloed around her head, glowing the same shade as her eyes. She looked like an angel, all soft warmth and tenderness. Looking at her was like stepping into a hot spring on a cold morning at sunrise.

"Hello, Sunflower," I tried to say, but my grin faltered, and my words garbled around the dirty rag in my mouth.

Instantly, the warmth and light were gone. Erisa was cold as night, and my arms and legs were bound once more.

"What's wrong, Lord Lusilim?" she jeered, pulling the gag away to place a kiss on the corner of my mouth. "Aren't you happy to see me?"

Her icy touch made my stomach turn in revulsion. I pulled at my restraints, snapping the metal links and freeing my hands. She slunk back as I reached for her, desperate to wrap my hands around her slender neck and squeeze.

"You're the reason I'm in here!" I seethed, kicking my legs free from their binds.

A mocking grin spread across her face, twisting her beautiful features into a terrible mask of unnerving satisfaction.

"Punish me then," she dared, "if you think you can catch me."

And then she was gone, melting into the shadows as though she'd donned them like a cloak. I scrambled to my feet, reaching the door in time to hear her derisive chuckle echo around the dim tunnels.

I ran toward the sound but stopped and whirled when it rang out again from behind me. Then again from my left. She was running me in circles, luring me through this maze of underground caves and passages.

"Come and find me, Theo," she taunted, and I saw a flash of yellow in the darkness before me.

I lunged, scrabbling for purchase on her clothes and hair. She was a writhing ferocity in my arms, taking us both down to the damp floor where she bit and scratched me in an attempt to get free.

Firelight from a distant torch flickered over her face as I finally got a hold of her throat. I clenched my fingers—squeezing hard enough to make my hands cramp—compressing her windpipe until the saccharine smile possessing her face finally dropped and the wild sheen faded form her eyes.

❖ ❖ ❖

Bile sprayed from my mouth, and I retched, forcing my already empty stomach to expel the remaining contents.

My bound hands were still tingling with the feel of Erisa's throat beneath them, the phantom warmth of her skin being stolen away by the frigid stone. A cold sweat coated my skin, causing shivers to wrack through my body.

I couldn't be sure if I was sick from the act of killing her and watching her die, or from the sheer ease of the action. I'd chased her down intent on ending her, *needing* to punish her for every wrong she'd committed.

I'd acted like a man possessed.

Erisa had lied to me, she'd attacked and abandoned me, making it perfectly clear that my death would be nothing but a convenience for her. And yet, presented with the opportunity, I wondered if I would even be able to repay the favor.

Trembling like a sick dog, I fell once more into a fitful sleep, the image of Erisa fading into the distance on the stern of the ship replaying once more behind my eyelids.

❖ ❖ ❖

"This will all be over if you just tell me what I need to know," Corbin repeated, his voice too loud in the confines of the cell. "You know I don't want to do this."

Malah had long since avoided attending his interrogations, so he had freely removed his crow mask upon entering. His face was full of false pity and concern.

"She's been sighted entertaining other men, you know," he lamented, as though he regretted being the one to impart the news. "But my sources can't say for certain where she's taking them to."

"Why don't you ask one of them, then," I spat out through gritted teeth. He'd tried various different techniques to try and get me to talk, from playing on my jealousy to trying to convince me that she was pregnant with my child.

Each of his statements had been painful to hear, but even if I wanted to give him the information he sought, I didn't have it.

"I told you, I don't know," I said again, meeting his hateful blue eyes. "But, if I were in your situation, I'd want to know where she was too. She's coming for you, Corbin, and if I were you, I'd start running."

His eyes widened for a split second, confirming my suspicions. He was afraid. He knew that his *precious* Feline was going to make him pay for taking Verrill away from her, and he wanted to know where she was to either capture her before she got to him, or to simply flee in the opposite direction.

"I think you've forgo—" His voice faltered as a knock sounded at the cell door.

"Your Grace," Malah's voice was muffled, but his anxiety was clear, "I know you told me that you were not to be interrupted, but there's currently a situation that I think you'll want to be aware of."

"I'll be seeing you later, Theo," Corbin threatened, staring at me for a long moment, before donning his mask and leaving me, once again, alone with the single lit candle.

FELINE SPOTTED WITH POTENTIAL SUITOR

OUR FAVORITE MOUSER HAS ALWAYS HAD A REPUTATION FOR TREATING HER MEN AS PLAYTHINGS, BUT HAS OUR FEARED FELINE FINALLY FOUND HER FOREVER HOME? THE MASKED MAIDEN WAS SEEN HAVING A SECRET LIAISON WITH A HANDSOME MYSTERY MAN YESTERDAY AFTERNOON, DURING THE SEASONAL TAX COLLECTION ONE.

AS ONE OF THE AUTARCH'S FAVORITES, THE FELINE SHOULD BE THE GOAL OF MANY AN UNMARRIED MAN, SHOULD HE BE BRAVE ENOUGH TO ATTEMPT IT. AND EVEN IF SHE HADN'T BEEN RUMORED TO BE A BEAUTY BENEATH HER VEIL, ALL CATS LOOK GRAY IN THE DARK. JUST TEMPER YOUR CURIOSITY AROUND THIS ONE.

❖ ❖ ❖

The rough scrape of metal against the stone floor jolted me from my slumber. The candle had just about burned out when the door opened. I stiffened, glancing up at the dark figure in the cell entrance and waited for the Autarch to resume his torment.

"Fuck, Theo."

Erisa's soft voice unraveled my nerves like a ball of yarn.

Not again. Let me have *one* fucking peaceful sleep. The hair on the back of my neck rose watching the demonic wraith move closer and I could feel my heart rate surge as I pulled desperately against the shackles around my wrists and ankles.

The room began to spin the second her fingers brushed against the skin at my wrists, closing my throat around the panicked breaths being forced from my lungs.

"Try and stop your trembling," she murmured, "I won't be able to pick the locks if you can't keep your hands still."

Her voice was softer and kinder than I'd ever heard it, but her scent was stronger than I'd experienced in any of my previous dreams, and the intensity of it made me dizzy.

Any moment now, she would take her dagger and plunge it into my abdomen.

The clink of my shackles hitting the cell floor shook me from my panic-induced spiral. I moved my wrists, bringing them in front of me for the first time since I'd arrived. Pain lashed through my stiff shoulders, but I could barely feel it over the adrenaline now coursing through my body.

My hands were free, and Erisa was busy working on the locks around my ankles. My heart was still racing as I sat up, causing my head to spin. The click of the shackles sounded deafening in the quiet cell, and I didn't wait for the walls or ceiling to stop whirling before I lunged for her. Erisa's eyes turned from triumphant to alarmed and she brought her hands up to protect herself.

"Theo, stop! What are you doing? We need to leave!" she hissed, scrambling to her feet and putting the small distance of the cell between us. The movement extinguished the dying flame of the candle, plunging us both into darkness.

"Shit," she murmured, and I felt her hands patting along my arms and tugging at them, trying to pull me to my feet. "Come on, we need to go *now*!"

I reached up and gripped her forearms, trying to use her as leverage to get to my feet, but my legs were useless and numb. They buckled and I dug my fingers into her skin to ensure she came down with me.

If I couldn't get on my feet to kill her, I'd do it on the floor.

Chapter 9

Erisa

Feline,
Everything is in place. We're ready to leave on your word.
Alekos

4 December

❖ ❖ ❖

Theo grunted in defeat when I incapacitated him against the wet floor. The cell stank of filth, and I hoped to hell that whatever liquid was currently seeping into my trouser leg was only water.

He fought and clawed at me desperately, as though he were possessed with an inherent *need* to hurt me.

"Theo, stop," I pleaded, trying to disable him as gently as possible. I knew from the sweat slicked across his skin and the tremors that still wracked through his limbs that he was having a panic attack. And from the roiling fever heating his skin, I guessed he was likely delirious too.

The first sight of him lying shackled and filthy against the floor had my stomach twisting and my vision turning red with fury. He was broken. I'd been too late, spent too long planning his rescue.

He thrashed against me, his rapid breaths almost wheezing from his lungs.

"I'm dreaming ..." he panted, mumbling to himself. "Just dreaming ... you're not here ... don't kill me ... don't kill me ... I'm dreaming, just dreaming." He threw his hand up to try and claw my eyes, letting out a howl as his shoulder rotated.

I knew I had to do something to stop this quickly; he was making too much noise. I briefly considered singing to him, to force his body to relax, but thought better of it. It would only make things worse when I stopped. Quick as a snake, I struck him across the face, my hand stinging as it connected with his dirty, gaunt cheek.

"Listen to me!" I snapped. "You're not dreaming, but if someone captures *me*, they'll put *you* into a sleep you won't wake up from."

In the darkness, I could just about make out the shine of his eyes as they locked onto mine. He was still panting and trembling, but at least his thrashing had ceased.

I gripped his biceps tightly. "Now, are you going to come with me quietly?"

Or do I have to knock you unconscious and drag you out? I added silently.

After a tense moment, he nodded and gripped my arms to try and haul himself up. As it turned out, I did need to drag him. His legs were stiff and weak, wobbling like a newborn fawn, and I cringed at the yelp he couldn't suppress as I tucked myself beneath his left arm trying to support his weight. We crept through the tunnels, stepping over the guards I'd felled on my way in, their bodies illuminated by the intermittent sconces lining the passage walls.

"Where are we going?" Theo breathed shakily, and I noticed he was speaking with a slight lisp. "Please ... I don't know where I am."

"I'm taking you home. To Zingal."

That seemed to pacify him slightly, but I couldn't help observing the way he cringed away from my contact. His eyes were wide, watching me as though he were waiting for me to attack. I wanted to move away from him, to stop touching him in order to make him more comfortable, but I knew he would never be able to walk on his own.

Every time we passed a light I had to turn my head away. He was emaciated, dirty, and feverish. I needed to get him to a healer as soon as possible. There were large patches of his skin that were practically falling away, with puss seeping through his blood-stained shirt.

We walked as fast as Theo could manage, the slanted floor bringing us closer to the surface with every step. The sound of shouting echoed around the adjacent tunnel, and I paused at the entrance to the dungeons, knocking three times against the door.

After a moment, one of my Katmuan Rats opened it, ushering us through the crisp night air and around the side of the upper level of the dungeons. I pressed us against the wall, allowing a dark shadow to envelop us as I waited for the next stage of the plan.

THE ECHO OF HIS FURY

Less than a minute later, the Rat returned, followed by a horse drawn cart loaded with sacks of silkleaf fronds, headed for the mainland.

At his signal, I half-ran, half-dragged Theo to the wagon, practically hauling him up onto the bed of the cart and tucking him in between two overstuffed sacks. This operation was so much harder than I'd anticipated. I had been ridiculously short-sighted not to consider the state he could be in. To think that Csintalan would treat him with any kind of respect.

Once I was up into the wagon too, I moved a bag to hide his feet and threw the waiting canvas sheet over us as the horse began to move forward.

Under the enclosed space of the sheet, the smell of him was feculent, making my eyes water and my stomach turn. Though he had finally stopped trembling, his eyes had glazed over, and his expression had turned vacant and unseeing.

It was too much for him to handle. The Autarch had broken him.

Every time my skin brushed against his, his hands would begin to shake, and his breathing would accelerate. I tried to stay as far away from him as the confines of the cart would allow, expecting him to finally snap at any moment.

The journey felt endless. I was too afraid to speak, or even breathe too loudly, for fear that Theo would be shaken from his daze and alert everyone to our presence.

After an eternity, the cart stopped.

"We're here, Feline," the Rat driving whispered, before removing the canvas sheet and shifting the sacks of silkleaf out of the way. He helped me pull Theo down to the ground and slipped under his other arm so that we could lift him from both sides.

Alekos was waiting at the gangway of the large boat, his eyes wide as he took in the state of the Lord of Zingal.

"We need to hurry, Feline," he fretted, "we're almost a half hour behind schedule."

"Help us get him inside then," I ordered, silently daring him to make a comment about Theo's appearance or odor. He was clever enough to remain silent.

The boat had been completely gutted for speed, but between the three of us, we managed to lower Theo onto some blankets in the cargo hold. The Rat who had helped us turned to go, needing to have the horse and cart at its designated drop point on time. I caught his hand as he turned to leave and pressed a full bag of silver into it.

"Thank you, Feline," he said, glancing toward the cargo hold. "Good luck."

As soon as he was gone, we prepared to leave. Theo had fallen asleep by the time we were sailing across the channel, back toward the mainland, and I couldn't help but take stock of all of his injuries and ailments.

Apart from the fingers on his left hand, nothing seemed to be broken, but his entire body was crumpled and destroyed. His tattered clothes revealed the surface wounds covering the majority of his skin, which were either infected or scabbing over and covered in dirt. He had abrasion wounds on either side of his mouth, and I guessed his slight lisp had come from biting his tongue.

I wished I wasn't able to imagine the torment Csintalan had put him through, but I was familiar with the Autarch's torture methods and felt sick to my stomach picturing Theo on the receiving end of his twisted schemes.

The journey across the water was uneventful, but slower than if we'd had access to a proper ship. I'd planned for every eventuality but willfully neglected to consider that I'd find Theo in such a poor condition that he'd barely be able to stand.

Luckily, the tormenting mists surrounding Katmu were unable to penetrate below deck, and the few tendrils that did manage to make it inside were easily wafted away from Theo's sleeping form. The whisps of the hateful vapor that managed to touch my skin reiterated how wretched I felt inside, rightfully blaming me for Theo's pain and suffering.

I was sitting beside him on the floor when I felt the boat begin to slow as it came into the port at the Anzillu harbor. Disturbed by lack of movement from the gentle waves, he began to mumble and twitch.

He began to pant. "Don't do it ... not again, please ... don't ... don't."

"Shh, it's all right," I whispered, and tried to stroke his filthy, too-long hair. But the moment I touched him, his sunken eyes flew open and rolled around wildly before finally settling on me.

"Are you here to kill me?" he asked quietly. He was completely still, apart from the slight tremors of fear shaking his body.

He's scared of me, I realized with an agonizing pang, and rose to my feet to get someone else to watch him, in the hopes that it would ease his discomfort.

"You're leaving me to die again." Theo's voice was barely audible; a hoarse echo of the rich, deep tone I was used to hearing from him.

"I'm just going to get you some help, I'll be back."

He looked torn, as though he couldn't decide if having me nearby was worse than being abandoned.

As I emerged onto the deck, I took in several deep breaths to try and steady myself. I had seen all kinds of atrocities in my twenty-five years, but the sight of Theo like that was hitting me harder than I dared even admit to myself.

Tasar was waiting on the walkway of the port and whatever he saw on my face had him calling for the reinforcements to come and aid us immediately. It took four grown men to remove Theo from the cargo hold. Now that the adrenaline in his system had abated, his body was too weak to support him and failed as soon as he was lifted to his feet.

He fearfully pushed away the hands trying to help him, eventually collapsing again from the exhaustion, hunger, and dehydration. However, his lack of consciousness made it easier to load him onto a makeshift stretcher and out onto dry land and into yet another cart that would take him to the nearest medic in Anzillu.

"I hadn't expected it to be this bad," Tasar murmured as we followed the cart on foot, keeping our eyes and ears peeled for any sign of attack.

I wanted to agree with Tasar, to lament at how Theo could barely even stand the sight of me, and how he would never be able to forgive me for landing him in that cell, even if it *had* been the only way to save his life.

"I should've accelerated the plan," I said instead. "I waited too long to get clarification from the Rats in Katmu."

"If we hadn't waited, we would've been sailing into a shitstorm, and I doubt any of you would've made it out alive."

Even though I knew he was right, his words did little to soothe the guilt that had wormed its way beneath my skin and burrowed deep into the pit of my stomach. It was my fault that Theo was in this mess, and even though a sick, twisted part of me considered his treatment an apt comeuppance for Verrill's death, I knew I would try and make amends for it. Because it hadn't been Theo that killed Verrill; Csintalan had thrown the knife, and I had been the target.

A loud screech sounded above us, and I whirled, daggers drawn, as a large crow swooped past our heads and landed next to Theo on the cart. I rushed forward to shoo the bird away, before noticing the scroll attached to its leg.

When I tried to collect the letter, it drew blood pecking my hand. I hissed and threw the creature back into the sky as soon as the scroll was free.

My darling Feline,
Once again, you have outmaneuvered me with your clever schemes. When I noticed the odd behavior of the pigeons, I knew you were behind it. After all, they are flying rats. But I must admit, your boldness and bravery have shocked me. I believe I taught you a little too well.

I don't care what you do with the boy, he's not much use to anyone now, just come back to me, my daughter. All will be forgiven.

Your Autarch
P.S. Happy belated birthday, Kitten.

A white feather fell out of the letter and into the palm of my hand and I stared at it in horror, watching as the iridescent sheen changed color in the light. Wrapped around the end of the quill was another piece of paper and bile burned my throat as I read the tiny words.

I reach for shadows, find the air—
You're everywhere and never there.

It was part of a song my mother would sing to me while she braided these feathers into my hair when I was little, saying that they came from her favorite songbird. Verrill would always pluck them out again later, but those moments were one of few times in my life where I had felt truly safe and at peace. And somehow, the Autarch knew.

Tasar was murmuring something, but I couldn't hear him over the pounding of my heart.

❖ ❖ ❖

For the third time today, I had to take a deep breath and resist the urge to kill Karasi.

Again. For good this time.

I could tell that even Didi and Dana had started to become frustrated with her incessant insistence that Theo should be taken out of Irkalla to heal properly, away from the threat of the Autarch.

"It'll only take a few days, and we have connections and places for him to be hidden," she prattled, and I had to force my hands not to throttle her with the bandages I was boiling.

"He belongs at home, and I won't hear another word on the subject," Dana maintained, and rose from her seat to leave the room, scowling at me on the way past.

Since I'd successfully brought Theo back to Zingal a few days ago, his family had reluctantly allowed me to stay in the estate, no longer able to justify their banishment based on Theo's safety.

They too had tried—and failed—to come up with a successful plan to save their Lord. I'd arrived to find them all half asleep over a poorly enlarged map of Katmu's islands. It was obvious that they planned to sail the entire fleet back to Malah's district, declaring outright war against him.

Fools.

"We had a solid plan," Nook had argued, "until almost all of Tasar's men decided to abandon us and flee back home."

"Ah, yes that might have been my fault," I said. "I needed Tasar to take control of the harbor in Anzillu. And besides, they'd

S.C. MAKEPEACE

only just escaped Katmu, they'd never agree to sail straight back there, and you wouldn't have had the authority to make them."

Upon seeing the defeated look in his eyes, I had dropped the subject. He already knew that their plan would have failed, and everyone had been so relieved to have Theo back that it wasn't brought up again. They all thanked me for going after him, no matter how reluctant the gesture had been.

"Are you taking more up to him?" Karasi asked coldly, gesturing to the bandages I was hanging by the fire to dry. Without waiting for my response, she continued, "I've heated some broth, you can take that up to him as well, but make sure he doesn't gulp it down too fast, otherwise he'll be sick again."

I nodded, trying to muster the courage while she was busy filling a bowl. Owing to his heavy dose of medication, I hadn't spoken with Theo since we arrived at the estate three days ago. He'd only regained consciousness this morning and I hadn't yet dared go into his room. But his dressings needed changing, and besides the healer, I'd been the only one to truly see the extent of his injuries, so had insisted on doing it myself.

Relief washed over me when I entered his room and saw that he was asleep. I placed the bowl on the side table to cool and sat on the bed beside him. Making as little movement as possible, I gently peeled away the bandages from his legs and feet. The skin on his right calf had been almost completely chewed away and I winced as the bandage snagged on some crusted fluid that had seeped from the wound.

I looked up to check that he was still sleeping, only to meet the pair of Lusilim green eyes that had become so familiar to me.

They were still bloodshot and dull, but undeniably open and alert.

"I didn't mean to wake you," I said quietly. "I just need to change your bandages and then I'll leave."

He said nothing, only watched in silence as I continued peeling away the soiled strips of fabric before spreading a thick layer of ointment over the wounds and redressing them. He didn't complain once, even though the pain must have been considerable.

I left his hands until last, wanting to delay the moment when I'd have to feel them trembling because of me. He sucked in a sharp breath when I touched his palm, but he didn't flinch away, even as I worked around the splints setting the fingers on his left hand. I kept my gaze focused solely on my work, spinelessly avoiding the contempt I knew would be waiting for me in his expression when I looked up.

"Karasi made you some broth," I said, finally breaking the silence when I fixed the last of the bandages. "I'll help you with it."

He scowled down at his freshly bandaged hands, as though debating whether it was worth risking his injuries to avoid accepting my aid. When he nodded, I took the bowl into my lap and used the spoon to feed him the contents.

He still hadn't looked at me by the time it was empty, just continued staring at the wall while I collected everything to take back downstairs.

"Thank you," he croaked as I opened the door. Without looking, I nodded once and went downstairs.

Ezra was in the kitchen when I entered, sitting at the table with a mug of tea.

"How is he?" he asked.

"Better, his fever finally broke last night. And he's awake, he'd probably appreciate some company."

And ideally from someone who isn't me.

He nodded and rose from his chair. But instead of going for the door, he came toward me. I only had enough time to put down the dirty bowl and bandages in preparation for his attack when he pulled me into his arms.

For a few seconds, I was frozen, unable to understand what was happening, but then I sagged against Ezra's chest, incapable of maintaining my rigid posture.

When was the last time someone had held me?

"He hates me," I whispered, horrified to hear my voice crack with emotion.

"Shh," Ezra hushed, and rested his cheek on the top of my head, offering me the first shred of comfort I'd received in weeks that hadn't come from myself. His hatred toward me had ebbed since I'd brought Theo home. And while I knew we would never regain our former friendship, it was nice to have at least one person who didn't constantly glower at me.

"It's all my fault. But I had to do it," I blabbered, unable to stop the words falling from my mouth. "I had to leave him on that beach. There wasn't enough time to get him to the boat. And the chain was being raised, I had to get to the ship and make them leave. The Autarch wanted *me*, if I'd helped Theo, they would have captured us both and Theo would've been killed. I saw the letter. He was only imprisoned because the Autarch knew I'd come to get him; he was using him as bait to get to me. It's all my fault;

I did that to him."

Ezra listened to my garbled sobs in silence, his only reaction stroking my shoulders supportively. He had always been the most emotionally intelligent of Theo's friends, but his ability to know exactly what someone needed in a time of crisis was extraordinary.

"He'll come around, you'll see," he said soothingly, with almost enough conviction to make me believe him.

Chapter 10

Theo

Erisa was humming. From my chair in the parlor, I could hear the soft, melodic notes drift in from the kitchen as she boiled the last remaining bandages my mother had taken off my skin this morning.

I wanted to tell her to stop, yet I yearned to hear *more*, to hear her *sing*. Even when the thought of it made my skin prickle and my stomach sour in disgust. It was an unhealthy obsession, like a silkleaf addiction, only all the more enslaving. I'd only heard Erisa sing a handful of times and was more than aware of the devastation it could cause. And yet, I craved it like an oasis in the desert.

Annoyed at myself for losing my train of thought, I turned back to the reports in my hands and frowned.

"How long was I asleep?" I asked Nook, who was scribbling something into his notebook.

"Three days," he said without looking up.

"And I've been awake for another … how long was I … What date is it?"

Nook stopped writing and clenched his jaw before looking up. "It's December thirteenth."

We were almost two weeks into December. I'd been in that dungeon for almost an entire month. The thought of that damp, dark cell made my breath hitch, and my heart accelerate.

"I'm so sorry, Theo," Nook muttered. "We tried to come up with a plan to get you out of there sooner, but every time we thought we had a solution, it would fall apart before it even began. Erisa told us not to meddle, and I just wonder how much sooner she would have been able to get you if we had only helped her instead of making her do everything alone."

"I can hardly blame you for not trusting her," I said, feeling the sores at the corner of my mouth crack as I gave him a wry smile. "I would've been angry if you had."

He nodded, unconvinced. I had no doubt that Ezra had told him the information that he'd given me a few days ago, that Erisa had left me to save my life. In theory it had made sense. The Autarch was only interested in finding out any information I had about her whereabouts. He hadn't even bothered himself with questions regarding my army, as though the subject was so far beneath him, it didn't warrant a second of his attention.

I believed that she had told Ezra the truth, but I couldn't help imagining the situation in reverse. If she had been the one stranded on that beach, and I'd had to make a decision between saving the hundreds of people on that ship or helping her, I would've landed in that sand and destroyed any of the Coastguard who dared to touch her. Even if there was a possibility that she would've been killed, I would've found a way around it.

S.C. MAKEPEACE

But she hadn't. And I couldn't even be angry about it. She'd chosen to save hundreds of my soldiers instead of me, which was a choice I would have gladly made ten times over. I was happy with the decision she had made, even if the reality of it stung more than I cared to admit.

I scanned through the district accounts, noticing that Karasi had been managing things exceptionally well in my absence, thanks to all of her prior training with Corbin. I curled my lip at the thought of the traitorous backstabber, once again unable to comprehend how anyone could treat someone they had pretended to love with such cruelty.

His double life made no sense. Why would he even bother to pretend with us after ordering Karasi's murder? I needed to make him pay for every atrocity he'd committed against my family, the need for revenge simmering into an inferno beneath my skin.

And I needed the shield to do it.

"I'm going to pay Aran a visit," I announced to Nook and rose from my chair, being careful not to break any of my freshly formed skin. "And potentially fix him a room in the house. After experiencing being locked away myself, I'm inclined to at least offer him the dignity of a bathing chamber."

"Umm … about that, Theo …" Nook hesitated, suddenly enraptured with a loose button on his tunic. "The thing is, while you were gone … We didn't want to worry you about it, with your healing and all … but the thing is … uh, well … Aran's gone."

"Gone? What do you mean he's gone?"

"Well, one morning, one of the guards went down to the dungeons to give him breakfast …" he mumbled, cursing quietly when the thread snapped, and the button tumbled to the floor. "We don't know how he did it, the door was still locked, he was just gone."

"When was this, Nook?" I tried my best to keep my voice low and even.

"A few weeks ago. We sent people out looking as soon as we realized, but you were imprisoned, and we had to focus on how to get you out."

"A few weeks ago?" I fumed, unable to keep my voice down. "Why did no one tell me about this sooner?"

"There was nothing to be done about it, he just … vanished." Nook looked desperately at Ezra and Suenna for help, who had appeared at the door, drawn to the commotion.

Ezra remained silent and Suenna melted back into the hallway.

"FELINE!" I bellowed, knowing that she would have been eavesdropping on the entire conversation.

She appeared beside Ezra and slunk into the room; chin held high as she levelled me with a look that told me to watch my tone.

"Where is Aran Seirsun?" I demanded. "We all know he's not clever enough to get himself out of that cell. Only a handful of people knew where he was being kept, and of all of them, I trust *you* the least."

"First of all, hurtful," she quipped. "Second of all, I've been a little *busy* this past month saving *you* from your own cell. And third, what would I possibly want with that pompous airhead?"

"Oh, I don't know," I said sardonically, "maybe because he has the last remaining relic needed to complete the shield and destroy the Autarch."

"A shield that we don't have," she reminded me bluntly. "Everyone leave. I want to have a word with Theo alone."

Nook and Ezra looked to me for guidance and gratefully sped from the room when I nodded. It was the first time I'd been alone with Erisa since I'd woken up to her changing my bandages days ago.

"I have the stylus," she said quietly, and held up a finger when I opened my mouth to demand clarification. "Aran Seirsun is a fool, and a predictable fool at that. Did you really think that I would let *him* hide one of the most valuable items in the kingdom, when Silas is looking for it? Because he *is* looking for it. He wants to destroy it, to ensure that we never complete the shield. When I came to question Aran, the bonehead told me exactly where I needed to go."

The fact that Silas was actively plotting against me stung, but by now, I was almost numb to betrayal.

"But I was there when you spoke to him, he refused to tell you anything about it," I said.

"No, but I had my suspicions, I just had to push the right buttons to get clarification. Aran always had an odd relationship with his mother, a little too close if you ask me. And he would never pass up an opportunity to gloat. So, when he said that his darling Mama would get the last laugh, I knew I was right. He'd buried the stylus with her, sealed into her tomb."

"You unearthed her body?" I asked, horrified.

"Oh, calm down, bones were the only thing left of the old hag … mostly. And it's not like I dug her up or desecrated the grave; I just broke into the tomb. And there it was, just as I'd suspected."

"And where is it now?"

"Upstairs in your closet."

"You mean I've had it here the entire time?" How could I not have noticed her planting something in my private quarters? Maybe I truly was as unobservant as she said.

"Of course not, I've been moving it around when I haven't been able to keep it on me. As soon as I collected it, I brought it here to hide. But then I overheard some of your plans to liberate your army and knew I needed to be clever. The Beldams informed me that Silas would be searching for the stylus to try and destroy it, so I couldn't leave it somewhere without supervision."

I wanted to question her about the Beldams and Silas, but I stayed quiet, not wanting to enrage her by throwing her off course.

"I knew that I needed to come along on your ridiculous mission if things were going to play out properly, but I also had a suspicion that Silas was following me. So, I brought the stylus to Katmu, not wanting to leave it unguarded anywhere on the mainland," she explained, looking delighted at my astonished expression. "I went ahead of you, clearing your path as best I could—you're welcome, by the way, for the guards at the Kusig docks. Then I followed you all to the ships and took your bag when the commotion began. I hid the stylus in the lining; you'll see a small gap in the stitching. I also dried my hair with one of your shirts, hope you don't mind. I would've concealed it better, but Ezra almost caught me, so I hid in the gunport until we reached Katmu."

"And … afterwards?" I didn't want to hear her recounting the moment she'd left me for dead.

"I admit, it was a little tricky to track it down after that, as I didn't return to Zingal on the same boat as your bag, but I knew that Ezra would bring it back to the house for you, along with your bow, I just had to find it.

"Luckily, your council were bickering too loudly to notice that I was rooting around in their belongings trying to find the right bag. Then, after a *charming* introduction to Torin fucking Sharru—who was living in your house, in case you didn't know—I tucked it into my corset and took it with me to Anzillu, where I left it in the capable, grubby little hands of twelve orphan children. Silas would never have suspected me to leave it so vulnerable, so it was perfect. I picked it up on the way back here, and it's been with you ever since."

Sighing, I pinched the bridge of my nose and closed my eyes momentarily. I had so many questions, none of which were voiced when I opened my mouth.

"Why did you stop changing my bandages?" I wanted to kick myself for asking something so trivial and unimportant.

Her eyes widened, clearly taken aback by the change in subject. She turned away, avoiding my gaze. "I saw the way you looked at me. Not just in the cell or on the boat, but even that first morning when you woke. You hated me, and you were scared of me. I thought you would be more comfortable with your mother helping you instead of me."

"I didn't hate—" I began, but backtracked when she raised a brow. "Okay, I did. Back in the cell, I hated you for abandoning me, first after Ocridell and then again on that beach. I spent every second blaming you for the fact that I was there, convincing myself that all we'd had meant nothing to you.

"I dreamt about you every night, so vivid that I could touch you, *smell* you even. You were so real. And just as I began to find even the slightest shred of happiness in your presence, you'd kill me. You'd pull out one of your daggers and run it through my chest, or my stomach, or my neck, without fail. I can't remember much, but the night you came to get me, I thought I was dreaming. I thought you were there to kill me again."

"I know it'll take time, but I'm going to try and make things right," she said, her eyes flaming orange from the fire in the hearth. "I'm not going to tell you that you can trust me, because you won't believe it. But I promise you that we'll get that shield and kill the Autarch. Together."

I wanted to tell her that I never wanted to do anything together ever again, but I knew that was nonsense, that if I wanted revenge for myself and my family, I would need the Feline's help to do it. And the ferocity in her voice left no doubt in my mind that she had every intention of honoring that promise.

But there was one thing I needed to know, that had been plaguing me relentlessly since the battle in Ocridell.

"Did you know who he was?" I asked. "Did you know that the Autarch was C—"

My tongue tied around his name, closing my throat before the truth could escape my mouth. Her baffled expression told me enough. I would explain who he was to me at a later date, but for now there were more important matters to discuss.

"Will you show me the stylus?"

She was gone in a flash, leaving me alone with my thoughts. I had no idea how to feel. A few months ago, I was so in love with her that I could barely think clearly about anything that concerned her. And now …

As confusing and ridiculous as it was, I was still in love with her. I knew that even I wasn't delusional enough to pretend otherwise. I may have hated her and lost every scrap of trust we'd built, but I couldn't deny my feelings, no matter how deeply I'd buried them.

As much as I'd hated it, it was probably a blessing in disguise that she had never once returned the sentiment. Even days before we could've lost our lives in battle, she wouldn't allow me to say it. For my own sanity, I had to believe that my feelings had been my own, instead of some forced manipulation from the strange, compelling power of her voice. But I just couldn't be certain.

"Hello, Theo, are you listening?"

Erisa was standing beside me, waving a hand in front of my face. In the other, she held the stylus. It was the exact same as the counterfeit Aran had given to us, but instead of being made from pure gold, it was crafted from an unremarkable blend of bronze metal streaked with silver, as though its creation was simply an afterthought.

She placed the writing utensil into my hand, and I immediately felt the thrum of power radiate across my palm, sending tendrils of warmth through the fresh pink skin of my wounds. This was the final component, the last relic left behind by the gods. The last remaining object needed to defeat the power they put in place centuries ago.

"Now for the shield," I said, handing the stylus back to Erisa, trying not to watch as she slipped it inside her corset. "Silas hasn't returned any of my letters. I'm assuming you've been to his house?"

She rolled her eyes. "Obviously."

Despite her snarky remarks and nonchalance, I could see that she was hurting. She refused to hold my gaze, and the dark circles beneath her eyes told me she was having trouble sleeping. I tried my best not to care, and hated myself for noticing.

"I think we should try the Beldams again," I said. "They helped us last time."

"They helped *you* last time," she argued. "I've been back there twice since then, and it was a waste of time. They told me outright that I wasn't welcome, but …"

"But?"

She chewed on her lower lip, hesitating. "They said I would seek their counsel once more, but also that they wouldn't give their answers away for nothing. I'm worried what the asking price for that kind of information will be."

Chapter 11

Theo

We waited a week for the remaining skin on my legs to heal before we began our journey to Khar'ra. I had written to Tasar to arrange for a tram to take us into Ersetu, and on toward Hudjefa.

Cyfrin met us at the station, with two horses saddled and ready for us to take. He greeted Erisa with a ridiculous flourish of admiration that set my teeth on edge.

I really didn't like the younger Wranmaris brother.

"What's gotten you into such a sour mood?" Erisa asked as we exited Ersetu through the recently broadened hole through the face of the volcano.

"I'm not looking forward to spending the next few days in the saddle," I lied. Though the thought of having to ride all the way to Khar'ra barely healed, just to ride all the way back again wasn't particularly appealing.

She didn't respond, and her silence stretched until we skirted past the edges of the Giŝtir Jungle.

"We should stop to make camp before the sun sets," she said, eyeing the small flat area between the trees.

"Here's good," I agreed, and dismounted to begin preparing the horses for the night. My shoulders were still stiff from being held behind my back for weeks, and even though I had regained some of my strength from before the capture, I had to admit that I was tired.

Erisa was finished with the tent by the time I'd fed and watered the horses, and I was about to start making the fire when the rain began to fall.

"You needn't bother with that," she called from inside the tent, "I'm not going to sit around in the rain."

I was secretly glad for the excuse to abandon the fire, uncertain if my bound fingers would have been able to strike a spark.

Opening the canvas door, I joined Erisa inside, where she was already unpacking the food parcels I'd prepared that morning. We ate in a comfortable silence, listening to the patter of rain against the walls of the tent.

"Why didn't you let them help you?" I asked after a while. At her confused look, I clarified, "Nook, Ezra, and Suenna, why didn't you ask them to help you rescue me? You know you could've trusted them."

She shook her head. "I couldn't have. I knew I had to rely on myself for something like that. I wouldn't have risked you—or them—for the sake of having some help. If they'd have been caught, they would have been killed. And then there would have been no one else to come and get you if I failed."

I couldn't even imagine that scenario, the pain of losing my friends was more than I could bear to think about.

"How did you even do it?" I said, wanting to steer the conversation in a new direction. "Malah showed me how heavily the dungeons are guarded on our last visit there, how did you do it by yourself?"

"I managed to make contact with a few of the Rats again." She huffed out a small laugh. "We used carrier pigeons to make the initial connection and then I went to Tasar and gave him the information he would need to secure Anzillu Harbor for himself. From then, all correspondence was relayed by small boats that coincided with the Rats shifts at one of the smaller docks on the main island.

"It took a few weeks to stabilize the connection and it was touch and go for a while, but we managed to keep the channel open and relatively uninterrupted. It's nowhere near as effortless as it once was, but it was all I needed to form a plan."

She picked at a hangnail, refusing to look at me. "I know how the Autarch keeps his prisoners. I knew your conditions would be poor, but I never imagined—" She finally met my gaze. "I needed *time*, Theo. I needed to make sure that we were successful. If I didn't have every detail exact—even down to the last second—I knew it would fail.

"I had one of my Rats strip a boat completely bare, so that it would be as fast as possible, and we sailed to one of the derelict fishing yards on the small island northwest of the main one. I met one of my Katmuan Rats there, and over the course of the next day he smuggled me onto the mainland hidden in a sack of cowhides—

the smell was unbearable.

"Malah and the Autarch," she paused to calm a swell in temper at the mention of the two men, "they would go down to the dungeons in what I initially thought was a sporadic pattern, but it actually just coincided with the change of the night guards, which happens on a time rotation. So, I waited, hidden in the dark until they came, and it was so tempting, *so tempting*, to just run up to the Autarch and slit his throat. But I knew that I could never make it through Malah and the fourteen guards afterwards, and that you'd be left there in that dungeon to rot. And it took every ounce of willpower in my body to do it, but I sat there, and I watched them walk by.

"The seven guards were still talking through their handover in the chamber off the courtyard, which according to my Rats, usually lasted about five minutes. It gave me just enough time to slip behind one of the fresh guards and steal the sword from his belt."

"You and your sticky fingers," I murmured with a laugh. I was suddenly nostalgic, thinking back to the many times I would jokingly chastise her for her thievery, in the happier months that seemed like a lifetime ago.

She peeked up at me through her lashes and gave me a small, shy smile and my heart shattered at the sight. There was a time when I had hoarded every smile from her as a treasure, and when she left me, she had smashed the lock and stolen each one back again.

But this one … this one I would keep forever.

"Anyway," she continued, "I had to create a diversion to

allow me to get the Autarch out and for me to get inside. You might have noticed that we didn't come out of the dungeons via the entrance. There's a hidden passage that runs along the outer perimeter. Apparently, a few hundred years ago, one of the prisoners got out and blocked the way to the main door, killing whatever Jirata Lord was in power then. His younger sister had the passage built when she took over, allowing for an emergency exit.

"I knew that you would be heavily guarded at all times, except for when the Autarch went to see you. I knew my best option was to try and get to you during the time he was meant to be in there."

Tentatively, she reached for my hand, hesitating when it began to tremble beneath her fingers. Her touch was so light it was barely there, yet it ignited my skin. I wanted to pull away, to sever the contact, but I was held captive.

"So, as the old guards finished their handover and were walking away, I threw the sword toward the commander. Swords are heavier than daggers and my aim was terrible, but it did the job. And as soon as they saw who it belonged to, they turned back in total confusion. And ... and that's when I began to sing."

She studied me carefully, but I kept my face blank, not wanting her to stop her explanation. "I've ... been practicing since Ocridell. I'd always been able to sense and amplify emotions, though I'd only ever tried it with ... Verrill. But with the Autarch—that was the first time I actually influenced someone's behavior.

"The guards were a different story though, I had never tried manipulating so many people before and trying to get them to *do* anything would've been impossible, so I influenced their emotions instead. I turned their confusion into anger. They were already tired, so their aggravation was almost easy to entice from them, and the newer guards were fresh, they were ready for a fight. Both sides launched into it, and I fanned the flame. It was overwhelming; their emotions felt like I was eating a volcano pepper, spicy enough to make my tongue burn. But I kept going, kept stirring them up, until eventually others joined in, and it was like the agitation was contagious. When I affected one, I affected them all.

"It progressed out to the courtyard where more weapons became involved, and that's when Malah came out to see what was going on. I switched my song over to him then—trusting that I'd enraged the soldiers enough that they'd carry on without me—and instilled absolute dread into him. Focusing on one person is easier, I was able to persuade him that he *needed* to go and get the Autarch, that he *needed* to see what was going on.

"I moved to the doorway, hiding in the gap between the two doorway pillars until they both came out. I didn't dare sing then, the Autarch would've known it was me immediately, I'm sure of it. So, I slipped in behind him, and he was so close ..." She closed her eyes, shaking her head in disbelief. "He was so close; it would have been effortless."

"Why didn't you do it?" I asked. "Why didn't you kill him there and then? The guards were distracted and Malah would've been no issue for you."

Her eyes reopened slowly. "There wasn't time to make a

decision. I had *minutes* to find you and get you out. I couldn't have …"

"What?" I pressed.

"I didn't want to do anything that could've jeopardized my chances of finding you," she admitted, her eyes fixed on the floor. "I left you before, I wasn't going to do it again." She smiled after a moment, looking at me again. "And besides, when I finally kill the Autarch, I want to take my time. I want him to look into my eyes and *know* that it's me."

The malice in her voice almost made me shiver. She went to pull her hand away from mine, as though she'd only just remembered she was holding it, but I tightened my grip, keeping her there. I tried to force the ridiculous trembling to subside, but my body refused to cooperate.

"Did you have Rats in the dungeon to tell you where I was?"

She shook her head and gave me a wry grin. "No, I had to be … creative in my methods of extracting information. It turns out that when a man is beside himself with lust, he'll tell you his deepest darkest secret, especially when you have a knife pressed to his throat."

I looked away, trying to mask whatever biting, unpleasant emotion was twisting in my gut.

Darkness fell quickly, as did the temperature. By the time we'd set out our bedrolls, Erisa was already shivering, which only intensified as the night wore on, making it impossible to sleep.

"Is this your first winter outside of Ersetu?" I asked when her teeth began to chatter.

"The first in about ten years," she said, and I heard her

pulling the blanket tighter around herself. I could imagine after spending a decade within the warmth of the volcano, sleeping outside in the winter months must be challenging.

The words were on the tip of my tongue, pushed back only by the strange combination of revulsion and desire warring inside me at the thought.

"Come here," I murmured, not meaning for them to escape. "We'll both be warmer."

I lifted the side of my blanket up to invite her onto my bedroll, my heart already racing at the thought of being so close to her, but I couldn't tell if it was out of fear or excitement.

She hesitated for a moment before nestling into my arms in a manner so practiced and natural that it stole my breath. Her proximity was overwhelming, and I was embarrassed to know that she could probably feel my heart hammering in my chest.

Adrenaline coursed through my veins, and I cursed my hands as they began to tremble once more against her clothed back. I hated her for making me look so weak, for causing such a pitiful reaction to her touch. And I hated myself for succumbing to it. I was suddenly glad for the fatigue the day's travel had brought on. If it hadn't been for that weariness, I would never have been able to battle through the desire-laced fear of having Erisa back in my arms to fall asleep.

Even though my body remembered and rebelled against the pain she'd put me through, everything just felt so *right*, that for the first time since being rescued from Katmu, I enjoyed a completely dreamless night's sleep.

And against my best wishes, I prayed for cold weather until

the end of our trip.

❖ ❖ ❖

"We knew you would return, Feline." The croaking voice came from beneath the left hood of the three women sitting on the floor in front of us.

"We need the location of the shield," Erisa stated calmly, though I could feel the tension rippling off her in waves.

"We told you; we would not give you something for nothing."

"What's your price?" I asked, but even with their hoods thankfully covering their faces, I could tell that none of them had even registered my question.

"It's a pretty voice you've got, Feline," crooned the middle sister, "there's untapped power in that siren song of yours. Yet, you haven't even scratched the surface of what it can do."

"What's your point?" Erisa said.

"We want it." The hag practically wheezed with excitement. A bony hand appeared from her robes, and she stretched it out, palm up toward Erisa. "Relinquish your gift over to us, and we'll answer your questions."

Erisa narrowed her eyes. "How many questions will you answer? And with no riddles or games or twisted truths. Just straight, clear, and truthful answers."

"Three."

Sweat began to gather in my palms and my heartbeat accelerated as my mind raced through the repercussions of this agreement. This should have been exactly what I wanted, a chance to interact with Erisa without the constant mental nagging and doubt that what I was feeling was entirely fabricated by her gift. Even if she hadn't realized that she was doing it, having the persuasive power stripped from her voice would tell me exactly how I really felt about her.

Yet, the thought of taking that part away from her made me sick. Not only had that gift saved her life on that cliff in Ocridell, but it was part of who she was, whether she used it or not. Verrill had cherished her song and giving that up would destroy her.

Did I accept the possibility that as soon as that gift was taken away, I might cease to love her, confirming that my emotions had been false the entire time? I knew the answer to that question as the deal hung between them. Like when a coin is tossed into the air, the true desired outcome presents itself to you while the coin is still suspended. And selfish as it was, I secretly preferred living in ignorance. I wanted to keep loving her, and if my compulsion to do that was severed, I knew that I would be devastated.

"De—"

"No! Don't do it!" I shouted, knocking her hand away from the old woman's. I met her confused gaze for a brief second before turning my attention to the women in front of me. "Name another price or I'll take the last remaining relic to Silas myself, and he can destroy it."

The sisters hissed and reared back, affronted by my incivility. It was a foolish gamble, and they could likely see that I was bluffing, but the pale, bony hand stiffened as it was drawn back into the mass of gray robes.

They had their own agenda for wanting to get rid of the

Autarch, and my threat clearly had the potential to jeopardize whatever that was.

The middle sister spoke first. "Insolent boy! If the cost of finding the shield is too high, then we suggest you look elsewhere for answers—"

"Silas has a woman with him," Erisa interrupted, reaching into her pocket to pull out a peculiar necklace made of golden leaves. "I thought you could use this to locate her."

The Beldams lifted their hoods in unison, revealing their haunting empty eye sockets and haggard faces. The blue tattooed eyes on their foreheads glowed bright in the light of the single candle between us. They chattered amongst themselves, as though we weren't there, animated by the new development.

"Could he have found her again?"

"It is no wonder I lost track of her if they are united once more—"

"You know what this means, sisters."

"We could use this, most definitely!"

The middle sister focused her inked eye on Erisa. "Do you know what that pretty trinket is?"

"An old necklace?" Erisa replied, irritation clear in her tone.

"That is the headdress worn by the First Queen, gifted to her by her lover. It is said to have remarkable protective properties, though that did not stop her from being butchered like a squealing pig, did it, sisters?"

The three of them cackled quietly at the gruesome thought, before the middle became serious once more. "We will give you one answer. We will tell you where the woman is, if you leave the headdress with us."

"Done," Erisa agreed, before I had a chance to intervene.

Even though Silas had actively chosen not to help us, he was still my friend. And I was sure that everything he did was for a valid reason, even if I didn't agree with it. This headdress was clearly linked to him in some way, and to the mystery woman he was supposedly traveling with. I had a sinking feeling that we'd just handed over something of great power to three malevolent entities. Because if the Beldams were this excited, whatever had stirred them was bound to be horrific.

The bony hand snatched the headdress, and all three women sucked in a deep breath of contentment. "The woman you seek is hidden in Ganzir."

"The Palace?" Erisa clarified.

"Indeed, and if this woman is who we suspect, Silas will not stray far from her side."

Once we had the information we needed, we left swiftly, not wanting to overstay our less than warm welcome.

The ride back was long and hard, broken only by a single night's stay in the wilderness. The night had been warm, and Erisa had stayed on her own bedroll on the other side of the tent. My disappointment overruled my relief and I fell asleep petulant and troubled, the only thing saving my mood the hope that tomorrow, we'd have the shield.

Chapter 12

Erisa

Replication of sealed correspondence

Karasi,

I know things between us have been strained recently after what happened, but I want you to know that I'm doing everything in my power to ensure that we—

※ ※ ※

"Stop that!"

Theo snatched the letter out of my hand and threw it into a nearby sconce, ensuring it burned before returning to me.

"Don't you know it's rude to read over someone's shoulder?" I chastised him, annoyed that I hadn't had time to skim the rest of the words.

"That belonged to my sister! Why would you need to read anything of hers?"

I scowled. "Torin Sharru tried to kill me. Not only that, but he's also second in line to the throne of another realm. I want to know who he's speaking to and what he's saying."

"It's a complete invasion of privacy!"

"You weren't complaining a few months ago when I was gathering intel on the Autarch's movements," I argued.

"Well, I … it was … now that's just—" he spluttered.

"Exactly. And besides, what Torin doesn't know won't hurt him."

"You can't possibly be monitoring everything that's sent throughout the realm," he said. "You'd never have enough time."

"I've only been reading the correspondence since … since the Fox died," I forced out, looking away for a second to set my expression. "He didn't really talk about it before, but he said that once someone decided to be a Rat, they were automatically loyal to him, some leftover bargain agreement from the time of the gods. He said they instinctively knew which letters would be of interest to whoever was in charge of them. I didn't really understand what he was talking about at the time, but now that *I'm* the one in charge, I can feel the bond he was talking about. It was how he was able to encourage them to follow me, even weeks before he died."

"But the Rats only came into existence within the last decade, I'm sure of it," Theo said, puzzled.

"That's only when they were given the name," I explained. "I vaguely remember hearing talk of a Master of Secrets when I was little. Verrill took over when he was fifteen, after we'd moved into the Palace. But it's true, they thrived under his command."

He nodded. "Who was it before?"

"No idea, I've never really thought about it."

We continued in silence toward the stables outside Tasar's

house, carefully navigating through the closely packed housing structures that made up the majority of his slums.

After putting the horses away, we made our way to the front door, which opened as we approached.

Tasar beamed. "Theo, my friend, I'm so glad to see you! Come in, come in. There's a pot of tea brewing."

Once again, I found myself in Tasar's ancient, sunken armchair, tracing the cracks in the leather surface with a long, pointed nail.

"I'm afraid we can't stay long," I said, interrupting whatever heartfelt reunion was happening between the two men. "We only came to tell you to prepare. If all goes well today, we're going to be moving in on the Autarch very soon."

Tasar looked from me to Theo. "What's happening?"

"Nothing you need to worry about," Theo answered with a smile. "Just something that might give us a bit of an edge in the next stage of our operation. You don't need to do anything yet but just be ready for things to get moving soon. We'll keep you informed, of course."

I let out a small sigh of relief, pleased that Theo was finally learning from his mistakes and not trusting simply anyone with every secret he'd ever heard.

"I'll arrange a meeting with my generals shortly then," Tasar promised. "Is there anything else I can do to help either of you?"

It pleased me to know that Tasar was finally beginning to tolerate me again. Conspiring with him on Theo's rescue had been difficult enough. It would make working with him in the future much easier now that his face wasn't set in a permanent scowl whenever I was present. Not that I could blame him, I had been the Autarch's pet for years and trust takes time to build. Again.

"We'll take some of that bread I can smell baking in your kitchen," I said. "Some cheese too, if you've got it. Oh, and we'll need a tram to Šarrum."

He made a disgruntled face but disappeared into the next room to honor my request. Before the door shut, Cyfrin snuck into the room, with all of the rakish charm his brother had lost over the years.

"Feline." He grinned. "I just *knew* someone important was in the house, don't ask meow." He winked, as though that would make up for the terrible joke. "What are you doing here?"

"We were just leaving," Theo grumbled before I could answer. He stalked from the fireplace to shove past Cyfrin and follow Tasar into the kitchen.

"Don't mind him, he's probably just hungry." I rolled my eyes at the dramatics. I could sense that Cyfrin had something on his mind. "What can I do for you?"

His carefree countenance faltered briefly, and he ran a hand through his copper hair. He was weighing his words very carefully.

"An ... *acquaintance* of mine in Tarprusa has informed me that tensions over there are ... running a little high. I know they haven't shown any signs of hostility, but it might be worth considering how compromised our border defense is right now."

Theo barged back into the room, holding a small package of food and a flask. "Time to go," he huffed, making a point to scowl at Cyfrin.

"Thank you," I said to the younger man and strode out of the house in the direction of the tram platform. When Theo caught up with me, I turned to him with a clipped tone. "If you try and order me around like that again in front of others, it'll be the last thing you ever do. It was disrespectful and you were rude to Cyfrin for no good reason. I know you're unhappy about the proposed marriage between him and Didi—and I agree, she should only marry who she chooses—but you need to get over your strange prejudice toward him. He's been a real asset to us these past few months, and if you continue to alienate him like that, he might just stop being useful."

He grimaced slightly at my tone and sighed, opening the food package and handing me a sandwich. "You're right, I'm sorry. I've been all over the place since you brought me back from Katmu. It's just hard knowing who to trust."

We ate as we walked, both lost in our thoughts. Though I'd already considered our tenuous relationship with Tarprusa, I hadn't appreciated how many of the soldiers would desert when given the opportunity to travel back through the volcano toward Anzillu. I supposed being held captive in Katmu was enough of a deterrent for remaining in service, and passing so close to home had been too much to resist.

Theo froze as we approached the edge of the platform, gripping my arm tight enough to leave bruises.

"What is it?" I asked, immediately alert and looking for the source of the attack. I followed the line of sight from his wide green eyes toward the slightly sunken tram tracks. A large, scrawny rat was nibbling on a discarded bone directly in our path. Even the vermin in Hudjefa were underfed.

I felt Theo's hand start to tremble against my arm, and the color swiftly drained from his face, leaving a light sheen of sweat over his now-pallid skin.

It took me a second too long to make the connection. Theo had never been afraid of rats before being captured, and the tiny bite marks that covered most of his legs and arms hadn't appeared on their own. A fresh wave of fury washed over me, and I imagined carving the Autarch up into tiny pieces, going slow to ensure he felt every second of the agony.

My hand was already launching a small dagger toward the rodent, and it landed with a soft thump in its mangy fur.

"Oh good," I said cheerfully, "my aim is still perfect. I like to improvise with some real-world practice sometimes."

I pried my arm free from his grip and walked toward the rat to retrieve the blade and nudge the poor, dead creature into a shadow at the edge of the walkway. Theo swallowed hard and gave me a small, grateful smile. This newfound fear was something we'd have to work on—there was a wealth of rats and mice in this realm, and as soon as tensions started to rise, they'd all begin to emerge.

❖ ❖ ❖

The Palace loomed above us as we approached from the western entrance. There had been no guards patrolling the gate, but I could feel the first of the protective enchantments tug at my skin as I climbed over the locked metal bars. The sensation was familiar, but without the usual sentries standing watch, the experience was slightly unnerving.

I had been briefly concerned that Theo wouldn't be allowed to pass, even invited as my guest, but it seemed that the Palace did not take into account who was no longer loyal to the Autarch. And for that, I was grateful.

The windows of my former home were dark, and I led us down the dimly lit path toward the front doors mostly by memory. I stopped in front of the elaborately carved wood and twisted iron, not knowing whether Neti, the god depicted on the surface, would let me through.

Taking a deep breath, I pushed the doors open and stepped over the threshold, keeping a tight grip on Theo as we walked into the expansive entrance hall. With a sharp pang, I realized that I was looking for Tohnain, expecting him to walk down the stairs, dressed impeccably, to greet me. I hadn't heard from Asila or her father since before Malah's betrayal, and I could only hope that he was keeping them safe.

"Come on," I whispered to Theo, feeling a slight pull from the stylus tucked into my corset, "let's try this way."

We walked softly toward the heart of the Palace, ending up at the entrance to the throne room, where a voice was coming from within, too low to hear from outside. I slowly pushed the large door open a crack, feeling immensely grateful that Tohnain had been so fastidious with oiling hinges.

Torches were lit all around the room, throwing the area into a golden glow of warmth. I dared to push the door another inch, giving me a clear view of half of the room. Sitting in an armchair in the near corner and sewing up a piece of clothing was the woman who I'd caught sneaking around Silas' cabin back in the summer.

And resting against the side of her chair was the shield. It was as large and imposing as I remembered, but the flickering torchlight illuminated a dent in the top left corner, warping the shining metal surface.

"It's here," I mouthed, turning back to Theo. He nodded, waiting for my instruction. Slowly, I opened the door wider, checking every corner of the room for Silas before stepping forward. Theo followed me inside, impressing me with how quiet he was on his feet.

The woman didn't look up, and I stopped a few paces away. I didn't know much about her, but she had seemed a timid little thing during our previous brief encounter. The last thing I wanted was for her to alert Silas of our presence, so I tried a more delicate approach and gently cleared my throat.

Startled, the woman looked up and gasped softly when she saw us. But instead of screaming, she mouthed something rapidly, barely moving her lips.

"I remember you," she addressed me, squaring her shoulders. She brushed her dark hair away from her face and assessed me with large, gray eyes. "You were in Silas' cabin. What are you doing here?"

"That's right," I replied, pretending to look around for him. "Where is Silas? And the Palace is my home, I should be asking what *you* are doing here."

"He's not far." The wideness of her eyes betrayed the steady tone of her voice. She rose from the chair, angling herself between us and the shield. Her gaze kept darting to the door, and I knew we were running out of time.

"We're not here to hurt you," Theo soothed, raising his empty hands as proof. "We just want to take back our shield and leave."

"I can't let you do that." Silas' deep voice reverberated around the large room.

I turned slowly, keeping one eye on the woman, and watched Silas stalk into the room. He looked even more formidable than when I had summoned him to the battlefield in Ocridell. His brows were furrowed, crowning his dark eyes that seemed almost wild with anger.

"How did you get into the Palace?" I asked him, matching every step he took to ensure I remained between him and the woman. "The wards don't let anyone through uninvited."

"Feline, I was here when Ganzir fell and this Palace was built," he rumbled. "The wards do not keep *me* out." The intensity of his glare softened as he briefly flicked his gaze to the woman behind me.

I watched him like a hawk, predicting him to strike within a split second. And I was ready when he did.

Silas lunged for me, and I feinted back, knowing that he would expect me to go for the shield. He grasped the empty air where I'd just been before his momentum barreled him into Theo. As I moved backward, I swept my right leg out in a wide arc, catching the dark-haired woman behind the knees and grabbing her arms as she fell forward.

Theo grappled Silas for the shield, but even if he hadn't still been weakened from his time in Katmu, he was no match for the inhuman strength and speed of his friend. Theo was thrown roughly to the side and Silas gripped the metal prize tightly in his hands and whirled back round to me.

His eyes flared when he took in the woman's position; kneeling with her arms pinned behind her back between my legs, and my dagger at her throat. My free hand held her hair out of the way, ensuring that nothing impeded his view.

"You know I'll do it," I hissed, pressing the blade into the soft skin of her neck hard enough to make her yelp. "Give the shield to Theo and let us leave, or I'll slice her ear to ear."

"You don't understand what you're asking for," he protested, the stress of the situation causing tension to ripple off him. "The shield should never be completed; it should be destroyed! Please stop this, Theo, I'm begging you! You have no idea what will happen!"

"Because you refuse to tell us!" yelled Theo. "We're supposed to be friends, Silas, you're the one who told us about the relics in the first place, tell us what will happen when we combine them!"

"I *CAN'T*," Silas thundered. "I am forbidden!"

I locked eyes with Theo, and he nodded, answering the silent question that had barely even formed in my mind.

"Give him the shield, Silas," I warned. "I'll give you three seconds."

I dragged the dagger ever so slightly, knowing from the way Silas' eyes darted down that they were following a single drop of blood welling against the blade.

"One," I counted.

Silas looked ragged in his indecision, but we all knew what

he was going to do.

"Two."

Hidden by her halo of coiled hair, I slipped my right hand into the front of my corset, catching the tip of the stylus with my nail and swiftly pulling it up, making sure that Silas was still focused on that single drop of blood.

"Three."

Silas lunged once more, and I shoved the woman abruptly in the opposite direction, while simultaneously throwing the stylus toward Theo, who had grasped the edge of the shield with his right hand and was pulling back against Silas.

Time seemed to slow to a crawl as the instrument spun through the air. Silas made his decision mid-lunge, choosing to break his grip on the shield, changing his course to catch the woman. But he realized his mistake too late.

Theo's fingers wrapped around the stylus and immediately slammed it down into its dedicated slot on the shield.

"NO!" Silas roared in unrestrained fury and reached toward Theo.

But there was nothing he could do. The shield was whole.

It started to glow, brighter and hotter, until Theo yelped and threw it on the ground. We all watched in horror as the luminous metal began to melt, bubbling away and sinking into the stone floor. The molten substance leeched away completely through the cracks between the stones, leaving no trace of its existence behind.

"What happened?" Theo fretted.

"You fools," Silas said quietly, unable to take his eyes off the empty floor where the shield had been.

A tremor caused each of us to stumble and a few chandelier candles fell from above, along with a fine sprinkling of dust from the ceiling. I had barely regained my balance when the next tremor hit. The ground began to shake in waves, as though the very earth below us had acquired a heartbeat.

The floor cracked and I gaped in horror as it began to open up, causing the enormous throne to start sinking slowly down into the trembling earth.

We were all running for the door as chunks of ceiling and stone began to fall. But just as we were about to reach the exit of the throne room, the monstrous carved dragons skulking down the pillars above began to move. Each one shed their stone scales like an old, obsolete skin and began to prowl down the pillars toward the floor, stretching their bat-like wings out wide. The other snarling creatures joined them a second later.

Silas' woman started to scream, and he pushed her on, trying to contain the horror in his own expression. We sprinted out of the room, heading for the entrance hall before the stone beneath our feet began to fall away, sinking into the earth.

Theo stumbled as the stone floor opened beneath his feet, catching his boot in the yawning expanse beneath. I gripped his elbow, hauling him back into a run.

"We need to get out," Silas called over the din of the demolition, looking intently into the woman's eyes. "The Palace is collapsing."

Yeah, no shit, I thought, too out of breath to form the words aloud.

The woman nodded and reached for Silas' hand, which he

grasped firmly. His step faltered and he looked over his shoulder at Theo. With his free hand, he grasped Theo's forearm.

And the crumbling floor, the falling ceiling, the entire world, vanished.

Chapter 13

Theo

M y body was being turned inside out.

I tried to open my mouth to scream, but I no longer had control over any part of myself. Everything was black and disorienting. I felt like I was one of the wooden spinning tops that children play with, my entire being pivoting violently around where Silas had gripped my forearm.

The moment I felt solid ground beneath my feet again, I fell, and my body slammed against the cold dirt as my vision continued to whirl.

It took a few seconds for the world to right itself, and I opened my eyes to find the unfamiliar woman next to me on her knees, vomiting. Erisa was lying on her back with her eyes closed, taking slow, deep breaths.

"What the fuck," I panted, pushing to my knees and finding Silas sitting on the ground a few paces away, resting his head in his hands. I took in our surroundings, noticing that, clearly, we were not in the Palace or Šarrum anymore. The dark surface of

Ersetu rose high in the distance, meaning that we were no longer inside the volcano. "What the *fuck*?"

The ground shook again, and Erisa flew to her feet, her complexion as sickly and pallid as I was sure my own was. A loud crack split the air, and we all looked up in astonishment to see the top of Ersetu fracture, cleaving across the surface. Rivulets of lava bubbled out of the fresh cracks and crept down the sides, glowing orange against the dark terrain.

"Silas," Erisa snarled, "where are we? And what the *hell* is going on?"

He raised his head, and for the first time, he looked haggard. I had only ever seen him look tired before, but now he appeared half-dead, as though his impossibly long lifetime was finally catching up with him.

"I transported us here." His voice was lethargic, as if the words were a great effort to get out. "I wanted to go further from the volcano, but I couldn't manage it."

"*That* is how you … *relocate* yourself?" Erisa demanded, then shook her head to refocus. She pointed to the lava still spewing from Ersetu. "Again, what is going on?"

"The gods are waking up."

The earth trembled again, as though reiterating his words. At the top of the volcano, spiny black wings began to emerge from the molten rock, followed by a great, scaled body crowned with a ferocious head. Four strong legs appeared next, and the dragon stretched its long neck to look up toward the sky. A high-pitched screech careened through the air, smarting against my eardrums, even from this distance. The beast leapt into the sky and thrust upwards with impressive sweeps of its dark wings, a long, thrashing tail following behind it.

I had only ever seen dragons from a great distance, but this one seemed bigger than I'd even heard stories about. I was transfixed as several of them emerged from the volcano and took to the sky, one after the other.

"The relics you found," Silas began, bringing everyone's attention back to him, "they were given by the gods before they went away. The items were kept separate to ensure that they stayed asleep. And you just ruined everything."

He glared at Erisa and me with renewed intensity.

Erisa was incredulous. "But you were the one who started us down this path. You were the one who first told us about the relics. You told us to go to the Beldams, knowing that they would tell us that combining the relics would give us the power to destroy the Autarch."

"The Beldams lied! Those old hags should have told you that each of the relics on their own could have harnessed the power to kill that ridiculous, *human* figurehead. To strip away his power and slaughter him as a regular man. You only needed to find *his* relic; the Orb."

"Then why didn't you tell us?" I demanded. "You knew what we were trying to do, why didn't you say anything?"

He sighed, putting his head in his hands again. "I couldn't. As in I physically couldn't. In the same way you can't speak the Autarch's name in front of someone who doesn't already know it, I couldn't speak of the powers the relics held. A stipulation of a farcical bargain I made long ago." His eyes flickered to the woman still vomiting in the grass.

Another crack of splitting stone reverberated through the still air, and we all looked back at the volcano. Ersetu's crater was cleaving down the center, causing fresh torrents of lava to spill from the fractures.

"What's happening?" I asked, afraid of the answer.

"Ereshkigal's rebuilding Ganzir," Silas answered gravely. "The Palace is gone."

My heart plummeted as I watched parts Ersetu collapse, a cold wave of dread washing over me. The crushing weight of what I'd done in the Palace hit me like a physical blow, and in those fleeting moments, I realized my actions had condemned hundreds, if not thousands, to death.

"What about the people inside the volcano?" Erisa fretted, shock and concern widening her eyes and pinning them on Silas. "There are people living by the Palace in Šarrum! What about Anzillu? And Hudjefa?"

"Hudjefa and Anzillu are likely too far away from the center to have been directly hit, but I don't know how well the volcano will hold above them. As for Šarrum … it's hard to say."

"Take me to Anzillu," she commanded. "Do whatever freakish trick you did to get us out here and take me back into the volcano. There are children—"

"No." Silas' voice was worn but firm. "I don't have the strength."

Instead of arguing like I expected she would, she hesitated, eyeing Silas with caution. She opened her mouth and for a sickening second, I thought she would try to sing to him as she had to the Autarch, to compel him to take her.

"Thank you, Silas," she said, grimacing as though the words sliced her throat on the way out. "I know you had no intention of saving me too, but I'm grateful all the same. I'd be dead now if it weren't for you. We would all be dead."

Silas appeared as taken aback as I felt, but he nodded and looked toward the unfamiliar woman still sitting on the floor. Her dark complexion still had a sickly sheen to it, but she had finally stopped vomiting.

"I'm indebted to you," I said, knowing that he had briefly considered leaving me too but decided not to at the last second. I was thankful that he had, but also that Erisa had still been holding onto my other arm when he took me. I cleared my throat before continuing, "I'm afraid I have another ask of you."

Silas looked at me wearily, as though he couldn't quite muster the strength to pretend to care about what I was about to say. I couldn't blame him.

"Erisa and I … we messed up. We caused this to happen by going after the shield and ignorantly trusting the Beldams, even though we had no idea what we were getting ourselves into. But you know more about the gods and the magic of the realm than anyone else. If you worked so hard to try and prevent this from happening, then I trust that it should be put right. Please will you help us?"

He looked back to the woman, her large gray eyes meeting his with an intensity that almost made me turn away.

"I'll help," Silas agreed. "But I need to take Ana somewhere safe first." After a moment, he turned, levelling a soft glare at both

Erisa and me. "I think I have a plan, but you'll both do exactly as I say for this to work. I mean it, you won't hide anything from me or go off on secret missions without my say-so."

Erisa and I both nodded and watched as Silas lifted Ana into his arms and tenderly brushed the damp hair from her sweaty forehead.

"Are you ready?" he whispered softly.

When she nodded, he glanced up at us briefly before another deafening crack rent the air, and they were gone.

❖ ❖ ❖

After ascertaining that Silas had dropped us somewhere between the Silent Canyons in Saqummatu and the recently excavated entrance into the volcano, we began our trek toward Hudjefa to check in on Tasar.

Erisa had begun the journey in a temper, upset over Silas' miraculous ability to take Ana somewhere, but not us. Her mood had soured further as the temperature dropped on the first night, and even though I was secretly thrilled with the opportunity to hold her again until sunrise, I could admit that the cold was almost unbearable without a tent.

The entrance to Hudjefa hadn't even come into view yet before Erisa's Rats had started scampering up to us and whispering reports into her ear about the events inside the heart of Ersetu.

The Palace was gone, and Šarrum was in ruins. Only the outer portion of the district remained intact, but the damage to the rest was beyond salvaging. The tremors had destabilized the outer surface of the volcano, leaving fractures above areas of Hudjefa and exposing the citizens below to the magma that ran down the sides.

"I'm guessing this wasn't what you meant by *getting things moving*?" Tasar asked when we finally arrived at his house, almost two full days after Silas left us. He looked more tired than usual, and stress had carved permanent lines across his forehead.

Shame forced my head down and my gaze to the floor. "Almost nothing went as planned."

"What's the death toll?" Erisa asked him.

"We're estimating around twenty thousand so far, mostly from Šarrum. But we're still searching the rubble for survivors."

"We'll go to join them," I began. "Where is the worst—"

"We'll do no such thing," Erisa interrupted. "As noble as the sentiment is, the last thing this realm needs right now is you being kidnapped again or being crushed to death beneath some falling rock. We need to be working on a way to fix this situation, and before the other kingdoms decide to take advantage of our vulnerability. The realm needs you strong, Theo."

I knew she was right, but the guilt had been bubbling away inside me over the past two days, and I wanted to be actively *doing* something to help. Instead, I'd have to return home, far away from the devastation and destruction, and wait for Silas to share his plan with us.

"When you talk about fixing the situation …" Tasar hesitated, as though he was too nervous for the answer. "What exactly is the situation? There have been disturbances all over Irkalla."

Erisa glanced at me and her sunflower eyes fractured with worry for a heartbeat before she turned to Tasar.

"I wouldn't usually believe in this nonsense, and were it not for what the Rats have told me I'd not even bother repeating it. But I don't have another explanation for what's happening." She hesitated, steeling herself. "The gods have woken up."

He was taken aback. "How—I'm sorry, the *what*?"

"We made a mistake," she explained. "We put too much trust in something we knew nothing about, in old magic we had no business meddling with. Now the realm is paying the price for that mistake. I've had the Rats begin to spread the word on what is happening. I don't want to leave people in the dark."

Tasar's spluttering began anew, but I cut him off.

"Why don't we print about it in the pamphlets and get the Rats to distribute them?" I suggested. "That way, we'll be able to spread the news more reliably."

"Pamphlets?" Erisa and Tasar said in unison.

"Yeah, the Autarch would leave them in my cell. They had reports on our infiltration of Katmu, my capture and your ..." I looked away from Erisa, "courtships."

She let out a strained laugh; a lilting, chiming sound that filled the small room all too briefly.

"From what we've heard since making it onto Katmu," Tasar began, "the Autarch was handing out printed propaganda to try and quell the tension rising through Malah's people. He stopped quickly though. I think he realized that it was having the opposite effect, because there's been a few uprisings over there since you were captured."

Before I could answer, someone knocked at the door. An exhausted middle-aged man was ushered in by Tasar. He rushed over to whisper something in Erisa's ear, but when he turned to leave, she caught his arm, halting him.

He waited patiently while she scribbled and sealed a note with the wax press on Tasar's desk.

"There's a bakery on the edge of the market in Anzillu's bazaar, with a yellow sign out front. I need to know if there are any damages," she said, passing him the rushed letter. "Give this to the owner—a woman called Aghna—and no one else."

He nodded and hurried away, slightly flushed from being given a direct order from the Feline herself.

"What's in the bakery?" I asked.

"An investment," she replied. I knew from her clipped tone that pressing the matter would be pointless.

"I'm still confused," Tasar said. "I don't understand what you mean by the gods, but if you're planning on going back to Zingal, you'll need to take horses. The tram line to Šarrum is ruined, and there's been—"

The ground began to shake again, rattling the crockery cabinets on the far wall. The candelabra on the table fell as people outside began to scream.

We all jumped to our feet and rushed outside in time to see the rocky earth that bordered Tasar's dying garden begin to move. The cracked soil parted violently as a dirty, pale hand emerged. Without thinking, I seized Erisa's wrist and pulled her behind me.

Crowds of people stood frozen in shock and horror as the

ashen, sickly creature clawed its way out of the ground. It was enormous, at least two feet taller than any human I'd ever seen, with long, thin limbs tipped with twisted claws that swam in an ocean of filthy rags.

But as the being straightened and looked around at its surroundings, it began to change. Within seconds, the elongated limbs had filled out, and the grotesque, animalistic face had morphed into one resembling a peculiar human, crowned with a head of dirty, dark brown hair.

I couldn't pinpoint exactly what made the face unnerving, all of the individual features were normal enough, but there was something off-putting and disharmonious about the way they all came together. It looked like an overgrown and underfed human, who had somehow managed to survive every disease known to man.

"I … am … Namtar," it rasped. Its voice sounded like rubble crunching underfoot, and the tone uncertain, as though it was trying out the language for the first time.

Without warning, Namtar punched upwards through the cavern's ceiling, causing dust and debris to rain down to the floor. Several people started to scream anew as the creature pummeled the rock above, until its fist broke through the surface of Ersetu and sunlight flooded the perpetually dim underground chamber.

Namtar was crowned in a halo of illumination, and the dust-streaked rays shifted my perspective.

I was in the presence of a god.

"Do you think we should kneel?" I whispered to Erisa, who looked at me like I'd just asked her to dance with it.

My knees threatened to buckle beneath me anyway, the weight of Namtar's stare demanding me to pay reverence. Several people yielded to the unspoken command, falling to the ground to prostrate themselves before the divine being.

He surveyed his surroundings cautiously, as though oblivious to the commotion and upheaval he'd caused. When his watery, bloodshot eyes found Tasar, he tilted his head slightly, assessing him from afar.

From the corner of my eye, I saw Tasar begin to tremble under the scrutiny. He opened his mouth to say something, but before any words could come out, Namtar leapt upwards, pulling himself through the hole in the volcano's surface and disappearing.

❖ ❖ ❖

The shock of the encounter had yet to wear off by the time Erisa and I returned through the entrance to Hudjefa and started heading back toward Zingal. We decided to exit the volcano entirely, instead of trying to reach the tram station in Ocridell on foot.

Since being inside Ersetu again, Erisa had been bombarded with reports of disturbances in the other districts. It seemed that Namtar had been the last god to awaken, which meant that one had likely arisen in Zingal.

Erisa shivered as the wind picked up on the approach to Ocridell. "We should find somewhere to stay for the night."

I agreed, thankful for the suggestion, but apprehensive of our success. We hadn't even entered the district border and there were more people than usual outside of the volcano, hoping to escape the carnage within. I recognized accents from Hudjefa and Anzillu, but mostly from Šarrum.

By the time we reached the run-down streets of the city, the wind was whipping around us, causing our borrowed horses to spook and prance.

"Let's try in there, I know the owner!" Erisa called over the gale, but her words were caught and whisked away on the squall.

I held the horses while Erisa enquired after a room inside, and felt the relief of her success warm me despite the cold. Even though we were civil and working together once more, there was still a distinct rift between us, one that seemed to grow larger and more apparent by the day.

Being so close to her again had clouded my judgment, and her rescuing me in Katmu had tricked my mind into associating her with safety and security once more, even though I knew it was far from the truth. She'd rescued me from that cell because she had put me there in the first place. She'd acted out of guilt from her past actions, rather than genuine affection for me. I had lost all trust in her, and yet, my insensible, traitorous heart craved her, even more now that she was emotionally distanced from me.

The small boarding house was crammed with people fleeing Ersetu, and the owners were run ragged trying to hand out bowls of hot stew for everyone. Families were camped out on the floor, unable to face the cold conditions outside, after living their entire lives within the heat of the volcano.

Erisa and I ate our meals standing rather than trying to battle our way to one of the overcrowded benches populating the main room. They were small portions, but hot and hearty enough to

THE ECHO OF HIS FURY

staunch the hunger brought on by the eventful day.

Erisa was quiet, and I could tell she was uncomfortable with the overpowering noise and stimulation in the busy, cramped space.

"Do we have a room?" I called over the din. When she nodded, I almost sighed in relief. The prospect of finding a section of a crowded corridor to sleep in had troubled me. "Shall we go?"

She nodded again and grasped my wrist to pull me through the dense mass of bodies, being mindful not to knock my healing fingers. Without a conscious thought, I twisted it around, pulling back slightly so that her hand slid into mine. Her fingers stiffened for a few seconds before relaxing into the hold between my own.

Her skin burned against mine, and despite the overwhelming chaos of the boarding house, her touch stole my focus completely, sending my heart racing.

Erisa led the way up five flights of stairs, to the top floor of the boarding house, where she dropped my hand to retrieve a key from her pocket. I immediately regretted the loss, chastising myself for the fatuity of the thought, and followed her inside the room. It was tiny, and the little space it did have was taken up by the thankfully decent-sized bed and a small wardrobe.

Erisa sighed and sat heavily on the bed, propping her elbows on her thighs and resting her face in her hands. "There's a bathing chamber next door, the key for it is kept on top of the doorframe."

I desperately wanted to comfort her but had no idea how. There wasn't a chair in the room, and I was suddenly conscious of how awkward I was being, just quietly standing and staring at her.

"How do you know the owners?" I asked, trying to break the

clumsy silence.

"This room was mine and—" She backtracked. "This room is mine; I use it when I'm traveling."

Her eyes went to the wardrobe and quickly shifted back to me, and I knew she wanted to be alone, so I excused myself to go and bathe. The water wasn't as hot as I'd have liked but there was soap and clean towels, and for the first time in the last few days, I finally felt clean.

Erisa was absent when I returned, but she had laid some fresh clothes out for me on the bed. They were a little tight, but I appreciated them all the same.

The wardrobe door was still ajar, and I couldn't ignore the compulsion I felt to go and look inside. My chest cramped uncomfortably when I opened the door and found the polished, gleaming wood of a lyre leaning against the back wall, behind a small wooden box.

Though I'd only seen it a handful of times before, I knew without a doubt that the instrument had belonged to Verrill.

Before I could dwell on it too much, I shut the door and slipped beneath the cool sheets of the bed. They weren't soft but they smelled freshly laundered.

Minutes seemed to stretch into years while I waited for Erisa to return. I didn't know whether I should pretend to be asleep or turn away and face the wall. She had slept beside me when we were camping outside, but everything always felt different indoors, especially within the warm confines of a plush bed.

Just as I was starting to relax, thinking Erisa might have found somewhere else to sleep, she returned, the creak of a floorboard the only indication of her presence as she crept into the room. Immediately my heart began to race, and I was suddenly all too aware of what my arms and legs were doing.

Do I need to move them? Will she think I'm odd if I do? Or if I just lay completely still? The ridiculous thoughts continued to pound away at my sanity as Erisa slipped under the covers. *And of course, she's completely relaxed and at ease.*

Although the bed was decently large, I couldn't help but fixate on every breath, every miniscule movement that she made. She was so close that I could smell the soap in her still-damp hair and feel the heat radiating off her in soft, warm caresses.

"I can practically hear the wheels turning in your head," she said, turning onto her side to face me, a smile evident in her tone. It was dim, but I could still see the glistening of her eyes as she propped her head up on her arm.

Unable to help myself, I turned onto my side, bringing our faces level. We were so close that if I leant forward by just a few inches, I would be able to brush my nose against hers.

"Erisa," I whispered, almost pleading, except I didn't know what for. I couldn't bear being this close to her, both from the need to touch her and from the lingering anguish of my imprisonment still tormenting me. I couldn't tell her how many times she'd visited me in my nightmares, or how often I'd hallucinated her twisting a knife deep in my gut. I knew that she hadn't been there, but in this moment, especially in the dark, my brain just couldn't disassociate her from that miserable place, where I could still feel the pain of those tiny teeth sinking into my skin.

She reached out to trace a finger along the stubble of my jaw, a gesture she'd performed countless times before, and yet somehow, this felt like the very first. I fixated on her touch, on the curve of her lips I could just about make out in the darkness, and on the breath that came from them when they parted under my scrutiny.

In this moment, the desire to kiss her consumed me, stronger than any longing I'd ever known. It was as if nothing else outside of this room—in this entire world—mattered except the press of her lips against mine.

Without thinking, I reached out to snake a hand around her waist, pulling her toward me to close the seemingly infinite space between us.

But my traitorous hands were trembling. And she stilled, feeling my ridiculous, broken fingers betraying the spike of adrenaline coursing beneath my desire. I hadn't even realized that it was there, but I silently cursed myself for it as she dropped her hand and dipped her chin so that her face was hidden from mine.

I pressed a kiss to her forehead and moved to extract my arm, but she caught my hand as it slid away from her skin. She brought it up to her face and placed a soft kiss on each of the healing knuckles, before relinquishing it back to me and turning to face the wall.

Her everyday ferocity made such simple, sweet acts all the more enchanting. A rare softness in her world of sharp edges.

Chapter 14

Erisa

Feline,

Anzillu is in turmoil. A being clawed itself from the below the ground in the middle of the bazaar. It looked human but was unlike any man I've seen before. It must have been at least fifteen feet tall, covered in unfamiliar armor and carrying a curved sword. I couldn't hear what it said over the screaming, but it appeared to be looking for something. After a few moments, it just vanished.

Tremors have caused a lot of the buildings to collapse, but the children are safe with Aghna.

Faithfully,
Alekos

26 December

❖ ❖ ❖

O cridell was a writhing throng of chaos. The frantic crush of bodies fleeing the volcano unleashed a raw, untamed energy that seemed to bleed into the very weather itself. Last night's gale still lashed at our clothes and whipped across our cheeks, as if echoing the havoc around us.

Theo and I were riding hard along the road toward the Zingali border when shrieks and shouts rang out from the travelers around us. We pulled our horses up to follow their horrified expressions and fingers pointed toward the heavens.

My stomach plummeted as I looked up, just quick enough to see a dark mass streak across the sky. For a split second, I thought it was a dragon, but as the creature soared upward on a gust of wind, I saw features that turned my blood cold.

It was a man, unbelievably tall, with enormous, tawny wings propelling him upward in strong, steady beats.

"Oh, gods," Theo breathed, the air quavering from his lungs as we watched the … *thing* loop backward, giving us a view of the rest of its body.

Its feet were scaled claws, tipped with razor-sharp talons, but my attention was caught on the strange, feral shape of its face and the deafening screech coming from the open mouth. I strained my eyes to see more, but it had already disappeared into the clouds overhead.

Theo turned to me, his eyes wide. "Tell me you saw that too."

I met his gaze and nodded. "We need to find Silas."

Fortunately, achieving that task was easier than expected. Silas was waiting for us in the kitchen at the Lusilim estate, watching us wearily as we dragged ourselves through the door in the middle of the night, half-delirious from exhaustion.

The sight of him snapped my attention back into sharp focus, the many sleepless hours forgotten. He had dark rings under his eyes and a slight gauntness to his face.

"You look as tired as I feel," I said.

"A pleasure as always to see you, Feline." Silas leveled me with a flat stare. He turned to Theo next. "You two have made quite the mess."

I didn't need him to tell us that, I had already received more than enough reports from the Rats detailing the devastation invoked throughout the realm by the rising gods. Ersetu was in ruins, cleaved in two and spewing lava from within. It was a miracle that any of Šarrum and Hudjefa had survived, especially now that temperatures within the volcano must be beyond unbearable from the shifting magma. Kusig hadn't fared much better; another god—a woman this time—had emerged from the center of the Golden City, toppling houses in her ascent, before striding to the old temple in the center of the district and barricading herself inside.

I had even received a few scribbled notes from Katmu, sent from the Rats we had managed to maintain somewhat stable communication with since Theo's rescue. The short reports described huge tidal waves lashing at the inner coasts, before a large human-looking man emerged from the ocean between the seven islands. Some letters said that he took one look at Ersetu in the distance and sank back beneath the surface, but others reported that he stormed the citadel, breaking through the gates with his bare hands.

Theo dragged two chairs toward the fire and gestured for me to sit in one of them, before turning back to his friend. "What's going on, Silas?"

Silas was quiet for a moment before saying, "What do you know about the gods?"

He said "gods" with a reverence that caused goosebumps to wash across my skin. The same deep-rooted tone of respect he'd used when talking to us about them all those months ago in his jungle cabin.

"Very little," Theo admitted.

Silas sighed and ran a hand through his hair, looking as though he didn't know where to begin.

"Before the God's War, the four realms were once united as a single land mass, a vast and thriving dominion ruled by the great Anu," he said, his eyes glazed as though he were no longer in the room with us. "Irkalla was just one part of the world—a world we called Ki—and would be the resting place for us mere mortals when we died. Each departed soul would pass through the gates of Irkalla and be judged by the Seven; Neti, guardian of the gates to Irkalla, Namtar, the god of fate, Pazuzu, ruler of the wind, Dumuzid, god of agriculture and his sister Geshtinanna, who would write down the names of every deceased to pass the gates into Irkalla. And, of course, Ereshkigal, goddess of the dead and her king consort, Nergal, the god of war.

"The Seven would judge a person for their crimes, and if they were found guilty, Ereshkigal's gallû would drag them down into the underworld to face their punishment."

"Gah-loo?" Theo asked, pronouncing the unfamiliar word slowly.

"Demons of the underworld," Silas answered, shivering ever so slightly in disgust. "Or lesser demons, I should say; ghoulish creatures created to do Ereshkigal's bidding. Pazuzu is also a demon, but powerful enough to have been elevated to deity status."

I shook my head, trying to clear it. "I still don't understand. Irkalla, Tarprusa, Aessurus and Atturynn were joined? And Irkalla was where people went when they died?"

I had heard the old stories, but the idea just didn't make any sense. How could we be living and breathing in a realm meant for the dead?

"Yes," Silas confirmed, "the realms were once one. Until Ereshkigal's sister, Inanna, decided that she was unhappy with just being goddess of love and fertility. The queen of the heavens tried to take Irkalla for herself, inciting the God's War. During one of the final battles, the two brothers, Enki and Enlil, cleaved the earth—*Ki*—in two, eventually forming the four realms.

"Ereshkigal was furious with Inanna and raised each soul from her underworld, ready to unleash them on her sister. But in doing so, she lost the loyalty of the mortals inhabiting her portion of Ki—Irkalla—and they sided with Inanna out of fear. Ereshkigal rewarded them by raising Ersetu from the ground, flooding the plains with fire and lava. The gods were so great that they never once stopped to think about the mortals perishing underfoot ... and you can't even begin to imagine how many of them died during that war."

His voice was so ragged and haunted that I was too stunned to speak for a moment. My voice was almost a whisper when I finally spoke. "You say all that as though ... as though you were there."

He met my gaze. "I was there. I was there the day the Cedar Forest, my *home*, was ripped through the middle, forced down into a warmer ocean. I watched as my beloved trees turned to wild, unruly jungle, trapped with Irkalla's horrors inside. But I was there *before* the war. I was there when Ereshkigal and Inanna were doting siblings. I worshipped at their altars, in their temples. I was there the day they decided to *help* me." His voice took on a vicious undercurrent, almost sneering around the words. "I was there the day they decided to taunt and trick and enslave me into this miserable existence—" He cut himself off, closing his eyes and taking a deep breath. "I was there. As I have been every day since."

❖ ❖ ❖

Sunlight pelted against my eyelids as the sound of frantic voices roused me from my sleep.

"Oh, but we've been so worried," that was Dana's voice, "the ground was shuddering so hard I thought the windows would rattle out of their panes. Lola was right in the thick of it, pushing Isadora's chair up that hill toward the bakers. She said she saw the great big thing emerge from the ground, shaking it so much that the wheels almost wobbled right off, nearly throwing the poor girl out—"

The voice trailed off into another part of the house and I pried my eyes open, holding up my hand to block out the glaring light streaming through the open curtains. I was lying on top of the bed in my room, still fully dressed. I had a vague memory of falling onto the plush covers last night, unconscious before my head had even hit the pillow, exhausted from the travel and wild revelations from Silas. My mind spun thinking about what he had revealed. Had it come from anyone else, I wouldn't have believed a word of it. But there had always been something different about Silas, something *other* that I couldn't quite put my finger on.

He had refused to answer any other questions last night, insisting that we all needed some rest before we could decide how best to proceed. Theo had been silent after his friend had disappeared into some wing of the house without another word. I could tell that he was upset with being so deceived, but as I'd reached a hand out to take his, he'd slipped into his room without so much as glancing my way.

The action had pained me more than I cared to admit.

I bathed and dressed quickly, opting for the practicality of trousers as opposed to a dress. I had no idea where we would be going over the next few days, and I needed to be prepared for anything. The house was quiet, and I found Theo looking over hurried letters and damage reports from the center of Zingal, where Dumuzid, the god of agriculture, had risen. He flicked through the pages, balancing a plate of fruit, cheese, and bread on his knee, his brows furrowing deeper with each item of correspondence.

I was swiping a sliced pear from his plate when a knock on the window had me whirling around. A small fist rapped impatiently on the glass again and I crossed the room to open it. I looked down to see Farzin smiling up at me, swamped in an old coat that trailed across the mist-covered ground.

"I've got a letter for you, Feline," he said proudly, before rooting around in his pockets and pulling out a crumpled, slightly damp note. There were some small, sticky fingerprints gluing the paper together and I tried not to wrinkle my nose thinking about what the substance could be.

"What are you doing out there, little Rat? Come into the warmth—no, through the door! Go round to the back door."

Theo was chuckling quietly to himself as I pulled the window closed, shivering slightly from the brisk air. His amusement leeched away when I placed the open note in front of him.

Replication of sealed correspondence
Lord Jirata,
As the closest district, I'm afraid Katmu must be the first to hear about the troubles we are currently facing here at the Prison. We have experienced a series of disturbances, which to my horror, have facilitated the escape of several inmates incarcerated here at Bīt Asiri.

I also regret to inform you that although there is an expanse of ocean separating you and the mainland from us, I have no doubt in these inmates' abilities to make it across.

I have sent this letter on a boat directly to you, in the hope that you receive sufficient warning.
Casen Stavrou, Governor of Bīt Asiri Prison

26 December
Copy made 27 December

I barely had time to return Theo's horrified expression before Farzin came barreling into the room, followed by five more of Aghna's wards. Several squeals of delight came from the adjoining rooms and the clatter of feet could already be heard overhead.

"Erisa …" Theo's tone was questioning.

I grimaced slightly. "I might have told them to come and stay with me when we were at Tasar's, before I knew I was coming back here."

"Where else would you have gone?" He didn't say it with any hint of malice or ridicule, but rather as if he couldn't think of any other place where I belonged outside of Zingal. While I knew he didn't mean it in the way he once had, it was still comforting to hear that I was welcome somewhere in this realm.

Silas strode in before I could answer, effectively scattering the children with his furious expression. The circles under his eyes were stark against the unfamiliar pallor of his skin.

"So, we've already established that this cursed realm is on the brink of collapse. But is someone going to explain to me why mere *moments* after I was able to finally fall asleep, I was then awoken by several pairs of little muddy boots jumping all over my bed?"

I could hardly blame him for his annoyance, I would have been livid. But I also couldn't pass up the opportunity to rile him up further. "Well, you're clearly well-rested enough to come in and complain about it. So glad to see you waking up so *chipper* and raring to start the day."

Silas took several measured breaths through his nose before turning to address Theo, disregarding me entirely. "The gods all over the four realms have begun to awaken, not just in Irkalla, and the rift between the two sides has already been reestablished. Some of the others will be coming here and we need to try and

S.C. MAKEPEACE

convince Ereshkigal to be sympathetic to the humans, otherwise Irkalla will be flattened like it was before. I have a plan to try and put them back in the ground, but we must have them all distracted when that time comes."

"And what exactly is this plan? How are you going to put them back to sleep?" I said, almost cringing at how ridiculous the notion was. But I was starting to get annoyed with Silas for his vague demands, and at Theo for not questioning them.

"I'm going to use the same method as before, it's the only way to do it."

I almost screamed in frustration, but finally, *finally*, Theo said something.

His voice was sharp. "Are you going to tell us what that method is, or are we supposed to just trust you blindly? You've only ever given me half-truths, Silas, and look where it's gotten us. You may not trust us, and that's your call to make, but we're here, desperately asking for your help and willing to do what needs to be done to make this right. The least you could do is provide some fucking *detail* about what we're walking into."

Silas' mouth lifted in a sad half-smile. "I do trust you, Theo," he made a point to not look at me, "but we'll need to go to Ereshkigal and beg her for mercy. I am old, I have methods of redirecting her away from the truth in my memories, but you won't be able to lie to her. If I tell you what I'm planning, she'll uncover that information from you, and she won't hesitate in thwarting me."

Theo took a moment to weigh his response. "What *can* you tell us?" he said finally, gently shaking his head. "We're

199

THE ECHO OF HIS FURY

completely at a loss for what's happening. No one I know truly believes in these gods and yet, we're supposed to just believe that the ... the *things* crawling up from the earth are the deities we grew up hearing fabricated stories about. They're nothing but old wives' tales, created to keep naughty children in line."

"I'm afraid so," Silas said and took a seat across the desk from Theo. "Do you remember what I told you when you first asked me about the Orb of Nanaya?"

"You said that each of the seven guardians of Irkalla left a relic," I answered, remembering the unpleasant encounter all too well.

Silas nodded. "The gods knew that their time was drawing to a close. Ereshkigal had already unleashed the horrors of her underworld and knew that without the Seven to shepherd them back in, the balance between the living and the dead would falter. So, she instructed each of the Seven to imbue their power into an object, commanding them to bestow these gifts onto a human worthy enough to harness them. The districts weren't established until many years later, but essentially, Neti took his key to Jirata in Katmu. Nergal took his shield to Elkas in Anzillu. Dumuzid took his daggers to Lusilim in Zingal. Geshtinanna took her stylus to Seirsun in Kusig. Pazuzu plucked a songbird from the sky and gave it to Anzû in Ocridell and Namtar cut the head off his pet snake and gifted it to Wranmaris in Hudjefa."

Immediately, I wanted to stop him to enquire about the last part, but he'd already glossed over it and continued.

"By then, Ereshkigal had almost run out of time to choose her successor, and word had spread about these gifts. Hundreds of power-hungry mortals fought to the death in the hopes of securing them, and she chose the most brutal of the lot, knowing that the realm would need a fierce leader, who could do what needed to be done. And finally, after bestowing the Ey—the Orb of Nanaya onto the new ruler of Irkalla, Ereshkigal returned to Ganzir and succumbed to her slumber."

My skin prickled and the hair on my arms stood on end as he finished talking. I looked up to see Farzin and several of the children stood at the door, enraptured with the tale.

"Who is Lamaštu?" I asked Silas, unable to shake the feeling that he'd omitted rather large portions of this story.

He stiffened. "Lamaštu," he practically spat the name, "was a vile creature. She was a demoness made to rule over the monsters of Irkalla, tormenting the most unfortunate of souls within the underworld. But she became greedy, and being as tricksy as she was, often broke free from her constraints to inflict that suffering upon the living. The gods shackled her into submission before they went to sleep, but I doubt that they will hold now that they're awake once more."

"Why do the Beldams have a mosaic dedicated to her in their inner temple?"

Silas' brows furrowed. "I wasn't aware that they did. I've never been … permitted to enter their grounds."

"How do you know that the others are waking up? And that they've taken sides?" Theo asked.

"Ereshkigal and Inanna, they …" Silas trailed off for a few seconds, grimacing. "They made me; I'm linked to them in a way I can't explain. But as soon as the relics combined, I could feel their power flooding back into them."

I'm not even going to try and wrap my head around that—no, fuck that, I have to ask. "They *made* you? What even are you?"

He curled his lip in distaste at my rudeness, but answered, nonetheless. "Yes, they made me. I was human, a very, very long time ago, but now … I'm not entirely sure. I've never met another being like myself; a mortal made immortal." He rose from his chair, clearly indicating that the discussion was over.

But something had been bothering me since I'd seen the shield at the Palace, and hearing him talk of the relics snapped something into place.

"You tried to destroy it," I said. "There was a dent in the shield. You tried to use Sharur to break it. Was that why the Elkas estate was in ruins?"

"I hadn't seen that old mace in centuries. Only the gods know where that fool managed to get it," Silas replied, bitterness creeping into his expression. He narrowed his eyes at me. "I knew it was unlikely to work, but if anything could help rid me of that damned shield, it would've been Sharur." He looked between us. "Are you ready to leave then?"

"Where are we going first?" Theo asked. His voice was steady, despite the anger and betrayal I knew must be stirring beneath.

Silas looked grim. "We've got an appointment with the goddess of death."

Chapter 15

Theo

A fter ensuring that the old lady Erisa had invited over—and her hoard of children—had plenty of food and warm clothes, I followed Silas and Erisa out to the front of the house. Despite the surprise, it was nice to have the house full. It so often felt cold and empty, and my mother and Didi were already doting on the orphans.

I had no idea where Erisa had found them, and I couldn't help but notice how she attempted to soften her sharp voice and scathing remarks when interacting with them. It was endearing in a way that felt dangerous.

"Hold onto my arm," Silas instructed as we stepped out into the frigid winter air. Erisa tucked the letter she'd been reading away when he held an elbow out to her. The bastard gave no warning of the shock waiting for us.

As soon as I touched the sleeve of his coat, the world turned black and upside down and inside out. Everything was spinning too fast, the force of it threatening to tear the flesh from my bones.

And then it was over.

My knees were weak, but I somehow managed to stay upright this time, maintaining a vice-like grip on Silas' forearm. I immediately looked for Erisa, afraid that he'd left her behind or dropped her somewhere alone.

I huffed out a ragged sigh of relief when I found her staggering backward, away from my friend, desperately trying to find her balance. Without consciously moving, I stepped forward and caught her by the waist, allowing her to right herself.

Her eyes were reeling but settled when they met mine. And widened again when she took in our surroundings. I pried my own from her face, looking up to see a huge set of obsidian doors towering before us. Carved into the surface were terrifying, ornate designs of ferocious beasts inlaid with bone that contrasted starkly against the black.

The heat was almost unbearable, and I could tell from the flames dancing up the dark, shining walls that we were back inside Ersetu. But I knew immediately that I had never been to this place before, that it hadn't existed until now.

"Where are we?" Erisa asked, her voice shaking slightly.

As if in answer, the huge doors opened, seemingly by themselves, to reveal a cavernous chamber beyond, split down the center with a deep crimson rug. It was at least ten foot wide and led straight to the far end of the room.

Erisa saw what awaited us at the end of the rug at the same time as I did, and Silas had to push us both forward.

Ereshkigal loomed larger and more terrifying with each step we took across the plush red carpet. She sat in a throne, similar to the one that resided in the Autarch's throne room, only larger and engraved in devastating detail. The twin lion heads almost looked as real as the long, taloned fingernails that rested on top of them.

I tried to lift my gaze as we approached, but my head bowed of its own accord, refusing to travel further than hem of the long, black robes that pooled on the ground as Ereshkigal stood. Erisa walked to my right, and Silas on my left, both of their heads bowed like mine. But I could see from the corner of my eye that Erisa was fighting it. Where Silas was reverencing willingly out of respect, she was trying her best to challenge the act.

We stopped at the foot of the slightly raised dais, and my neck locked, forcing my eyes to remain trained on the floor. I tried to turn my head to look at Erisa, but whatever influence had tucked my chin demanded that my entire focus remain on the being in front of me.

I needed to know she was all right though. My neck threatened to snap as I tilted it as much as I could manage. In my peripheral vision, Erisa gnashed her teeth and locked her spine until her hands were shaking. Tremors slowly began to wrack her entire body.

She was going to get herself killed.

"Please, Erisa." The low groan escaped my throat before I could stop it.

Erisa's last thread of defiance snapped, and she bowed, suppressing an agonized yelp. My own hand trembled as I fought against the invisible binds to reach for her, barely able to brush my little finger against her wrist.

"Syrus." Ereshkigal's voice was booming and cold, rattling

my bones.

To my left, Silas flattened himself at the goddess' feet, his forehead against the floor and his arms outstretched toward her, palms facing up.

"It has been a long time." She began to move, circling us slowly. "A very long time since you betrayed me."

"Forgive me, my Queen," Silas begged. "Forgive me, I was tricked, I—"

"I know what you did, dog!" Her terrible voice turned my blood to stone. "You conspired with that wretch, Nanaya, to put us all into the ground." She stopped in front of him, towering over us all. "You should have come groveling the second you felt us return. As punishment, I will claim Morana as my own. This death will be her last, and you shall remain tethered to the earth."

"No!" His voice quavered, suddenly agonized. "Please, I—"

"Go and find your prize, it seems you've lost her again. And who knows how much time is left?"

"My Queen." The pure, primitive fear in his voice struck me like a cold wind. "Please."

"Leave, the sight of you irks me."

Silas turned his head, locking eyes with me for a heartbeat before the air around him warped and snapped him out of existence.

"You may look at me." As soon as she said the words, the invisible snares securing my body released me, allowing me to raise my eyes and take in the sheer majesty of the being before us.

I hadn't necessarily *not* believed that the gods were real since they emerged, but seeing Ereshkigal this close forced the truth of their existence upon me like ink on white linen; staining my ignorance with evidence that could never be washed away.

The goddess was enormous, towering twenty feet above us. She was beautiful in a feral, animalistic kind of way. Golden hair cascaded down to her rib cage in loose waves, each strand tipped with a glowing red that seemed to burn like embers in the reflection of her glossy black eyes. Her angular face was pale, as were her hands and bare feet, which were just visible beneath the dark sleeves and hem of her robes.

"Your … Majesty," I hesitated, not certain how to address her. "I am Theo—"

"I know who you are, Theodoraxion Lusilim," she said, cutting me off. "Nothing happens in Irkalla without my knowing. Even asleep, I see everything. I knew of your birth before the first Autarch had even claimed the Eye of Nanaya. Your fate was sealed to ours. We would always rise within your lifetime, Theodoraxion."

My mouth felt as though it was full of ash, refusing to be swallowed down. I tried to clear my throat. "Then you know what we've come to ask of you," I managed to choke out.

There was so much power emanating from her that even the weight of her gaze had my knees threatening to buckle.

"You've come to beg for mercy on behalf of the humans in this realm," she said, and it was clear that she had no intention of granting it.

"Yes," I answered. "I have."

She dipped her chin to look down at me properly. "Then beg."

From just those two words, I could feel my body trembling under her command, influenced by the immense power of her presence. My knees bent without permission and slammed into the floor.

My arms were stretching forward, my chest almost touching the crimson rug when I heard Erisa hiss, "Get up, you fool … Theo, get up. I won't … let you."

She had to fight to release the words, and I fought with her, desperately trying to heave myself upright. I managed to stop mere inches from the floor, but lifting myself back up would be impossible.

Erisa started to groan; a half-whining, half-growling noise of frustration and pain.

And then my body was on fire.

I could *feel* her, a current of lightning surging through my veins. I latched onto it, feeling her hatred toward Ereshkigal for forcing me to do this. She couldn't bear to watch me debase myself like this.

You beg on your knees for no one but me, she seemed to say.

My body was torn, crumbling beneath the power of the goddess before me, and yet wanting—no, *needing* to submit to Erisa's will.

Sweat ran down the back of my neck as I straightened my arms, pushing my torso back off the floor. I focused solely on that low sound emanating from Erisa's throat, allowing it to coerce one trembling leg up after another, until I slowly, painfully, rose back to my feet.

Ereshkigal snorted in amusement, and the pressure trying to

force me back to the floor ceased. My body sagged with reprieve, a heavy breath almost sobbing from my lungs.

I glanced over at Erisa, who had paled, her face shining with sweat. Whatever she'd had to do to get me back to my feet had taken a toll on her.

Ereshkigal tutted. "Foolish girl, I ought to punish you for that." She paused for a moment, considering. "But I do so admire a strong will, and I am not even sure that *I* could break yours, Erisa Anzû." Her obsidian eyes slid back to me. "Such a disappointment. I would have killed you the second your nose touched the floor, boy. I had hoped for a stronger champion, but I suppose you are only human after all. I know what you are all planning, how you want to trick us into slumber once more."

"Humans are nothing if not audacious," echoed a cold, booming voice.

I looked left, trying to find the source. In the shadows skirting the edge of the immense room stood what I had previously thought were statues.

Only now, those statues were moving.

A huge, hulking man stepped toward Ereshkigal, not quite as tall, but almost twice as wide. He had dark waves that fell to his shoulders and skin that shone a deep bronze in the torchlight. Everything about him exuded power; from his strong physique to the lethal curve of the scimitar gleaming at his hip.

"Do you really think that *you*," he sneered around the word, "would possibly have any sway over *our* fates? You are nothing to us, mere mayflies in comparison. You ought to be overcome with reverence for your queen. You ought to be at her feet, weeping with gratitude that she would even deign to look upon you."

Ereshkigal smiled as he ran a hand down the length of her hair, his eyes full of deep adoration. "Come, Nergal, we have been away for so long, these ones are clearly unaccustomed to the usual propriety we are used to."

As she spoke, two more figures advanced into the light. They were both smaller than Ereshkigal and Nergal, standing at around sixteen feet tall. I recognized the gangly, strange-looking man as Namtar, who we had witnessed clawing his way from the ground in Hudjefa.

The woman on his right—who I assumed, through process of elimination, was Geshtinanna—looked kinder than the others, almost timid in comparison. Her dark brown hair was woven into an intricate braid around the crown of her head, and her watery blue eyes were wide as she approached the other gods. The power emanating around the room now was unlike anything I'd ever experienced before, like I was being crushed from every angle.

I looked around for the others to join, fearing that I couldn't take anymore additional force, but found the room empty. There were only four of them present; Neti, Dumuzid, and Pazuzu were nowhere to be seen.

"They have chosen to ignore my summons," Ereshkigal said, as if in answer to my unspoken thought. "It appears they are still upset with me for failing to prevent our misfortunes."

"Traitorous ignoramuses," hissed Nergal.

"Still," she continued, "what's done is done. We must now look forward." She paused, ensuring that our attention remained solely on her. "Even though I no longer possess the Eye of Nanaya,

I am still aware that there will only be two outcomes. In the event of my … departure, Irkalla will need a strong leader once again." She sneered down at me. "I expected more of you, Theodoraxion Lusilim. But perhaps you will surprise me yet."

"We came to ask for your mercy," Erisa called out to the towering figures, her voice steady and her chin held high. I could tell that the confidence was mostly bravado, but the sight of her still made my heart swell with pride. "Irkalla is home to the living now. There are families and children here, living in—"

"And how many of you pray?" Ereshkigal cut in. "How many of you give thanks to your gods? You curse us freely for your hardships, forgetting that you would have nothing if not for us. You humans are no different from the ungrateful recreants who sided with my sister during the last war."

"You were *gone*," Erisa argued. "Hundreds of years, and generations of humans have passed since then. How could you possibly expect us to keep believing after all that time?"

Ereshkigal's eyes flared dangerously, but it was Geshtinanna who spoke next. Her voice was soft and quiet. "If I may, my Queen. I think we oftentimes forget how fleeting human existence can be. Where a hundred years is a mere moment for us, it is more than an entire lifetime for them. They are so delicate and momentary, it is no wonder that they do not possess the ability to comprehend that which they do not see in front of them."

Her gently worded insult seemed to placate the goddess of death enough that she smiled at the smaller woman, a gleaming show of white teeth that made her appear almost feral.

"Very well," Ereshkigal said, looking down at us, "respect

can be relearned. I will not punish the humans here in Irkalla. But I expect you to do what your ancestors did not." Her black eyes bored into mine. "You command an army, Theodoraxion Lusilim. You will use that army to fight for me when my sister comes to try and claim my throne. One human is nothing to us, but a horde of thousands is a nuisance, and I can already sense my *dear* Inanna gathering her forces."

I squared my shoulders. "But I—"

"This is not a negotiation, human," Nergal interjected. "We will be considerate of your kind, merciful even, but you will fight alongside us. If you do not, we will assume you are consorting with the enemy."

"You must leave now," Ereshkigal declared. "You have an army to ready."

Namtar began shepherding us away from the throne, pulling us back with invisible threads toward the monstrous doors. Erisa thrashed against them.

"And what of the Autarch?" she demanded.

Ereshkigal let out a bitter, humorless chuckle. "Who do you think has promised my sister her army?"

Chapter 16

Erisa

Feline,
A great tidal wave has flooded Saqummatu. It came down from the side of Ersetu and washed through the Silent Canyons. Mercifully, the water stopped before it reached Zingal, but everyone living in the caves was likely swept away by the current.

Rumors have already been circulating of a woman rowing her boat along our new river.
R

28 December

✽ ✽ ✽

Namtar released us from whatever invisible binds he'd put us in as soon as the towering double doors closed with a resounding boom.

I breathed a sigh of relief, glad to be away from so much overwhelming power in that room. Ereshkigal had been almost unbearable on her own, but when the others had moved closer, I felt as though my skin was peeling away in ribbons.

Namtar looked down at us with his haunting, blood shot eyes.

"You must go now, humans." His voice sounded as awful as it had when we first heard him speak in Hudjefa. The only difference in the gravelly tone now was the confidence, as though he'd had time over the last few days to master the language.

"Where were the other gods?" I asked, making no move to leave the seemingly endless hallway yet.

He assessed me coolly, tilting his head ever so slightly, as if truly looking at me for the first time. "Dumuzid, Neti, and Pazuzu have decided not to join us here in Ganzir. Perhaps you possess the power to convince them otherwise. Or perhaps not."

"With my voice?" I asked, astonished.

Namtar snorted, an ugly, crackling sound. "That silly little parlor trick? Don't be absurd. I simply meant that it will be interesting to see if something so small and inconsequential as a human can sway the fates."

"You're the god of fate though, aren't you?" I countered. "Surely you already have the answer to that. Can't you just influence the outcome?"

"I am the god of fate," he confirmed. "The one true, inescapable fate that awaits you all. I am what you will see when that final, unavoidable fate snatches the last remaining breath from your lungs. You may hide from me, Erisa Anzû, but know that I will find you eventually, and then that fate will claim you."

A shiver ran through me at his words, a strange prickle of awareness that I was unable to explain, even to myself.

Theo's voice echoed off the walls. "How do we get out of here? We don't know the way."

I barely had time to see the huge god before us raise a single dark eyebrow, before he waved a hand lazily and we were gone.

There was no spinning, no whirlwind of darkness or deafening roar to endure this time. Within the blink of an eye, I found myself standing—right way up, for once—in front of an enormous tree in a large meadow.

I knew immediately that we were in Ocridell, because right there, at the base of the broad trunk, were two small letters carved into the bark: E and V. We had stolen the idea from the small AC initial whittled into the surface on the opposite side of the tree.

I still couldn't believe that Verrill was gone; that the only proof of his existence lay in a handful of trinkets scattered across the realm. It was a comfort to know that even after everyone who knew him was gone, and his belongings were lost to history, this small, poorly carved piece of him—of us—would remain.

"Well, that was a lot more pleasant than when Silas does it," Theo called to me over the wind.

When I didn't respond, he walked up behind me and followed my line of sight. After a heartbeat of hesitation, he snaked his arms around my waist. The movement was uncertain to begin with, but the second I melted into his embrace, and he knew that this was what I wanted, he relaxed and placed a soft kiss on my temple before resting his head against mine.

My heart slammed against my ribs at the contact, my body felt starved of it—of *him*—and of the simple ways in which he could bring me comfort. He slipped a thumb beneath the hem of my coat and began tracing small circles against my skin, raising goosebumps in his wake.

Over the howling gale, I could hear him taking in slow, deep breaths of air, as though trying to slow his own rapidly beating heart.

All too soon, the moment was over, when a screeching sound keened overhead and a hulking figure dropped from the branches.

Theo spun us around, curling around me to turn his back to the rush of leaves and feathers that rained down in a torrent. When a moment passed and no one attacked, he straightened, allowing me to wriggle free from his arms.

At least fifteen feet tall, Pazuzu stood proud above us, enormous wings outstretched, shrouding us in his menacing shadow. Each feather gleamed, a light brown so shiny, they were almost golden. His hair was the same shade, falling to his muscular shoulders in thick, unruly waves.

But his face.

His dark brown eyes were the only human thing about his face. Where a nose and mouth should have been, snarled the muzzle of a lion, covered in a smooth coat of sand-colored fur.

His chest was bare, proudly displaying the vicious scars marring his smooth skin. The loincloth wrapped around his waist was no mere strip of fabric, but a work of art, fashioned from silken fibers dyed in rich hues of red and gold, each shimmering thread a testament to his high station. Beneath the hem stood strong legs, that transitioned seamlessly into the taloned feet of an eagle just below the knee.

"Are you done gawping at me, human?" he growled, displaying a set of long, sharp canines. With a near silent swish, he tucked his wings in behind his back and crouched down, sitting on his haunches. He rested his human hands against the floor, suddenly meeting me at my eye level. "Does my inability to glamour my true form frighten you?"

"No," I lied, trying in vain to quell the surge of adrenaline commanding me to run. Small, furry ears poked out from his mane, and I was almost certain he would be able to hear how my heart thrashed in my chest.

He sniffed the air and chuffed out a laugh. "I can smell your fear, little Feline. You cannot lie to me. Why have you come here?"

I looked to Theo, because why *were* we here?

"Namtar sent us," Theo said, meeting Pazuzu's gaze head on.

The ruler of the wind exposed his deadly teeth in a snarl. "That meddlesome fool. I suppose his queen assumes that because I did not answer her summons, I will side with Inanna."

"Is Ereshkigal not your queen too?" Theo asked.

"I am a demon of Irkalla," Pazuzu's long whiskers twitched in irritation, "of course she is my queen."

"I thought you were a god?" I said, silently cursing myself for the inability to stop the question from coming out. His jaw—the one that could easily snap me in two—was mere feet away.

A long, lion's tale thrashed behind him, another marker of his agitation.

And he's got a tail too? I thought. *How unfortunate.*

"To you humans, I am a god," he rumbled. "But to them, I am a demon."

There was no hint of bitterness in his words, just the matter-of-fact tone of a long-since accepted fate. But I noticed a gleam in his dark eyes; a flash of denied defiance buried deep below the surface.

Theo must have noticed it too, because he asked, "So they're right then? You'll side with Inanna like—"

A growl reverberated from deep within Pazuzu's chest, causing the hair on the back of my neck to rise. "Do not try your manipulation tactics with me, human. My mind is my own, and if I choose to play a part in this war to come, it will be on my own terms. You may have been the one to wake us, but do not think that my gratitude will spare you if you continue that thread of thought."

As if emphasizing the threat, his fingers lengthened into lethal claws that dug into the earth beneath him as he began to prowl forward. Theo yanked me back as those talons swiped through the air, missing us by inches. I stumbled as he pulled me into a run, lengthening my strides to keep up with him.

"I suppose now would be a bad time to ask him for a lift to Zingal," Theo panted, daring a glance behind to where I could hear the monstrous creature thundering after us.

I choked out a laugh, but it was swallowed in the gust of wind that blew us clean off our feet, sending us sprawling into the dirt. I looked over my shoulder and opened my mouth to scream as Pazuzu soared toward us, teeth bared. But before I could make a sound, he shot past, trailing a swirl of dust in his wake.

A warning.

Theo crawled over to me, coughing the dust from his lungs. He looked me over, checking for any obvious sign of injury and meeting my gaze when he found none.

We stared at each other for a moment before bursting into

uncontrollable laughter, the ridiculousness of the situation finally catching up with us. I couldn't remember when I had last laughed so hard my sides had ached, and Theo's booming guffaws made me howl even louder.

His laughter was like a balm, a sound that settled deep into my chest—warm, effortless, and grounding. It held the familiarity of a place you return to after being away for too long, like the weight of a childhood blanket, or the rhythmic beat of a long-forgotten song. It wrapped around me like an embrace, a quiet reminder that some things, some feelings, are always there, waiting to welcome you home.

It made me realize just how homesick I'd been without him.

He quieted when he noticed my attention on him, an arresting grin still splitting his face. My breath caught as he moved closer, bringing a hand up to cradle the back of my neck as his lips stopped a hair's breadth from mine. Waiting. Assessing.

I closed the gap and kissed him. It started off gentle and hesitant, like a struck match only just given permission to burn, before developing into a fervor that rivalled the fires of Irkalla rumbling deep within Ersetu's belly. His hand tightened around the nape of my neck, pulling me closer with bruising force as I sighed into his mouth.

A cracking sound whipped through the air, loud enough to break through the invisible bubble separating us from the rest of the world.

Theo broke away first, his breaths coming in short, hard pants as he rested his forehead against mine. His eyes were a blaze of ardent green, boring into me with a vibrancy that had been missing since the battle in Ocridell.

"Feline!" The roar was nearly animalistic, warping the usual tone of Silas' voice into something dark and dangerous.

We turned to see him stalking toward us, and the expression on his face rang enough alarm bells in Theo's mind that he yanked me to my feet and angled himself in front of me.

Silas looked even more haggard than before, as though he hadn't slept once in the last decade. He pinned me with a searching glare, and the feeling of it on me was sickening. It was similar to the sensation of the Beldams observing my past, present, and future, only more intense and direct. I could feel it crawling beneath my skin, reaching with tiny tendrils of awareness that prickled as they emerged out of every pore.

It lasted no more than several heartbeats, but they seemed to stretch out endlessly, one dragging sluggishly to the next.

"What was that?" I demanded, trying to shake off the feeling.

"I can't find her." His tone was low and menacing. But it was obvious that whatever he had been looking for within me, he hadn't found it.

We didn't need him to clarify who he meant. Theo and I had both seen the way he had hovered over the gray-eyed woman—Ana—like an overbearing protector.

"And you think *I* have her?" I asked incredulously. "I think we've got bigger problems right now than some wayward girlfriend!"

He took several measured breaths to regain his composure. The act aged him dramatically, making him appear more like the true age he refused to claim. The thought made me pause.

"So, this woman, *Ana*, can't mean very much to you in the grand scheme of things then," I mused. "Her lifespan will just be a drop in the ocean for you … assuming she's human of course."

"Do not *dare* speak of her, Feline," Silas snarled, and I could practically see steam coming out of his nostrils. "You know nothing of her."

"Erisa," Theo warned under his breath.

I rolled my eyes. "Oh, come on, we were both thinking it. She didn't exactly look robust when she was vomiting her guts out after we escaped from Ersetu."

Theo shook his head, his eyes wide, pleading for me to be quiet.

"I don't have time for this," Silas seethed, disregarding my presence entirely and turning to Theo. "Bīt Asiri Prison has been breached and Lamaštu has escaped her imprisonment. She's already been wreaking havoc across Irkalla, but if she continues, she'll anger the gods into retaliation and that will only divide them further. It's what she's aiming for, I'm sure of it. She thrives in the chaos of her own making."

A shudder crept over me, refusing to be suppressed. I wasn't sure if it was due to the state I was in during the time, but ever since I had seen the mosaic of Lamaštu in the Beldam's inner temple, the mere mention of the demoness sent a shiver down my spine.

"You need to go to the other gods," Silas continued. "You need to convince them to stand with Ereshkigal when Inanna comes, because if they remain divided, not only will Irkalla be flattened, but there is a chance that what I'm planning won't work if the underworld is not strong enough to claim them back."

"What do you mean, not strong enough?" Theo asked.

Silas ran a hand through his hair, restless to get away. "Irkalla is the home of the dead, and while gods cannot die, they can be forced into a state that can almost replicate it. But the wells of power holding that realm apart from the living thrive off the beings that feed it. If the Seven are not *all* put to sleep, Irkalla— the underworld version—could become unstable and begin to fragment away. If even one of them wakes up again, it could potentially tear the fabric of the realm apart, leaving no boundary between the living and the dead."

I still didn't quite understand his point. "And what does that have to do with the sides they take? Why is the will of the Seven so important?"

"They are the guardians of Irkalla," he said, as though it were obvious. "They are what hold the underworld together. If they decide that Inanna is a more worthy cause than Ereshkigal and her entire realm, it is possible that they could exploit that loophole, and that would allow them to remain awake."

"So, you're saying that your plan, whatever it is, isn't strong enough to hold them down, they need to want to stay down as well?" I couldn't help the accusatory tone in my voice. "Because they seem to be pretty content with staying very much awake."

Silas pulled in another deep, measured breath. "No, I'm saying that they need to care more about the fate of their underworld than they do about fighting for Inanna. If all Seven go down, Irkalla will thrive off their power, and the gods that rule over the other kingdoms will be forced back into the death-like state as well. They've woken throughout all four realms."

Theo met my gaze, mirroring my own trepidation back at me. Pazuzu had been absolute that his view would not be swayed by a mere human, and I was almost certain that if we attempted to approach him again, he would do more than threaten us.

"Is Ereshkigal worth fighting for?" Theo asked, finally looking at Silas. "What makes Inanna so bad that they would choose one sister over the other? What's the point of all this?"

Silas snorted, an impatient, exasperated sound. "There is no good and evil, Theo. The gods have had complete control over all since the beginning of time. If Ereshkigal became vexed, she would command Namtar to wash a plague over her opponent's crops and people. But does the blame lie with her for the order, or with Namtar for the act? Or does it lie with the one who incited Ereshkigal's rage, knowing what her act of retaliation would be? Gods do not have the same morals as humans, they do not think of what it's like to be crushed underfoot, any more than you would think about an ant beneath your boot. Does accidentally stepping on a beetle make you a monster, because that beetle has young to tend to?"

"But to kill thousands of humans—" Theo argued.

"Is no more than the disruption to thousands of creatures when you plow a field," Silas countered. He sighed. "I'm not trying to disagree with you, my friend. I'm just trying to make you understand. I've had a great many years to become acclimated to their ways, and hundreds of years since to ruminate over them. Ereshkigal may seem like a tyrant and believe me, there are times when I have wanted to rip her and Inanna to shreds, but she is neither good nor bad. She is just powerful and entirely used to getting her own way.

"The *point* is, if Irkalla doesn't receive the power it needs from the Seven when I force the gods into the ground, you'll learn just how fragile the veil between life and death truly is. And if they remain awake, the war they began centuries ago will rage on, and millions will die in the crossfire."

Theo nodded, not wholly understanding. He glanced toward me for a brief second, before turning back to his friend. "And Neti, Dumuzid and Pazuzu … if we can't convince them?"

"You must."

Chapter 17

Theo

I couldn't remember ever being this tired. The winter sun hadn't even fully set by the time Erisa and I made it to the nearest inn with an available room. There was still an influx of people from the volcano who had nowhere to go since we had awoken the gods. But seeing how the people of Ocridell had welcomed them into their homes and provided shelter eased some of the guilt I felt.

It would take a long time, but there was hope for them now in their new home, and it breathed a fresh breath of life back into the wilting district.

"We're going to have to try and see Dumuzid tomorrow," Erisa said, looking longingly at the plush mattress and soft quilts in the center of the room. This was one of the nicer inns we'd stayed at, with a large bed, a hot meal and our own adjoining bathing chamber. Although I had to wonder whether the good fortune of our lodging was due to luck—or the innkeeper's fear of the Feline.

Erisa had avoided getting too close to me since we'd kissed. Maybe she regretted it, or thought that I did. Every time she looked at my hands, at the freshly healed skin and weakened fingers, her expression hardened, and her eyes dimmed with self-reproach as she withdrew into herself.

I nodded in agreement, trying to focus on anything but her every movement. The energy between us was too charged, too volatile, and from the way she refused to meet my gaze, I could tell that she felt it too.

Trying to pull myself together, I turned away, heading for the bed to take my boots off.

"Oh no you don't," she snapped, pulling on the back of my shirt as I went to sit down. "You're still covered in dust; go and get clean first."

I turned back around, unable to help myself. "Only if you join me," I teased, giving her a wink.

She froze, utterly still for what felt like an age, and my breath caught with hers. My heart skipped a beat when her lashes finally lowered, and her gaze flicked to my mouth. I wasted no time crashing it into hers, reigniting the fire that had been simmering away since surviving our encounter with Pazuzu. I fisted a hand into her hair, angling her head up to deepen the kiss, not even caring if it shook or not. If it did, neither one of us noticed.

I was completely absorbed in her, and in the way her body molded to mine in such a perfect, familiar way. Reaching down, I picked her up and threw her onto the bed, her earlier protests completely forgotten in the frantic fumbling of buttons and laces.

She was more glorious than I could've remembered, each

S.C. MAKEPEACE

perfect dip and curve had faded to a soft blur every time I tried to imagine her. And oh, how many times I had imagined her. I recommitted every detail to memory, searing the swells and hollows onto my mind as I traced each one with my fingers and tongue.

She felt like the embodiment of somewhere I had once called home, each heavy breath she took seemed to carry the weight of a long-awaited return to a place I had cherished but lost. I could survive off her exhales alone. The ache of familiarity and desire rivalled the undercurrent of pain churning deep below the surface; a haunting awareness that if she left me again, I would be shattered beyond repair.

"You're never leaving me," I rasped into her neck, biting the soft skin at her throat to emphasize the point. "I won't let you go. Not again."

"You'll have to catch me first," she purred, dragging her nails over my skin as I sank deeper into her embrace, allowing myself to be consumed by the irresistible force drawing us together.

She cried out, the sound causing a lashing of ecstasy to wash over me.

That's ... new, I thought, barely able to string a mental sentence together before I lost myself in her completely. I chased the high, coaxing out every sigh and moan from her until she sang for me. The resonance sent a ripple of pleasure cascading down my spine, turning my vision black.

❀ ❀ ❀

"You've been practicing," I said, massaging soap into Erisa's

227

scalp, relishing in the way she leaned back into my touch with her eyes closed, sighing in contentment.

Somewhere in the last few hours, the deep-rooted fear my body had harbored for her had surfaced, and she had transformed it into something else entirely. If my hands trembled at her touch now, it would be from desire alone.

Water lapped over the sides of the tub as she chuckled softly. "I don't know what you mean."

"You've never influenced my emotions in that way before," I murmured, placing a kiss on her temple. "Should I be jealous that that guard in Katmu experienced it before I did?"

"If it makes you feel any better, I did slit his throat."

Somehow, that did make me feel a little better. It was irrational for me to be upset over the fact that she had used her voice to make another man so crazed with lust, when she had used it to free me from that dungeon. But still, I *was* jealous. And even though, as far as I was aware, Erisa had only sung normally to him, I could see why the Fox had hoarded her voice as a treasure.

As we rinsed the soap from our skin, the events of the day finally caught up with me, and I sighed in contentment when I finally sank into the soft mattress of the bed, draping Erisa over my chest.

"Do you think you could sing to one of the gods?" I asked, playing with a damp strand of her dark hair. "Would it be enough to sway them?"

She shook her head, looking up at me. "I don't think so." She paused for a long moment, as though deciding whether to carry on or not. "The Autarch always forbade me to sing. I had no idea why, he just said that it upset him when I did it. I always thought that was odd because when I would sing to … Verrill," she whispered his name, "I could tell when he was happy and I could amplify it, turn joy to elation. But I thought that was just with him, I had never tried with anyone else.

"Then, on that cliff in Ocridell, I was desperate. I was already crying out, not quite singing, but almost the same, when I felt the Autarch's frustration, like a bitter taste in my mouth, as opposed to the sweetness of Verrill's joy. The thought of influencing someone's intentions as well as their emotions had never occurred to me until that point, but I tried anyway. I forced the Autarch to stop, made him *want* to stop. And it worked, for a brief moment it actually worked. But there was so much going on around me, and so many emotions bombarding me that the connection severed …"

Her voice trailed off, and I tilted her face so she was looking at me again.

"You did everything you could," I told her. "It wasn't your fault what happened next, it wasn't anyone's fault but that backstabbing bastard who threw the knife."

"I'm going to kill him." Her voice was soft, but the intensity of the promise shone in her eyes. "I'm going to kill him for what he did to my family, to Verrill, and to *you*."

I leaned down to press a kiss to the crown of her head. "I know you will."

"I missed you, Theo," she whispered, closing her eyes and brushing her long lashes against my skin.

"I missed you too, Sunflower."

And even though the world was in chaos and the realm was

falling apart, I fell asleep, feeling totally at peace for the first time in what felt like an eternity.

❖ ❖ ❖

With the tram lines beneath the volcano completely devastated by the gods, our options for returning home to Zingal were both limited and slow. A kind farmer had recognized me on the road and had offered us a ride in his cart to his land, situated in the outer borders of Zingal, where we would continue on foot. He had insisted on taking us all the way to the Lusilim estate, but I had declined his offer, much to Erisa's dismay.

"It'll take him longer to journey there and back than it would for us to just walk," I said as she clambered into the wagon behind me, scowling at the wet mud traipsed across the wood by the man's old black and white farm dog.

She eyed the canine warily, waiting for it to shake and shower her in dirt, but it just flopped onto a pile of empty grain sacks and closed its eyes. I seated myself in the back corner, opening my arms for her to settle herself between my legs, her back against my chest.

Even though we'd woken early, it would still be at least a day's ride and despite the many worries I had about the coming days and weeks, I allowed myself to enjoy this moment. Just basking in the warm, jasmine scented mirage of Erisa's good graces.

I'd made love to her again when we'd awoken, slow and gentle, losing myself in the vibrancy of her eyes and the sweetness of her expression. I still enjoyed her fire, her tenacity to be hateful and difficult, but in those brief moments where she softened for me, it drew me in, like a moth to a flame.

I knew that whatever walls I'd tried to build around my emotions toward her were crumbling rapidly, even as I tried desperately to piece them back together. Whatever this was between us was still too fresh, too delicate to relax into, and I knew that I was a fool for even hoping that things would be different this time. I knew from experience that she could flip at any second, and my life would hang in the balance once more.

But for now, I closed my eyes, rested my cheek against the crown of her head and pretended that all was well. There would be more than enough time for fretting and overthinking tomorrow, and every day beyond that.

"—told me there was magic in that tree." Erisa's voice roused me from my slumber late afternoon.

"What was that, Sunflower?" I said, stretching out my stiff limbs as best as I could in the confines of the wagon.

"I said, my mother always told me there was magic in that tree," she repeated. "In the big one we found Pazuzu in. She said it was her favorite tree in the entire world."

Although her voice wasn't sad, there was a tight edge to it that tore at my heart. I pulled her closer, tucking her head beneath my chin. "Maybe she knew that a god nested there."

"My favorite tree is probably gone." Her voice was a whisper, barely audible. "The glowing one beneath Ersetu … you're the only one I ever showed that to."

My chest tightened, and even though I tried not to be moved by her words, I still felt a sad smile creep across my face. I hoped the tree was still there, and that she could show it to me again.

"We'll find it." It was a reckless promise to make, but with the war of the gods looming on the horizon, and the fate of Irkalla riding on our ability to sway them, we needed to cling onto every scrap of hope we could find.

❖ ❖ ❖

We parted ways with the farmer and his dog on the approach to the outskirts of Zingal, when he stopped at a small boarding house to rest for the night. As Erisa and I had dozed throughout the day, we decided to continue on by foot during the night, after scarfing down a small bowl of stew and some stale bread at the inn.

The air was crisp and the night clear, brightened by a waxing crescent moon, high in the sky. While I was grateful for our thick cloaks, it didn't take long for Erisa to start grumbling about the cold, a habit from her years under the volcano she had yet to break.

Our trek was long and arduous, and I felt naked without the comforting weight of my bow at my shoulder, especially during the darkest hours of the night, when strange, eerie noises surrounded us from all sides. Not that I had been able to shoot it properly since returning back home from Katmu. My broken fingers had stripped me of even that dignity.

But they would heal.

It had made me appreciate the functionality of my body in a way I'd never had to consider before, and once again I thought about Karasi. She'd had to relearn everything in the last half decade, and cope with the knowledge that she would never get her hand back. And she'd had to do it alone, without the support of her family and friends.

I looked to the woman responsible for my sister's pain, unable to quell the small flare of resentment I felt toward her over everything she'd done to my twin. But as always, that resentment redirected itself back, settling deep within myself.

Because I knew I was a hypocrite. I didn't care about any of the other people Erisa had hurt or killed—either under the Autarch's order, or by her own volition—because they had nothing to do with me. If Karasi hadn't been my sister, I wouldn't have thought twice about her maiming a poor woman for life, or the impacts it would have on that woman's family.

Deep down, I knew that how Erisa lived her life was wrong and immoral. I was simply too enraptured by her to care. And while I could recognize that flaw within myself, I decided to make peace with it, to take every day as it came, and try not to dwell on the past. Erisa was actively helping me solve this monumental mess we'd created, and that had to count for something.

She was never going to be good, or perfect. But she was mine, she was perfect *to me*, and that's all that mattered.

"What are you looking at?" she snapped, scowling at me for staring too long.

But how could I not? The dawn light had flamed the sky orange, reflecting the deeper tones of her eyes across the horizon.

"I'm in love with you, Erisa." The words spilled from my lips, unrestrained and unbidden, each one racing free, driven by the urgent need to be heard. As if the floodgates of my dissident mouth had been blown wide open, my thoughts and sentiments poured out loud for her to hear. "You don't need to say anything,

I just needed you to hear it. I love you, Sunflower. There's nowhere in this world that you could go that I wouldn't follow or find you. Ever since I met you, you've blown apart the structure of my life, dismantling the foundations of everything I've known and all the guidelines I've been taught to follow. Loving you goes against everything I believe in, but I just can't think straight when it comes to you. In my world of rules, you are the exception."

"Theo—" she whispered, but I shook my head, cutting her off.

I crowded her against the trunk of a tree, feeling the rough bark beneath my palms planted either side of her face. "You consume my every thought; even when I was in the depths of despair in that dungeon, it was the nightmares of you that kept me alive. The anger of my hatred toward you, because it was never hatred. You're foul-tempered and cold and aloof, but godsdamn it, I love you with everything I have. There is no one else for me."

Her eyes were wide, shock plain across her beautiful features. "Theo, I …"

I smiled when her voice trailed off into silence, understanding that she would never be able to voice something like that, and even hearing it was uncomfortable enough for her. "Even if you felt the tiniest shred of that for me, I'd die a happy man."

"If you *die*, I'll find a way drag you back, so that I can kill you myself," she said, fisting the front of my shirt in her hands.

That was enough for me. And with the weight of voicing my emotions finally lifted from my shoulders, I couldn't help the grin from spreading across my face. Erisa squealed as I lifted her up by the waist and spun her around, unable to suppress the swell of joy threatening to burst from me.

Erisa's laughter was like the delicate chime of bells. "Put me down, you fool."

So, I did, and kissed away each insult as they fell from her mouth.

❖ ❖ ❖

The sun was warming away the chill of the night as we passed over Tolani Seko's land. The dew was evaporating into the air in thin wisps of steam, creating a sparse blanket of mist across the field. The grazing aurochs lifted their heads as we approached on our way toward the center of Zingal.

"Theo," Erisa whispered, pointing toward a hill in the distance, "look."

Holding my hand up to block out the sun, I followed her direction. Sat at the top of the hill was a hulking great figure, basking in the morning rays, overlooking the vast plains of farmland.

Dumuzid. It had to be. He was associated with Zingal and had supposedly gifted his daggers to one of my ancestors hundreds of years ago.

It took us about an hour to reach the foot of his hill, and he watched us climb the steep face of it with a lively, amused expression. He looked remarkably young compared to the other gods, as a human man would, approaching his twenty-fifth year. His golden blond hair was cut at his shoulders, complementing the radiant hue of his tanned skin.

"Ah, I wondered when you would show up, Theodoraxion Lusilim," he called out as we reached him. He clapped his huge hands together, his bright blue eyes wild with mirth. "The mighty Lord of Zingal, here you are, not quite bowing at my feet, but your presence is appreciated all the same. I suppose *acting* Lord is more accurate, your lovely sister is still alive, thank the gods." He gave me a wink. "Still, you should have been the first to greet me. Zingal is my domain after all, and you, my dear chap, are but another sheep under this shepherd's care, bleating out for my guidance."

Erisa turned to me slowly, disbelief dripping off her every feature, and I could practically hear her questioning this creature's sanity.

"I … err … Apologies for not coming to see you earlier, Dumuzid," I stammered, at a loss for how to reply to his speech, or how to address him directly.

"Oh, think nothing of it, my good friend! Now, out with it—what troubles you? How can this humble poet, master of words and melody, be of service to you?"

I had no idea what to make of this man—if he could be classed as a man. As far as I could tell from the way he was sat, he was certainly as tall as Nergal had been, and though he was slender like Namtar, nothing about him seemed lacking. He exuded health and joviality, as if everything had always just fallen perfectly into place for him and he was just happy to be alive.

"We're under the impression that you've decided not to attend to Ereshkigal in the Pal—in Ganzir," I said, glancing to Erisa for guidance, but she looked as lost as I was. "Am I right in thinking—"

"Ah, you're about to ask me to leap into the fray to fight for our Queen Ereshkigal's noble cause," he cried, cutting me off. "Or perhaps serenade the troops into a frenzy, making them yearn for victory. I must say, the promise of a good battle does stir the blood—I just hope that there's no dragons involved this time …"

Dumuzid trailed off, his brow furrowing in remembrance of what appeared to be an unpleasant memory. Before I could reply, he turned back to smile at me. "Well, as much as I'd love to join the charge, I'm afraid it is an impossibility. You see Ereshkigal's sister, Inanna—bless her heart—is my wife! And oh, what a vision she is, a rare beauty! Curves that could make a poet weep and forget his own name. But her temper is sharper than the edge of Nergal's scimitar when she's displeased with me, and disappointing her so greatly would be a fate worse than a thousand battle cries."

I could remember hearing stories about Dumuzid's romanticism and his love for Inanna, but I couldn't recall ever hearing that they were married.

Erisa called up to him, batting her long lashes and angling her hips to show that she too had the curves of a goddess. "But surely stirring her into such a temper would make your *reunion* all the more passionate. Imagine how wild it'll be when the time comes for you two to make up after this little spat."

Dumuzid's face lit up and he clapped his hands again, his delight radiating out of him like a ray of spring sunshine. "Oh, you wicked, delightful little creature! If that were the case, I'd be off with you to Ereshkigal's side in a heartbeat. But alas, such a betrayal would only hurt my lovely Inanna, and I fear she would punish me by relieving me of my favorite appendage, which would make me … ill-equipped for such future ventures, so I dare not part with it so recklessly. Still," he looked wistfully to the horizon, "the thought of such devious schemes does tempt the heart!"

"But you've sided with Ereshkigal before?" It was more of a question than a statement, as now I wasn't entirely sure.

Dumuzid waved a hand dismissively through the air. "Different times, different stakes. And oh, how my love wept. I can't do that to her again. I'm sure you understand, my friend," he said looking from me to Erisa and waggling his brows.

"Please," I implored, my tone practically begging, "can't you at least try to convince Inanna not to engage in this war? What is she even doing it for?"

"Oh, Theo—can I call you Theo?—I would never attempt to unravel the enigma that is a woman's will. Our poor, simple man-brains are as ill-suited to grasping the complexities of their minds as a fish is to playing the lute. Best to admire the mystery and leave the thinking to them!"

And with that, he rose to his feet, towering over us completely, and bounded away down the hill, causing the ground to shake with every step.

❖ ❖ ❖

"Silas isn't going to be happy," I muttered to Erisa as we reached the back door of the Lusilim estate. We were both exhausted and irritable from walking through the night and the lack of success with Dumuzid.

Erisa scowled at me. "Silas shouldn't have put this on us. How were we ever going to convince one god—let alone *three*—to change their minds about something they've probably been ruminating over for the last few hundred years? It was an impossible task to begin with."

I knew she hated failing at anything, and with so much riding on this, I didn't doubt that she was feeling the defeat deeply.

We entered the kitchen to find a throng of excitement. My mother, sisters, and Suenna were crowded around Vashti, taking it in turns to place their hands on the now-noticeable swell of her belly. Nook watched over the scene with a content smile and a glassy sheen over his eyes.

Karasi bounded over to me. "Oh good, Theo, you're here. We were just discussing when we should arrange the gathering to celebrate Vashti and Nook's baby." She glanced to Erisa, and the smile vanished from her face. "*You're* not invited."

Before I could reprimand her for being so childish, Erisa sneered at my twin, "Perfect, that means I won't need to make up an excuse," and pushed past her, disappearing up the stairs.

"Don't you dare even think about telling me off," Karasi cut in as I opened my mouth. "You have an uncanny ability to forget that she tried to kill me, I'm just reminding you of that. And of the fact that she isn't even sorry about it."

I merely nodded, not wanting to offend my sister, but equally, and cowardly, not wanting to get involved in the tension between them. I knew it would be beyond foolish to ever have a hope that they might eventually become civil toward each other, but the constant bickering and ribbing gave me a headache.

"Plan it sooner rather than later," I advised, thinking about the looming threat of war that the rest of them were blissfully ignorant of. "I imagine that over the next few weeks, we'll need all the happy news we can get."

"What do you mean?" she asked, her eyes wide with concern. "Is there news on the Autarch? Is he coming?"

I rubbed a hand over my face. "Something like that. I need to sleep, Kara, we've walked halfway across the damn realm today. Tell the others I'll brief them tomorrow; I don't want to spoil everyone's day with the news now."

Chapter 18

Erisa

Replication of sealed correspondence
To the great Autarch of Irkalla,
It has come to our attention that these recent disturbances are a result of you and your realm meddling in things you cannot even begin to understand. As you well know, relations between our domains have been somewhat tenuous in recent years, and I'm afraid this further solidifies the justification of our reluctance to engage with Irkalla.

That being said, Gods will not respect the manmade boundaries between us, and we have no intention of being caught unawares. We request that you tell us your plans and impart knowledge of your movements so that we may arrange ourselves accordingly.

I expect to receive either a response detailing your realm's recent failings and what you are actively doing to remedy the situation, or an invitation to a meeting with myself, where we can discuss the subject directly.
Ramin Tamzi, royal advisor and representative to the noble King Ardeshir Nazrali of Tarprusa

27 December
Copy made 30 December

❉ ❉ ❉

T ensions were high the morning after Theo and I returned to Zingal. Despite sleeping for longer than was necessary, I was still tired, and my legs ached from the vast distance we had walked over the last two days. My body was weary from travel, and I felt as though I hadn't been able to fully relax in months.

Theo had called his court into the dining room for an urgent meeting, and even though we'd only spent a few hours apart, the sight of him almost took my breath away. He had openly admitted his feelings to me, and I hadn't been able to say anything in return. I didn't know how I could express to him that when we're together, I finally felt at ease. That since Verrill's death I've turned angry and bitter and resentful. But that Theo had the ability to me forget how much I'm hurting and how much my need for revenge consumes me.

But I was never very apt at expressing my emotions, and he should know how fond I am of him simply by the fact that I haven't grown bored and disposed of him yet.

I tuned back into the conversation he was having with his friends and family.

"But I don't understand," Josefine whined in that aggravating pitch, "the gods are back because you combined all of the old relics, but that wasn't supposed to happen?"

"No." Theo shook his head. "We were tricked. The Beldams in Khar'ra told us that if we combined all of the relics then we'd have the power to destroy the Autarch. Either they were wrong—which I doubt—or they wanted to bring the gods back for their own schemes."

"And now the gods are fighting?" she said.

"It's more that they're continuing a fight that was started hundreds of years ago, when Inanna tried to claim Ereshkigal's throne here in Irkalla."

"And you expect us to believe that Silas—*our friend Silas*—was responsible for putting them into the ground," Nook said, raising an eyebrow, "*hundreds of years ago*."

"That's just what he told me."

"I think," I began, pushing away from the wall and walking toward the table, "that we're all focusing on the unimportant details. The fact of the matter is, that not only are these gods at war with one another, but that they are dragging us into their mess as well. If Ereshkigal is to be believed, the Autarch has already promised his army to Inanna, for when she decides to take another stab at the throne. And now *we* are being called to defend ourselves and our realm against them.

"The odds are completely against us. Dumuzid has already made it clear that he isn't on our side, and it's pretty safe to assume that Neti will be fighting for Inanna too, given that Katmu is his domain. Pazuzu claimed to be neutral, which leaves Ereshkigal and Nergal as the main beings standing in the way of Irkalla being crushed. Geshtinanna looks shy enough to cower before a butterfly and I've seen corpses looking healthier than Namtar. Our army barely survived the Autarch the first time around, and that was *with* help. We're heading toward an absolute disaster."

"Nice of you to spout problems without the offer of a solution," Karasi snapped.

What is she even still doing here? I thought. She was still operating in secret, hiding from the Autarch—as if he didn't have anything better to do than to be concerned about one woman he'd tried to kill years ago—and conducting all kinds of secret dealings with Torin. *Still, at least* he *isn't here. What a freak.*

I had to grit my teeth to stop my lip from curling into a sneer at her. "My *solution* is that we cut and run. If Silas is right, then Irkalla is gone. We'd be better off leaving as soon as possible, using the Rats to spread the word, warning the people about what's to come so that they can make that decision for themselves too. I'm sure your *Prince Sharru* would be willing to accept refugees."

"I'm not abandoning Irkalla," Theo said, his voice steady and unwavering. "This is our home, and you know as well as anyone else that hundreds of thousands of people will be left here to die."

He met my gaze, a silent promise to argue about this later, in private. It wasn't that I didn't care, I *did*. I cared about my Rats, about the families who would be torn apart across the realm. But if we fought in this war, the same destruction was bound to happen.

"We need to talk to Tasar about this," said Ezra, looking at the map of Irkalla spread across the dining table. "Before we can decide on a course of action, we need to get an idea of numbers, both on our side and the Autarch's."

"The last I heard was that Malah's Coastguard have been working overtime on their fleet. Building as many ships as possible," I said. "I imagine the Autarch intends on filling them with Henri Elkas' men and possibly Aran Seirsun's, because Malah certainly doesn't have enough."

"Has anyone seen anything of Aran?" Ezra asked. "Have we been able to locate him?"

I nodded. "The Rats intercepted a letter sent by him to the Autarch, letting him know that he was back in his district and that the entire city has been closed down. No one has been allowed in or out for weeks, and as we still have the majority of his ships in our possession, he has nowhere to go." I had to hide a smirk as I continued. "The letter went unanswered."

"How easy would it be to take the Golden City, I wonder," Nook mused to himself. "If Aran has nowhere to go …"

"It wouldn't be worth the effort," Suenna replied. "Aran's men won't turn on him, and getting past that wall would be a ridiculous waste of time. It would be possible to attack from Zagina Bay, but that's probably their most defended area."

"Suenna's right," Theo added, "the reward wouldn't be worth the risk. I have no interest in taking other districts just for the sake of it. For now, we'll just have to include his numbers in with the Autarch's. He certainly wouldn't dare to try and side with us after last time." He looked at me. "How soon could we get word to Tasar that we need to meet with him about this?"

"I sent a message to him last night," I said, feeling a thrill of warmth at his answering smile. "I expect he'll receive the message this afternoon and leave Hudjefa straight away—I made it clear that the matter was urgent."

The discussions continued well into the evening, and we ruminated over the potential movements of the Autarch as well as any involvement from Tarprusa. Even though I had already sent out a few chirps to the Rats to look out for an emissary from our neighboring kingdom, I was still uneasy over the letter I had received late that morning.

"Do you think we ought to send someone over there? Or try to make contact ourselves?" Ezra asked when I showed them all the note.

I frowned. "I'm not sure. If we're already too late and the Autarch has made some sort of agreement with them, we run the risk of them betraying us to him. I was planning on asking Cyfrin Wranmaris about it when he arrives with Tasar. I think he has a contact over there who might be able to tell us more about the current situation."

Karasi cleared her throat quietly and chewed on her bottom lip before speaking. "Torin can talk to King Ardeshir; they're on good terms. I'd just need to get a message to him."

"Where is he?" I asked.

She scowled at me. "That's hardly your concern, Feline."

But even as she said it, a faint blush crept over her cheeks, because if she needed the Rats to deliver a message—especially across the border—then obviously it *was* my concern.

Catching the rift in the air, Dana quickly commanded everyone to go and rest. I was relieved, the exhaustion of the day was catching up with me and I longed to go to bed. Still, I forced myself to go into Theo's office again and scribble a few quick letters, one of which was addressed to Asila.

I still hadn't heard anything from my friend since Malah had taken her away to his district, and not knowing if she was safe had been driving me crazy. I'd sent numerous letters to her with my Katmuan Rats, but had never had a response.

After sealing and sending my latest correspondence, I made one last detour into the kitchen, where I found Farzin standing on the counter, rifling through the cupboards.

"You're up to no good, little Rat," I said, fighting a smile.

He jumped at my voice, but relaxed as soon as he saw it was me, and a devious grin spread across his face. Knowing that this frightened little boy had grown to be so comfortable around me made my chest swell almost painfully.

"What would you say to another little job?" I asked, reaching into my pocket.

He lifted his chin. "I would say 'what's in it for me?'"

"Absolutely the right answer," I commended, pressing a silver coin into his outstretched palm. "I've taught you well."

Like the rest of the scrawny children, he now looked remarkably healthy. I made a mental note to cut Aghna some slack. Luckily, this job I had in mind for them would give her a day or two off from her childcare duties.

Farzin practically squealed in delight when I explained what I needed him and the other children to do, before I handed him a plum tart from the top shelf and sent him off to bed.

I made my way upstairs and stopped outside Theo's door, uncertain what to do. I had slept in his chambers with him yesterday, but I had been so delirious from exhaustion that I hadn't even realized where my feet were taking me, and I'd been barely awake by the time my head had hit the pillow.

He had been gone when I awoke.

I hesitated outside the room for a long moment before silently scolding myself for being ridiculous and pushing the door open. Theo was standing by the bed, folding his shirt, and I couldn't help but appreciate the sight of him as he turned to smile at me.

He was devastatingly handsome. Even after all this time and all that had happened between us, he still had the ability to make my heart falter in my chest.

I didn't know what to say. I was hovering.

"I … um … goodnight," I stammered. Why the hell was I *shy*? I was never shy.

I squared my shoulders and turned back for the door, wanting to lock myself away for this abhorrent display of foolishness.

Before I could take a step, Theo dropped the shirt and was across the room in two long strides. He pushed my back against the door, closing it and trapping me inside the cage of his arms.

"And where do you think you're going?" he murmured, dipping his head to trace his mouth along my jaw to the shell of my ear. "We've been living on borrowed time since the battle in Ocridell, who knows how much of it we have left? If you think I'm going to let you out of my sight for a single second of it, then you're sorely mistaken."

"You think awfully highly of yourself, Lord Lusilim," I whispered, tilting my head to give him better access to my neck. "Did it ever occur to you that I would rather be alone than in your presence?"

He nipped at my earlobe, sending a shiver down my spine. "No, you're exactly where you want to be."

"Or maybe I'm just bored and you're the best distraction this dreary, backwater district has to offer," I purred, running my hands over his bare chest, greedily taking in the toned definition of his muscles. He hadn't yet managed to reclaim the brawn he'd lost during his imprisonment, but the progress he had already made eased some of the worry I felt.

Theo pressed a kiss to my throat, and then another to my sternum, before swiftly unbuttoning my shirt, replacing the fabric with kisses. "One day you'll say something nice to me, something kind and sweet."

He knelt down in front of me and reached for my foot, bringing it up to rest on his leg as he slowly untied my laces. He removed the boot and then my sock, before gently placing my foot back down on the ground and reaching for the other one.

"Then you'll know I've been possessed," I said, raising a brow as he looked up to smirk at me. "You wouldn't like it anyway. You enjoy it when I'm mean to you."

He let out a soft chuckle as he straightened up and moved to the fastening of my trousers. "I can't deny that. But I'll take you in any way I can get you, Sunflower. Whether you're benevolent or cruel, vindictive or merciful, I'll love you all the same. Just when I think I've seen the very worst of you, you manage to surpass any of my imaginations, and yet, I still can't get enough."

He slid the last of my garments off while he spoke, leaving me completely bare before him. I opened my mouth to retort something hurtful, but instead a single note of a song escaped my lips. Theo's eyes brightened and he flashed me a spectacular grin when he realized what I was doing.

I morphed the note into another, reaching out to him through the sound and tasting his desire on my tongue, like sweet, spiced wine, made from the dark lava berries found deep within Ersetu.

I amplified that desire, spinning the threads of it in my mind until his pupils dilated, flooding the deep green of his irises. He looked up at me as though I'd caught lightning in a bottle and hung the stars with the contents. He followed my every movement as I walked around him slowly, still entranced by my voice. When I reached the bed, he stood and followed me, rapidly shedding the rest of his clothes.

The note of my voice ascended, and I willed him to stop, halting him a foot away from where I sat on the edge of the bed. I traced my fingers lightly over my skin, feeling it flame beneath his gaze as he followed my touch. He remained motionless, obeying my lyrical commands willingly. His enthusiastic encouragement fed into the feedback loop, almost overwhelming me with the intensity of it.

But he knew how to play; how to cheat. As soon as I had trailed my fingers lazily up to the tops of my inner thighs, he flooded me with emotion, bombarding me with affection, desire, admiration. And love. So much love it was all consuming.

I shattered his invisible bonds before I could even understand what he was doing, willing him to be closer, to touch me. Even his underlying satisfaction and smugness couldn't dampen the inferno searing through my veins, and he wasted no time in joining me on the soft sheets of the bed.

I was on fire. Every press of his lips against my skin was molten and scorching. His need for me was feverish, as though I was the last breath of air in a world suffocating in smoke. His soul was bound to my song, as adoring and willing as his physical movements were wild and punishing. Even as the notes faltered and skipped as my body wound tighter, he fed more emotion through that channel between us, pushing me higher, silently begging me to keep singing.

So I did, until my voice was hoarse and our bodies were slick with sweat. Until I saw stars and spiraled into obscurity, beckoning him with me.

And no one had ever followed so willingly, whispering heartbreaking declarations of love and sweet promises of things we both knew we could never have.

※ ※ ※

Theo groaned, halting in his tracks. "You've got to be kidding me."

The morning air was crisp, and my breath produced a small cloud as I chuffed out a laugh. As instructed, Farzin stood beside a bench in the main gardens, proudly holding up a wooden crate.

He was beaming from ear to ear. "I did it, Feline. You only asked for one, but I found you three!"

I moved past Theo, giving his arm a gentle squeeze as I went to the bench. "Good job, little Rat. I should think that means your reward has tripled, then."

The small boy nodded enthusiastically, and I pulled three large toffees from my cloak pocket and handed them to him. He scampered away back toward the house, leaving me alone with Theo.

I sat down on the damp wood and looked at Theo. "Aren't you going to join me?"

He shook his head, his eyes wide and startled, staring directly at the crate. "I can't … I can't do it."

Small chirps sounded from within as I shifted the crate to the end of the bench, and I could see the three large rats sniffing at the perimeters, trying to find an exit. Making sure that I was sitting in the center of the bench, I patted the empty space beside me.

"Come on," I said, "just come and sit with me, I'll stay here to protect you."

He flashed me a warning glare, making it clear that he didn't appreciate my teasing. But he still took a step forward, torn between his fear and the determination to not disappoint me.

"I won't let them out of the cage," I promised when he stopped just a few paces away. He met my gaze, saw the truth in my words and closed the gap, seating himself beside me, as far as possible from the crate.

He tried to hide the trembling of his hands by shoving them into his pockets, but I caught the one nearest to me and held it firmly in both of mine.

Theo couldn't take his eyes off the rats. "What now?" he asked, clearly afraid of the answer.

Smiling, I shook my head and sat back into the bench, tilting my head back and closing my eyes. "Nothing, we're just going to sit here."

I tried to look as serene and restful as possible, hoping that it would help him to calm down. It took him several long moments, but eventually, little by little, he started to relax. It was only when the trembling in his hand started to ease that I spoke to him.

In my attempt to keep the topics light, we spoke only about joyful subjects, like Nook's expected baby, and unimportant, trivial things, like the perfect thickness of a winter cloak and the bitterness of the weather.

"You're the one who dragged us outside for hours," he teased when I complained once again about the cold.

"I thought it would be better to start out in the open, rather than indoors." I had wanted to begin in an area that was completely open, so that he wouldn't be reminded of that horrible, enclosed cell in the Katmu dungeons.

"Thank you," he whispered, placing a small kiss to the back of my hand. "I know you're trying to help, but I don't know if I can do much more than this … I can still feel them … their teeth …"

I turned to look up at him. "Then this is all we'll do. I promise we won't move on until you're comfortable, we'll go slowly and practice every day. I'm not going to let you be ruled by this fear."

He shook his head. "We haven't got time for this; there's so much we should be doing and planning. The Autarch could strike with Inanna at any moment and we're so unprepared it's almost laughable. I can't spend hours every morning sat next to your crate of horrors."

"Then," I said, squeezing his hands once more, "we'll just have to set aside ten minutes every day. We'll get through this, Theo, together."

I didn't think I needed to mention that I planned to have the rats moved into the house, he'd find that out soon enough.

His eyes roamed happily over my face as he smiled. "Together."

Chapter 19

Theo

"So, to put it bluntly, we may not have enough?" I asked Tasar, raking my hands through my hair. He had arrived in the late hours of the afternoon with his brother Cyfrin in tow.

"As it stands, I think not," Tasar confirmed. "If it were purely based on the Autarch's forces—even including Aran's men—then we'd be on equal footing, but they're making such a vast number of warships that I can't help but suspect that he intends to fill them somehow. And if we are taking that fleet as an indication for his true number, then we ought to prepare for something far worse than what we faced in Ocridell."

I repressed a shudder. "Do we have a way to disrupt their production line?"

"I've already been doing what I can," Erisa announced from where she was perched in an armchair beneath the window. "There have been several fires started in the lower decks of the finished boats, and shipworm has been introduced to the supply chain of wood going in, but that's about as much as we can do without being detected."

Erisa was always very secretive about the things she did and the schemes she concocted, and I was used to how proactive and capable she was, but I had to admit that I was impressed by her initiative. I let it show in my expression and relished in the small, almost shy smile that curved her mouth.

"And there's no chance that someone will betray us?" I asked. "Who's relaying the information?"

"The Rats are fiercely loyal to the Feline," Tasar said, sounding almost skeptical at the truth of his words, as if he couldn't quite comprehend it. "I've had some fascinating dealings with them. They'll only engage with my men holding the harbor if they believe that it's what the Feline would wish for. I wouldn't necessarily say that her word surpasses that of Malah's, but rather they would never put themselves in a position where they would have to obey one word against another. Like how the Zingali Rats will pass messages under your nose, while still maintaining their regular duties."

His words weren't exactly comforting, but worrying about the logistics of the communication channels was a poor use of my time. The system the Rats operated under had always been reliable enough when Verrill had been in control, I just had to hope that whatever loyalty had bound them to him would be as strong with Erisa.

"Have you spoken to your commanders?" I asked Tasar.

He scratched at the pale wash of stubble across his chin. "I have. I've made it clear what's at stake—not that they would be able to ignore the state of the realm or our district right now—and they've all agreed to fight. Of course, each individual soldier will have to make that same decision for themselves, but having their superiors lead the way will be a massive help." He looked to his brother, who had been sat silently throughout most of the meeting. "Cyfrin has already been planning how to get them back here. Hudjefa is half caved in and the remainder that was left intact was already well over capacity, so I thought it best to get as many moved as possible to begin their training afresh."

Cyfrin cleared his throat. "The first division will be arriving at the barracks in the Zuamsik mountains by tomorrow afternoon."

"Excellent," I replied, nodding in appreciation. As uneasy as I felt about the younger Wranmaris brother, I couldn't deny that he'd been invaluable. I turned back to Tasar. "Bring as many over here as you like, fighters or not, your people are welcome in Zingal."

Tasar smiled. "Thank you, my friend. I'm sure many will take you up on that offer, but I have suggested that the majority join the other subterranean districts in heading to the exposed half of Ocridell. There's plenty of space that needs occupying there."

Our discussions carried on long into the evening, with Cyfrin excusing himself at sunset so that he could go and meet up with the Hudjefan forces moving toward Zingal.

"We need to discuss what is to happen if we succeed," Tasar began, looking first to me and then to Erisa. "Unless either of you are aware of how an Autarch gains the power and the title, I am going to assume that if we kill him, it will disrupt the natural order of things. Not to mention that Malah Jirata, Henri Elkas, and Aran Seirsun will need to be dealt with; even if they don't survive, are we to trust that their successors will not bide their time and begin this war again?"

"We're a long way off from succeeding," I said. "I think it's better we cross that bridge when we come to it."

He shook his head. "That's folly and we both know it. This needs to be properly thought out, with the good of the people of Irkalla at the forefront of the discussion. If we go into this with no plan to handle the aftermath, we might as well roll over and let the Autarch gut us now. Because it's bound to happen. As soon as we kill him, there'll be a squabble for the throne. There's still no leading family governing Ocridell, and what's left of Elkas' district consider him a laughingstock. That's already two more positions to fill."

"What are you saying?" Erisa asked.

Tasar's voice was low and precise. "I'm saying that we ought to reconsider the way in which this realm is run. Šarrum is finished, and I suspect that by the end of this, so many will have fled Ersetu that there won't be anyone left to govern beneath the surface." He looked over to where Erisa was assessing him coolly. "I'm not saying we make any decisions yet, just that you give it some thought. And ... I'm just saying that if we decided to abolish the Lording families ... I wouldn't be opposed to the notion."

Erisa narrowed her eyes. "If you're unhappy in your position, Tasar, you could always abdicate to Cyfrin."

He chuffed out a laugh. "We both know that he is ill-suited to lead a failing district."

"You want Theo to take over," she said, a ghost of a smile pulling at the corners of her mouth.

Tasar looked to me, holding my gaze, before nodding.

"Absolutely not," I protested. "You can't pass Hudjefa on to me, it's not how the succession works."

"Don't be dense, Theo," Erisa chided. "He's not talking about Hudjefa, he's talking about Irkalla; all of the districts."

I was taken aback. "You can't be serious. I wouldn't know the first thing about governing a realm, and besides, the other Lords," I looked to Erisa, "and Ladies, would never agree. We both know that I'm not even the proper Lord of Zingal, Karasi is still alive!"

"Not to sound callous," Erisa chimed in, examining her nails, "but this *is* your rebellion; if we won, you could just … *take* that control."

I opened my mouth to protest but Tasar cut me off.

"Just food for thought, my friend. I simply want you to know that I will back you, when the time comes."

Despite offering him a room for as long as he needed it, Tasar insisted that he needed to return to his people early in the morning, even though his home was practically in ruins.

It pained me to think of all of the lives I had disrupted beneath the volcano. Although I hadn't directly caused part of Ersetu to collapse, I had still combined the relics. The fact that we had been tricked by the Beldams was inconsequential; it was still my fault.

❖ ❖ ❖

The days of planning and scheming were long, but the weeks flew by as uncontrollable and unpredictable as a derailed tram, catapulting us further toward an unknown destination. Despite numerous efforts to locate them in order to sway their decisions, Dumuzid and Pazuzu were nowhere to be found. The only indication of their presence was in the flourishing of the crops across Zingal and the erratic, gale force winds that whipped up through Ocridell and across the surface of the water now settled in the Silent Canyons of Saqummatu.

Erisa was consistent to the point of fanaticism with my progress on conquering my fear of the rats. She would bring the crate of vermin to me daily, making me sit with it by my side, on my lap and clutched to my chest. I'd had several setbacks; times when I could feel a brush of fur or a small, curious nose against my fingers, but she simply calmed me down and continued as though nothing had happened.

She hid our strange routine from the others remarkably well, somehow sensing my embarrassment and masterfully redirecting any kind of interest they showed with a particularly nasty look or a spiteful comment.

But she never worsened the shame I felt on my days of failures, nor did she make any dramatic, celebratory flourish at my progress, only rewarded me with small, proud smiles.

And oh, how I chased those smiles.

I had managed to put my hand inside the crate for ten seconds the day the letter arrived. Erisa had taken the rats back to the barn and had returned inside with a note.

Replication of sealed correspondence

Aran,

If I have to read another letter of your sniveling and whining—prattling on about how unfair your treatment has been—I'll tell the Autarch to cut you off entirely. I suggest you pull yourself together, quit behaving like a spoiled brat, and start offering ideas that we could actually use.

Don't forget that he doesn't need you or your men, so, if you want to remain relevant, I suggest you stop gazing into the mirror and start figuring out how to transport your forces, since you were foolish enough to allow your fleet to be stolen. Though, I admit, I'm not holding out much hope.

Malah Jirata, Lord of Katmu

13 March
Copy made 14 March

"Brutal," I said, passing the letter back to her. "I'm guessing Malah didn't grow too fond of Aran during their joint betrayal."

"No, Theo, look," she pointed at the words on the paper, "look at where his handwriting is different on certain letters. My Rats wouldn't have bothered making a copy of this if it wasn't important."

I was about to say that it was important because Malah had all but confirmed that the Autarch was sourcing an army from elsewhere if he didn't need Aran's men, but then I noticed what Erisa had fixated on. Random letters were written clumsily and slanted, a change from his usual neat handwriting.

Erisa voiced the words as I was working them out. "Asila safe. Top tower. Left room."

I turned to face her, unease twisting in my gut at the flame of excitement lighting up her eyes. It was the same look she always got when she began to scheme. And I had an idea of where this one was taking her.

"Oh no, you can't go there. Erisa, think about who sent this letter. It's a trap."

"I have to, she's one of my only friends. I have to try and get her. If it was a trap, then he would have said that she's in danger."

"But he gave you her location," I argued. "Please, Sunflower, think about this; he obviously knew that you were going to see that letter and knew that you wouldn't be able to resist going to Katmu. The Autarch has tried time and time again to capture you, and you'd just be walking right into his open arms."

She scowled at the insinuation. "I'll be careful, I always am. And besides, I don't need your permission, I'm going, whether you like it or not."

I bit down on my tongue to stop the sad sigh from escaping my mouth. "I know you are, I'm just asking you to think about it logically. Take a few days so that we can prepare properly. The last thing we need is—"

"We?"

I tried to smile, but the thought of returning to Katmu made my stomach sour. "Yes, we, because *obviously* I'm going to come with you."

Even as I spoke the words, I couldn't believe that they were real. This was madness to even consider. I had only interacted with Asila a few times, and even though she seemed lovely, and Erisa was clearly very fond of her, there were just too many things that could go wrong. And that was before we would even make it to the Citadel.

Her eyes widened. "No, Theo, it's too risky, he won't kill me, but he won't hesitate if he sees you."

Nausea was starting to make my head spin ever so slightly. I placed my hands on her shoulders. "Erisa, I can't ... I just ... the thought of him putting you down in that ... *place*. I can't do it, I have to be with you, I have to come so that I can know you're safe."

"I don't need you to protect me," she snapped, but even as she said the words, her eyes softened.

I took a few steadying breaths, and ran my hands up and down the tops of her arms, trying to comfort myself more than her. "I know you don't, but if you're going, then I *need* to be there. I told you that I'm not letting you out of my sight for as long as we have left. I'd follow you into whatever ring of hell you get dragged down into and burn with you there for the rest of eternity."

"Theo," she breathed, her sunflower eyes impossibly large and bright. She looked innocent and defenseless for less than a second, before her harsh mask of practicality snapped back into place. "Fine, if I can't stop you from coming with me then we'll need to do this properly. I won't be able to just slip in and out if I've got you tagging along."

I relaxed ever so slightly at her teasing, though the reality of returning to the place that still plagued my nightmares had my heart racing. I had tried my best not to think of the collection of small islands at the bottom of the realm. Everything that had happened there felt like a fever dream. I could barely remember the fighting at the Stacks, or the bloodbath of the third island before I was captured on that beach, kneeling in the sand.

But the sight of Erisa abandoning me refused to fade from my mind. The sharp sting of pain the memory invoked was quickly washed away as I pulled her into my arms, burying my face into her hair. No matter how much it had ruined me, I couldn't deny that I was grateful for it. Her reasons for leaving me there had been solid; it was either save my soldiers or save me. And I was glad that she'd made the right choice.

"So, how are we going to do this?"

She pulled back slightly to look up at me. "How do you feel about climbing?"

Chapter 20

Erisa

Feline,
The Autarch is on the move. We haven't been able to get much from the Rats in Katmu, but all we know is that the army is stirring. Malah's people are reluctant to engage but are loyally standing behind their Lord.

Aran Seirsun has moved his remaining ships to Katmu—obviously under the direction of the Autarch—and is now situated within the Citadel himself.
Alekos

18 March

❖ ❖ ❖

"He's abandoned his district then," Theo sneered, disdain and disappointment evident in his tone. "He's left it completely vulnerable and open to attack. Pathetic, cowardly man."

Moth turned to take a chunk out of my arm as I reached to retrieve the letter from Theo, and Fergus tossed his head in response. "Missed me," I said to the piebald beast, before addressing Theo. "He must know that it would be foolish for us to waste resources in taking it. Let's just hope that the other realms don't catch wind of his desertion. The fool has left all of Irkalla exposed to invasion. If one of them exploits the weakness and obtains a foothold in Kusig, we don't have a hope in hell of defending ourselves, especially when the realm is split in two."

Theo looked horrified at the idea. "We'd be flattened. Let's just trust that the gods have caused enough disruptions across Tarprusa and Aessurus that they don't have enough disposable resources to orchestrate an invasion. I'd like to trust Karasi in her belief that Atturynn won't attack, but Torin has been absent for weeks now, and I'm starting to feel uneasy."

Theo already knew my stance on the Atturynnian princeling, so I didn't feel the need to rehash my own nervousness regarding that dubious alliance. Torin Sharru seemed, at best, unhinged, and I would be perfectly happy if I never encountered him again. Besides, from the look of hatred in his eyes the last time, I wasn't sure I would survive it.

The spring sunshine warmed my cheeks as we rode toward Anzillu. Even though it had only been mere months since the gods had begun their disruptions of the land, repairs and improvements had already been made to the roads and dwellings surrounding Ersetu. It had been a long time since I had seen Ocridell so alive and flourishing. Countless families had fled the volcano, braving the harsher, exposed climate to begin building a life above ground.

During one of our many ventures to find Pazuzu, Theo and I broke down the gates to my family's old estate in the hope that people would find refuge within the remaining walls. Within days, the place had begun to transform, like the restoration of an old painting. The grounds were being cleared of overgrown vegetation and rubble, and supplies were brought in for the rebuild. According to the Rats, almost all of those supplies had been donated, and the quiet community of Ocridell had started coming together, volunteering and helping the effort to renew the heart of the district.

I tried not to think of Verrill as we passed through the streets of our old home, but I couldn't help but imagine what his reactions would've been to the events that had transpired since his death. I missed him terribly, like part of my anatomy had been taken from me. I could still function, but I knew I would never be quite whole again.

Half a year had passed since I'd watched his lifeless body fall from that cliff, and though I still thought of him every day, somewhere along the way, I had accepted the fact that he was gone. I no longer looked around to catch his eye when I found something funny, or started letters recounting my day or asking for advice, only for the ink to trail away halfway through as I remembered that no one would be reading the words. I was secretly glad that I hadn't found his body, that I didn't have a headstone to sit and weep against, because I wondered how much of those six months I would've wasted pressed against the cool slab of stone.

"It feels like it'll be cold tonight," Theo murmured, looking at the cloudless sky and shaking me from my reverie.

I watched him ride on ahead, momentarily overwhelmed by the swell of emotion I felt. I knew that he was the reason I had remained sane. My anger and need for vengeance would have only carried me so far before I crumbled. But Theo's presence, stable and unwavering as it was, had kept me grounded. Had kept me alive. Even when I had tried hating him, blaming him for Verrill's death, I knew that he would still be there when I needed him.

Once again, the wave of gratitude I felt for Karasi for stepping in and stopping my blade caused my stomach to turn. I didn't believe in regretting past actions, but I did regret that. If she hadn't defied every odd known to man and showed up when she did, I would've killed Theo, clouded by agony and anger and consumed by madness for a mere moment.

Fergus pranced uneasily, sensing my rising panic brought on by my own shameful memories. I took several calming breaths to recollect myself before urging him forward to catch up with Theo and Moth.

"If we press on, we should make it to Alekos' house before nightfall," I said to him, allowing my gaze to linger on his face for a few seconds too long.

He noticed, and gave me a roughish wink before clicking his tongue and setting off at a canter down the worn track toward Ersetu.

Alekos was waiting for us when we finally made it to his small dwelling in Anzillu. It had been a long and difficult journey, navigating our way around the bottom curve of Ersetu to reach the exposed part of the district. Horses were seldom seen within the volcano even before the gods had emerged, and now, with the collapsed tunnels and half-blocked entrances, maneuvering around on horseback was more trouble than it was worth.

While he took the horses around the back, Theo and I were

quickly ushered into the house by his wife. It was only after she'd shut the door that we lowered our hoods, and I was able to look at the woman for the first time. Her ebony hair coiled down past her shoulders, peppered with streaks of pale gray.

"Rania," I said, nodding to her in greeting.

Her dark eyes assessed me warily. She was scared but hid it behind an almost convincing mask of bravery. "Feline." She nodded slowly before turning to Theo. "Lord Lusilim. Welcome to our home."

Theo thanked her and we followed her through the house and into a small parlor. The heat from the fire was almost stifling and I quickly shed my cloak.

"What are you burning?" Theo asked, trying to look at the roaring flames, but unable to get closer than a few feet.

"The Autarch has been importing wood from the Cedar Forest for months," Alekos answered, walking in through a back door. "He's amassed vast quantities of it and has been using it to build his new fleet in Katmu. We've stolen what we can from the imports, handing it out to those in need from the volcano, but it behaves … strangely. Even though it hasn't been dried, it still burns like nothing I've seen before. I'm sure it's saved more than a few families who have fled Ersetu this winter."

I watched as the flames danced in the fireplace, slowly bending and twisting into impossible shapes, punctuated with flashes of blue and green and purple.

Theo smiled and pointed. "Huh, it looked like a flying snake for a second."

"Why is he importing wood instead of sourcing it from the

Gištir Jungle?" I asked Alekos, having to turn away from the searing heat of the flames.

He shook his head. "I'm guessing that he didn't want to trouble himself with securing a foothold along that coastline. The Jungle is volatile after all; it protects itself."

❖ ❖ ❖

"Are you ready?" Cyfrin said at the door of the cabin. His carefree demeanor slipping ever so slightly into something akin to fretting. But when I nodded, he didn't move to let us leave, only frowned as though deciding how to phrase his next words. "Look to the skies, Feline … be wary about who's watching."

My brows furrowed, but we didn't have time for this nonsense. "Thanks," I muttered, and pushed past him and through the door, pulling Theo with me.

The boat was small, and we crossed the deck in just a few strides. Making sure Theo's hood was up and secured, I clambered onto the wooden planks of the small docking yard and immediately made for the stacks of barrels along the loading area.

"What did he mean by that?" Theo whispered into my ear.

I shook my head without looking at him, scanning the area for any sign of life and finding nothing but the soft lapping of waves and our shallow, quiet breaths.

The past few days had been a whirlwind of planning and preparation, scheming with the Katmuan Rats and Tasar's men holding Anzillu Harbor. We waited until there was a natural break in the shift changeover to bring the boat into view, where the Rats were scheduled to be on guard. I could hear them approaching now, coming to their stations ten minutes late so that they wouldn't see the boat that Cyfrin had silently sailed away. Their argument was that if they didn't see the boat, they wouldn't feel compelled to report it.

Their logic was shaky at best, but if I wanted to take Asila and her parents safely back to Zingal, I had no choice but to trust in their loyalty to me.

I could hear footsteps approaching our hiding place, and a deep voice shattered the silence. "Clear night tonight, should have no trouble seeing across the waters."

A signal from the Rats, letting us know that the coast was clear. I glanced back at Theo, wishing that I could leave him behind and go alone. Because if I trusted this Rat and led us both right into Csintalan's trap, then I would be the one responsible for our capture.

All of Theo's progress with overcoming the trauma he sustained on this wretched island would be destroyed. He would be killed. And it would all be my fault. But the brave, foolish man saw my hesitation and nodded toward our exit, giving me a slight push forward, urging me to go.

I slipped out from behind the barrels, holding my breath as we came out into the open night, knowing that if I'd been betrayed by the Rats, someone would call out to alert others of our presence.

But there was no sound but the creaking wood of the planks underfoot. The wall of the Citadel towered ahead of us, and I locked eyes with a few of the Rats as we passed them, touching a finger to my ear in thanks, and watching them bow their heads slightly as they returned the gesture.

Theo and I sidled our way through the stacks of cargo, keeping as hidden as possible until we reached the wall. We crept along the perimeter of it, trying to keep quiet so as not to alert the guards standing on top, until we came to the first door. I paused for a few seconds, trying to find any cause for concern in the deafening silence surrounding us.

Finding none, I moved past the door, and continued on until the doorway of the second appeared. Theo brushed the backs of his fingers across my shoulders to let me know that he was there and was okay to proceed.

I reached round to the door and gently knocked twice, then three times. After a few long seconds, the door creaked open.

"Now," whispered a voice on the other side.

We slunk through the barely open door and into the courtyard of the Citadel, the moonlight casting menacing shadows from the statues and large fountain in the center. I looked behind to see that the Rat who had let us through the door had disappeared.

We clung to the wall as close as we could, slowly walking around until the main tower dominated our vision. I pictured the layout in my mind, hoping that nothing had changed since Theo and I had stayed all those months ago. I identified our target. There was a light coming out of the top left room, the soft orange glow illuminating the stone ledge of the balcony.

I moved to take a step toward the tower, but Theo stopped me.

"Look," he breathed into my ear, and pointed to where several crows were perched on the heads of the statues and on the top of the fountain, "what are they doing?"

His question should have been "Why aren't they doing anything?" because they were completely motionless; so still that, in the poor light, I had assumed that they were part of the decoration.

I didn't have an answer for him, but despite how uneasy the frozen birds had made me, we didn't have time to dwell on it. I reached down to give his hand a quick squeeze, before setting off across the courtyard.

The second the moonlight unveiled my cloak of shadows, the crows silently took to the skies, startling me. Had I not been watching them, I would've missed it. One of them crossed the path in front of us and I barely had time to reach for a dagger sheathed at my hip and launch it at the creature. Its eyes flashed red as it fell and instinctively, I knew that we were in trouble.

Theo must have known too, because he grasped my elbow and hauled me across the courtyard with him, bounding me forward and practically throwing me onto the first balcony. I scrambled up, balancing and jumping from one to the next, silently thanking the years I had spent precariously hopping between the tips of stalagmites beneath the volcano.

Theo was slower, and his grunts of exertion sounded deafening in the near silence. My heart was hammering in my chest by the time I gripped the back of his shirt and helped to pull him over the railing of the top floor balcony on the left side of the tower.

Without wasting a second deliberating, I yanked the door open, and threw myself inside, expecting Asila to scream or cry out in surprise. Instead, she was sitting at a dressing table, calmly twisting tiny turquoise beads into her braids.

"Well, better late than never I suppose," she said, raising a dark brow at me in the mirror. After a second, her expression cracked, and she turned to beam at me before standing up and launching herself into my arms. "I've missed you so much! Malah said you would come, and I've been waiting for weeks! Did you get the messages in his letters?"

She said it all so fast that I couldn't help but laugh. I held her at arm's length, inspecting her for injuries or any sign of mistreatment, but fortunately found her looking radiant as ever.

She looked over my shoulder. "Verrill?" she asked, searching the room expectantly, waiting for him to join in her rescue.

My stomach plummeted and I felt as if someone had tipped a bucket of cold water over me. Had Malah not told her that Verrill had died?

I shook my head, unable to find the words. "He …"

Whatever Asila saw on my face caused the delight to drip away from her own, leaving an expression of horror in its wake. She opened her mouth, but before she could say anything, someone crashed into the large wooden door of her room.

"Shit." I seized her hand and pulled her toward the balcony. We needed to go. But as soon as we reached the open night air, my heart sank. The silence immediately filled with shouts and the whooshing of arrows flying toward us.

Theo yanked me back just in time as another flew by, so close to my face that I could almost feel the feathers of the fletching caress my cheek. I looked around for a door, a passage, or any other route of escape that didn't involve making Asila risk her life.

The pounding at the door was getting louder, and the little bottles on her dressing table were beginning to shake and fall over, toppling to the floor.

This wasn't part of the plan. We were supposed to slip in and out without anyone seeing us. I'd chosen this time specifically to coincide with the largest number of Rats on guard. But whoever was waiting for us on the ground didn't belong to me.

"We'll have to jump to the balcony below," I told them both, "it's not too far down. The guards on the ground will obviously see, but we might be able to—"

"Erisa," she cut in, pulling me round to face her. "I'm not coming with you."

It took immense effort not to shake her. "What do you mean? Of course you're coming. I came here to get you and your parents and take you all back to Zingal."

The wooden panels of the door began to groan, threatening to splinter under each blow and a quick glance behind me showed me that dozens of guards were running across the top of the wall toward the balcony.

"I'm not coming," she repeated, and rushed through her words as the door groaned ominously behind her. "The Autarch is using me to influence Malah, but I can't leave him. The Autarch won't do anything to me really, he wouldn't hurt my father like that." She reached into one of the drawers in the dresser and took out a letter. "Here, this is from Malah, he wanted you to come and take me away, but I can't go, he'll be all alone otherwise and I'm afraid that if I'm taken away, the Autarch will punish him for it."

She tucked the folded paper into the hidden pocket of my

corset, one that she had designed and made for me, and pushed me toward the balcony.

"You have to go, Erisa, please," she said, flinching as the door gave way behind her, "you don't know what he has planned for you."

Before I had to make the decision, Theo wrapped an arm around my waist and hauled me out of the room, just as several of the guards spilled in and swarmed Asila. We locked eyes for a heartbeat, and she nodded, urging me to go.

My heart was thundering in my chest. There were guards all around us, some of the faster ones on the wall had almost made it level with the balcony and I could hear others scrambling up the same way we had come. I prepared to launch myself over the railing and onto the wall, but stopped myself, backtracking.

Theo's fingers. Once we were on the wall, with the stairways blocked, the only way down would be to climb, stuffing the tips of our fingers into the cracks between the stones. And while Theo's broken fingers had healed, he'd never be able to support his body weight with them.

I gave myself a second to assess the situation, eliminating two more exit plans based on the guards' positions and numbers.

"Boost me up," I said to Theo, already reaching for the gutter above my head. He didn't hesitate, grasping me around the thighs and almost throwing me onto the roof. I didn't even have time to check that the coast was clear before one of the guards from Asila's room began to grapple with him. I sunk a dagger into the man's shoulder and then another into his throat, giving Theo the time he needed to spring off the railing and up over the edge of the roof. I pulled him up, sending a silent prayer of thanks to whoever was responsible for ceasing the barrage of arrows that had rained down on us before.

We scrambled to our feet and ran across the slanted tiles, slipping from the moss covering the surface. The cool sea breeze bit at my skin, but I could barely register the chill. I glanced to Theo, whose eyes were wide and frantic.

I hurled myself at the trapdoor leading to the servants' quarters, wrenching at it with everything I had. It didn't budge, not even when Theo threw in his weight beside me. It was sealed tight. This was *so* not part of the plan. We were trapped, and I had no idea how to get us out. The only way was down.

Movement from the corner of my eye caught my attention; sheets of colorful fabric flapping in the wind, their vibrancy paled by the dim light.

"This way, I have an idea," I said pulling him to the edge of the roof and lowering myself to a crouch. After confirming that no guards had seen us from below, I lowered myself down onto the protruding window ledge, balancing on the tips of my toes.

The faint shouting intensified from behind us and Theo swore. The guards had made it onto the roof. To avoid being slowed down, we hadn't brought any real weapons; my knives were all I had, and a quick pat down my body informed me that I only had three left. And Theo had one dagger in his belt. It would have to be enough.

I reached my right hand out, grasping the thick rope and giving it a sharp pull to test the fixings. The banners hanging between the us and the next tower swayed, dancing above the empty space below.

"Get your dagger ready," I called to him, and shuffled myself closer to the wall. "Now, Theo!"

He didn't question or hesitate. He was no novice to danger, and he trusted me to know what I was doing. He leapt into the air at the same time as I threw my knife toward the bolt securing the rope into the wall. I watched the blade slice through the rope as I jumped, watching it begin to unravel, snaking itself free from the metal ring it was hanging from.

My hands grasped the coarse material less than a heartbeat after Theo and I cried out as it ripped through my palms, my stomach turning as we plummeted toward the ground. It rushed toward us eagerly, and just as I thought it would claim us, the rope went taught, swinging us up.

We were too far from the ground to drop now. I waited, watching as the flat roof of a guardhouse approached. This was it.

Two more seconds. One more second.

"CUT IT!" I screamed to Theo.

And we were falling again, carried forward by the residual momentum of the swing. I tucked myself into a ball, bracing myself for impact. But no amount of preparation would've been enough.

I felt several ribs break as I crashed into the dusty stone surface of the roof. I rolled over and over, shielding my head with my arms. And when I finally stopped, the world kept spinning.

I couldn't breathe. The air wheezed out of my lungs in groans and pants, not allowing any more to enter.

"Erisa," Theo grunted, pulling me upright, "we need to

move, they're coming."

But I still couldn't breathe. And the pain in my chest was all consuming. I could feel my heart rate spike, making my head spin and black spots obscure the edges of my vision. Theo lifted me to my feet, and I whimpered as he pulled my arm over his shoulder and slipped one of his own around my waist.

"I'm sorry," he said, breaking into a limping run, "but we have to go."

My breathing, though painful, returned after a moment and I was finally able to take in small breaths. We half-staggered toward a small trap door in the roof of whatever building we had landed on. Neither of us knew what waited for us down there, but we didn't have any choice, the guards would've seen us fall from the tower and it was only a matter of time before they caught up with us.

Mercifully, at the bottom of the old, rusted stairs, there was an empty dormitory, with several bunk beds lining the walls. We raced through the dormitories, down two more flights of stairs, through what I assumed were the kitchens and living spaces, until we found what appeared to be the back door.

"Ready?" I panted, turning to Theo. "They're probably waiting for us."

He surged forward in answer, dagger in hand and a wild determination in his eyes. The door opened onto a courtyard clearly used for drills and fighting practice, and Theo swiftly grabbed a sword from one of the weapon racks as we sprinted past. There wasn't time for me to search for any more knives, and I had never been adept at using broadswords, so I kept on running. I decided that if I made it out alive, I'd master the sword, become just as deadly with it as I was with my daggers.

We needed to get to the other side of the main wall. Once we passed it, we could slip into the bustle of the loading docks and remain hidden. It loomed above us on the other side of the building, only about fifty paces away, and as I pulled Theo around the corner of the guardhouse, I stopped short, immediately backtracking.

Running toward us from the main tower were what looked like over a hundred guards, all armed and desperate to reach us.

"This way," Theo growled, setting off toward the far end of the courtyard.

A few seconds later, a set of stairs climbing the edge of the wall came into view. It was how the guards were able to patrol the top, but there was no way down on the other side.

My entire body burned as we battled our way up the stone steps and if not for the sheer flood of adrenaline coursing through my body, I was certain that it would've shut down entirely. There were a handful of guards still patrolling the wall, but I managed to subdue them with a breathy, panting tune long enough for Theo to dispose of them.

By the time we reached the very top, I had run out of breath and ideas. We ran along the top of the wall, hoping to find any possible route down, until our path was blocked by guards who had climbed up after us.

Soon, we were surrounded on all sides once more, and down on the ground, fifteen feet below us and surrounded by soldiers, stood the Autarch.

Chapter 21

Theo

We were fucked.

"Erisa," I whispered, "I love you, but this plan of yours was horrendous."

Every way I turned, I could see the seafoam blue uniforms of Malah's Coastguard. Each exit was blocked, and my mind wouldn't quiet long enough for me to try and formulate a plan.

The Autarch—Corbin—stood looking up at us from the ground, the beak of his black crow mask glinting in the moonlight. The face that I'd seen looming over me, night after night, watching as the rats gnawed away at my skin.

I was going to die here. Erisa was going to be taken and tortured and I wouldn't be able to stop it from happening. My hands were already trembling as I glared down at that cruel, evil man, remembering everything I had endured at his hand in that dark, damp cell.

There was no way in hell I was going back there. And I would do everything in my power to ensure Erisa didn't either. I tightened my grip around the sword I was holding and drew in several calming breaths.

But before I could launch into action, the Autarch spoke; a deep, booming voice that traveled effortlessly to our elevated position.

"Stop this nonsense, Kitten. We both know that you're trapped up there. Come down quietly and let's talk about this like adults. I promise I won't hurt you," I could feel his attention shift to me, "or your charming Theo."

Erisa looked at me, and for the briefest, most horrifying of moments, I thought she might actually be considering his offer. But then she turned back to the Autarch, opened her mouth, and screamed.

It was the worst sound I had ever endured, convincing me that liquid ice had entered my bloodstream and was freezing my blood solid. Every artery, vein, and capillary felt like it was brittle and shattering, destroying me from the inside out.

I stumbled away from her, falling to my knees like every other person within a ten-foot radius. Those beyond her reach simply screwed their eyes shut and clamped their hands over their ears. Even those milling about on the other side of the wall cried out.

But the Autarch ...

Even out of range, he had gone down; fallen to the floor under the direct focus of Erisa's lethal voice. I watched in astonishment as he brought a hand up to unbutton the collar of his tunic, pulling the fabric down to expose his neck. His body trembled and I could tell that he was fighting with every fiber of his being, but she was relentless, forcing him into submission. He took a knife from his belt and brought it up toward his throat.

The second it touched his skin, the guards around him finally seemed to notice what was happening and several of them dropped to his side, frantically trying to pull the blade away. It took four of them to straighten his arm, but still he continued to try and slit his own throat.

It was then that I realized what Erisa was doing. She knew that there were too many of them for her to succeed in killing him this way, it was merely a distraction. And we were already out of time.

A glint of silver caught my eye; the chain of a market stall swaying slightly in the breeze. I knew it was going to hurt, but I didn't give myself time to deliberate or hesitate. In one swift motion, I rebelled against the ice-scorched breaking of my blood vessels and snatched Erisa around the waist, took two bounding strides, and leapt off the edge of the wall.

I twisted mid-air, holding Erisa close and shielding her as much as possible before we hit the awning. The aged fabric ripped, and the supporting beams collapsed, causing us to fall again. We landed hard, splintering the wooden tables and fruit buckets and scattering the remaining goods across the floor.

My breaths came out in ragged, choked pants and I rolled over to find Erisa crawling toward me. Her lip was split and a cut across her brow was dripping blood into her eyes, but she was alive. We reached for each other, pulling ourselves free from the debris of the broken market stall and stumbling our way into the street.

We began to sprint when the arrows started to rain.

I felt a sharp slice across the top of my arm and another at my calf, but I ignored them, we just needed to make it round the bend of the street. What sounded like thousands of footsteps were thundering after us; the guards were following us again.

Large talons sunk into the back of my neck and I flailed my arms, batting away the enormous crow, but it kept coming back to attack.

"We can't … let it … follow us," Erisa heaved, breathless from the exertion. "It will … see … where we hide."

Almost effortlessly, she flung out her left hand, sinking a small knife into the ebony feathers of the creature. I didn't stop to watch it fall as we sprinted to the end of the street.

"But we're … not staying … here." I struggled to catch my breath.

"I was just … saying that … so that the Autarch—" Her words were swallowed in a sharp intake of air, and she stumbled.

I grasped her arm and hauled her around the corner, ready to continue our escape to the docks when she stumbled again.

My heart stilled when I looked down to see the arrow protruding from her lower abdomen.

"No," I croaked, flapping my hands uselessly over her stomach, unable to touch her. "No, no, no, no, no."

"Theo," Erisa whispered. Her chest was heaving, and she raised her eyes to meet mine. They were as wide as the moon above us. She was frightened.

Footsteps and shouting forced me to snap out of whatever absurd stupor had come over me. If we didn't move now, we'd be caught in less than a minute.

As gently as I could, I lifted Erisa into my arms, cradling her against my chest and launched back into a run. I darted through the smaller streets and alleys, praying to every single one of the gods, begging for them to help us.

Although she remained silent, every turn and jolt made me wince, knowing how much pain she was in and how each step must have made it worse. With each step, I prayed—*begged*—for a way through this, for a way to save Erisa.

We arrived earlier than originally agreed, but Cyfrin was ready with the small boat, letting it bob gently in a hidden alcove of the loading docks. He looked up when he heard my pounding footsteps, and his eyes widened in horror as he took in the sight of Erisa. Immediately, he lowered the gangplank and began calling out to the sailors he had brought with him, instructing them to set sail as soon as I flew over the plank and into the boat.

We were already moving by the time I lowered Erisa onto the tiny bed in the cabin, positioning her on her side, so that her injury and the arrow would remain elevated. When I eased my arms out from under her, I found them covered in blood.

"Here," Cyfrin said, appearing at my side. He handed me some scraps of clean cloth and a bottle of what looked like spirits.

"Theo," Erisa breathed, her voice weak and faltering. "Is it bad?"

"Shh," I murmured, smoothing the dark hair around her face. "It's fine. You're fine. It's just a scratch. I just need to clean you up a bit … it might sting a little."

She huffed out a shallow laugh and rolled her eyes. "One

little arrow doesn't … phase me." But her eyes didn't reopen, and she lost consciousness the second I pressed the spirit-soaked bandage to the wound.

❖ ❖ ❖

The two-hour journey back to the mainland was hell. The seconds seemed to stretch on endlessly, mocking me, taunting me with the knowledge that every single one was precious. That every single one that slipped by, was another one closer to Erisa bleeding out.

Ereshkigal, please, I begged silently, *please let her live. I'll fight for you; I'll happily die in battle in your name if you spare her.*

Erisa was too quiet and too still, except for a small whimper when we passed through the mists surrounding the islands and some of the malevolent tendrils of vapor made their way inside the cabin.

She's going to die, they whispered to me. *She's going to bleed out and there's nothing you can do to stop it. She's going to die without ever telling you that she loves you.*

Look at how shallow her breathing is, how waxen her skin has become.

That arrow was meant for you.

This is all your fault.

Cyfrin had stayed by my side the entire time, helping me clean and keep pressure on the wound without knocking the arrow. He'd pulled the blanket around Erisa, trying to keep her temperature up and her body stable, catching her every time the boat jolted over a particularly large wave.

I knew I had misjudged him in the past, assuming the worst based on nothing but my own prejudices, but I couldn't quite find the words yet to express my gratitude for him being there with me.

"You knew about the birds," I said, breaking the long, heavy silence between us. Now that the adrenaline was wearing off, my injuries were beginning to make themselves known. My body was battered and exhausted, but I couldn't focus on any of them until I knew that Erisa was safe. "You told us to watch out for them."

Cyfrin gave me a small, tired smile. "Call it intuition."

I could tell that he wanted me to drop the subject, and I didn't have the energy nor the curiosity needed to push the matter, so the silence persisted until we approached the harbor in Anzillu. Between us and the two crew members, we managed to gently transfer Erisa onto a door we'd ripped from its frame and carry her out of the cabin and across the gangway onto solid ground.

The harbor was teeming with Hudjefans, and Tasar himself rushed toward us as we disembarked. He was followed by Alekos and a short, aging man carrying a large leather satchel.

"The Rats informed me to bring a healer," Tasar said, nodding toward the unfamiliar man. "What happened? Where are the others?"

He looked around for a sign of Asila and her parents, who were, after all, the reason we'd taken the risk to venture into Katmu in the first place.

I shook my head. I couldn't speak right now—not even to marvel at the Rat's intuition to know that Erisa was in trouble— she needed medical attention immediately. We carried her from the harbor to Alekos' house, and although the distance was short, it still pained me that we were wasting precious time. But I couldn't help but agree that we needed to get her under cover, and into a place suitable for the doctor, Ivan, to work effectively.

It wasn't until she was placed in front of the roaring fire with Ivan's equipment sterilized and fresh bandages laid out that I could finally breathe a sigh of relief. I had already ordered the Rats to fetch another healer, but aside from that, there was nothing else for me to do but watch and wait.

"They were onto us from the start," I said, turning to Tasar. "I don't know how they knew that we were there, but as soon as we made it to Asila's room, they surrounded us. Erisa tried to bring her with us, but she refused, saying that she didn't want to leave Malah."

Tasar's brow furrowed. "So, it was a trap?"

"I'm assuming so. But Asila said that she'd been waiting for weeks, and there's no way that the Autarch could've known when we would be there."

"Did the Rats betray you?"

"The Rats would never," hissed Alekos from where he sat on the opposite side of the room. "Secrets are never whispered into wrong ears. We instinctively know what information needs to go where and we are bound to keep it safe."

"Even when money's involved?" Tasar questioned.

"Our entire operation hinges on the fact that we cannot be bought or swayed," Alekos snapped. "It would only take one person to question our integrity for our whole way of life to collapse. You also seem to forget that we Rats are paid handsomely for our services. I meant it when I said we are bound.

I couldn't tell you secrets that were not meant for you, even if you offered me all the gold in Irkalla. We answer only to our Master, which currently, is the Feline."

"And your loyalty just switches, does it?" I said, voicing one of my longstanding concerns. "If you were so loyal to the Fox, how can you then just transfer that over to the Feline so easily?"

Alekos narrowed his eyes, but I was too tired to care if I had offended him. "You have never chosen to be a Rat, so I cannot explain the connection we feel toward each other and toward whoever is in charge of us. I have been a Rat for almost five decades, back when we were operating under a different name, and I have seen several spymasters come and go within that time. Each one *chooses* their successor, whether consciously or not, and we feel that shift in energy. We were loyal to the Feline before the Fox had even died, his choice was made long before his death and his own loyalty to her was so fierce that it influenced us just the same."

An idea sparked to life inside my chest. I leaned forward eagerly. "And now? Do you feel anything like that now?"

He smiled and shook his head, immediately catching on to my train of thought. "No, our loyalty hasn't begun to wane yet; she will not die today."

My head started to spin, and the relief I felt almost made me sick. And I decided in that moment that I would never again question the loyalty of a Rat. It would be so tempting to interrogate every single one, asking if they had noticed a change in the intensity of the bond they shared with Erisa, any sign to indicate that that bond would be ending. I would drive myself mad, waiting and fearing for the day that one of them would say yes.

The next few hours whirled by in a flurry of exhaustion and disappointment. After gently wiping away the blood and grime from Erisa's skin, I cleaned myself up as best as I could, trying not to think about how we had failed to extract Asila from Katmu. Only once Ivan's work had been double checked by another healer, did I allow him to tend to my own injuries.

Apart from a few bruised ribs, a sprain in my left ankle and several cuts and scrapes, I was mostly unharmed. He had given Erisa a concoction to keep her asleep and watching him add wild eytelia root into the mixture had me fighting a smile. It seemed like several lifetimes ago that Erisa had attempted to poison me with it on that cold night in the Zuamsik mountains.

The trajectory of both our lives had changed that night, and I couldn't be more grateful to that pale, bitter powder for orchestrating that shift.

I watched her as she slept, wondering how different things would've turned out had I not unceremoniously rifled through her bag, looking for nefarious items. She would've succeeded in dosing me so thoroughly that I would've likely slept for days. I would have woken up alone—probably robbed of every valuable I had—fearing for my life and the future of my district.

But maybe she would still have taken the Orb of Nanaya from the pouch around my neck, and she would have still made the same choice to return. Maybe our paths were always destined to fuse, and we were always fated to end up together.

I liked to think so.

Silently, I picked up the corset Ivan had cut off Erisa's body and searched for the letter Asila had slipped into it. When I unfolded it, another letter, hidden within, fell to the floor.

I opened the outer one first.

Erisa,
I know that if you're reading this it's because you came to rescue me, and I didn't come with you. Please forgive me and know that I am so grateful that you would even try. Even though I'm told next to nothing, I still know how much of a risk it would have been for you.

The Autarch is desperate to capture you and as far as I can tell will do anything to achieve it. Malah is unable to tell me much, but he says that you are safe in Zingal. Oh Erisa, I know you must hate him, but he really does treat me the best he can under the circumstances.

The Autarch took me and my parents back in July and he used us—well, me—to control Malah. I think he knew then that you had betrayed him, and he wanted to have leverage over as many of the Lords as possible. He took me and threatened to hurt me if Malah didn't do what he asked.

He's also locked away the rest of Malah's family and I'm worried that if I leave, he'll threaten his little sister, Calia, or just kill Malah and force her to do his bidding, as she's next in line. I don't want to leave him to fight this alone, and I don't want to abandon my mother and father. I don't even know where they're being kept in the tower.

When you win—because you *will* win—please show mercy to Malah, he was just doing what he thought was right.
Your friend,
Asila

I unfolded the next letter.

Feline (and by extension Theo),

I cannot begin to express how sorry I am for the way things have turned out. I was a fool for not seeing how my open flirtations with Asila would have put a target on her back. Please know that putting her in danger was never my intention and I'm hoping that if you are reading this then you figured out the messages in my letters and managed to take Asila away from Katmu.

The Autarch took her and her family after I had already pledged my loyalty to you, and I know that my betrayal is unforgivable. I was forced to abandon you in your hour of need and that killed me. I have never known a deeper shame. I should have taken more precautions to ensure that my family, as well as Asila's, were hidden from the Autarch, and the responsibility for that error lies solely on me.

I know I will never be able to make up for the losses you suffered in Ocridell indirectly at my hand, but I'm hoping that when Asila gives you this letter, I can impart some knowledge that will help you eradicate this tyrant from Irkalla.

For months, the Autarch has been importing goods from the Cedar Forest in Atturynn. These shipments have been comprised mostly of chopped wood, which he has been using to build a fleet. The wood doesn't behave normally, and he's been having a difficult time getting it to cooperate. My men have been dragging their feet; they are as unhappy with this alliance as I am and were grateful when I told them to give you an easy, yet believable fight when you rescued your forces from my district.

Theo, I cannot put into words how appalled I am with your treatment during your imprisonment in my dungeons, and how appalled I am with myself for allowing it to happen. I hope that the little codes I added into those pamphlets offered you a brief moment of peace. I am watched every single moment of the day by the crows controlled by the Autarch; he can see through their eyes somehow. It has taken me almost two weeks to write this letter, so I apologize if it is disjointed.

The Autarch has promised to fight on behalf of the goddess Inanna, and in return, she is supplying him with another army to command. I'm sorry I cannot give you more information than this, as he doesn't trust me and refuses to tell me how many are coming or from where. But from the number of ships he wants built, I advise you to gather as many forces as you possibly can.

Neti and Dumuzid have sworn allegiance to Inanna, as far as I can tell, Pazuzu is still undeclared. I don't know when this letter will reach you, but as of early March, we are sorely unprepared for battle. Use this time wisely—while you still have it.

I hope that any of the information I've included is helpful to you both. Please know that you have my unwavering support, even if I am unable to exercise it.

Your loyal friend,
Malah
P.S. I was heartbroken to hear about the Fox, and I cannot comprehend the pain that that must have caused you. I haven't had the heart to tell Asila yet, but I'm glad that she will have you to mourn the loss with her when she finds out.

Chapter 22

Theo

It was three days before Erisa was able to be moved. Ivan kept her mostly unconscious, wanting to limit her movement to minimize the risk of internal bleeding. Tasar and Cyfrin dopped in and out, checking on her progress, and we all agreed that we would move her back to Zingal the next night.

Cyfrin and Tasar had already left on Moth and Fergus to procure a suitable carriage to take us from Ocridell to Zingal, but we would need to get her through the volcano first. While Alekos prepared a small, thin wagon to use, I ensured that his wife, Rania, was watching over Erisa before slipping out of the small house.

Without the trams, it was a long trek from the harbor to Ersetu, especially when most of the tunnels had collapsed, and new, unfamiliar passageways had formed in their stead. It took me several hours to navigate through the new twists and bends, but as the temperature rose, I knew I was getting closer to my goal. My sprained ankle radiated pain all the way up my leg, but I forced myself on, not knowing when I'd next get the chance to make the journey.

Eventually, the dark walkways widened, opening out into a colossal underground cavern, partially lit by enormous sconces, their flames licking up the infinite walls. As I stepped out into it, my breath caught. Where the Palace had collapsed, something truly formidable and monumental had taken its place. Made of lavastone and obsidian, the spires and turrets pierced the gloom of the cave, disappearing into the darkness before I could see the tops. The very stone itself seemed to be alive, each roughly cut slab held together with moving magma, glowing bright orange and illuminating the sheer size of the castle.

Something huge moved in the shadows, the ground shuddering with heavy footsteps. I squinted my eyes at what looked like black scales glinting in the poor light of the lava. I had assumed whatever was lurking out of sight was one of the gods and foolishly hadn't turned to run back the way I'd come.

Before I could do just that, a harsh, rumbling whisper seemed to fill the entire cave. "Stay where you are, human."

I froze, my blood turning cold with fear as I watched a large, scaled foot step into the light of a sconce, its shiny, black talons honed to lethal points. My heart stuttered as the rest of the body came into view.

Stories of dragons had always intrigued me, but in all the ones I had ever heard, never had they described something so truly monstrous as this. Even seeing them at a far distance, I had imagined them to be ten feet at most; impressive but still comprehendible. This creature was something else entirely.

Standing at least forty feet tall, its scaled body rippled with the faintest shimmer as it shifted, the impenetrable void of its black hide reflecting the barest hint of an iridescent sheen. Its wings were vast and membranous, stretching out endlessly like the blackened sails of a ghost ship, edged with sharp, ragged ridges.

My breathing sped, and the hot, faintly sulfurous scent filtered into my lungs. The beast's head was crowned with two twisting horns that curled like the jagged obsidian spires of the Palace behind it, ancient, long-forgotten markings etched into the surface. A streak of sharp spines ran down its long, serpentine neck, leading to the end of the thick, thrashing tail.

But it was the eyes—glowing a fiery reddish-orange, like molten lava—that commanded my attention. They illuminated the darkness, burning with an ancient, unforgiving intelligence that seemed to pierce right through me.

A low growl rumbled deep within its chest, vibrating the ground beneath my feet and clattering the small pebbles scattered across the stone floor.

The dragon opened its mouth, revealing a set of devastating teeth. "Why do you approach Ganzir?" it said, lashing out a long, forked tongue to taste the air.

I tried to speak, but the words stilled in my throat. "I … I came … I wish to speak to Ereshkigal."

"You seek an audience with my Anunngal." Its voice was deep enough to rattle my bones. "What have you done to deserve the honor?"

I had no idea what an anunngal was, or what an appropriate answer should be. "I have come to thank her, to declare my loyalty."

The dragon narrowed its large, glowing eyes. "You are the one who woke us; the human who disrupted our slumber."

"I was tricked. The Beldams—"

"The Ladies of Khar'ra have always chased their own desires. To trust them was to succumb to human ignorance and witlessness. You are a short-sighted species, so eager to trust, and now it seems you have squandered the ability to see when you are deceived. Even from beings as guileful as the Three Ladies."

I eyed the sharp teeth and lethal talons, knowing I was pushing my luck, but couldn't help asking, "Why would they want me to wake you? Why couldn't they do it themselves?"

The nightmarish creature studied me. "Long before your lifetime, three sisters made a deal with a demoness. They longed for everlasting life and the power to see what others could not. Jealous of the gifts they had seen another receive, they sought more than a human ever ought to wish for and came to Irkalla to ask my Anunngal to grant them the same. When, of course, she refused, the sisters turned to another. Lamaštu played on their pathetic, human insecurities, bestowing twisted promises upon them in exchange for a favor."

A heavy silence blanketed the cavern. "What was the favor?"

The monster growled at my impatience, causing the hair on the back of my neck to stand on end. "Do not mistake my tolerance for acceptance, human. You are still breathing only because I permit you to do so." A very hot, very dense cloud of steam chuffed from its nostrils, almost scorching my skin. "Lamaštu prolonged the lives of the sisters and gave them the Sight, allowing them to see into the past, present, and future. In return, they were bound to worship her above all others, to do everything in their power to wake her from her sleep.

"Once the deal was struck, Lamaštu plucked the sisters' eyes from their sockets, taking one sight in exchange for another. And while she did give them everlasting life, she did not mention that their beauty and vitality would leech away, withering their bodies into corpses kept alive only by spite, and the will of a more powerful being. For the last few centuries, the sisters have been waiting for you, Theodoraxion Lusilim, to fuse the relics and wake the Gods once more so that they can beg Lamaštu to restore them to their former selves."

I waited several moments before making a sound this time. "They couldn't do it themselves? And I don't understand, why me?"

The dragon shook its head, snaking its long neck and rippling the glossy scales. "No. The sisters could *See* the relics, but they were unable to touch them. Ereshkigal sees all that happens in Irkalla, human. You were always meant to wake us, one way or another."

Not daring to speak, I allowed the beast to examine me for several more tense, heart-stuttering moments. Eventually, its enormous head turned to the towering doors of Ganzir. "You will enter now."

Not wanting to argue or disobey, I hurried toward the grand entrance, not daring to turn back until I reached the threshold. But the dragon was gone; melted back into the shadows of the infinite cavern to join whatever other horrors lurked within.

I found the throne room with surprising ease. It was clear that the human Palace had been modelled directly from Ganzir, just on a much smaller scale, and even though the rooms and hallways now dwarfed me, the layout remained the same.

Erisa's absence was tangible and aggravating; I could almost hear the sarcastic little quips she'd be making about the strange décor or the choice in rug. I couldn't remember the last time I'd had to brave something like this alone. My friends had always been by my side since the beginning of my Lordship, and I felt a renewed sense of awe at how much Erisa had been forced to endure and overcome by herself.

Ereshkigal was seated on her throne at the end of the regal chamber when I entered. Nergal stood on her right, Namtar and Geshtinanna on her left. The long red carpet stretched between us for what seemed like miles, and each limping step I took across the soft fabric felt like it was taking me farther away from my goal.

After an age, I reached the foot of the dais and knelt on one knee with my head bowed, not wanting to be forced into paying my respect this time around.

"You may stand, Theodoraxion Lusilim," Ereshkigal said. Her voice was still as harsh and as powerful as before, setting my teeth on edge.

I rose to my feet and looked up at the goddess of death. "Did you answer my prayers? After Erisa was wounded, I prayed to you. Did you hear me and save her?"

"I heard you," she replied.

I hesitated, not knowing if she would answer the other part of my question. "I wanted to thank you … for allowing Erisa to live."

She assessed me coolly with her shining black eyes. "You ought to be more careful with your promises, human. Whether I fulfilled your wish or not, the outcome remained the same, and you are therefore bound by your word. You will fight for me, Lord Lusilim, to the death in my name, if need be, do not forget that."

My heartrate spiked, and my head spun as I tried to remember all of the frantic, desperate promises I'd made over those two awful hours in that boat. But even if I had known then that I was damning myself, I knew that I still wouldn't have changed a thing. And whether Ereshkigal had or hadn't saved Erisa, I was grateful all the same.

"Why did you choose me to be the one to wake you?" The question was out before I had a chance to stop it.

Ereshkigal's head tilted slightly. "An animal will not drink from a stagnating pool; change is necessary for life to flourish, and old cycles must be closed for new ones to open. I was forced to leave Irkalla in a state of turmoil, relying on the most ruthless of humans to govern my beloved lands in my stead. The Lording families worked well for a time and stabilized the realm just as I had hoped they would, but the time has come for something new. You were not chosen specifically, human, you were merely a catalyst for change; an individual with enough belief in what Irkalla *could* be to set the wheel into motion."

Hearing that the gods would have been woken eventually lifted a weight from my shoulders. If I hadn't fused the relics, someone else would have. I had no idea how these beings created or manipulated destiny, but I knew that I just had to accept that I was simply one small part of a much larger plan, one grander than I'd ever be able to comprehend.

"Rally your forces, human," Nergal commanded, resting a huge hand on the hilt of his scimitar. The metal blade flashed in the firelight. "Inanna is sparing no effort in gathering hers. It will not be an easy win, particularly as Dumuzid has declared for her, and Pazuzu is nowhere to be found."

"My brother is a fool," Geshtinanna said. Her voice was quieter than the others but still held an immense undercurrent of power. "And Pazuzu will have been occupied with hunting Lamaštu. I hear she has been wreaking havoc across the realm once more, and I for one am grateful that he is the one chasing her down, she is tiresomely tricksy. I hope he manages to dispose of her for good this time."

"There can be no right without wrong," Ereshkigal mused. "The quiet of the night makes the melody of the morning song that much sweeter." She focused on me once more. "You will leave now, Theodoraxion Lusilim. Every moment you spend here is one that you could be using to prepare. Inanna will not attack until after Dumuzid has enjoyed his Tammuz celebrations, but do not expect her to wait much longer after that, my sister never did have the virtue of patience."

My heart faltered. Tammuz. That was a matter of weeks away.

"But if you know the future of Irkalla, can't you just see what will happen?" I asked.

"I can glimpse into many possible futures," she answered, "each with an outcome so vastly different from the next. Every decision, no matter how small and seemingly inconsequential, has a rippling effect that has the power to affect the entire realm. An inconsequential choice that was made with good intentions can warp into something ugly when left to decay.

"The current Autarch once made a decision to take in an orphan girl and her friend instead of leaving them to fend for themselves. While his reasoning for helping her stemmed from his own selfish delusions, taking the boy too was a kindness, one that will inevitably lead to his downfall. Make your choices wisely, human; for even the smallest of them hold the power to influence the course of history." She looked to her left. "Go now. Namtar will escort you."

I bowed my head. "Thank you."

The sickly-looking god stepped forward, bending down to stretch a thin, pale hand toward me. I froze, not knowing what to expect. As soon as one of his fingers touched the top of my head, it felt like ice cold water had been thrown over me, trickling down my spine. I shivered violently, but when I blinked my eyes open, I found myself back in Anzillu, standing outside the red door of Alekos' house.

It was dark, and I had no idea how much time had passed since I'd left to venture into the volcano. Erisa was still unconscious by the fire when I stepped inside the parlor, but her clothes had been changed into ones suitable for the colder temperature outside. Ivan had left a small bag of medical supplies to see us through the journey to Zingal. Despite me offering him a small fortune, he declined to come with us, insisting that Erisa was over the worst of it, and would heal without issue if she rested properly.

The door swung open, and Alekos barged in, laden with armfuls of blankets and bags. "Where have you been? We should have left already!"

"I'm sorry," I said, lightening his load and following him back outside. "I had something to attend to."

A small wagon waited out the back, but it had clearly been modified from its original state to look more like an enclosed stretcher on four large wheels. Alekos arranged the blankets into the bed of the wagon, cushioning the hard wood in preparation for Erisa to travel comfortably. I hooked the bags onto each of the four outstretched poles, trying to distribute the weight as evenly as possible.

Transferring Erisa from the makeshift stretcher to the wagon was more of a challenge. We lifted her gently onto the blanketed bed, ensuring she was secure, before preparing to leave.

Alekos took the front of the wagon, using the poles to turn while I pushed from behind. It also allowed me to always keep an eye on Erisa, to check that she hadn't slipped or woken up. Ivan said she would wake during the journey, offering us more of the sedative to take with us, but I'd refused. I had no idea if the Autarch had sent anyone over from Katmu to finish us off and I wouldn't leave Erisa unconscious and unable to defend herself.

The journey was hard and strenuous, and my body was already exhausted. My ribs and ankle pained me more than I cared to admit, leaving me breathless after particularly rough areas of terrain. We decided to go through the outer slopes of the volcano. There were more people who could recognize us, but the pathways were flatter and more direct.

I was both horrified and relieved that we were not the only ones carrying an unmoving body out of the volcano on a stretcher. With the waking of the gods and then the rapid reconstruction of Ganzir since, tunnels throughout Ersetu had been collapsing in on themselves regularly, burying people beneath the rubble. My mouth filled with bile as we passed several lifeless bodies discarded in a large alcove, the youngest looking no older than five. I wanted to stop and help, but the risk of being recognized was too great.

The Feline had amassed quite the collection of enemies over her reign as Palace executioner, and since she and I had been seen together publicly many times, it would take very little effort to connect the dots about who I was currently transporting out of the volcano. I couldn't risk someone taking the opportunity to enact revenge while she was unable to defend herself. I readjusted the top blanket once more, letting the corner of it cover the exposed side of her face.

We traveled continuously until we saw daylight filtering in through the end of the tunnel up ahead, only pausing for a few moments at a time to take some refreshments. As soon as we made it out into the late afternoon sun of the exposed half of Ocridell, I breathed a sigh of relief. We were by no means safe, but I felt more comfortable out in the open air as opposed to the confines of the subterranean tunnels.

Erisa's eyelids fluttered at the change in light, and she groaned, but didn't fully wake.

"You took your time," Cyfrin called out as we approached

the inn we'd agreed to meet at. He helped us move her and the bags into the large carriage he and Tasar had procured for us from only the gods knew where. It was spacious enough for Erisa to lay on one of the benches with her legs tucked up.

Alekos made a swift exit before we departed, brushing off my words of gratitude and insisting that he owed the Fox and the Feline everything. Cyfrin and Tasar were to ride behind, wanting to come to Zingal anyway to discuss the next steps of our operation, and I had to admit that I was glad for the extra support. I was exhausted and fully intended on sleeping for the next few hours, after cleaning the burst blisters on my hands from pushing the wagon.

Erisa roused when I readjusted the cushion under her head. "Theo," she whispered, her voice hoarse from misuse.

"Welcome back, Sunflower," I said, sitting on the floor of the carriage to rest my face on the bench next to hers.

Her eyes locked onto mine. "Where are we?"

"We're going back home," I murmured, pressing my forehead against hers. "But you're safe, try and get some more rest."

But she was already drifting back to sleep, the drooping of her eyelids beckoning mine to join them in their descent.

Chapter 23

Erisa

Replication of sealed correspondence

Lord Wranmaris,

I never did take the time to congratulate you on your successful acquisition of Anzillu Harbor. Henri Elkas is still not over the snub, poor fellow, his pride took quite a hit with that one. I'd enjoy the interdistrict drama much more, however, if it didn't have a knock-on effect on my own.

Of course, I'm aware of the rather tenuous relationship you and Lord Lusilim have with the rest of us Lords, which is understandable. But as my mother always said, "Closed mouths don't get fed, but open ones might catch a crumb." So, I'm requesting that you allow some smaller boats from my district to make port at the harbor to purchase goods we are sorely in need of. It would also be beneficial to allow correspondence to flow more freely between us and the mainland, it's been rather hit and miss, and rerouting mail through Tarprusa is incredibly tedious.

My warmest regards,
Malah Jirata, Lord of Katmu

21 April
Copy Made 24 April

❖ ❖ ❖

Nothing aggravated me more than being still.

For weeks I had done nothing but lay in bed and trawl through boring reports and correspondence. I was sick of it. I longed to get up and train; to prepare myself for the war that was looming on the horizon. But I knew it was a foolish idea.

I had been healing slowly but surely, and I had to remind myself daily how lucky I was that my injury wasn't much worse. An inch or two over, and the arrow could've pierced an internal organ, or nicked my spine. It was a miracle that I was still alive, and I knew that Theo was entirely responsible for saving me.

He had stayed by my side as much as the time restraints of planning a war would allow. Despite my injuries, I hadn't missed a single meeting regarding the movements of the armies. Not trusting Theo to recount every minute detail, I'd hobbled downstairs every time one was called, providing what knowledge I had gained from the Rats.

It was still unclear where Inanna had sourced the Autarch's army from, but there was no denying that it would be a problem. Dozens of ships were sighted leaving Katmu every few days, returning with what was no doubt hordes of soldiers. We had attempted several attacks on the empty ships leaving the Isles, from setting up netting traps to sending large boats filled with explosives into the center of the fleet. Our success had been discouraging to say the least; whatever the Autarch had had these ships crafted from had made them damn near untouchable.

Occasionally, Pazuzu was seen disrupting the fleet, beating

his mighty wings to blow the vessels off course. The rumors gave me hope that he might come to aid us when the time came.

"You should be resting," Theo chided, coming up behind me and pressing several light kisses to the side of my neck.

I threw the next dagger, hitting the target perfectly. "You smell disgusting."

"I haven't seen you in three days and this is how you greet me?" He chuckled, his breath tickling the shell of my ear. "I guess I'll just leave you to it then."

I reached behind me to sink my nails into his forearm, keeping him pinned in place behind me while I threw my remaining blades in quick succession. I didn't need to look back to know what smug expression he would have plastered on his face, but I wanted to see it anyway. I turned and wrapped my arms around him, burying my face into his chest.

Even though he did smell truly revolting—especially under the heat of the midday sun—I had missed him over the last few days and was happy that he was back again.

Theo dropped to one knee in front of me, raising the hem of my shirt to take a look at my wound, which was now a deceivingly small pink scar. From the outside, it looked like it was almost healed, but internally, it was still giving me hell. When it wasn't numb or sending tingling, shooting pains across my abdomen, it *hurt*; a bland soreness that just wouldn't go away. I had sustained plenty of injuries in the past, and none of them had plagued me like this one.

Seemingly satisfied with his inspection, Theo kissed the raised, pink mark and stood back up, taking my face in his hands.

"I missed you."

I tried not to smile and failed miserably. "How was everything at the barracks?"

He dropped his hands and led us to a small bench beneath the shade of a large tree. I barely managed to suppress my wince as I lowered myself onto his lap.

"Suenna's got them running drills twenty-four hours of the day by the looks of it," he said, clearly beaming with pride for his friend. "She's got that entire place running seamlessly and I'm almost certain that all of the other generals are scared shitless of her. The soldiers are a far cry from the scrawny looking Hudjefans that arrived in Zingal a year ago. I'm very pleased with their progress."

"And the weapons production?"

"Still running at capacity. Tolani Seko has cleared the metal scraps from both Zingal and Ocridell, and has already moved it all onto his land and begun processing it."

I hesitated, not wanting to spoil the moment. "Do you think we'll be ready in time?"

His green eyes met mine, the color of springtime. "I don't think we'll ever be ready. All we can do is keep up the preparations and try to boost morale as much as possible."

I knew that he was referring to the Tammuz celebrations that would be happening the following week. Everyone in Zingal was practically giddy with anticipation for their favorite holiday, and even though I'd only experienced it once, I had to admit that I was excited too.

"You don't think it's risky?" I asked. "The Autarch will know that our defenses will be lessened for the week; it would be the perfect time for him to attack."

Theo frowned, creating a line between his brows. "Ereshkigal said that the fighting would begin after Tammuz. Do you think I've made a mistake banking on that too much?"

I reached up to smooth that line away, before trailing my fingers through his hair. He was waiting for my answer, desperate for a second opinion. Not from a lack in confidence, but from the deep-rooted desire to do right by his people. Every decision he made had a direct impact on the lives of thousands of individuals, and not for the first time, I felt both grateful and ashamed that I had abandoned my own responsibilities. I wasn't suited for those kinds of obligations like he was; I was selfish and only able to concentrate my compassion toward my small handful of loved ones.

"No," I said, resting my cheek against his forehead, "I don't think you made a mistake. Having something to celebrate before the fighting begins will renew their spirits, as well as yours. We just have to hope that Ereshkigal knows what she's doing."

Besides the general ongoing disruptions throughout the realm, we hadn't heard anything from the gods. Whatever they were planning, they had left us in the dark. Now that the shock of their return had finally ebbed, no one was certain how they ought to react to the deities walking among us again. The long-forgotten temples had become populated once more, filled with people prostrating themselves before the statues and leaving gifts at the alters. Fortunately, gifts of a sacrificial nature had yet to appear, but I had a feeling that as soon as the fighting truly began, people would turn desperate.

Aside from the accidental deaths of the humans being unfortunately in the wrong place at the wrong time, the general population had embraced the new changes the gods had brought. Each district had flourished with new life since their true rulers had returned, bringing back a vibrancy and vitality that had never before been experienced in Irkalla—at least not in this generation.

Though few people had actually seen her up close, Lamaštu had quickly become a name to fear among the people of Irkalla. Everywhere she was rumored to go, tragedy often followed; pregnancies failed, crops died, and water supplies turned toxic. She would lure groups of hunters into dark corners of the realm, and the few that returned often came back with some form of ailment or disease, barely able to tell the tale. She was often rumored to be sailing a boat across the waters of the Silent Canyons, causing such a stir that people had begun avoiding the area altogether.

Families with young children and expectant mothers had taken to carving small amulets of Pazuzu and hanging them over their thresholds, in hopes of keeping Lamaštu from knocking at their doors. I was skeptical about them, to say the least, especially knowing of Pazuzu's unpredictable nature, but it was already a general consensus that he was the one to stand in between them and the demoness.

"Anything from Silas?" Theo's voice had gradually lost hope in the answer with every time he had asked me that question.

I shook my head, giving his shoulder a comforting squeeze. Trying to make use of my sedentary hours, I had combed through letters day in, day out, hoping to find something that would give any indication of Silas' whereabouts. But he was either dead—which was unlikely—or he knew exactly how to avoid my methods of detection.

Of all the Rats that I had sent to his cabin in the Gištir jungle, only a handful of them had even managed to find the place, and they had all claimed that it was completely empty.

"The group I sent to Khar'ra came back this morning," I said, leaning back so that I could see his face. "They said that the bridge to cross the moat had disappeared, but that they could hear chanting and wailing coming from the temple across the water. One of them tried to wade through but was unable to physically put his foot into it."

"And the rest of Khar'ra?" he pressed.

I frowned. "Eerie, apparently. Even the ones who had been there before said that it made their skin crawl and that the people felt like they were desperate for something. They weren't exactly fun when we were there, but at least you could hold a conversation with one. But now, all they're doing is rushing around aimlessly, flailing desperately like drowning spiders."

"I didn't expect much from the Beldams," Theo admitted, shaking his head. "They only declared loyalty to me to use us to fuse the shield. I should've seen it coming, should've known that it seemed too easy."

"I'm not sure which 'easy' part you're referring to, but I won't sit and listen to you mope about what happened." I gave him a sharp look. "You said yourself that if it hadn't been you, it would've been someone else to wake the gods, that Ereshkigal had ensured it would be so. There's no point blaming yourself. Let's just be grateful that we have the chance to turn this shitshow around into something positive for the realm. If we win, there's an opportunity to reform the way Irkalla is run, and I can think of no one better to lead us through that transition."

And before he had the chance to argue, I kissed him.

❖ ❖ ❖

The atmosphere of Zingal on the first morning of Tammuz was palpable. Everyone had been so on edge in the lead up and during the preparations that when the day finally came, and there were no sightings of war ships on the horizon, it was as if the entire district breathed a sigh of relief. We could relax, if only for a few hours.

As was usual for the Lusilim estate, a huge celebration had been set up across the grounds, hosting so many people, food stalls, musicians, and entertainers that it made my memory of last year's festivities seem like a traveling circus act.

As soon as dawn had broken on the first morning of May, the revelry had begun, with the sound of trumpets and drums rousing me from my sleep in the early hours. Even Theo couldn't explain why the energy was so charged this year, but as soon as I stepped outside, I found the atmosphere almost intoxicating.

By midday, I was breathless and exhilarated, being whirled around into yet another dance. I had barely even noticed my injury at all, allowing myself to be swept away by the merriment of the day.

It wasn't until I paused for refreshment and felt the ground trembling beneath my feet that I paused to stop and question why everyone was in such high spirits. As the shaking increased, so did the volume of the music and the speed of the dancing. I could feel myself getting swept up in it once more, but a flash of movement in the distance caught my eye and halted me in my tracks.

Leaping and dancing over the brow of the hill at the far end of the estate was Dumuzid, lute in hand and a jubilant expression on his face. The tables shook and cups toppled to the floor as he bounded toward the main bustle of the estate, but as I looked around, no one seemed to be frightened, or even concerned. Each twang he made on the strings just seemed to pull the humans around him deeper into their merriment, and I couldn't help but fall prey to it myself, thrilled with his attendance rather than wary as I knew I should have been.

I found Theo in the crowd, and he beamed at me, spinning me around before dipping me low enough that my head spun on the way back up. I hadn't drunk much yet, but Dumuzid's presence was as intoxicating as several pitchers of wine, and I could practically see how he riled the exultation of the crowd into a joyous frenzy with his dancing and lute playing. For a brief second, I wondered whether this was how it felt when I sang, to have your emotions completely in the hands of another but being too thrilled by the sensation to care.

Theo spun us around the clearing—missing Dumuzid's huge feet by mere inches at times—keeping in rhythm with the flutes and drums around the perimeter. My pale yellow dress was plastered to my skin with sweat and my braid was coming loose from its binding, but I felt more alive than I ever had before. Ezra and Suenna were a blur, twisting so furiously between the other couples that it made me dizzy to try and keep track of them. I watched Nook kneel to press a kiss to Vashti's swollen belly, before grasping Didi by the elbow and towing her into the center of the excitement, making her squeal in delight.

Unable to stop myself, I began to sing to the tune, so wrapped up in my own elation and wanting to excite it into the others around me. The result was enthralling; Nook whooped, and Theo had us moving so fast that my feet barely touched the floor. I played each thread of their emotions like my own instrument, plucking and strumming until they were drunk on the feeling.

I reached for an unfamiliar golden thread of pure joy that led straight to Dumuzid, but when I tried to manipulate it, whatever power allowed me to influence those of the humans simply glanced off.

Dumuzid shook his golden hair out of his eyes and grinned down at me. "I wish you could have that same influence on me, Siren! You rally them into such spirits!" He beamed at the revelers celebrating around him. "Oh, how I've missed this!"

Caught in the bright light of the sun, he appeared to be almost glowing from within, and every single person that danced within twenty feet of him seemed to take in some of that light, radiating it back out in smiles and laughter.

The god of agriculture left the Lusilim estate in the early evening, traveling toward the center of the city to no doubt enjoy the festivities hosted there. The farther he went, the more I felt the exhaustion beginning to set into my limbs and the pain slowly returning to the wound in my side.

By nightfall, I was dead on my feet, and from the looks of

everyone else, I could tell that they weren't far behind.

❖ ❖ ❖

Normality somewhat returned for the rest of the week, but the differences from before Tammuz were hard to ignore. Whatever Dumuzid's presence had done during the festivities had transformed the district. Crops had flourished, the fish caught along the coast had doubled in size, and the weather had been so pleasant that I could practically taste summer approaching in the air.

The end of week celebrations were just as riotous as the first, but the youthful god did not make an appearance this time, and I was more than a little relieved. Whatever influence he had had on Zingal and its people seemed too good to be true; the flu that had been sweeping through the battalions of soldiers had ceased, and even the weariest of them had perked back to life.

Despite my overexertion, my wound had improved dramatically, and every morning I expected whatever magic Dumuzid had woven throughout the district to wear off and for the puncture to reopen worse than before. My muscles were still weak, but since Tammuz, the pain had lessened more each day, to the point where I could mostly return to normal.

Tasar was now a permanent fixture at the Lusilim estate, and he and Theo would talk for hours on end about battle strategy and army reserves. Cyfrin flitted between here and the Zuamsik mountains, where he and Suenna oversaw the main bulk of the training. They liaised with Tolani and Josefine, ensuring that every single soldier was fed, clothed, and armed.

Nook, Ezra, and Theo were playing cards in the parlor when I approached the door, rat cage in hand. Aghna's children had somehow managed to domesticate a couple of them and they would take them out to play and teach them tricks. I would have been concerned, had Verrill and I not had much more dangerous hobbies at their age.

I leant against the doorframe, watching the three friends for a few moments. It was so rare for them to find a moment to laugh and be themselves again. So much had happened in the past year, and I was glad that they could find pockets of time to spend with each other. It was just a shame that Suenna was too often at the barracks instead of at the estate with them.

Nook was leaning in close to the others. "—and so I told him, 'That's not a satchel, that's a cry for help.'"

Theo laughed, and the grin on his face widened when he saw me at the door. Then, it fell off his face completely when he noticed the rats.

He subtly tried to move his chair back as I came into the room. "Do I have to?"

"Yes," I said, not leaving any room for arguments. He knew he needed to overcome this fear, to not let the Autarch win.

The brief thought of Csintalan had my blood boiling for a split second before I quelled my rising anger. There would be a time, likely in the near future, when our paths would cross again. And when that time came, I would let that anger fuel me into claiming every last drop of vengeance I was owed.

"Come on," I said to Theo, "you've been doing so well. Farzin feeds them by hand now. Are you going to be outdone by a six-year-old?"

"I'm eight!" came a disgruntled cry from the adjoining room.

Theo eyed the rodents and grimaced. "I'm secure enough in myself to not be swayed by that." He glanced at me, and I frowned. "All right, bring them over here."

I placed the cage on the table in front of him and held out a carrot to him. He took it warily and slid it through the slats of the crate, holding the other end and keeping his fingers as far away as possible. I knew the carrot would be tough for him; it would be very easy to imagine it being a finger, and I knew from bandaging his hands myself that he had experienced that horror directly.

Theo was tense, but after Nook and Ezra continued the conversation they had been having, he began to relax. I couldn't deny that I was proud of him. He'd come so far in such a short time, and after what he had endured in those dungeons, I was surprised he even tolerated being in the same room as a rat. But I would persevere with him, make him overcome this and beat the Autarch. I had enough stubbornness for the both of us.

"Only a few months to go now," Ezra said, beaming at Nook.

A gleam sparked in Nook's eyes, and he nodded. "Vashti thinks it's a boy from the way she's carrying, but I'm sure it's a girl. I've been trying to convince her that the name Ettie—"

A snapping sound split the air, like the crack of a whip, silencing Nook immediately. I knew that sound, we all did.

Silas had arrived.

Chapter 24

Theo

I pushed away from the table, already on edge from being forced to feed those damned rats. I knew it was beneficial to overcome this weakness, but I hated it; hated every reminder of the time I'd spent in that dungeon.

Erisa was the first one out of the room, racing upstairs to the source of the sound. When I made it to the top of the landing, she was standing outside Karasi's open door, gripping Silas roughly by the hair and yanking his head back to hold a blade to his exposed throat.

"Where the hell have you been?" she hissed.

Immediately, a lashing of hot—and completely irrational—jealousy washed over me before I banished it from my mind.

"Take your hands off me before I remove them from your wrists," Silas snarled, reaching up to follow through with his threat. She seemed to come to her senses and release him before he managed to make contact.

Karasi snorted and gave Erisa a derisive look as she passed

by them both. "Pity, she ought to know how it feels."

She was dressed in her traveling cloak and was hastily shoving clothes and other essentials into a bag, heading for the stairs.

"Where are you going?" I asked, catching her elbow to stop her.

She glanced at Silas. "I'm going to Atturynn, but I need to leave *now*." And she pulled away and hurried off down the stairs.

Bewildered, I turned to Silas. "What's going on?"

He took a step away from Erisa, watching her like she was a coiled snake ready to strike, before turning to address me. "Aessurus' entire fleet have just left their shores. I came to advise Karasi that if she intended on asking Prince Sharru to come to our aid, now would be the time."

"Oh wonderful," Erisa's tone was laced with disdain, "Torin is coming to the rescue. Excuse me while I jump for joy."

"You'll be grateful if he does agree, Feline," Silas warned. "If we don't have northern support, we'll be outnumbered four to one."

Erisa narrowed her eyes. "I like those odds better than pinning our hopes onto that rabid dog! He's completely—"

"Stop!" I shouted, unable to sort through all of this information fast enough. "What do you mean, their entire fleet has left? Is Aessurus where the Autarch is getting his army?"

We had already considered this as the most likely scenario. It was between Tarprusa and Aessurus, and the Rats had reported nothing from our neighbor. But we'd expected there to be signs first, or some sort of clarification that we hadn't been jumping to

THE ECHO OF HIS FURY

conclusions. We knew very little about the Aessuri fighting style, or how their army operated.

"It would appear so," Silas answered. "And not only that, but in amongst Aessurus' white, I saw a collection of black sails … from Nicaieri." He said the last part in a tone so grave, it made my skin prickle.

"I didn't know they even had soldiers," Nook said from the stairwell.

Silas weighed his words carefully. "They're not exactly soldiers; they aren't trained in combat, they specialize in something … different. Nicaieri tends to keep to itself. It's a small realm with no real value or wealth and the conditions there are … disturbing, to say the least. But centuries ago, something unsettling began to emerge from the gloom and despair there.

"They call them Intunecas and while I've never seen them in action before, I've heard that they're deadly. It is the only gift that people native to Nicaieri will possess, but it allows them to ensnare the senses of someone so absolutely that the individual will temporarily forget everything they've ever known, even their own name."

A chill ran through me at the thought of yet another thing we needed to prepare to face. But another thought occurred to me. "The other realms have these," I gestured to Erisa, "rare *gifts* too?"

He didn't need me to clarify that I was referring to the way Erisa could manipulate your mind and emotion simply by using her voice.

Silas snorted. "Of course, they're just a lot more discreet about them. In fact, I'd wager that Irkalla has a rather small population of gifted humans compared to the other realms. They're rare here, but that's not the case for the others."

Perfect, I thought, *I'll just add that to the list of things to stress about.*

"You said you saw the boats," Erisa said. It was almost a question, but with an underlying accusatory tone.

"I was in the north," Silas replied, as though that was enough of an explanation. "And I need to go back, this was not meant to be a long visit."

"Couldn't you just take Karasi with you then?" Ezra said skeptically. "Why did you send her off alone if you're just going to be returning there now?"

"She wouldn't survive the journey," Silas replied. And within a heartbeat, he was gone.

❖ ❖ ❖

The next few days blurred into each other, with the news of Aessurus' forces coming to our shores causing a flurry of panic and rapid preparations. The heightened stress levels and general unease felt throughout Zingal rippled outward, affecting the rest of the realm, and within the week, even those who had refused to leave their homes within Ersetu had heard that the approaching war was finally coming.

Silas had not returned since imparting the news that the fleet had set sail from the northern kingdom, so we had little indication of how much time we had until they reached the shores of Irkalla. And even then, we were unable to tell if they would go straight for the attack of if they would regroup with the rest of their forces in

Katmu.

"We ought to go through the back up plans once more," Erisa voiced during one of our late-night meetings. "Silas said that without the aid of Atturynn, we'll be outnumbered four to one, so at least we have a rough idea of numbers now."

"We should still aim to meet them head on here in Zingal," I said, "we know the land and we have already evacuated everyone from the eastern side of the district and repurposed those buildings for the army."

Nook nodded. "Luring them to Zingal would be the best-case scenario. Let them tire themselves out before they get to us," he threw several punches at an imaginary opponent, "then we'll deliver the final blow."

"But we should still adjust our plans to suit the lands of the other districts as well," Erisa said, ignoring Nook's foolishness. "I think we should also discuss the possibility of it happening in the Wilds too, especially if the Beldams decide to cause trouble."

Everyone agreed and we set to work adjusting our plans and battle formations to suit the terrain of each district, from the tunneled network of Hudjefa to the isolated stretch of land in Kusig. The Silent Canyons in Saqummatu were now not so much of a concern as they were still flooded with water, courtesy of Lamaštu, but the Gištir Jungle and all of its horrifying creatures and strange atmospheres would pose more of a problem.

Once we had all agreed on the various strategies, I set to work on organizing who would be going where. I relied heavily on the advice of my counsel, letting their superior knowledge and experience guide me in the right direction. So much was hinging on this critical stage, and if I didn't get this right now, it would mean the loss of thousands of lives.

Every spare second I had, I was out in the training yard, going through rigorous drills, or joining in on the regimented practice routines of the soldiers. It was tough, grueling work, but I needed my skills to be as sharp as everyone else's, otherwise I would just be a liability.

Erisa was still regaining her strength, working on her sword skills day in, day out, sparring with the soldiers and slashing down targets from Fergus' back. Though she would brush it off every time I mentioned it, I could see that her injury would still occasionally cause her issues. I didn't voice my concern that she was pushing herself too hard; she was perfectly capable of making her own decisions and from experience, I knew not to question them. But I couldn't help but worry that she would cause more damage by trying to force her body past its new limits.

From previous interactions with the northern kingdoms, we knew that Aessurus kept its fleet hidden somewhere along its northern coastline, concealing its location while still allowing space to maneuver in the event of an unexpected attack. Based on the currents and weather, we estimated that it should take between two and three weeks for them to get to Irkalla, depending on the route they were taking. Erisa had sent Rats along Irkalla's coastlines with the instruction to report back whenever they caught sight of the first ships.

For sixteen long days, we heard nothing.

Then, on the seventeenth morning, Farzin rushed into the parlor, his chest heaving from running and passed Erisa a letter.

She read it in silence before looking directly at me. "They've been seen along the coast of Khar'ra, they must have gone around the top of Atturynn. This says they're about a day away from us."

Even though I knew it was coming, I could still feel my chest tighten and my heart begin to race. Fear lashed through my bloodstream and prickled across my skin, causing my hair to stand on end.

"Send out word to the others," I said, picking up some paper from the desk to scribble a message to go to Tasar's men at Anzillu Harbor.

Erisa was already gone by the time I was finished, and I gave the message to Farzin, who skipped off eagerly to pass it along.

Another fear struck me right in the chest as I watched him charge from the room. Like everyone else, I had grown incredibly fond of the wild, unruly children Erisa had brought to the estate. The orphans had breathed life into the empty rooms and had filled the silence with shouts and giggles. It had felt more like a home in the last few months than it had since I was little.

Aghna agreed to keep them away from the fighting, much to the children's dismay. They wanted to be involved, particularly Farzin, but I refused to even entertain the idea of them passing notes between the ranks. It was too risky, and if I thought anywhere else in the realm would be safer, I would've sent them away.

We had spread the word throughout the rest of the districts that civilians who did not want to engage in the fighting should pack up their essential belongings and be ready to evacuate at a moment's notice, but as we didn't know which angle the Autarch would attack from, we couldn't tell them where to go. Many had already left, traveling to Saqummatu where they could be in the center of the realm and be able to flee in any direction.

Tasar was the first to appear from my summoning. "This is it then," he said, watching me pace across the length of my office. When I didn't answer, he pressed on. "We've done all we can to prepare, Theo, and made the best of a bad situation. All we can do now is just adapt to the challenges as they begin to unfold."

I wanted to tell him that it was all very well and good in theory, but in reality, everything was so much more complicated than that. I knew that the best course of action would be to wait like we planned and let the Autarch make the first move, but now I knew that the enemy was approaching our shores, the thought of doing nothing made my skin crawl.

I needed to be doing something; to be taking some sort of action.

Erisa was the last to join the meeting. "I've instructed the Rats to stay on the coast, to monitor the progression of the fleet. They're going to be relaying information as it arises, although there will be a delay of around a day when the news gets to us, so I imagine that Aessurus will already be in Irkalla as we speak. Though from what I've been told already, Silas' estimation on their numbers doesn't seem to be far off."

The silence that blanketed the room was full of unspoken unease. Everyone felt the wave of trepidation that washed over us with those words. The enemy was already here, and we had no idea when they would strike, if they hadn't already.

"Any news from Karasi?" Tasar asked, breaking the heavy

hush of the office.

I glanced to Erisa, who shook her head.

The small thread of hope in my chest snapped and I sighed, addressing everyone. "We proceed with our plans assuming that we will not have the support of Atturynn. Even though it would've been a tremendous help, we didn't bank on having their forces with us, so this doesn't change anything. Now, we just have to wait for an update on where their fleet drop anchor."

❖ ❖ ❖

Aessurus did not attack. After a day and a half of fretting and pacing, a Rat arrived at the Lusilim estate informing us that the warships had sailed straight past the mainland to Katmu, dropping anchor within the Shrouded Isles.

Four tenuous weeks of waiting and watching passed without so much as a whisper from them. Whether they were simply establishing themselves or using their inaction as a tactic to derail our plans, no one knew, but it kept everyone on edge.

We had made the most of all the borrowed time we were granted, running through drills and keeping up a constant routine of training. Erisa had been more absent than not, running all over the realm gathering information from her network of Rats. Despite hating being apart from her, the intel that she gathered was invaluable. She had sent numerous reports back to Zingal describing the movements of the Autarch's expanded forces across the islands and where he was keeping the Aessuri soldiers.

I was sitting at the small table in my chambers, studying a map of Irkalla and using some loose papers to fan the hot afternoon air from my face when Erisa returned. Creeping in through the window behind me, I was met with her faint jasmine scent before I felt her arms slip around my middle.

Gods forbid she would enter the house like a normal person instead of climbing up the drainpipe.

I straightened, grasping her wrists and hugging her closer to me for a second before turning to face her. She looked exhausted and I resisted the urge to ask if she had any news to deliver.

I leant forward and pressed soft kisses to her cheeks and forehead. "How are you, Sunflower?"

"Tired." She sighed, leaning into me for a second before rummaging around in the small bag at her hip. "I've got something to show you, though."

I shook my head, taking her hands in mine and pressing each knuckle to my lips. "I don't care about that right now; you need to rest."

"But it could be important," she protested, "Malah sent—"

"Shh," I slid my hands down her body, resting them at her waist, "let me take care of you."

Gently lifting her, I moved us to the bathing chamber where I sat her down on the edge of the large tub and began unlacing her boots. The rush of running water filled the room, but she didn't make a sound as I slowly undressed her and lowered her into the hot water. I trusted her judgement enough to know that if the news she had was truly important, she wouldn't have allowed me to distract her from it.

I stripped out of my own clothes, and submerged myself behind her, pulling her between my legs so she could rest against my chest. She closed her eyes and sighed in contentment as I lathered the soap into her hair. I massaged the suds over her scalp and worked through the knots and tension in her muscles until she was boneless in my arms.

When I made a move to stand, she pressed against me, pinning me back down and turning her face to mine. I kissed her, unable to resist the temptation of her mouth smiling lazily up at me. I could see her heart beating, causing the deep bronze skin of her chest to rise and fall ever so slightly.

"You're so beautiful," I whispered, once again overcome with the depth of my love and affection for her. While I was able to go about my normal duties just fine in her absence, having her safely back at home comforted me in a way I couldn't explain even to myself.

When the water started to cool, I wrapped a towel around Erisa and led her into the bedroom, picking up her discarded bag on the way.

"It's the brown letter," she said, settling herself beside me on the soft sheets of the bed and closing her eyes.

Retrieving the note, I opened it, absentmindedly playing with the damp strands of her hair that splayed across my chest.

Replication of sealed correspondence

Tasar,

Since my last letter was ignored, I must assume that you have decided not to permit us use of Anzillu *Harbor for* the trading *of* essentials. I *am* not entirely surprised, *but* I have to admit that I am somewhat disappointed.

I *am* not requesting this *for* my soldiers, but *for my* citizens. They have already been running out of some essential items that cannot be imported easily from any other kingdom, and they are suffering for it.

I ask again that you allow the harbor to reopen for civilian trading only.

Regards,
Malah Jirata, Lord of Katmu

1 July
Copy made 3 July

The hidden letters were barely different from Malah's usual handwriting, and I had to reread the letter a couple of times before I caught them all. My heart sank when I confirmed the message: Watch from behind. More from the back. Stay alert.

I spent the next half an hour poring over the words, desperate to find an explanation somewhere in the slanted scribbles.

"They must have reserves somewhere," I said to Erisa when she finally woke. "Do you think they're hiding the rest of their fleet around the back of the Isles, so there's no chance of us seeing them, even with the Rats?"

"I'm not sure," she admitted. "The Autarch has to know that we're getting intel from the Rats at the Citadel, but if he suspects Malah in any way, I doubt he'd even trust him with all of the information. And it could all be a ruse anyway." She placed the letter back down. "I mean, the entire thing is nonsense, because there are boats constantly sailing between Katmu and Anzillu Harbor, that's how I'm able to get—" A knock at the door made her pause, and she shook her head when I went to stand. "It's for me."

How she knew that it was a Rat at the door, I had no idea, but when she returned to my side, her face was drawn and severe.

"Cyfrin has sent word from Ocridell."

Chapter 25

Erisa

Feline,
The Autarch is on the move.
They're coming.
C W

5 July

❖ ❖ ❖

While the news of the impending attack had sent a fresh flurry of panic throughout the district, our regimented drills and practices for the last month had prepared us for this exact moment. We would do nothing, baiting the Autarch to cross the realm to meet our army in the outer stretches of Zingal.

The only thing that had changed was sending out the regiment to evacuate the civilians from the coast. As the fleet crossed the channel and surrounded the edge of Kusig, we had time to move people from Ocridell into the camps we'd set up just north of the Silent Canyons in Saqummatu, where they would remain behind the fighting.

We assumed that as Aran Seirsun had sworn fealty to the Autarch, the people of Kusig would be left unharmed by the army traipsing through their district. We had welcomed the few that had managed to escape the golden city in the previous weeks, but there was little we could do to help the remaining people locked behind the gilded gates.

Our war camps had been erected in eastern Zingal, stretching up and around the district, all the way into the Zuamsik mountains, where our reserves had been kept. A small number had remained behind at the barracks to set up an overflow medical area that would be protected by the mountains from the rear. The more severely injured would be taken there to be treated out of the chaos of the fighting. Several thousand non-fighting citizens had come to help in the effort of keeping the camps maintained and the soldiers fed.

I had a constant communication channel with my Rats around the realm, and the flurry of scribbled notes and copied reports had long since become overwhelming. Three days after I had received Cyfrin's letter announcing the beginning of the attack, I had already ascertained that not only were we outnumbered, but that the Autarch hadn't even bothered bringing the full fleet to fight us. A few Rats who had managed to report from Tarprusa had sent word of another group of ships anchored on the horizon. We couldn't be sure that they were from Aessurus, but we had to assume the worst.

Despite Nook begging her to stay behind, Vashti had refused, insisting that most of the medics had been called to the frontlines and that she was going to treat the wounded until she was unable to do so.

"Thanks," she puffed when I bent down to pick up the bag of rolled bandages she'd dropped. "If you could put them over by the others, that would be great."

"Do you not think it would be better for you to go to the barracks?" I asked, finding it impossible not to notice every wince she made as she waddled on her swollen feet.

She cradled her enormous belly, smoothing the stretched fabric of her dress over her bump. "No, I want Nook to be there for the birth, I don't want to do it alone. And I'm not due for another few weeks, there's still plenty that I can do to help out here. Once he's born, I'll go to the barracks, but for now, I'm staying."

"Still think it's a boy?"

She grinned at me. "Oh yeah, I'll prove Nook wrong. Have you seen the size of me? There's a strapping young lad tucked away in here. I'm certain of it."

I was supposed to be further into the center of the camp, overseeing the distribution of reserve essentials across the divisions, but found that I couldn't leave Vashti alone to set up her medical tent by herself. Nook, Ezra, and Suenna were busy organizing their own divisions of soldiers and I didn't want to take anyone else away from their duties.

"I'll be right back," I said to her, and slipped out of the tent to head in the direction of the food preparation area.

As soon as the smell of roasting meat filled my lungs, several small children surrounded me, led by Farzin. Theo had tried to order them away, but Aghna couldn't control them all. I spotted the elderly woman filling up the bowls for each person in the long line.

"I'm taking the children to help set up Vashti's medical tent," I called over the din of the camp.

"Good," she said, shooing me away, "it's about time they had something useful to do to get them out of the way."

But even though her words were sharp, I still saw the way she counted each of the children following me out of the mess area, her fondness for them softening her severe look.

❖ ❖ ❖

"And they haven't seen any evidence of Inanna or the others?" Theo asked me during the late morning council meeting.

I shook my head. "No one has seen or heard from any of the gods, on our side or theirs. The Autarch is protected at the center of their camp, hiding himself away with the other Lords."

I didn't bother to mention that no sighting or word from Silas or Karasi had reached the Rats during the night, and no one thought it worth asking.

The Autarch's army was situated in Ocridell, spreading along the coastline where the first battle had been held almost a year prior. We had already sent spies down into Kusig where his reserves were being kept to attempt to hinder their ability to join the rest of their comrades. Not that that would change anything. From the sheer numbers alone, we knew that defeating the Autarch and Inanna would be no easy feat.

Not wanting to get Theo's hopes up, I had sent several Rats into Ersetu to try and gain an audience with Ereshkigal, to ask her for guidance or for her to give us *anything*. But they had come back unsuccessful. Whatever entrances had previously led to Ganzir were now collapsed or missing entirely.

"It's been four days since they reached Ocridell," Theo said. "If he's going to try and wait us out, he'll be in for a nasty surprise when he realizes the roads and tunnels into the volcano are blocked. He'll be hard pressed to even find a way into the underground half of Ocridell and even if he raids the city, no one will have left anything useful behind."

"We don't know what they brought with them though, or if they'll be getting new provisions sent in from Aessurus," Ezra stated. "We can't guarantee that we're able to wait them out. I say we give it two more days and re—"

"Feline," a voice called from the opening of the tent, cutting Ezra off.

Everyone's attention turned to the young, anxious looking woman, and I nodded for her to continue with delivering her message.

"They're coming from the mountains," she said, her wide eyes darting between each of us. "The Autarch's army—they've taken the barracks and are coming for us through the mountains!"

Chaos ensued.

❖ ❖ ❖

"Tarprusa must have let them through," Theo growled as we ran toward the rear of the camp, where the soldiers were already setting up our lines of defense.

"We knew it was a possibility," Cyfrin called over the shouts around us. His long legs easily kept stride with Theo. "It just seemed too unlikely that they would side with the Autarch and Aessurus. Especially with the hostilities between them."

I eyed Cyfrin carefully. He had told me that we needed to be wary of our shared border with Tarprusa back at the beginning of winter. The passing comment he'd made about the crows when we'd gone to rescue Asila from Katmu had seemed strange, but now I wasn't so sure that it was entirely coincidental. The younger Wranmaris brother had always had a reputation for being a little strange, but now I was almost certain that he was gifted with some sort of premonitory ability.

I grabbed his arm when we reached the front, leaving Theo to charge on ahead to begin barking orders.

"Tell me the outcome," I demanded, meeting his pale green eyes. They flared wide, clearly not needing me to explain what I meant.

Cyfrin shook his head. "I can't … it's always so vague and disjointed. I can't tell anyone, even my warnings cause too much of a ripple effect sometimes … if even the smallest decision is made, the result could be disastrous. You weren't supposed to get shot in Katmu … I saw the Autarch—" He shook his head again, as if trying to dispel the image. "I could've killed you."

He pulled his arm from my grasp and loped away before I could say anything else. I didn't have time to dwell on what Cyfrin had told me, or what the implications of such a gift could be.

Theo had already begun to organize the division that was going to be standing in between the surprise attack of the enemy and the rest of our retreating army. We had situated our camp against the Silent Canyons, using them as a natural protector from a side attack, but now that the threat was behind us, we were pinned against them, without sufficient room to fight.

Everything was being packed away and loaded onto wagons, ready to be transported east toward Ocridell, in an attempt to avoid the main city of Zingal. Owing to the regimented drills and practices Suenna had enforced over the last few months, the entire camp was packed and moving within the day, before we had even seen the first of the Autarch's army.

We walked through the night with the rear guard, ready to jump into action at the barest hint of an attack, but only scouts had been seen. I had managed to call a few over to us, luring them with my voice and getting them to tell us how many there were in pursuit before slitting their throats.

Theo hadn't wanted to kill them, but we had no use for prisoners.

We adjusted the size of the rear guard based on the answers we received from the scouts, adding to the number as much as we dared to ensure that we would be able to hold off an attack when it came. News from the Rats in Ocridell told us that the Autarch was making his way toward us, clearly intending to pin us between him and our pursuers.

Once we were past the Silent Canyons, our army traveled east, skirting beneath them to shield us from the back once more. We had no intention of being trapped and forced to fight in opposing directions, so chose the open expanse of land in northern Ocridell as our next location to stop at. It wasn't our preferred terrain, but we had created battle plans for every corner of the realm, and we were ready.

Late the next morning we saw the first wave of the division that had been chasing us from the mountains. We had split the rear guard into three, with two thirds utilizing the rocky, towering edges of the canyons to flank the approach from an elevated level. They were hidden, arrows at the ready to attack as soon as the final third of the rear guard lured the enemy soldiers toward them.

Fergus pawed the ground and tossed his head impatiently, sensing the tangible trepidation washing over the rest of the cavalry unit. I glanced up at the cliff towering over the entrance to the clearing we were in, desperate to catch one last glimpse of Theo. But he was hidden out of sight with the other archers, waiting for the enemy to round the corner.

As we had expected, they arrived on foot, not able to navigate the mountains on horseback, and turned down the narrow passage between the two cliffs. They ran toward us, and from the uniforms, I could tell that these were the expendable dregs of the Autarch's army; the remaining soldiers from Kusig and Anzillu.

When they caught sight of us ready and waiting, a few of them faltered, clearly not expecting to face a fully mounted unit.

"Come on," I murmured, watching the bend in the passage. We needed more to come through for the ambush to be successful. The man leading the charge—who I recognized as a member of Aran Seirsun's court—let out a feral cry and lifted his sword in the air.

Several hourlong seconds crawled by, with the enemy sprinting toward us, weapons raised, before the first arrow was shot. Hundreds more followed, raining down on the bulk of the unit from both sides of the passage. Rocks were tipped over the edge, instantly crushing several people at once as they fell.

The ones who made it through were less than two hundred feet away when I heard Nook swear under his breath. I looked up to see approximately ten hooded figures bringing up the rear of the unit, with soldiers all around them protecting them with shields.

Their hoods were—

"CHARGE!"

My train of thought vanished into dust as Fergus leapt forward beneath me, snatching the reins from my fingers as the thunder of hooves rivalled the pounding of my heart in my ears.

We hit the mass of bodies as though it were a wall, and before I was even halfway through the crowd of scared, adrenaline-fueled soldiers, I had thrown almost a full row of knives from the leather harness strapped across my chest.

Pulling my thin, curved sword from its sheath, I swung it in the precise, efficient moves I'd spent countless hours practicing. Fergus moved as though he could hear my thoughts, never once shying away from a shout or the clang of metal.

But when a different kind of scream rang out across the clearing, my blood ran cold.

The hooded figures—shrouded entirely in black, despite the summer heat—stood motionless among the Autarch's soldiers with their hands outstretched. Between throwing my knives and slashing with my sword, I watched in horror as tendrils of murky black smoke traveled from their fingertips and engulfed individuals around them. As soon as it touched the target, it spread across their skin and splayed over their eyes like ink within seconds. They stopped fighting immediately and were slain by another just as quickly.

"They must be those Intur-things that Silas was talking about," Nook yelled to me, taking down two of Aran's men at once. He had lost his horse somewhere but was moving so fast between opponents that he'd turned into an orange blur.

The Intunecas. I turned Fergus away from the swirling black cloaks and pulled another knife ready.

Having ran out of arrows, the archers had finally made it down the cliff to the battle, and as they approached the Intunecas turned to them. I cantered around the edge of the fighting, opening my mouth to sing to them, but as soon as the first note escaped my throat, something cold touched my wrist.

I felt myself topple off Fergus' back, catching a glimpse of a hooded figure a dozen paces to my left. How had I not seen them?

Seen who?

The tingling cold spread up my arms and across my chest, stealing the air from my lungs. When I blinked, I opened my eyes to empty blackness.

Everything was gone, the fighting, the …

The what? Where had I been?

Who was I?

There was nothing but an empty void.

An empty void of endless black … and a thread. A black thread, shimmering ever so slightly against the flat abyss.

I considered it, tasting it; feeling the essence of it thrum against my consciousness.

And I pulled. It warped under my command, so I tugged harder, manipulating and contorting that thread until I recognized the metallic tang of anger, laced with the sweetness of fear, spreading across my tongue.

My tongue.

I had a body; I could feel my arms and legs. A hooded figure flashed in my mind's eye. The clearing. The fight.

I felt the gift of the Intuneca wrapped around my will like a strangler vine.

Reverse it, I thought. *Turn it back on itself.*

Almost immediately, my senses returned. Nook was dragging me backward across the dusty ground, away from the chaos of the fighting around us. My throat was hoarse from screaming, and there, lying crumped in a puddle of blood, was the Intuneca.

"That was the most horrific thing I've ever seen," said Nook, pulling me to my feet. His eyes were wide. "Do it again."

As soon as I caught the obsidian thread of the next Intuneca, I understood why. As soon as I began to sing, my own thread of power wove its way around hers, ensnaring it in the same way it entoiled itself into the senses of others. As soon as I caught her, I began to scream, twisting the ability and unleashing her own power onto herself.

As the woman's gift reversed, she screamed with me, throwing her head back in agony as the black smoke entered her veins and spidered its way beneath the surface of her ivory skin. I held her gaze for less than a second before her eyes burst from her head in a spurt of blood and smoke. It dripped from her mouth and ears and oozed from every pore.

I stared at the dead woman, fire lashing down my throat from my screams, and felt entirely repulsed. Never before had I been able to merge my gift into another's or even influence how they wielded it. But the Intunecas' gifts weren't so different from my own; they addled the mind in a similar way, taking things away instead of pushing them in.

But no matter how wrong it felt, my friends were in danger. So, swallowing down the bile rising up my throat, I turned to the next and began to scream.

Chapter 26

Theo

We hadn't expected an easy win, but we hadn't been anticipating fucking *smoke wielders*. They'd rendered my soldiers entirely defenseless with just a swish of their hands, offering them up to Aran and Henri's men for slaughter.

I thought that half the rear guard would end up discarded in the dirt with their throats slit until I saw Erisa fucking *burst* one of them like a piece of overripe fruit.

Just when I thought she couldn't get more gloriously terrifying. I watched in absolute awestruck horror, unable to even believe what I was seeing. Several people within a few feet from her—from our side as well as the Autarch's—wailed in pain, hunching over to cover their bleeding ears as she screamed.

The enemy disbanded quickly after that, the strange, hooded figures from Nicaieri fleeing after Erisa felled the fourth of their brethren. We captured the remaining soldiers, agreeing to hold them hostage and put them to work around the camp.

I sent a small group of people after the hooded Nicaierians, but I had little hope of being able to capture them too. I had to just accept the risk that they would try to sneak up to the camp and kill us in our sleep. When we finally returned, I gave the guards patrolling the outer perimeter instructions on how to raise the alarm if they did see them approach.

The sun was beginning to set when my council joined me in the main meeting tent to discuss the skirmish.

"We lost more than we'd hoped to," Ezra said, bringing back a final report of numbers after organizing the removal of the dead from the clearing. "Do we know how many Intunecas the Autarch has in the main bulk of his army?"

Erisa shook her head when he looked at her. "The Rats haven't been able to get a definite number, but they've estimated around a hundred."

Her dirt-streaked face was pale, almost sickly, and I couldn't help but notice how hollow her expression was. I hoped that it was merely exhaustion draining the usual fire from her features, but I knew it had something to do with the immense power she'd displayed in the clearing.

"I want a constant relay of communication from the Rats watching the Autarch," I said, aligning the small crow figurines on the map of Irkalla stretched over the table. "I need to know exactly where his forces are at all times and be signaled immediately when he so much as raises his banners."

Erisa nodded and silently slipped out of the tent. I longed to go after her and offer some comfort, but there were things I needed to take care of first.

I looked to Suenna. "Have we managed to take back

possession of the mountain barracks?"

"Yes," she confirmed, "though we didn't have much to do; by the time we got there, the reserve unit we left there had rallied and done most of the work for us. The Autarch clearly didn't intend on keeping it, he must have just needed to use it as a way through the mountains."

Not for the first time, I silently wondered how he came to know about the barracks in the first place, after we'd managed to hide it for so long.

"I suggest we move these two battalions over here," Ezra said, shifting the small, Zingali date palm figures across the map. "They can be flanked by this cavalry unit on the right, putting us in a stronger position from an attack here."

"But we need to determine if they're mounted first," Cyfrin remarked. "If they're on horseback they'll be able to skirt around here and …"

Several hours of strategic development passed in a blur, and the night was cold when I finally made it back to the tent I shared with Erisa. She was already wrapped up in blankets on the bedroll, but I could tell that she wasn't asleep.

As soon as I laid down, I pulled her into my arms and when she turned to face me, I was shocked to find her cheeks wet when I kissed them. I held her tighter, knowing that if she wanted to tell me about it, she would in her own time.

Eventually, she said, "I didn't know I could do that … I didn't even mean for it to happen."

"Shh," I whispered, stroking her hair, "I don't think anyone would've expected that to happen. It's never easy to take a life, and I understand if you feel guilty or upset by it."

She had killed gods only knew how many people, and I couldn't help but be surprised that these had affected her so much. They were brutal deaths, but I had seen her commit other atrocities that were almost as bad.

She shook her head against my neck. "It's not that ... it's just ... for most of my life I've thought of my gift as just a silly trick; a way to heighten emotions or to do a bit of light persuasion. I hadn't even realized until the battle in Ocridell that I could influence someone's behavior. That's probably why the Autarch forbade me to use it ... he must have known somehow, so stopped me from practicing." She took a long, measured breath, and I knew she was keeping her anger at bay. "If I had just used it, I could've developed my ability so much sooner, instead of having to rely on lurking in the shadows and throwing silly little daggers. I could've ... I could've saved Verrill."

I cradled her as she sobbed silently, tracing small circles at her temple with my thumb, wishing I could ease the headache that was surely blossoming there.

"There's no way of knowing what would've happened," I said. "Most gifts develop with age, maybe last year, you wouldn't have even been able to do what you did today."

"I put my faith in him for years, and the whole time, he was lying to me, holding me back from becoming stronger," she whispered. "I just wish I'd not been so trusting."

I didn't need her to tell me who she was referring to.

"Me too," I muttered, kissing her damp cheeks once more, "me too."

❖ ❖ ❖

Horns blared through the silence of the dawn two days later. They repeated the same short, four beat signal we'd used for decades with the Visszhangok birds along the coast of Zingal.

Danger. Danger. Danger.

Erisa and I were sprinting down the hill we'd been watching the sunrise on and running toward the outer perimeter when I saw Nook barreling toward us.

"A small group of Intunecas has attacked from the south, alongside a squadron of soldiers." He paused for a brief moment to catch his breath. "It's hard to tell if they were the ones who ran before, but the Autarch has begun his march toward us. His banners are on the horizon."

Before I could register this information and separate it from the chaos of the camp around us, a young girl ran up to Erisa and passed her a note. Erisa read it quickly before looking at me.

"The Atturynnian fleet has come," she said, a fierce look lighting her eyes. "They've dropped anchor at the Gištir Jungle."

Erisa had moved most of her Rats away from the coast to focus on watching the Autarch, so this news had to be, at the very least, half a day old. Which meant that if Karasi had indeed succeeded at convincing the Prince of Atturynn to come to our aid, they could have already made it ashore and be marching toward us.

"Keep me updated," I said, before boosting her up into Fergus' saddle. Our eyes locked for a brief moment before she cantered away. I watched her go, a sick, twisting feeling of dread settling in my stomach telling me that our time was quickly running out, the few precious moments we had left slipping away like fading echoes in the wind.

Nook and Ezra were leading the horses forward, and Nook handed me Moth's reins. "We've got this, Theo," he said, grinning from ear to ear. "There's victory in the air; I can feel it!"

"Be careful," I said, seating myself in the saddle, looking at my two friends. "Both of you."

"Until the end," they voiced in unison. Ezra's expression was as severe as Nook's was elated.

My echoing response was lost in the clattering of hooves as we sped toward the outer perimeter of the camp. When we arrived, the fighting was in full swing, and we immediately jumped into the thick of it.

The strange, hooded Intunecas were wreaking havoc, leaving my soldiers confused and defenseless to attacks.

Disgusting, cowardly behavior.

I reached for my bow, and sent arrow after arrow at the Nicaierians, managing to land a few successful shots around the soldiers protecting them.

This squadron of the Autarch's army consisted almost entirely of soldiers from Aessurus. Their white armor was an interesting choice, as it quickly blossomed a deep crimson, highlighting the uninjured fighters as targets. I wasn't complaining; having something bright and shiny to aim for made a world of difference.

Bodies were strewn about the dirty ground, and it was starting to get difficult navigating Moth around them. The camp medics were working themselves ragged trying to pick through the survivors and carry them off to their tents to be treated.

To my horror, from the other side of the battleground, I saw a near-lifeless body being heaved by four small children, one of which was crowned in curly dark hair. Farzin was directing the other orphans, and they shifted the body toward the nearest tent, where they were being urged back to safety by none other than—

"VASHTI!" Nook thundered, genuine fear, for once, replacing his perpetually carefree and jesting expression.

Before he could take his first step toward her, an ear-splitting screech rent the air. Drawn to the chaos of the fighting was a being so horrifying, it could only be Lamaštu. She wasn't quite as large as some of the smaller gods, but still towered above us, standing at least thirteen feet tall. Every feature was disjointed, like someone had taken spare parts from various animals and mashed them together.

Her lioness face was fierce and snarling, with the long, gray ears of a donkey standing tall from the top of her head. She was naked, covered only by the writhing, hissing snakes that encircled her body, draped around her neck and hanging from her waist.

Vashti screamed and pulled the small group of children close to her, backing them up as the demoness approached. I urged Moth into a gallop, trailing behind Nook and Ezra, as Lamaštu sank down onto all fours, prowling closer on her taloned hands and clawed feet.

"Such pretty babes," she shrilled, her voice warped and grotesque, like she was forcing her throat to produce sounds it was never created for.

She raised a hand, the razor-sharp edge of her claws glinting in the sunlight.

"NO!" Nook shouted, but the blow never landed.

An immense gust of wind knocked everyone to the ground. Moth stumbled, throwing me out of the saddle. The fighting around me ceased and tents were uprooted and flung into the air by the gale swirling around us.

Lamaštu screamed, a ghastly, dreadful sound, as Pazuzu landed heavily in front of her. Vashti and the children scrambled through his legs as he lunged for the demoness, attempting to sink his teeth into her throat.

She swiped her claws across his chest, throwing him off balance and causing rivulets of strange blood to trail down his exposed skin. He roared, shaking his maned head in anger before lunging again. But Lamaštu was already gone, sprinting away on all fours at an alarming speed. In another sweeping gale, Pazuzu beat his wings once and took to the skies.

"Haha! Yes!" Nook yelled, punching the air, sword in hand and a triumphant grin lighting up his face. "Now that's what I call a—"

But whatever he was about to say never came. Blood trickled from his mouth, replacing the unspoken words and turning the ever-upturned corners of his mouth into a crimson frown. He fell to his knees. A sword protruded from his chest, held by a white-clad soldier who had taken advantage of his celebratory lapse in focus.

A strangled cry came from my right, and I watched as Ezra scrambled to his feet and ran to our friend. But we both knew that he would be too late. Nook would never have left a joke unspoken; he was already gone.

By the time Ezra finished with the soldier, not a single thread of his uniform remained white.

Eventually, somehow, I rose to my feet, numb and unfeeling, refusing to come to terms with the fact that there would soon be a little boy or girl in the world who would never have the pleasure of knowing their prankster of a father. My mind shut the thought down, and I turned my head so that I would no longer see Ezra lying over Nook's body, weeping into his red hair.

I would not break down now. The fight was far from over, and my soldiers needed me. I would not break down now.

Most of the troops from the Autarch's side had dispersed after being knocked down by the gusts of wind from Pazuzu's wings, but the threat of their ruler had not ceased. He sat astride his back horse, crow mask in place, at the brow of the hill ahead of me, and although I couldn't see his eyes, I could feel them watching me.

As if he had heard my thoughts, the Autarch lifted his sword, and the enemy began their descent toward us.

Chapter 27

Erisa

Feline,
Soldiers bearing Atturynnian banners are fast approaching the camp, led by Torin Sharru, Prince of Atturynn and second in line to the throne.

We have confirmed that Karasi Lusilim is with them, hidden within the ranks.

We await your next instruction.
R

❀ ❀ ❀

"Look! There they are!" Tasar cried, pointing ahead of us. He faltered, squinting his eyes. "What are those?"

In the far distance, the Atturynnian army approached. It looked smaller than we were hoping for, but I was grateful that Karasi had managed to convince Torin to come at all.

I strained my eyes, finally understanding Tasar's question. Barreling straight for the camp were thousands of creatures, running alongside the soldiers dressed in blue silks and silver armor. Several of the soldiers themselves were actually *riding* the beasts instead of horses, and I realized with a sinking sense of dread that I had encountered some of these monsters before, deep within the Gištir Jungle. It had seemed like lifetimes ago, but I was sure that these were the kinds of things that Verrill and I had hunted and been hunted by in the ghoulish, shadowy corners of that wild woodland.

A glance behind me showed that the Autarch had raised his banners and begun to march toward the vanguard of our army. From our elevated position on the cliff, I could see across the expanse of our forces, stretching out over northern Ocridell.

"Nook's cavalry unit hasn't moved," I murmured, voicing the concern out loud to Tasar. "And Ezra should have signaled for the left flank to fall back behind the first wave."

"They probably know something we don't," Tasar said, but I could hear his own unease in his voice. "We ought to … What is Theo doing?"

I followed his gaze to the large green standard waving at the forefront of the troops, charging forward on the all-to-familiar piebald stallion. My stomach dropped through my feet.

"That fool's going to get himself killed," I hissed, turning to Tasar. "Go and direct the Atturynnians to the left flank, we'll need them there by the time they arrive. I'll see you down there!"

He nodded and gave me a grave look. "Be safe, Feline."

I spun Fergus around and urged him into a canter. I shouted to Tasar over my shoulder, "Call me Erisa, all of my friends do!" and flashed him a quick smile before vanishing around a bend.

All I could hear and feel were the rhythmic pounding of

hooves beneath me and the wind whipping against my ears. The air was thick with the acrid scents of dust, blood, and smoke as I drew closer to the chaos. As I neared the battle, the distant screams and animalistic howls began to rise, cutting through the deafening roar of the wind.

As I rounded the outer edge of the camp, I slowed enough to shout orders to the lieutenant of Nook's regiment, instructing them to take their position and defend the vanguard from the side. I didn't stop, joining the calvary unit as they sprung into action.

The ground shuddered and several horses spooked, throwing their riders.

It shuddered again. And again.

Charging in from the east, and followed by Namtar and Gestinanna, was Nergal, fitted in gleaming armor and crowned with a bull-horn helm. The god of war, as formidable as he was glorious, stormed forward, unintentionally stepping on humans and crushing them underfoot on his way into the battle. The lethal, curved edge of his scimitar flashed as he raised it above his head and let out a war cry that rattled my bones.

But his cry was lost in another, one even more piercing and feral. A great shadow rolled over the land, blocking out the sun for several heartbeats. When I looked up, my blood ran cold. Soaring through the sky, whipping the dust from the ground and into our faces, was a dragon.

The enormous beast had to be the one protecting Ganzir that Theo had told me about. The sheer size of it was bigger than I could even comprehend. And sat astride the dragon, in the space between the broad shoulders and the wings, was Ereshkigal. The goddess of death was dressed head to toe in black scaled armor, blending in seamlessly to her steed.

Every pair of eyes was on the lethal duo as they swooped low over the Autarch's army and the dragon opened its huge mouth, unleashing a torrent of fire from its long throat. The sickening scent of charred flesh hit me almost as quickly as the deafening cacophony of screams erupting into the air.

I hadn't even had a chance to feel the relief at the obvious victory we were about to receive from the arrival of the gods before another bellowing sound rang my eardrums. Flashing almost pearlescent white in the sun, was a—

"What the fuck is that?" someone cried behind me.

The creature careening through the air toward Ereshkigal was almost as big as her dragon, but with a slender, serpent-like body. It soared high, feathered wings outstretched like an eagle's, wide and powerful, cutting through the sky with an elegance that belied its size. Two feline and two avian legs, tipped with sharp talons hung beneath, ready to slice. But it was the eyes that caught me; their piercing blue glow, burning like a distant, roiling sea storm. I didn't know what it was, only that it was ancient and unforgiving.

The serpent looped around, revealing a rider of its own, and I knew immediately it was Inanna, goddess of love and queen of heaven. I had never seen anything or anyone so beautiful. Several soldiers fell to their knees at the sight of her, laying their heads against the ground in reverence.

"Get up," I shouted to them, lacing as much persuasion into my voice as I could, but even I had to admit that it sounded hollow.

Inanna's effect was intoxicating, and my eyes were drawn to her once more.

She was like a vision, glowing with an ethereal light that seemed to bend the air around her, accentuating the lavish curves of her body, criminally hidden beneath the pale golden armor, so refined it appeared to be forged from sunlight itself. Perfect curls of shining hair cascaded down to her thighs, framing a round, angelic face. Like the serpent, her eyes were liquid lapis, but so full of life that if she gazed upon you, heaven itself would pause to watch.

An arrow whistled past my face, stinging my ear as it grazed the skin. My attention snapped back to the present, and I was horrified to find that many of our troops had been caught in the same trap, sitting like statues with their mouths hanging open, ready for the enemy to pick them off one by one.

Ahead of me, Theo's banner waved, signaling the moment when the two armies would collide. I spurred Fergus forward, my heart pounding. At the crest of the hill, Dumuzid and who I assumed was Neti emerged, charging down to meet the other Gods in a thunderous clash. The impact was immediate, a brutal collision of flesh and steel as the human army surged into battle at the very same instant. Above us, the vicious snap of the flying monsters' jaws echoed through the air, while the sisters' battle cries rang out, their ancient feud reigniting with a fury that had not been seen or felt in centuries.

Inanna's serpent plummeted toward us; its massive form so close I could see the deadly gleam of its crystalline teeth as its enormous maw gaped wide. Fergus jerked to the left, narrowly avoiding the torrent of freezing mist that surged toward the rest of my unit. I gripped the gelding's neck, my heart racing, but I couldn't stifle the shriek that tore from my throat. The icy vapor plummeted into my right arm, fusing to my skin in a cruel, burning frost—an agony of cold I had never known before.

Once I'd pulled myself upright again, I forced myself to look behind; to face the fate that I had just barely escaped. Soldiers and horses were frozen in place, their forms caught midstride, and their screams of agony perfectly encased in the unyielding ice.

"Thank you, Fergus," I gasped, patting his shoulder, unable to calm my racing heart. He didn't slow for a second, charging head on into the battle.

By the time I reached Theo, only one of my throwing knives remained, and my arm was on fire from both the burn of the ice and from wielding the sword. His banner was long gone, but the fire in his eyes when they met mine would have inspired entire continents to take up arms to defend their lands.

"Atturynn is here," I shouted, seeing the flash of relief in his expression. I plunged my sword into the neck of one of Aran Seirsun's men and kicked him to the floor so that I could pull Fergus up next to Moth. "Tasar is bringing them up the left flank." I quickly glanced around us, not being able to make out much in the chaos. "Where are the others?"

Theo gave me a strange look; one I wasn't able to decipher before he launched into another attack, jumping from Moth's back and swinging his sword with such skill and precision, I almost pitied his opponents.

Horns blared and the ground trembled. I whirled around to

witness the sea of blue rolling in from the weakened left flank of our forces. But the ground wasn't shaking from the heavy footfalls of the Atturynnians, or the beasts they were riding, but from the earth itself. Tree roots and jungle vines erupted from below the surface, snapping and whipping at the Autarch's army, slicing them in two, or pulling them back into the ground.

Torin Sharru rode a bright white charger, his palms outstretched and facing down, directing the roots beneath him. He had brought the Gištir Jungle with him, and it seemed to obey him as though he were speaking the very language of the trees.

And behind him, on a strange beast of his own, was Silas. He was shouting out commands in a language I had never heard, and the snarling, gruesome monsters of the Wilds were obeying. They leapt into the fray, latching onto the Autarch's men with teeth and tentacles and suckers. Skuvlas swung from Torin's moving branches, snatching humans from the ground and drilling into their skulls with their pointed snouts. They discarded the drained, shriveled bodies before reaching for the next.

Despite the reinforcements, we remained woefully outnumbered. The Autarch's forces pressed forward with relentless fury, his Intunecas slicing through entire squadrons with terrifying ease. The battle stretched on, each passing moment feeling like an eternity, as if the sun had been frozen in the sky, unwilling to move.

I longed for the calming embrace of moonlight, knowing that only when the darkness came would we be forced to cease the fighting and rest. Yet, time itself seemed to stand still, caught in the spell of the conflict, as though it too were paralyzed by the chaos unfolding below.

With a deafening roar, Ereshkigal's dragon plummeted from the sky, a massive mass of black scales and searing fire. Its wings folded and snapped under the weight of its colossal body as it crashed to the earth, crushing hundreds of humans beneath it in a single, brutal sweep. The beast bellowed in rage, its howl reverberating through the air before it soared upward once more, unleashing torrents of fire at Inanna's serpent. Meanwhile, Ereshkigal, brushing dust from her bloodied form, glared up, fury blazing in her eyes.

"You hide behind Sirrush like a coward, sister," she shouted at Inanna. "Do not fool yourself—just because he sat atop the heavenly gates, it does not mean he will not turn against you, as he did with Marduk."

At her words, the serpent, Sirrush, let out a wrathful cry, swinging his long body around and launching toward Ereshkigal with terrifying speed. His jaws parted to shower her in a flood of deathly ice. But the goddess of death stood unyielding, her hand raised as she absorbed each shard of glowing blue frost, her power crackling in the air. With a mighty roar, she slammed that hand into the ground, splitting it apart.

The earth shuddered as the queen of Irkalla screamed, tearing the very fabric of her realm apart in a furious rage. "YOU DARE ATTEMPT TO END ME, SNAKE!"

The world seemed to unravel in an instant—chaos exploding in every direction. Hundreds, if not thousands, of soldiers from both sides plummeted into the yawning chasm that had opened in the ground, swallowed whole by the fiery pits of hell below. From the depths of the abyss, shadowy, almost-invisible demons clawed their way up, and twisted, smoke-formed creatures materialized, their ghoulish forms contorting with malice.

All around, the dead stirred. Corpses, discarded and forgotten, began to rise once more. Slain bodies dragged themselves forward with weapons clenched in limp, waxy hands, their hollow eyes locked on the battle.

The Autarch's soldiers, overcome with terror, shrieked and turned to flee, their ranks splintering in wild panic. But Inanna, with a mere wave of her hand, silenced them. Their screams ceased, and their fear was replaced by cold, unwavering focus. They returned to the battle, as though her command had snapped them back into line.

Our own army did not fare so well, and I briefly considered deserting with them, yearning to follow my instincts that were screaming at me to flee from this unnatural danger. But then I thought of Theo and of our friends and decided that I would rather die on this bloody battlefield than abandon them now.

And then, in amongst the mayhem and disorder, I saw him. The only man in the world that would incite enough hatred in me to change my mind.

The Autarch stood several hundred paces away from me on his black stallion. As if sensing my gaze, the crows head mask turned to me.

Fergus took one step, and then another.

Whatever the Autarch saw on my face made him hesitate for the briefest moment, before he turned to flee. Without a second thought, I raced after him, blind to the havoc around me.

This was my chance.

I didn't stop for a single heartbeat; not when Theo called out for me to stop, not when I saw Dumuzid pulverizing Namtar into the ground. Not even when I rushed past Tasar, bleeding out in Karasi's arms, her forehead resting against his.

I followed my prey into the city of Ocridell, until it became too impractical to navigate the winding streets on horseback. Dismounting, I paused for the briefest moment, long enough to run my hand down Fergus' face, to silently thank him for his bravery, before taking off again on foot.

My body screamed in exhaustion as I pulled myself up onto the houses, jumping between the crumbling roofs of my childhood.

Somehow, deep within my bones, I knew where the Autarch was going. Because even though his life had been split into two lies, each half had started and ended with my mother.

My knees shook from the impact as I jumped down from the final roof, finding the large meadow sprawling in front of me.

"Csintalan," I called, finally forcing myself, for the first time in months, to reconcile the man I had grown up worshipping with the coward who had lied through his teeth, betraying everyone I cared about.

He froze, turning to me. He pulled the mask off his head to reveal the icy blue of his eyes, awash with tears. He lifted his hands, to show that he held no weapon. "Please, Erisa, my child."

I threw my remaining knife, sinking it cleanly through his chest. He stumbled back, landing roughly on the lush, calm grass of the meadow floor.

I had expected a fight, some extreme display of magic and power to end the Autarch, but here, in this field of wildflowers, he was just a man.

The wound was fatal; I could already see the pooling of blood beneath him, and he began to drag himself away from me, toward the serene, shady haven of Pazuzu's tree. My mother's tree.

Traitorous tears spilled down my cheeks. I knew Csintalan was dying, but as much as I hated myself for it, I couldn't watch it happen.

Turning my back on the man who I had looked up to and loved like a father, I walked away, the weight of unbidden sadness heavy in my chest. Torturing him would not bring Verrill back, nor would it erase the agony he had inflicted upon Theo. Instead, I left, leaving him to die in the way I knew he'd fear the most: alone and afraid, without a friend in the world to witness his passing.

Chapter 28

Theo

The earth quaked once more beneath my feet, throwing me to the ground. But this one felt different, like this shuddering hadn't come from Ereshkigal cleaving the land apart. My body begged me to remain in the dirt, to rest at last, but I clenched my teeth and hauled myself back to my feet.

My people needed me, and I would fight to the death before ever giving up on them.

"Feel that, sister?" Ereshkigal cackled, gesturing around her. "Your Autarch is dead. The champion leading your great army is no more."

Inanna picked herself up from where her sister had struck her to the ground. The goddess looked around, horror and fury marring her perfect face when she realized that whatever spell she had woven throughout the Autarch's men had been broken.

In the distance, I saw the dark blue banner of Malah's district fall as he led his Coastguard away from the fight. Aran Seirsun's men had been wiped out hours ago, and what was left of Henri

Elkas' troops disbanded immediately, their Lord nowhere to be found. The soldiers the Autarch had brought in from Aessurus fought on bravely, still revering the queen of Heaven and fighting in her name.

I ran over to the edge of one of the chasms, where Silas was battling at least ten soldiers at once. But as I got closer, I realized that there were only two of them, twins dressed in white and somehow making copies of themselves. These shadow versions were immaculate replicas and moved entirely on their own, slashing at Silas with their phantom swords.

My friend howled in rage as he struck yet another of the false opponents, watching it dissipate into thin air.

Plucking an arrow from a fallen soldier, I nocked my bow, aiming to hit as many of the identical attackers as I could. The arrow sailed through the air, scattering three and landing solidly into one.

Immediately, Silas plunged his sword into the soldier's chest. The other twin made the grave error of retaliating, outing his presence. Silas wasted no time in swinging his sword and cleaving his head from his shoulders.

"Is it true?" I shouted to my friend. "Is the Autarch dead?"

I had seen Erisa go after him, and knew from the sheer determination in her eyes that she would try to end him once and for all. But no one knew how to kill an Autarch. I had tried to go after her, to help, but by the time I'd fought my way through the mass of frenzied bodies, they had both disappeared.

"He's dead," Silas confirmed. "Can you not feel the change in the air? The magic binding so many unspoken rules and allegiances is unravelling—"

"YOU!" Inanna shrieked, pointing a finger at Silas from several hundred feet away.

A scream tore from Silas' throat and he fell to the ground, writhing in pain. He ground out one word, one name, again and again. "Nanaya … Nanaya … Nanaya!"

But Inanna was still locked in a ferocious battle with Ereshkigal, and her momentary shift in attention allowed her sister to deliver a blow that sent her stumbling down into the fiery chasm.

The air in front of me shimmered, and a woman, at least thirteen feet tall, just appeared, materializing out of nothing. From her size and the swell of power around her, she had to be another goddess. Like Inanna, she glowed from within, harnessing beauty like a second skin and wielding it like a weapon. Her golden hair was like spun silk, woven into intricate braids and draped around her head and face like a blindfold, completely concealing her eyes.

The unfamiliar goddess crouched down on one knee and reached for Silas, shimmering them both out of existence as soon as she touched his skin.

On the other side of the chasm, behind where they had both been, I could see Erisa running back toward the fighting. My stomach twisted and I almost vomited in relief at the sight of her.

Our eyes met and we ran toward each other. Before I could yell at her to stop, she jumped onto one of the thick underground roots, balancing precariously over the eternal fires of Irkalla below. One wrong move and she would be lost forever.

I stepped forward as she jumped from the first creeping vine to the next, wanting to reach across the gap to help her over, but the earth crumbled beneath my feet, forcing me to retreat. Erisa caught the movement, and a low murmured note fell from her lips. Immediately I was fixed in place, unable to interfere. I obeyed without protest, not wanting to direct her attention to anywhere but the placement of her feet.

Until one of those vines wrapped itself around her ankle. Erisa stumbled slightly, caught off guard by the trap. As soon as I tried to push at the boundaries of her power, she increased the volume of her voice, immobilizing every muscle in my body.

My temper and fear rose as another thin rope of tree root snaked its way up her other leg, holding her in the very center of the makeshift bridge. She glanced behind her to where Torin Sharru knelt on the ground, covered in blood and dirt. His black eyes were focused on her, a mask of hatred across his face as he twisted his outstretched hands.

Erisa glanced back to me, her eyes softening even as her song harshened, ensuring that I couldn't move. The large roots beneath her began to split and splinter, falling away and lowering her deeper into the ground.

No, I pleaded silently, pure rage igniting the blood in my veins. *No, don't do this to me. Let me move!*

I fought against her siren call with every ounce of strength in my body, willing my traitorous limbs to move.

My fingertips twitched. My fist clenched.

But then the last vine holding her pulled taught, and her eyes filled with panic and regret and her song cut off as she accepted the inevitable. She called out. "Theo, I lov—"

The snapping of the vine seemed to ring through the air. The earth swallowed her, and her words were lost to the emptiness of the chaos surrounding us. Words that I would crawl through the deepest pits of hell to hear in full.

I was frozen, not by her song this time, but by the enormity of what I knew I was about to do.

Time is such an intricate concept at the best of times, but when facing the end of it, contemplating it seemed almost easy. Like staring at an empty sandglass representing the time you have left of this earth, each invisible grain making up moments of your life, spilling down through the bottleneck of your present moment, never knowing if that will be the last to fall. Whether that moment will define your final thought, or if it will be buried beneath a thousand more, forgotten and inconsequential. They would be a rapid cascade in joy, and a slow trickle in pain. And in the blink of an eye, the grains of your moments would slip away, leaving only the remnants of memories behind.

I had always hoped that I would have years, decades with Erisa, that the sunrise we saw this morning would not be our last, and looking into her sunflower eyes a second ago would not be the final time they would capture mine.

And though I could not see them, I knew only a few grains remained in my sandglass, that those singular, precious moments were slipping by faster than I could catch them. I needed to make the most of that little bit of sand I had left.

So, I jumped.

Chapter 29

Erisa

There was nothing but pain. Hot, scorching pain branding my skin and tearing at my limbs. I could feel my flesh bubbling, melting off my bones.

Who was I? What was I?

A face appeared in the inferno that had trapped me.

Green eyes. Dark and light, like the veins of a leaf illuminated by the sun.

Theo.

Sporadic memories returned. A campfire. A piebald horse. A red orb. A single candle in a dark room. A kiss. A hand winding through my dark braid.

I no longer had eyes, could no longer see Theo. I had been ripped from him, pulled down into the depths of Irkalla. The memory of him hurt more than the excruciation bombarding my body, the heartbreak in his eyes when he knew I was telling him goodbye, and the echo of his fury burning like acid across my tongue.

But I relished that bitter taste, it was the only thing tethering me to my sanity as the world went dark and hot and cold.

And then …

Nothing …

Nothing but agony.

Chapter 30

Theo

I fell for an eternity, spiraling through endless black until I lost all sense of direction. The world was empty, except for one haunting, harrowing sound.

Erisa. She was screaming. Her endless wail rang in my ears, filling my entire existence.

The ground hit me out of nowhere, knocking the wind from my lungs and shaking my bones loose. Blinking my eyes open, I found myself in what looked like a dark tunnel, lit only by small, smoldering pieces of coal scattered about the floor.

The screaming had stopped.

Not knowing which way to go, I called out into the void, "Erisa!"

Silence.

Before I could overthink it, I walked forward, taking one step after another, trying to pick out any discernable feature in the sparse passageway.

The noises started almost immediately. Eerie whispers

echoed inside the walls, accompanied by the soft scraping of claws against the dusty ground. Footsteps bounded up from behind me and I whirled around, but there was nothing there.

My heart was hammering in my ears, almost blocking out the low cackle of whatever invisible creature had just passed me. I had no weapons, nothing to help defend myself against whatever lurked down here.

The air was stale and rancid, as though nothing living had passed through this tunnel in thousands of years. And it was cold, so void of life and warmth that a shiver ran through me, chattering my teeth.

Unsettled by the concealed beings, I began to jog, trying to get away from whatever was surrounding me, hidden out of sight. But the faster I ran and the harder my heart pounded, the louder the phantoms became. Excited by my fear, they heckled and taunted me, chasing me until I found myself running flat out down the twisting passage.

Every time I chanced a glance over my shoulder, there was nothing there, but I could feel them all around me, matching my speed and nipping at my heels. The coals rattled against the floor as I sprinted as fast as I could, straining my eyes to see through the dim light.

The darkness of the tunnel grew, and I realized too late that I had reached the end. I was trapped with nowhere to go. Skidding to a halt, I turned, raising my fists in a last-ditch attempt to protect my face.

The ghoulish, decaying faces were visible for less than a second, their black tongues lolling out of their hanging jaws and their eyes melting from their sockets, before every illuminating coal extinguished, cloaking a heavy blackness over the tunnel.

Before I could even take a breath, the floor beneath me vanished, and I fell once more into unending emptiness, landing hard on damp, freezing stone. Shackles pinned my wrists and ankles to the floor, restricting my movement completely. Large flames licked at the dark walls, illuminating the small, dank cell.

Bile rose in my throat, turning my insides to acid. I was back in Katmu. I was trapped again. The pitter patter of tiny, scurrying feet forced the meager contents of my stomach up and I retched, covering myself in vomit.

The rats ran in front of the flames, throwing long, menacing shadows up the walls around me. The cell spun as I felt the first of the rodents touch the fabric of my trousers and black spots obscured my vision as I felt the brush of whiskers against the skin of my leg.

I barely registered the screams tearing themselves from my throat, oblivious to everything but the panic that was consuming my entire body. The air was stuck in my lungs, coming in short, sharp pants as the rats piled on top of me, one after another.

Tell me what you can hear. Erisa's voice cut through the chaos in my mind like a beacon in a storm.

"Shackles," I replied aloud, pulling against the clanking metal restraints. "Water dripping."

And what can you see?

I focused on anything but the rats. "Stone … Flames … and a door, above me."

What do you feel?

"I can feel … my fingers, and my toes. I can feel …" I trailed off, wanting to say that I could feel the rats biting me, that they were tearing into my flesh like before. Only … they weren't.

Habit forced me to complete the final mental task in Erisa's checklist without needing to be prompted. I tried to recount the last few moments before the panic set in, only I couldn't remember what they were.

This isn't real, I thought, and repeated the revelation over and over in my head until my heart calmed enough for the ceiling to stop spinning. Slowly, I shifted my limbs, relieved to find nothing binding them anymore.

But as I focused on the trap door above my head, the wooden slats of the hatch groaned and split under the impact, and hundreds of brown, furry bodies came cascading down onto my face. I threw myself backward into the stone wall behind me, trying to flatten myself against the damp surface as I watched the small cell fill with wriggling bodies.

This is hell, I realized. *I've died and this is my eternal punishment.*

A scream came through the empty doorway at the far end of the cell. I hadn't remembered seeing it before, but the exit was there, right in front of me. I searched desperately for a way to get around the moving wall of rats. But they filled the cell, pressing me further and further into the stone.

Gritting my teeth, I plunged forward, gagging as I batted away the furry bodies that had suddenly turned into tiny, rotting corpses. Even as the teeth sank into my skin, I kept going, because that was *Erisa* screaming, and I had to get to her.

Suffocating under the crush of rodents, I crawled forward, keeping my mind focused solely on the doorway in front of me. My body was threatening to shut down, to collapse in on itself, to save my mind from this torment. But somehow, I kept going, kept pushing through the waking nightmare.

Even as my mind begged me to let it leave my body, I refused, knowing that if I let myself disassociate for even a second, I would never be allowed to leave this place. I fixated on everything that would keep me present, the freezing dampness of the stone; the rough scrape of it against my palms and knees; the sound of my ragged breaths leaving my lungs.

Despite the frigid temperature of the air, sweat coated my skin, sticking to the mangy fur of the rats pressed against me. The sensation was unbearable, the tiny hairs clinging to my skin and refusing to be brushed away.

It could have been minutes or entire weeks before I made it to the arch; I had no way of measuring the time in this hellish place. But once I was free from the rats, I sobbed in relief, scrambling to my feet and through the doorway.

The cell exited into another larger chamber, and I found myself on a small stone outcropping in the center of an underground lake. The water was dark and stagnated, illuminated from within by what looked like phosphorescent reeds.

"Theo!"

Erisa's voice shattered the silence, and my head snapped up to see her being pulled beneath the surface of the murky water.

I waded into the lake, fighting through the reeds and debris that were looping around my legs, slowing me down. The water had a strange, velvety texture, as though not entirely liquid. A glowing hand broke through the surface, grabbing my knee.

I yelped, trying to get away from the dozens of reeds that were never reeds at all, but the emaciated limbs of corpses. Their bony fingers snatched at my ankles and clung to my trousers as I splashed deeper into the water, toward the ripples coming from the other side of the lake.

All too soon, my exhaustion became all consuming, making the strange liquid—now up to my waist—feel like molasses. The luminous bodies swarmed me, grabbing at me with their decaying fingers and trying to use me to climb out of the water. Most of their faces were gone, leaving only papery, waxen skin over ivory skulls.

When the water reached my chest, I caught sight of my hands. They had wasted away, losing all muscle and strength. I stopped for a second to look down in horror as the surface of the water settled, revealing the gaunt reflection of my face, crowned with white, thin hair and sunken eyes.

No wonder this water felt like wading through syrup when it was sucking the life out of me. Even as my heartrate accelerated in panic, the beats felt weak.

A flash of white—a hand—came up out of the water a dozen feet in front of me. A living hand. Ignoring every instinct telling me to turn back and get out of the water, I forced my frail body on, kicking and pushing with my feeble limbs.

Holding my breath, I dove beneath the surface, reaching out to grasp Erisa's sinking body around the waist. My lungs screamed for air as we dropped to the bed of the lake, the weight of her unconscious body dragging us both down.

My body was skin and bone, so near to death that the corpses of the lake had lost interest in me entirely. Erisa was the same, her black inky hair turned white and the haleness of her body diminished. With the last ounce of strength left in me, I pulled Erisa to my chest and pushed up on my feeble legs, kicking off from the sandy floor toward the surface.

When our heads broke the surface, the water was gone. I knelt over Erisa, watching her body convulse, coughing the strange, murky liquid from her lungs. We were both normal again, no longer knocking on death's door.

The earth tilted, causing us to tumble down the rough terrain. I seized Erisa under her arms, grunting with effort as I secured a foothold. Looking up, my heart stuttered at the infinite climb I knew we would have to make. We were at the base of a steep hill, where a shining light haloed around the summit. Menacing growls and the snapping of teeth echoed from below us, sounding closer with every frenzied beat of my heart.

Steeling myself against the fear and exhaustion already wracking my body, I began to climb, hauling Erisa's unconscious body up to the safety of that shining light. Sweat coated my skin as I fought against the relentless onslaught of gravity, which seemed to intensify with every shaking step, wanting to pull her back down.

But I refused to let her go. I dragged her up to the top, crying out in relief as the steep slope leveled out and that glorious light washed over us.

The light flickered out.

Before I could react, the ground shuddered, rumbling loudly in the silence of the dark, empty space we were in. Something white flashed past, too quick to make out. It was followed by a dozen more, sporadically searing across my vision in blazes of bright light.

Were they ... souls?

The ground continued to tremble and groan, rattling my entire body until it felt like I would fall apart at the seams.

Something vast and solid appeared in front of us, partially illuminated against the flare of the spirits flashing through the darkness. Each burst of light brought the mass closer, until I could make out a huge, scaled face assessing me with orange, slitted eyes.

"You should not be here, human." The dragon growled, the sound rumbling deep from within its chest, where a warm glowing light appeared.

Unable to do or say anything, I watched, transfixed, as that ball of fiery light rose, traveling up the long, scaled neck. Just as the great maw of the beast opened, I twisted away, hauling Erisa into my lap and leaning over her as the scorching inferno consumed us.

Chapter 31

Theo

A bead of sweat ran across my cheek and dripped from the end of my nose, landing on the dirty fabric of Erisa's shirt.

I was upside down, hanging from my ankles and gripping Erisa's wrists with all my strength as she hung suspended over the fiery chasm. Her eyes were wide, begging me not to let her fall.

As if that were even a possibility.

The vines around my ankles tightened, and more snaked around my legs and torso, lifting us both back up toward the lip of the chasm. Bits of dirt and rock cascaded over us as the earth trembled and groaned and began knitting itself back together.

A blood-curdling scream rang out somewhere above us, but Erisa's hands were slipping from mine, and I didn't dare break focus. I kept my gaze locked onto hers until the vines pulled me over the edge, gritting my teeth as I was dragged roughly across the ground. As soon as I was over, the roots loosened, allowing me to kneel and haul Erisa up to safety.

I pulled her into my chest, fisting my hands into her hair as I almost sobbed in relief, thanking the gods, the world, the stars, and the heavens for keeping us alive.

Feeling his gaze on me, I lifted my head and met Torin's black eyes. They were wide with something akin to fear, as though he had seen a ghost. I stared back at him, not sure if I wanted to kill him for making Erisa fall or thank him for pulling me back up with his tree roots. It hadn't escaped my notice that none of the vines had touched Erisa on the way back up.

Without a word, he turned and melted back into the chaos of the fighting. Or rather … the running. The soldiers from Aessurus were scattering, retreating south with the Atturynnians hot on their tails.

"Are you all right?" I asked, pulling back to hold Erisa at arm's length, inspecting her for any visible sign of injury.

"I'm fine," she said shakily, but her eyes were still impossibly wide. "We should—"

Another sonorous scream reverberated through the air. "YOU TRAITOROUS WRETCH!" Inanna raged, charging from the far end of the battlefield in long, bounding steps. Her beautiful face was twisted into an ugly, menacing guise of wrath. "I dismissed the last time as simply a juvenile mistake, but now I clearly see that *I* was the one mistaken. You have planned this from the beginning, Nanaya!"

She stormed toward us, leaping over our heads and across the wide split in the earth with ease, heading straight for the smaller, unfamiliar goddess with hair braided across her eyes. Silas was running toward the goddesses, joined by several jungle monsters who tried, in vain, to halt Inanna's progress.

But the queen of Heaven barely seemed to notice them, raising her long, curved knife high in the air and bringing it down on Nanaya. Something shifted in the air, and a flash of blinding white light seared into my vision at the point of contact, so intense that I cried out and covered my eyes.

A roar, so bone-chillingly anguished, settled over the clearing. It was the kind of sound that you couldn't forget, one that penetrated deep into your skin like a piercing frost, as though it encapsulated every single second of pain ever endured since the birth of the gods.

Time seemed to halt, as though the world was suspended in this wash of illumination. By the time my vision eventually returned, Inanna and Nanaya were gone. I looked around, as did dozens of others, trying to find where any of the gods had gone. But only Ereshkigal remained, kneeling on the ground with her palms flat against the earth, knitting the tears of her realm slowly back together.

Silas was knelt over a body, cradling it in his arms. It was Ana, the gray-eyed woman he had hidden inside the Palace in Ersetu what now felt like a lifetime ago. He wept into her neck, but she remained still, unmoving.

When the blazing chasm was almost closed, Ereshkigal looked over to the heartbreaking pair for a long moment. An unknown emotion flickered in her dark eyes, before she darted them briefly to me, and stepped down into her fiery pit of hell.

Chapter 32

Erisa

Feline,

I have consolidated the reports and included them with this letter. Aran Seirsun and Malah Jirata have both arrived back in their districts and are beginning work on rebuilding morale amongst their people.

Henri Elkas has still not been recovered, and the family have now accepted the likelihood of finding him alive to be extremely slim. As with the rest of the citizens that escaped Ersetu, most from Anzillu remain in Ocridell or Zingal, with only a small number seeking refuge in Katmu and Kusig.

Šarrum and Hudjefa are no more. As per your request, we sent teams in to recover what we could, but almost all of the tunnels have collapsed in on themselves, making it impossible to enter the volcano. This means that, regrettably, whoever was still inside during the final earthquake likely did not survive. We are still collating a death toll, but I imagine it will take a few more weeks to get a definitive number.

Cyfrin Wranmaris went to Anzillu Harbor to meet with Malah Jirata. I'm yet to receive specific details of what they spoke about, but from what I can gather, it was an amiable conversation, with

Cyfrin formally relinquishing responsibility of the harbor back to Malah.

Our house is fine, thank you for asking. Somehow, we managed to get away with minimal damage, and we have been involved with the reparations of others who were not so fortunate.

As always, your faithful friend and servant,
Alekos

23 July

❖ ❖ ❖

Somehow, the true aftermath of war is often forgotten. While the gruesome fighting and staggering death tolls are recorded, the rest of the suffering is overlooked. Like the way a body smells and bloats after lying out in the sun for three days, waiting for someone to scrape it off the ground. Or the rasping caws of vultures circling overhead, swooping down to fight over the unclaimed corpses below. The mourning families, the raided houses, the orphaned children, the sheer, unrelenting loss of life. The wail of a redheaded baby girl who would never know the delight of her father's smiles.

And in the end, no matter who claimed the victory, both sides remain defeated.

There was no celebratory cheer when the remainder of the Autarch's army fled the battlefield to return home, or when the final warship set sail back to Aessurus. There was just grief and confusion and the bone-shattering *relief* that it was all over.

The realm was quiet during the week that followed. No one could quite come to terms with what had happened, and the last few months felt like they'd been a fever dream. Were it not for the collapse of Ersetu or for the water remaining in the Silent Canyons, it was as if the gods had never been here at all.

The reign of the Lording families had come to an end. Now that two of the districts had been completely buried beneath the volcano, we each made a vote to reform Irkalla. Malah Jirata was more than enthusiastic and seeing as Aran Seirsun was barely brave enough to tie his own shoelaces anymore, he seemed almost grateful to be relieved of the burden. Henri Elkas was presumed dead, and Anzillu's decision was made by his cousin, a girl no older than eighteen. Cyfrin Wranmaris represented Hudjefa, declaring that Tasar had wanted Theo to take the lead the entire time, and that he could think of no one better to guide the realm out of this dark period.

While the Lords would remain as advisors, it was unanimously decided that until we were in a stable enough position for the citizens to decide for themselves, Theo would be the one to steer Irkalla into a brighter future, beginning with rebuilding the realm and reestablishing broken connections and relationships between the districts.

The citizens of Kusig and Katmu kept to themselves, unsure of their standing now that the Autarch had been defeated. It would take time to bring the two sides together again, but all we could do was hope that the realm could become stronger and better than before.

"So are the gods just ... *gone?*" I asked Theo again, unable to remember much after falling into the chasm. Apart from a bright light, which seemed to stretch on for hours.

He watched Suenna coo over baby Ettie, who slept soundly, cradled in the protective embrace of Lola's arms. Her hair was shock of vibrant red hair against the pale white of the blanket.

"I have no idea," he admitted, shaking his head. "They were here for six months—what's that to a god? It's no time at all, so what was the point? All that carnage ... and for what?"

It wasn't the first time he'd expressed this frustration. I could tell that the guilt was eating him alive, it was still too fresh and the reminders of what we'd lost too raw to rationalize right now.

I took his hand. "I suppose we have to just trust that Ereshkigal knew what she was doing, and that she achieved what she wanted in the short time she was here. She did say that she had intended for this to happen."

He sighed, glancing at me. "I don't suppose you've heard anything?"

I shook my head. I knew who he was asking about. No one had seen Silas after the battle, when he'd held the dark-haired woman—Ana—in his arms. He had simply vanished, in the way he always had. While Silas hadn't opened up to Theo about who this woman was, I knew Theo wanted to comfort his friend, that he worried about him being alone.

"I'm sure he'll come back when he's ready," he murmured, gently pulling me from the room. "Have you decided what we should do with Cor—with Csintalan's things?"

Now that the Autarch was gone, the magic that had bound me to silence had evanesced. I was able to tell Theo what Csintalan's real name was, or at least the name I knew him by. We had traveled back to the meadow in Ocridell and had buried his body where he had died, under Pazuzu's tree. The grave had been shallow and messy, but Theo had insisted that it was the right thing to do. We left no headstone or marker; only a mound of dirt that would, in time, settle into the meadow, indistinguishable from the rest.

We had taken Csintalan's crow mask and his staff. They no longer thrummed with power, but were simply empty shells of things that once were. They were still sat by the kitchen door, where I'd dumped them on our return to Zingal.

Picking them back up, I led Theo outside, heading straight toward the huge inferno raging in the lower half of the grounds. The flames were nearly ten feet in the air, burning away all of the rubble and old medical supplies from the infirmary that had been set up on the Lusilim estate.

I handed Theo the crow mask before throwing the staff into the fire, watching as the warped metal softened and began to distort the shape even more than before. Theo looked down at the glossy black feathers of the mask, turning it over in his hands before tossing it into the flames.

Regardless of what he had done to us, we had both loved him once, and saying goodbye to him like this felt like the closure we needed to move on from the pain he had caused.

For a long moment, we stood there in silence, watching the final remnants of the Autarch—of Corbin, of Csintalan—fade away into the embers, leaving nothing but smoke and memories behind.

❖ ❖ ❖

The sun was low on the horizon, setting the sky ablaze with a fiery hue. It reflected off the newest gravestone in the Lusilim urnfield, turning the pale stone a vibrant orange. The earth had settled into a smooth, raised mound—a peaceful and serene resting place.

I hesitated at the gate, not wanting to disturb the three friends, who knelt next to the upturned soil. Theo and Suenna sat on either side of Ezra, and though they were silent, with their shoulders barely touching, the connection was there; the flow of unspoken support coursing between them.

Suenna was the first to stand, squeezing Ezra's shoulder as she turned to leave, wiping away tears from her puffy eyes. She gave me a sad smile as she passed and headed back up to the house.

Theo turned to watch her leave and caught my eye. He murmured something to Ezra, who nodded but didn't move as Theo rose to his feet. I watched Ezra carefully as Theo joined me by the gate, unable to ignore how the sight of his heartbreak reminded me of losing Verrill. I knew it wasn't the same, that what Ezra and Nook had shared was a different kind of love, but my heart hurt for Ezra, knowing that nothing anyone could ever say would make up for that loss.

"How is he?" I whispered to Theo.

"As good as can be expected," he said. Concern drew shadows across his face as Ezra placed a hand on the grave. "He lost his best friend."

"And how are you?" I asked, cupping his cheek to turn him to me. I knew the loss of Nook had affected him deeply, but he hadn't openly talked about it with me. "You lost him too; you're allowed to grieve."

Theo sighed and pressed a kiss to my palm before taking my hand in his. He led me up to the crest of the hill and we sat on the warm grass, overlooking the rolling grasslands of Zingal.

"I think I still haven't fully accepted it," he said quietly. "All of this death and destruction … none of it would have happened if I hadn't rebelled against the Autarch." I opened my mouth to argue but he continued, "I know that Ereshkigal said it was her plan to destabilize the district Lords and the ruling system, but if someone had told me that so many would die for this … that Nook and Tasar …" He trailed off, staring into the distance.

"But what if you weren't the one to do it?" I asked. "What if someone else had fused the shield together, and instead of thinking of the people, they used the situation and manipulated it for their own benefit? Not once did you try and use those relics for selfish reasons." I thought about myself and how I was ready to abandon everything when the gods first woke up. "Your intentions were good and pure, and regardless of the outcome, Irkalla was at the heart of every decision you made, and that is something that you should be proud of."

He turned to me and gave me a soft smile. "I just wish there was a way of knowing if what happened was the best possible scenario. If Irkalla was always meant to reform, I wish I could know if I'd made the right choices."

Cyfrin Wranmaris flashed in my mind, and I shook my head. "Theo, I think that there would never be a way of knowing something like that. If you had known, you would have tried to change things, and even small decisions can have monumental ripples. There's no point looking back and regretting past actions or decisions because maybe you would've spared Nook, but maybe in the process, you would have condemned thousands of others."

"But all that plotting and scheming to get rid of the Autarch ... all that loss ... and you just killed him. None of it needed to happen."

"If he hadn't lost the war, I don't think I would have been able to," I whispered, not quite sure how to put my thoughts into words. Csintalan hadn't been the Autarch when I'd killed him, that spark deep within him had already gone out, as though he was ready to embrace death on his own terms. "Life is short, Theo. Mourn what is lost, but look forward to what we still have to come ... because there were moments when I thought we had reached the end."

Theo wrapped his arms around me and pressed a kiss to the crown of my head.

"Life *is* short," he agreed, "and I intend on making the most of every second I have left of it." He let out a small, low chuckle. "You still haven't told me that you love me."

I had nothing to say to that, because how could I say that I *had*? That I whisper it into his ear when he's deep in sleep, or every time he turns away and leaves the room. How could I tell him that it's a mental shout, loud enough to be all encompassing when he holds me like this, or that I scream it into the void of my despair whenever we're apart. How could I tell him that my love for him transcends my need to say it out loud, because everyone who I had ever uttered those words to had left me in the end?

"But it's all right," he continued, gently brushing a stray

piece of hair behind my ear, "I don't need you to tell me for me to be able to hear it, Sunflower. And I can say it enough for the both of us."

One day I'd feel safe enough, be brave enough to say those three tiny, monumental words. But for now, we sat, staring at the sun-kissed planes of our broken realm, looking forward to rebuilding a brighter future.

Epilogue

T he Princess Soraya Nazrali of Tarprusa paced across the pale moonstone floor of her balcony, looking out to where the moon illuminated the white caps of the Zuamsik mountains. For decades those cursed, frost-covered peaks had stood in their way, barricading their route into Irkalla, mocking the Tarprusans, taunting them with that impenetrable shared border.

"I ought to flay you on the Palace steps for your treason," her father, King Ardeshir of Tarprusa muttered from behind her. "Consider yourself lucky that I'm simply confining you to your rooms while I decide your punishment." He ran a hand through his thinning hair, at a loss for what to do with his beloved child. "Gods … if anyone found out … there'd be war … outright rebellion."

"Yes, Father," Soraya replied, dutifully bowing her head in respect.

With an exasperated sigh, he retreated back into the warmth of the Palace, leaving his daughter to continue her pacing, her gaze fixed on those mountains.

He was a foolish old man, too comfortable with the pleasant confines of their lavish home and too flattered by the bootlicking clowns sitting on his council, agreeing with any inept, uninspiring idea he produced.

She loved her father, but he had lost his drive—his ambition to truly *rule* Tarprusa. That was why she had done the unthinkable. She hadn't wanted to commit treason, but he had left her no choice but to take matters into her own hands.

As much as she disliked disappointing the King and putting him in a difficult position, she couldn't bring herself to regret her actions. Irkalla had all but fallen apart, the recent civil war making it ripe for the taking.

She would do what needed to be done; would forge ahead where her father faltered. She would change the fate of Tarprusa.

The Princess Soraya of Tarprusa cast one more look at the Zuamsik mountains.

And she smiled.

Acknowledgments

I don't even know where to begin with this one. I could write another whole book thanking each person who has helped me and cheered me on during this process. I have been absolutely blown away by the sheer amount of support and encouragement I've received from so many people.

To my family and friends who read The Place of Her Name without even knowing what you were getting yourself into, I'm sorry and I'm eternally grateful. To anyone who knows me, you know I'm worse than Erisa at expressing emotions, so I'd just like to say that if you've spoken to me about these books or even shown the barest hint of interest, you're the best and I love you forever.

I'd like to thank my amazing editor, Hannah, once again for the transformation of the manuscript, without your knowledge and guidance I would be completely lost.

Through writing this series, I have met some of the most incredible people and formed friendships that I will hold onto forever (Hanna, I'm looking at you). I have been exposed to some incredible authors through writing, and I could not be more pleased. The support and solidarity within the indie community is second to none, and I thank every single writer who has offered their encouragement and expertise.

Printed in Dunstable, United Kingdom